Brett Battles lives and writes in Los Angeles. He grew up on a navy base in the middle of the desert, where his father was a civilian physicist working for the military. He is currently Executive Producer for E! Entertainment Television and has three children.

The Cleaner is his first novel. Brett Battles' second Jonathan Quinn novel, *The Deceived*, will be published in July 2008, also by Preface.

BRETT BATTLES

THE CLEANER

preface

Published in the United Kingdom by Preface Publishing in 2008

7 9 10 8

Preface Publishing
The Random House Group Limited
20 Vauxhall Bridge, London SW1V 2SA

www.randomhouse.co.uk

Addresses for companies within The Random House Group Limited can be found at: www.randomhouse.co.uk/offices.htm

The Random House Group Limited Reg. No. 954009

A CIP catalogue record for this book is available from the British Library

ISBN 9781848090071

The Random House Group Limited supports The Forest Stewardship Council (FSC), the leading international forest certification organisation. All our titles that are printed on Greenpeace approved FSC certified paper carry the FSC logo. Our paper procurement policy can be found at: www.randomhouse.co.uk/environment

Typeset by Palimpsest Book Production Limited,
Grangemouth, Stirlingshire
Printed in the UK by CPI Bookmarque, Croydon, CR0 4TD

To Mom and Dad
For all the obvious
and not so obvious reasons

Acknowledgments

To paraphrase John Donne, no writer is an island. While much of the work authors do is done alone, the final version of any work is touched by many. This book is no exception.

Thank you to Jon Rivera, Kathy Karner, Ann Epstein-Cohen, Pam Epstein-Cohen, Patty Kiley, and Jeremy Quayhackx, for acts of kindness that went beyond mere friendship. Also, to those members of the group whose suggestions and insights are weaved throughout this story: Derek Rogers, Brian Perry, Ken Freeman, Eloise Freeman, and Allison Stuart. Thanks to Tammy Sparks, Theresa Imback, Dawn Butler, Darren Battles, Mark Paoletti, Janet Joe, Jean Galbraith, Aki Norita, Hunter Athey, Bruce Lambert, and Raquel Rancier, who braved early drafts and provided feedback and encouragement. And to authors J. T. Ellison, Sandra Ruttan, and J. B. Thompson for doing the same. Also thanks to authors John Ramsey Miller and John Gilstrap for providing invaluable assistance and advice. Your unselfishness and help are appreciated more than I can ever express.

For advice on medical issues, I owe a large debt to Dr Phil Hawley, Jr. The same is also true for Andreas Kanonenberg and Christiane Freuss-Turgel, who helped with German language issues. As for any medical errors or German language mistakes, I wish I could blame them, but I can't. Those would be my fault.

Without the following people, this book would still be sitting in a box in my closet; Nathan Walpow for providing an unexpected introduction; Jim Pascoe and Tom Fassbender at Ugly Town for taking the initial chance on me, then arranging my transition to Bantam Dell; Shannon Jamieson Vazquez for enthusiastically bringing me into the Bantam Dell family; Danielle Perez for being a wonderful editor, friend, and champion; and Nita Taublib for being such an enthusiastic supporter from the moment she read my manuscript. Also, thanks to my agent, Anne Hawkins, who has become my guide and biggest supporter; it's amazing what a chance meeting will produce.

Finally, there are four people who deserve extra-special recognition. My mentor and friend, Bill Relling, who gave me more than any writer could ever hope for. I only wish he were still around to see the results of his work.

And Ronan, Fiona, and Keira, you are each so much more than a father could ever hope for.

Chapter 1

Denver was not Hawaii. There were no beaches, no palm trees, no bikinis, no mai tais sipped slowly on the deck of the Lava Shack on Maui. Instead there were people dressed like they were expecting the next ice age, directing planes down taxiways lined with mounds of freshly plowed snow. There wasn't anyone wearing a bikini within five hundred miles. Worse yet, while it was only 3:00 p.m. local time on Thursday afternoon when Jonathan Quinn's flight began disembarking, a layer of gunmetal-gray clouds made it seem like it was almost night.

It was definitely vacation over, back to work.

After he exited the plane, Quinn made his way toward the front of the terminal, pulling his only piece of luggage, a carry-on suitcase, behind him. Not far beyond his arrival gate was a small kiosk. He stopped and bought an overpriced cup of coffee.

As he took a sip he glanced around. There seemed to be an equal amount of people walking to and from the gates. A typical busy afternoon in a typical busy international airport.

But it wasn't typical people he was looking for. He did a lot of traveling and knew from experience that you could never be sure who you might run into. In his business, that wasn't necessarily a good thing. But his arrival appeared to have been unobserved. He took another sip of his coffee and moved on.

Instead of following the crowd and proceeding to the passenger pickup area, Quinn found a seat next to a set of arrival and departure screens near the ticketing and check-in counters. He pulled out the book he'd been reading on the plane, *South of the Border, West of the Sun* by Haruki Murakami, and started in where he'd left off. When he finished the book an hour later, two dozen additional flights had arrived. He closed the novel and returned it to his bag. Time to call in.

'I thought you said you'd arrive first thing this morning,' the voice on the other end of Quinn's phone said, irritated.

'Selective memory, Peter,' Quinn replied. 'Those were your words. Is my ride here?'

'It's been there since eight a.m.,' Peter fumed. He told Quinn where to find the car, then hung up.

The ride turned out to be a blue Ford Explorer. The vehicle came equipped with leather seats, an AM/FM radio, a CD player, and two men, neither of whom felt it necessary to give Quinn their names. He designated them the Driver and the Other One.

As Quinn climbed into the back seat, the Other One tossed him a nine-by-twelve-inch padded envelope. It was about an inch thick and weighed maybe a pound. Quinn started to open it.

'Don't,' the Driver said. He was glancing at Quinn in the rearview mirror.

'Why not?' Quinn asked.

The Other One turned toward him. 'Not until we're gone. Instructions.'

Quinn rolled his eyes and set the envelope on the seat beside him. 'I wouldn't want you to get in trouble.'

They drove in silence for the next hour, through Denver and into the foothills of the Rocky Mountains. It was dark now and Quinn was getting hungry. The last meal he'd had was on the plane somewhere over the Pacific Ocean, if you could call the less-than-inviting beef Stroganoff he'd been served a meal. But he kept his hunger to himself. He knew if he didn't, his two new companions might decide that they were hungry, too. God forbid he would be forced to eat with them.

Instead, he tried to imagine that the pine trees they drove by were palm trees, and that the cloudy sky was just the regular afternoon rainstorm moving onto the island. After a few minutes, he gave up and just stared out the window. The dirty snow along the side of the road was a poor substitute for the beaches of Kaanapali.

Finally, the Driver exited I-70 and drove a mile down a two-lane road into the darkened wilderness, before turning left onto a narrower, snow-packed road. A hundred yards ahead, a green Ford Taurus was parked off to the side, tucked up against the encroaching woods. The Driver stopped behind it and turned the SUV's engine off. If Quinn didn't know better, he would bet he was about to be removed permanently. Deserted road. Two silent goons. A getaway car. Classic assassination scenario.

Game over, buddy. Thanks for playing, but you lose.

And though he knew he had nothing to worry about, he tensed a little, preparing himself just in case.

Without a word, both the Driver and the Other One opened their doors and got out. As they did, a blast of cold air swept into the SUV. Quinn watched as they walked over to the Taurus and climbed in. A moment later, the sedan roared to life. Without even giving the engine time to warm up, the Driver executed a quick U-turn, then sped off, back toward I-70.

Quinn chuckled to himself. This sort of cloak-and-dagger bullshit was really kind of amusing, if you thought about it. Asinine, but amusing.

He got out of the Explorer, his teeth clenching against the frigid air. The leather jacket he was wearing was a lousy barrier to the cold, but it was all he'd had with him when his vacation on the islands was cut short.

He hurried around the front of the vehicle and got into the driver's seat. The moment he had the door closed and the engine started again, he flipped the heater on full blast, letting the warm air fill the cabin. One of his first stops would be a place he could buy a winter coat, maybe even a couple of sweaters. Thermals, too. God, he hated cold weather.

Once he was reasonably warm, Quinn reached into the back and retrieved the padded envelope. He poured the contents onto the passenger seat. Inside were two business-size envelopes, a folded map, and three sheets of paper. Two of the sheets were a wire-copy news report about a fire in some place called Allyson. Apparently a vacation rental had burned down, and the person who'd been staying there – an unnamed man – had died.

Quinn picked up the final piece of paper and scanned it. It was the job brief containing his instructions and a limited amount of background information. Peter, as always, was trying to control what Quinn knew. Still, it was more information than the news article had revealed.

The dead guy's name was Robert Taggert. Quinn's assignment was to determine if the fire had indeed been an accident – which the local authorities were leaning toward – or something else.

That was all there was. Nothing else on Taggert. No helpful hints as to what Quinn should look for. Just an address – 215 Yancy Lane – and a contact name with the local police force. On the surface, a piece-of-cake job. No reason for Quinn to have been brought in. Which to Quinn meant there was probably more to it than the brief was letting on.

He grabbed the map and unfolded it. The location of the fire was marked with a small red X. It was at least a couple hours' drive from Quinn's current position. He set the map down and opened the first envelope. Cash, about five grand. A week's worth of expense money if nothing too costly came along. Longer if Quinn didn't have to pay anyone off. And if this really turned out to be a one- or two-day job, a little extra cash for his own pocket.

The other envelope held two identifications, both with Quinn's picture. The first was a Colorado driver's license. The second was an authentic-looking FBI ID. He'd played a Fed before, but it had been a while.

His new name, he was amused to see, was Frank Bennett. Peter had a thing for classic pop singers. Quinn guessed that 'Tony Sinatra' would have been a little too obvious.

He set everything back down, then reached under the driver's seat looking for the one thing that hadn't been in the packet. When he pulled his hand back out, he was holding a soft leather case. He unzipped it and found what he expected inside, a 9mm SIG Sauer P226 and three fully loaded magazines. It was his weapon of choice. He put his hand back under his seat and pulled out a second pouch, this one containing a sound suppressor designed to attach to the end of the gun's barrel. Anything else he needed would be in the standard surveillance kit that was undoubtedly in the back of the vehicle.

He stored the gun, mags, and suppressor in the glove compartment, then put the Explorer in drive.

Chapter 2

Breakfast the next morning was scrambled eggs and sausage, in the restaurant at the Allyson Holiday Inn, where he'd spent the night. He sat alone in a booth, with a copy of the local paper on the table next to his plate.

It was full of the usual stuff small-town papers were interested in. A couple of short blurbs made up the international section: one about curbing ethnic tensions in Europe, and another on the continuing chaos in Somalia. The national news items were longer stories, with footers directing readers to other pages for the rest of the story – an ailing Supreme Court justice, a corporate fraud trial in Chicago, and a rundown of the expected highlights in the President's upcoming State of the Union address.

But it was the local stories that commanded the bulk of the front page. Rather, one local story. The Farnham house fire. The story was a follow-up to the piece that had been included in Quinn's brief. It contained nothing new. Just old information reworked to sound fresh and feed the curiosity of the local population. The fire investigators were calling the blaze an accident. Faulty wiring. One tourist dead. There was little else. Taggert's name still hadn't appeared. That seemed a bit unusual, but Quinn suspected Peter might have something to do with it.

A waitress walked by carrying a pot of coffee. She stopped when she saw what Quinn was reading. 'That was awful, wasn't it?' she asked.

He looked up. Her nametag identified her as Mindy. 'The fire?'

'Yeah,' she said. 'That poor man.'

'Did you know him?'

'No,' she said. 'He might have come in here to eat, I guess. A lot of tourists do. Coffee?'

'Please,' Quinn said, pushing his cup toward her.

She refilled it. 'What I can't help wondering is if he has a family somewhere. Maybe a wife. Maybe some kids.' She sighed. 'Awful.'

'It sure is,' Quinn said.

She shook her head. 'They say it happened while he was sleeping. Probably a nice guy, just enjoying a vacation, then suddenly he's dead.'

She moved on, refilling a few more cups of coffee on her way back to the register. *Happens all the time,* Quinn thought to himself.

The Allyson Police Department's headquarters was located about a mile from the Holiday Inn. Quinn's contact was the chief of police, a guy named George Johnson.

Quinn flashed his FBI ID to the desk sergeant and was quickly ushered into Chief Johnson's office. The chief stood as Quinn entered.

Johnson was a tall man. He'd probably been in good shape once, but now carried a few extra pounds from too many years behind a desk. His face showed the strain of his job, too, eyes baggy and dark, jowls heavy and drooping. But his smile was genuine, and his handshake was firm. Quinn took both as signs of a man who liked his job despite its difficulties.

'Agent Bennett,' Chief Johnson said. 'I can't say that I've ever really had to deal with the FBI before. But I guess this is a day of firsts for me.'

The chief motioned to the empty chair in front of his desk. As Quinn sat down he wondered what Chief Johnson meant by 'a day of firsts,' but knew better than to ask right away.

'What can I do for you?' Johnson said as he eased himself back into his chair.

'Quite honestly, Chief, I'm not sure you can do anything,' Quinn began. 'I'm not really here on official Bureau business.'

Johnson eyed Quinn curiously. 'Then why are you here?'

'It's about the fire you had the other day.'

'The Farnham fire,' the chief said as if he'd expected it all along.

'That's right,' Quinn said. 'I'm here about the victim. Robert Taggert.'

The chief paused, obviously surprised Quinn knew the man's name. 'What about him?'

'He's apparently a relative of a special agent back in D.C. Somebody a bit higher up the food chain than I am. Since I was in the area on other business, they asked me if I could swing by and check things out. It's more soothing someone's concerns than anything else. I'm sure you have everything well in hand.'

The chief was silent for a moment. 'Is that why that other guy was out here earlier this morning?'

Now it was Quinn's turn to hesitate. 'I'm not sure I know who you're talking about.'

The chief opened the center drawer of his desk and pulled out a business card. Reading, he said, '"Nathan S. Driscoll. Department of Alcohol, Tobacco and Firearms."'

'May I see that?' Quinn asked.

The chief shrugged, then handed the card to Quinn. 'I've never talked to anyone from ATF before either,' the chief said.

The card was high-quality, printed on government-issued card stock, and complete with the ATF symbol embossed on one side.

'I don't know him,' Quinn said. 'But could be he's here for the same reason I am. If my guy back in D.C. was desperate enough, I'm sure he'd call in as many favors as he could.' Quinn handed the card back to Johnson. 'What time was he here?'

'Left no more than thirty minutes ago,' Johnson said.

Outwardly Quinn forced himself to smile. 'I hate to make you go over this stuff again, but would you mind?'

The chief shook his head. 'No problem. But like I said to Agent Driscoll, there's really not much to tell. It was an accident. That's it.'

'I heard that. But Andersen – that's the guy back in D.C. – he wasn't satisfied. I guess when all your information is coming from what you read in the paper, you just want to make sure you're not missing something.'

'If he's getting his information from the paper, how did he know Taggert was the one killed?'

'That's a great question,' Quinn said honestly. 'I have no idea.'

The chief seemed to give it some thought. 'Maybe it was the sister.'

'The sister?' Quinn asked.

'Taggert's sister,' the chief said. 'She's the only one we told.'

Quinn nodded. 'That makes sense. Is there anything else you can tell me?'

The chief shrugged, then said, 'It's not much.'

'Anything will help.'

Johnson pulled a thin file off the top of a stack on the right side of his desk. He perused its contents for a moment, then gave Quinn a halfhearted smile. 'As I said, it's not much. The fire was apparently electrical. We think it started in the living room. A space heater that caught fire or something similar. Taggert was in the upstairs bedroom. He was probably overcome by smoke before he could get out. By the time the fire department got there, it was too late. Once the flames were finally out, there wasn't really much left of anything.'

'How'd you identify the body?'

'We checked with the agency that handled the Farnham place, Goose Valley Vacation Rentals. When he signed the rental agreement, he left an emergency number. That's how we were able to contact his sister. She forwarded his dental records to us. We got 'em the next day. They were a match.'

'I'm curious. Why was his name never released to the press?' Quinn asked.

'The sister requested we keep it quiet. Since he wasn't a local, I didn't see that it was much of a problem.'

'Could I get her number from you?' Quinn asked.

'The sister? Shouldn't your friend have that? I mean, if they're related?'

'Probably. You'd think he'd have given it to me, wouldn't you?'

Johnson pondered for a moment. Then he glanced down at the file again and leafed through a couple of pages until he found what he was looking for. He jotted a number down on a piece of paper and handed it to Quinn.

'Not much else I can tell you,' Johnson said. 'It was an accident. These things happen.'

'Has there been an autopsy?'

The chief nodded. 'That's standard.'

'Who handled that?' Quinn asked.

'Dr. Horner. At Valley Central Hospital.'

'Would you mind if I talked to him?'

'Not at all,' the chief said. 'Though I don't think he'll be much more help than I am.'

'You're probably right. But I just need to cover my bases.'

The chief pulled out another piece of paper and wrote something on it. He handed it to Quinn. It was the address of the hospital. 'Thanks,' Quinn said.

'Anything else?' the chief asked.

'Not that I can think of.' Quinn stood up, and Johnson did likewise. 'I'd like to get a look at the accident scene, if that's okay? Since I'm here and all.'

'Be my guest. Do you know where it is?'

'I do.'

'Just be careful when you're out there. Officially, it's still a potential crime scene, though we're really just wrapping things up.'

Quinn held out his hand and the two men shook again. 'Thanks, Chief,' he said. 'You've been a big help.'

A storm front had moved into the area while Quinn had been talking to Chief Johnson. The clouds were dark and low, and heavy with moisture. It wouldn't be long before snow started to fall, Quinn realized. He needed to get a move on so that he could survey the fire scene before any snow disturbed what evidence might be left.

As he drove through town he used his cell phone to call the number the chief had given him for Taggert's sister. After four rings, an answering machine picked up.

'Hello. After the beep, please leave us a message, and we'll call you back.'

The voice was female, but flat and unmemorable. The message itself was laughably generic. Quinn didn't recognize the speaker, but he was willing to bet whoever she was, she was not related to Taggert.

He found the Farnham place with little trouble. There was a sign posted at the end of the driveway warning unauthorized individuals to stay off the property. A rope that had probably been strung across the entrance lay off to the side, out of the way.

Quinn turned off Yancy Lane and drove up the snow-packed driveway. A white Jeep Cherokee was already parked in front of what was left of the Farnhams' vacation home. Quinn parked his Explorer several feet away from it, then took a look around.

It had been a large house before the fire, at least two stories tall. Now the only things still standing were a blackened fireplace, a stone chimney pointing up at the sky, and a few scorched walls. Otherwise, it was an uneven pile of charred junk.

It was clear there had been little the fire department could do once they'd arrived on the scene. Their efforts had undoubtedly been directed more at containing rather than extinguishing the blaze. Though, with several feet of snow on the ground and an air temperature probably hovering at no more than twenty-five degrees, the likelihood of the fire spreading was pretty much nil.

More of a marshmallow roast than a rescue operation, Quinn thought.

He zipped up the Gore-Tex jacket he'd bought the night before, then climbed out of the Explorer. If it was possible, the clouds seemed darker and heavier now, the storm threatening to break at any moment.

What struck Quinn first was the silence. There was no hum of cars on the distant highway. No crack of wood being split by one of the neighbors in anticipation of a cold night. No yelling of children at play or hints of distant conversations. There wasn't even a breeze blowing through the trees. Even the snow crushing under his feet and the whisper of his own breath seemed muffled and far away.

Everywhere a silence, a stillness. The only movement other than his own was the blanket of clouds rolling and dipping in an eerily soundless dance above his head.

But where his sense of hearing provided him little, his other senses more than made up for the deficit. The odor of burnt wood, melted plastic, and death hung in the air as if refusing to leave, claiming the site for its own. And on Quinn's tongue, a tangy, acrid taste coating its tip and the roof of his mouth.

His first stop was the Cherokee. He pulled his hand out of his pocket and put it on the hood of the vehicle. It was still warm. He returned his hand to his pocket and walked over to the house.

Chief Johnson had said the fire department believed the blaze started somewhere in the living room. Quinn located where he thought the front door used to be, and quickly spotted a path just beyond it through the debris.

He followed the trail into the remains of the house. At various points along the path were fresh scrapings of wood and cleared spots where the fire investigators had examined possible points of ignition. Quinn knew what he was looking for, but so far he hadn't seen it.

Near the center of the house he found an area that had been cleared of extraneous debris, exposing a spot on the floor near the remains of a wall. He leaned down for a closer look. There was a melted mound of plastic that had congealed into a lumpy, blackened mass on the floor. It could have been anything from a pile of CD cases to a lamp, or possibly even the space heater Chief Johnson had mentioned. Without cutting it apart, there was no way to tell.

Quinn stood up and looked around. As he suspected, the spot was the lowest point the fire had touched. There was no question this was where the blaze had begun. He could see the patterns made by the flames as they moved outward and then up what was left of the walls toward the second floor. But as to how the fire started in the first place, there was no definitive indication.

The job brief had said the second-floor room in which Taggert had died had collapsed onto the family room in the back of the house. Quinn back-tracked out of the living room the way he had come in, then walked around the perimeter of the burnt remains until he was in the backyard.

At the far end of the debris, a man was leaning down, looking at the snow a few feet away from the house. His back was to Quinn, and on his jacket were three large letters: ATF.

Quinn stared at him for several moments, his face expressionless, then returned his attention to the house. His best guess was that he was standing only a dozen or so feet away from where Taggert had been found. Unfortunately, there was nothing much to see. A half-burnt dresser was about the only identifiable piece of furniture left; other than that, the back of the house was just an additional mound of junk.

He spotted another path through the wreckage, this one no doubt created to recover the body. But it didn't look inviting. And there really was no reason for Quinn to take a closer look. Any useful information had likely been destroyed in the fire.

He closed his eyes, freeing his mind from any distractions, and tried to mentally visualize what had happened. If this wasn't an accident, then someone had wanted Taggert dead. In that case, whoever had set the blaze would have wanted to make sure it took. Quinn pictured the arsonist-assassin as he went methodically through his tasks. He would have arrived either via the driveway or by way of –

Quinn opened his eyes and turned around to face the rear of the property. Directly in front of him, the snow had been thoroughly packed down, probably by the fire crew. There was a point in the snow about thirty feet away from Quinn where the foot traffic tapered off to a few scattered tracks, and another ten feet beyond, where the snow was just a flat surface, undisturbed since the last storm. This went on for a hundred feet to the back of the property. There the forest began again, lining the rear of the Farnhams' property, then wrapping around the sides of the clearing and coming all the way back to the house along either edge.

It was beside the row of trees along the left side of the property where Quinn spotted something. It was an indentation in the snow, perhaps only a pinecone or a branch that had fallen from a tree and created a depression in the cover of white. Or perhaps something more.

The man in the ATF jacket stood and turned in Quinn's direction. He was in his mid-twenties, a good ten years younger than Quinn. He was also a couple inches taller, topping out at about six feet. His brown hair was short, but not drastically so. When he saw Quinn, he smiled and started walking over.

'Thought I'd run into you here,' he said as he got close. 'Look what I found.'

He held out a silver bracelet. Quinn reached his hand out, but instead of taking the piece of jewelry, he grabbed the ATF man by the wrist and pulled him forward. At the last second, Quinn released his grip. The man's momentum was still carrying him forward as Quinn shoved him in the chest. The ATF agent immediately lost his footing and fell to the ground.

'What the hell?' the man said.

But Quinn had already started walking away.

Chapter 3

Quinn headed toward the depression he'd spotted in the snow. Behind him, the ATF agent pulled himself up off the ground and ran to catch up.

'What are you all mad about?' the man asked.

Quinn stopped. 'What are you doing here, Nate?'

'What do you mean, what am I doing here?' Nate asked. 'You told me to come.'

'I told you to come to Colorado,' Quinn said. 'I didn't tell you to come to the accident scene. And I especially didn't tell you to impersonate an ATF officer and go visit the police.'

'What's the big deal?' Nate asked. 'Thought it was a good chance to put some of my training to work. I don't think it harmed anything.'

Quinn was tempted to do more than just throw Nate back to the ground for that comment. 'How do you know that?' he asked. 'How do you know you haven't done any harm? Maybe Chief Johnson is sitting in his office right now wondering why he had two visits in one day from federal officials about a fire he thought was just an accident. Maybe while you walked around here you stepped on something that might have been an important clue. Have you talked to anyone else?'

Nate shook his head. 'No. Just the chief of police.'

'Give me the bracelet,' Quinn said.

'What?'

'The bracelet. The thing you were showing me earlier.'

'Right,' Nate said. He looked down at the hand he had been carrying it in. It was empty. 'I must have dropped it when you pushed –' He stopped himself. 'When I fell.'

'Get it.'

Quinn waited as Nate retrieved the bracelet and brought it back. This time when he held it out, Quinn took it.

He draped it over his left palm so he could get a better look at it. The bracelet was a series of solid, half-inch square links with some sort of design on the face of each. A few of the links had melted some from the fire, but otherwise it was surprisingly still intact. Quinn stuck it in his pocket.

'Think it means anything?' Nate asked.

'I want you to go back to your car and wait for me.'

'How am I supposed to learn anything that way?'

Quinn looked Nate in the eye. 'Today's lesson: Do what you're told.'

Nate stared back for a moment, then looked down. Without another word, he turned and began walking away.

Once Nate was gone, Quinn continued toward the line of trees at the edge of the property. As he neared it, the first flakes of snow began floating down from the sky.

'Great,' he muttered under his breath as he picked up his pace.

When he arrived at the depression, he bent down to get a closer look. Immediately he knew it wasn't caused by a pinecone, and definitely not by a branch. It was a footprint. Several, actually. Now knowing what to look for, he could see more indentations running along the trees leading back to the rear of the property.

At first Quinn couldn't tell whether the footprints were heading to or away from the house. A closer look revealed they were doing both. Someone had approached the house from the forest, then returned, keeping his – or her – feet in the same indentations. In fact, the person may have made more than one trip. Or maybe more than one person had used the same tracks. It was impossible to tell. Snow boots, though. Sorels, if Quinn guessed right.

As he followed the tracks, making a new set of his own beside them, the air began to thicken with falling snow. The prints were deep enough, though, that it would take some time before they completely disappeared.

A hundred yards from the house, Quinn found that whoever had made the tracks had stopped, either coming or going, and used the cover of several pine trees to shield him from the house. The person had stomped around a bit, probably to stay warm.

'You watched the fire from here,' Quinn said to himself, picturing the scene in his mind. 'Made sure it was doing what you wanted.'

But why had he gone back?

Because now that Quinn had had a chance to

look at several of the depressions, the top set of footprints definitely were heading back to the house.

He tried to reason it out, but no answer came to him. He decided not to worry about it for the moment, then continued following the person's footprints deeper into the woods.

He immediately noticed there was something different about these new tracks. There weren't multiple passes on them. Just one set, heading toward the house.

Okay, Quinn thought. *So, our guy approaches the house from somewhere off in the forest. He starts the fire. Walks back into the woods. Finds a tree to hide behind to make sure he's done a thorough job. Then what?*

The only possible answer he could come up with was that the fire didn't take the first time.

Or, he suddenly realized, *someone else had shown up, potentially ruining the arsonist's plan.*

Except there hadn't been any report of another body. Just Taggert. The only thing Quinn could definitely determine from the tracks was that the assassin hadn't left the scene the same way he'd come.

Quinn sat in the driver's seat of the Explorer, still parked in front of the Farnham house. He was talking on his cell phone to Peter, head of an agency simply called the Office.

'Definitely not an accident,' Quinn said.

'Witnesses?' Peter asked.

'Don't appear to be any.'

'And Taggert was the only victim?'

'Yes,' Quinn said. 'Unless there's something else you think I should know.'

'Nothing,' Peter told him. Quinn sensed a lie. 'Did the chief have anything else?'

'He did drop something I was unaware of,' Quinn said.

'What was that?'

'He said they talked to someone who claimed to be Taggert's sister. Know anything about that?'

'Just wrap things up and send me your report,' Peter said, ignoring the question.

'Not interested in cause of death?'

'No. You found out everything we need to know.'

'What did you do?' Quinn asked. 'Hire someone you didn't trust to get rid of this guy? Now you're worried maybe he didn't do as good a job as you'd hoped?'

There was a momentary silence from the other end of the line. 'We didn't kill Taggert. He's no use to us dead.'

'Who was he?'

'You don't need to know that.'

'All right, whatever, Peter. I should be out of here by the end of the day. You'll have my report in the morning.' Quinn paused. 'There's a few more things I want to check.'

Peter waited a moment before responding. 'What?'

'There's no car. Nothing here and nothing in the police report. Taggert couldn't have just walked in.'

'Maybe he took a cab.'

'Out here he'd need his own vehicle.'

More silence on the other end. 'Cadillac,' Peter finally said.

'What?'

'He was driving a white Cadillac.'

'Thanks,' Quinn said. 'That'll help.'

'Whoever started the fire probably took it. They're long gone by now.'

Quinn was thinking along the same lines. But it wouldn't hurt to check it out. He did find it odd, though, that Peter seemed so anxious for him to close the case.

'What else?' Peter asked.

'Huh?'

'You said a few things.'

'Just a figure of speech,' Quinn lied.

'I'm sorry, Agent Bennett. There wasn't a car there when the fire department arrived,' Chief Johnson said. 'We shouldn't have missed that. I'm not going to apologize. We're a small force, and we don't get a lot of people dying like that around here. Still, I should have noticed it.'

'I wouldn't worry too much,' Quinn said into his phone. 'Maybe a friend brought him up. Or maybe he just hired a ride.'

'I guess that's possible,' Johnson said. 'I'll look into it.'

'Maybe Taggert's sister will know something. If nothing else, she might at least know what kind of car he drove,' Quinn said, hoping to delay any search by the police until he'd been able to conduct one of his own.

'Good idea. I'll try her.'

'Let me know if you come up with anything,' Quinn said. He asked the chief to fax him a copy of the final report, giving him a number that would send the document straight to Quinn's e-mail in-box. They said their goodbyes, then Quinn hung up and got out of the car.

The snow was continuing to fall, lighter than before but steady. To his left, he heard the door of the Jeep Cherokee open and close. A moment later, Nate joined him.

They stood side by side looking at the remains of the Farnham house, the sound of their breathing the only noise breaking the silence.

After nearly two minutes, Nate said, 'Did you find anything?'

Quinn didn't answer right away. When he did, his voice was calm. 'What were my instructions when I called you?'

'I know. I fucked up. I should have just waited in my hotel room until you called, just like you told me.'

'Why?' Quinn asked.

Nate hesitated, then said, 'Because I could have messed everything up?'

'Because,' Quinn said, his voice calm as he turned to look at Nate, 'that's what I told you to do.'

'I'm sorry.'

Quinn looked at his apprentice, his face neutral. 'I've told you what sorry gets you.'

Nate glanced down at the ground, then back up at Quinn. 'Sorry gets you killed.'

Quinn turned without another word and started making a perimeter search of the parking area. Nate silently followed him a few steps behind.

Quinn didn't really expect to find anything else.

What tracks hadn't been covered up by the new snow had undoubtedly already been destroyed by the rescue vehicles during the fire. He stopped after only a few minutes. If Taggert had a Cadillac, there was no longer any sign of it.

So, Quinn thought. *Where is it now?*

He stared into the wilderness, mulling it over. If Peter was right, the car was probably hundreds of miles away, dumped in a random parking lot. But there was another possibility. And the more Quinn thought about it, the more likely it seemed.

Back in the Explorer, he started the engine and pulled out onto Yancy Lane. Glancing in his rearview mirror, he saw Nate following him in the Cherokee. At least there was something the kid didn't need to be told.

Quinn picked up his phone and called local information.

Chapter 4

Quinn knew if the killer hadn't driven out of town, then his most likely destination had been the nearest alternate transportation, whatever would have gotten him out of town faster. There was really only one place they needed to check. The Goose Valley Community Airport.

And there it was – a white, late-model Caddy. It was parked at the far end of the almost deserted airport parking lot, so it wasn't a stretch to guess that the airport had closed for the day because of the coming storm. It wasn't a big facility in the first place. Quinn knew there couldn't be more than a handful of flights a day, mostly private.

Quinn parked the Explorer next to the Cadillac, Nate pulling up alongside him in the Cherokee. No one would see them, and even if someone did, it was doubtful they'd come over to see what Quinn and Nate were doing. Not in this weather.

Quinn got out of his car and stepped over to the Caddy.

'Who does this belong to?' Nate asked as he walked up.

'Not important,' Quinn said.

Quinn checked the doors. Locked. He walked back over to the Explorer and retrieved a long, flat piece of flexible metal from the surveillance kit. The metal strip was straight for about a foot and a half, then bent up and down like a T wave on an EKG, forming a hook at the end.

He carried the instrument over to the Caddy and handed it to Nate. 'Open it,' he said, pointing at the car.

Nate smiled, then slipped the modified slim jim between the window glass and the weather stripping on the front passenger door. Within thirty seconds, the lock released and Nate opened the door.

'You're better than before,' Quinn said. 'But you still need work. You've got to be able to get in under five seconds. Any make or model. Otherwise, there's a good chance you're dead.'

Nate's smile didn't falter. 'But I did do better.'

Quinn shook his head, a smile briefly touching his lips. 'A little.'

The inside of the car looked tidy, but not unusually so. Chances were Taggert's assassin was a day-player like Quinn – hired per job, but not part of any bigger picture. If searching the car hadn't been on the killer's to-do list, then it wasn't done. Why waste the effort on something you weren't getting paid for?

Quinn popped open the glove compartment. Inside he found an unused owner's manual, a maintenance log, a couple of maps, a disposable camera still sealed in a plastic bag, the vehicle registration, a rental agreement – so it wasn't Taggert's personal car – a pair of expensive Ray-Ban sunglasses, and two fully loaded magazines. He left the sunglasses, but stuffed the mags and rental agreement into his pocket.

Next he checked under the car's front seats, hoping to find a gun that matched the ammo. But there was nothing.

Nate was still standing outside the Caddy's door. Quinn looked out at him.

'I'll pop the trunk,' Quinn said. He removed one of the mags from his pocket and held it up. 'We're looking for a gun. A Glock 9mm.'

'Okay,' Nate said.

Quinn released the trunk, then began searching the rest of the interior of the Caddy while Nate checked out the back. Quinn had barely begun when he heard Nate's footsteps returning around the side of the car. He looked over as Nate leaned in.

'What is it?' Quinn asked.

'You need to see.'

Quinn was annoyed, but said nothing as he followed his apprentice back to the open trunk.

'She's dead,' Nate said, unnecessarily.

Taking up a good portion of the trunk space was the body of a woman wrapped generously in silver duct tape. There was none of the smell Quinn would have usually expected, but that was no doubt due to the cold.

He recognized her almost immediately. Even bound as she was, there was no mistaking her. It was Jills. Helpful Jills, informative Jills, happy Jills. Sometime coworker, sometime acquaintance. Quinn clicked his tongue against the roof of his mouth.

Now he knew why the arsonist had come back to the house. Taggert hadn't been alone.

Quinn had no idea if 'Jills' was her first or last name. It wasn't the kind of question you asked someone in this business. It probably wasn't her given name, anyway. Just like Peter wasn't Peter's. Or like Jonathan Quinn wasn't his.

She was a courier mostly, though Quinn had heard she'd done a little operations work recently. Never on one of his gigs, though.

Operations was a dangerous life choice. Which was why Quinn liked what he did. No one bothered with the guy who came in after the fact, nosing around a bit, making things pretty for the locals. Quinn's line of work was about as safe as it came in the world of freelance espionage. Not without its hazards, but he was usually able to sleep soundly at night.

I guess this is why Peter asked if anyone else had died, Quinn thought as he stared down at her. What harm would it have done to tell Quinn that Jills was part of the program?

One thing was for sure. It looked like Quinn was going to have to do a bit of serious cleaning after all.

'You're sure it was Jills?' Peter asked.

It was almost noon. Quinn stood near the window in his motel room at the Holiday Inn, alone. The storm didn't look like it was going to let up soon. He was concerned that the roads back to Denver might close down in the next few hours, so he'd sent Nate off to pick up his stuff. As for Quinn's own bag, it was packed and waiting in the Explorer.

'No question,' Quinn said. 'But whoever did it beat her up pretty bad first.'

Peter was briefly silent. 'You took care of it?'

'It's handled,' Quinn told him. He'd called a disposal guy based in Denver he'd used before. Jills and the Cadillac would disappear within a couple hours. He'd arranged for her cremated remains to be delivered to the Office, but he decided not to share that information with Peter.

'What about the local police?'

'They don't suspect anything. I'm assuming Taggert's sister gave them a false lead on the car.'

Peter wasn't biting. 'Good,' was all he said.

'What was Jills doing here? Was she working with him, or was she working for you?'

'How should I know?' Peter said, sounding a bit too rehearsed.

'So you're saying this wasn't your operation?'

'I never said it was.'

Why was Peter trying so hard to sell him? Quinn wondered.

'And Taggert wasn't your responsibility?'

'Not our responsibility,' Peter echoed.

That cinched it. Peter was lying about something. If he wasn't, he wouldn't have even answered Quinn's questions in the first place. There was definitely more going on here than Peter was letting on.

'I'm heading out now,' Quinn said. 'I'll e-mail you my report tomorrow when I get home.'

'Stay available,' Peter said. 'We might have something else coming up soon.'

'If I've got nothing else going on, we can talk.' Quinn hung up.

Chapter 5

Peter had always been a pain in the ass. But he did provide Quinn with consistent work, and seldom argued over fees. Since Quinn was planning an early retirement, that was enough. He'd long ago decided steady work at top dollar offset the annoyance factor that came with working for the Office.

The real problem was Quinn had actually stopped working for anyone else. It wasn't planned, it just kind of happened that way. Whether Peter was aware of the situation or not, Quinn didn't know. It was none of Peter's business, so Quinn never told him. The less Peter knew about Quinn's life, the better.

The same could also be said about Quinn's knowledge of Peter and the Office. The only thing Quinn knew for sure was that their main headquarters was located somewhere in D.C., nothing more. If pressed he would have guessed the Office to be some secretly funded agency of the U.S. government – maybe NSA, maybe military intelligence. But he wasn't sure. And honestly, he didn't really care.

That wasn't to say Quinn didn't have standards. He considered himself a patriot, though a jaded one. If he thought for one moment he was doing anything that would harm his country, he'd drop it. So far that hadn't happened with the Office. And until it did, he was content to do his job and take his money.

His standard rate was 30K a week, U.S., with a two-week minimum whether he worked all fourteen days or not. He averaged one job a month. It meant that, even without bonuses, Quinn was bringing in almost three quarters of a million a year. With bonuses he easily made double that. Not bad work, if you could get it.

Quinn and Nate left in the Explorer as soon as Nate returned. But instead of heading directly out to the interstate, Quinn turned the SUV toward downtown.

'I thought you wanted to get out of here,' Nate said.

'I need to make a couple stops first.'

As far as Peter was concerned, the Taggert investigation was over. But that wasn't the way Quinn worked. If there were still leads to be followed, he'd track them down. He would never leave a job half done. If Peter didn't want to know about it, so be it.

Valley Central Hospital was located about a mile from the police station in Allyson. As far as medical centers went, it was small even for the size of area it served. The building was a gray stone structure, only two stories high, and taking up the length of a short city block.

Quinn parked the Explorer in the sparsely filled visitors' lot. Immediately, Nate unbuckled his seat-belt and reached for his door.

'What do you think you're doing?' Quinn asked.

'You want me to come with you, don't you?'

Quinn thought for a moment. 'If you come along, you don't say one word. Understood?'

Nate smiled and nodded.

The receptionist in the main lobby told Quinn that Dr. Horner was in the morgue. As was typical, death had been relegated to the basement. Quinn and Nate took the stairs, and asked a passing nurse for directions. She pointed toward a small office halfway down the hall. There they found a man in his early forties, big but not fat, a college athlete who had started to go to seed, sitting at a desk and talking on the phone. A blue plastic badge on his chest identified him as Dr. Shaun S. Horner.

'I don't think so,' Horner was saying into a phone as Quinn and Nate entered. The doctor nodded a greeting, and gestured to an empty chair beside the desk, apparently not realizing there was only one place for two people. Quinn sat.

'No, no. Cardiac arrest,' Horner continued. 'No, ma'am. No signs of anything else . . . I'm sorry. That's all I've got. Okay. Thanks.'

Horner hung up the phone. 'Insurance investigator,' he said to Quinn. 'Looking for something that'll get them out of paying a claim, I think.'

'Doesn't sound like she got what she wanted,' Quinn offered.

'I can tell them what I know, but I can't tell

them what I don't.' The doctor extended his hand. 'Shaun Horner.'

Quinn grasped the man's hand and shook. 'Frank Bennett.' Quinn turned toward Nate. 'And this is . . .' He paused, then said, 'Agent Driscoll.'

'I thought so,' Horner said. 'Chief Johnson called to say you might stop by. What can I do for you, Mr. Bennett?'

'Actually, it's Special Agent Bennett.'

'Right. Sorry.'

Quinn smiled. 'It's about the Farnham fire.'

The actual morgue was two doors down from Dr. Horner's office. It was also small, boasting only ten body drawers and a single autopsy table. 'Seldom have more than three or four bodies here at one time,' Horner was saying. 'I had six once. But that was my record.'

'How many do you have now?' Quinn asked.

'Only two,' the doctor said. 'One's your fire victim. The second's a woman who lived across the valley. Slipped and fell on her own front porch.'

The doctor led Quinn and Nate to a drawer at the far end of the room.

'You've had burn victims here before?' Quinn asked.

'A few,' the doctor said. 'And if you ask me, I can wait awhile until the next one. It's not pretty.'

Without asking if his visitors were ready, the doctor pulled open the drawer. The body, or what was left of it, lay uncovered on the long tray. It was a charred mass of flesh. Quinn didn't even flinch at the sight of it, but Nate turned away, gagging.

'You okay?' the doctor asked.

'It's his first time,' Quinn said.

'I'm okay,' Nate said, clearly not looking at it.

'Maybe you want to step outside for a minute,' Horner said.

Nate shook his head and resumed his spot beside the doctor as Quinn took a look at the body.

Taggert was lying on his back, his arms and legs bent upward in the pugilistic posture caused by shrinking tissue common to most burn victims. In some areas the flesh was completely burned away. Elsewhere the skin was sunken where the muscles and organs had cooked and contracted.

'Asphyxiation?' Quinn asked.

The doctor hesitated. 'Actually, no.'

Quinn looked over at Horner. 'No?'

'There appeared to be very little smoke damage to his lungs. I've sent some tissue off to the lab in Denver to be sure.'

Quinn made a mental note. That was one sample that needed to get lost. 'If he didn't die of the smoke, then what?'

The coroner shrugged. 'My best guess is that when he realized there was a fire, he panicked, tripped, and hit his head on something. Maybe a bedpost or a nightstand.'

'Was there damage to his skull?' Nate asked.

Quinn shot his apprentice a quick look, but said nothing.

'Some,' the doctor said. 'Which could have happened after the house collapsed. But that's doubtful.'

'Why?' Quinn asked.

'There was a lot of blood loss that occurred around the wound,' Horner said. 'Since his lungs seemed clean, I'm pretty sure by the time the house fell apart, Mr. Taggert here was already dead.'

'You don't find that unusual?'

'Not really,' the doctor said. 'Given the circumstances, I mean. He was probably terrified. The house was burning up around him. Most people make mistakes under that kind of pressure.' Horner looked at Quinn for a moment. 'If you're really asking if someone else did this to him, I guess it's possible, but unlikely. Frankly, Agent Bennett, that kind of thing doesn't happen here in Allyson. You've been spending too much time in big cities.'

'Sorry,' Nate said, once they were back in the Explorer driving away. 'I just couldn't help myself. I mean, it's obvious he was murdered.'

Quinn pulled the SUV to the curb and turned to Nate. 'Why?' he asked.

'The wound. That's what killed him. Someone hit him over the head.'

'So the wound tells us conclusively that he was murdered?'

'Well, sure,' Nate said, only now he didn't sound so confident.

'It couldn't have happened the way Dr. Horner said? Taggert panicked and hit his head?'

'Sure, it's possible. But it doesn't seem likely.'

Quinn stared at Nate for a moment, then looked back out the front window and put the Explorer back in gear.

'What?' Nate asked.

Quinn said nothing. Taggert had indeed been murdered, and the evidence had been right there in front of them at the morgue. But it wasn't the blow to the head that had led Quinn to this conclusion.

Quinn had known what happened the moment he'd seen the body. Taking the contractions in the arms and legs caused by the heat into account, the fire had frozen Taggert in the position he'd been in when the flames consumed him. If he'd died of smoke inhalation, the body would have been curled up in an obvious defensive posture. Even if he died from a head trauma, it was unlikely that his body would have landed so neatly laid out.

No, Quinn knew someone had posed him like this. Someone had wanted the Office to know this was a murder.

They drove across town, eventually parking in a lot just off Lake Avenue. Quinn was relieved to see the 'Open' sign hanging in the window.

He looked over at Nate. 'You stay here.'

There was no protest. Quinn zipped up his jacket and got out.

The building was an old, one-story house that had been converted into an office. Hanging on the wall near the front door was a sign that read, 'Goose Valley Vacation Rentals & Realty.' There was a covered porch where Quinn dusted the snow off his jacket. He then opened the door and went inside.

The front room had at one time probably made for a comfortable parlor, but now it was crowded with three desks, several bookcases, and a row of black metal filing cabinets. A radio was playing an old Neil Diamond song softly in the background. Against the far wall, a fire burned in a brick fireplace.

Only the desk closest to the fireplace was occupied. Behind it sat a woman Quinn judged to be in her mid-forties. Her blonde, frosted hair fell to just above her shoulders. She was wearing a smart-looking blue business suit. She smiled broadly as Quinn entered.

'Good afternoon,' she said, standing. 'Didn't expect anybody else today.'

Quinn offered a friendly chuckle as he approached her desk. 'Yeah, weather's getting a little crazy out there. Don't worry. I won't keep you long.'

'I heard we're in for almost two feet of snow by tomorrow.' She stuck out a hand. 'I'm Ann Henderson.'

Quinn shook her hand. 'Miss Henderson, I'm Frank Bennett.'

'Please, just Ann.' She indicated the guest chair, and they both sat. 'What can I do for you, Mr. Bennett?'

He pulled out his ID and showed it to her.

'FBI?' She looked perplexed. 'Is something wrong?'

Quinn smiled again and shook his head. 'I was just hoping you could help me with something.'

'Of course. Whatever I can do.'

'I'm looking into the fire at the Farnham house.'

Her face turned somber. 'A tragedy. It's such a shame.' A question formed in her eyes. 'I heard it was an accident.'

'It looks that way.'

'Then why would the FBI be interested?'

'Truthfully, my involvement is totally off the record. Mr. Taggert was a relative of someone in the Bureau. I'm just here checking things out for him.'

She relaxed visibly. 'I'm sorry to hear that. Mr. Taggert seemed like a nice guy.'

'Did you know him?'

'Not really. I only spoke with him twice. Once when he called to set up the rental, and then again when he came by to sign the agreement and pick up the key.'

'That's why I stopped by. My colleague was hoping I might be able to get a copy of the rental agreement.'

She eased back. 'Why would he want that?'

'Just trying to be thorough, that's all.'

'Is he planning to sue or something?'

Quinn laughed good-naturedly. 'Not at all. The family just wants to put this behind them. I'm just helping wrap up the details so they can move on. I can guarantee you there will be no lawsuit.'

Once again her relief was visible. 'Well, I guess it's not a problem.'

She got up and walked over to one of the filing cabinets. She pulled open the third drawer from the top and started flipping through the files. After a moment of searching, she removed a thin manila folder. 'Just give me a minute,' she said. 'The copier's in the back.'

'Could I take a look first? To make sure it's worth you making the effort?'

'Sure.'

She handed Quinn the file. There were only two sheets of paper inside. The first was a standard, boilerplate rental agreement. According to the information Taggert provided, he lived in Campobello, Nevada. Quinn had never heard of Campobello, but he was far from familiar with every city in Nevada. It was undoubtedly a false address anyway. Under emergency contact was written 'G. Taggert, sister' and the same phone number Chief Johnson had given Quinn.

'So you were the one who provided Mr. Taggert's sister's number to the police.'

'That's right. Mr. Taggert almost didn't give it to me, though. I had to promise not to call his sister unless it was an absolute emergency.'

Quinn nodded, understanding, then looked back at the file. There was other basic information, but nothing that would be of use. Quinn flipped to the second sheet. It was a photocopy of a Nevada driver's license. Robert William Taggert. Due to expire on November 22 of the following year. The photograph was grainy, but the image was discernible. A man in his late fifties, with short-cropped hair, and a thin, weathered face.

'This is Mr. Taggert?' Quinn asked.

She peeked around the edge of the folder. 'That's him.'

'Can I also get a copy of this?' he asked.

'Don't you have a picture of him?'

Quinn shook his head. 'Nobody thought to give me one,' he said truthfully.

Ann shrugged. 'Just take that one. If I make a copy the picture will only be a black smudge.'

'Thanks,' he said. He folded the paper, careful not to crease the photo, and slipped it into his pocket.

Quinn and Nate were able to make it to Denver just in time to catch a 7:00 p.m. flight home to Los Angeles. While Nate was shoehorned into the cattle section in back, Quinn relaxed with a glass of Chablis in the comfort of his first-class seat. After they'd been in the air for an hour, Quinn pulled out his computer and wrote his report.

By the time he finished, it was only a page long. He liked to keep things brief. 'Overload with facts,' Durrie, his mentor, had once told him. 'They can never fault you for that. Leave out all the cream puff stuff and opinions. Nobody wants that shit. And if you find somebody that does, they're not worth working for.'

Good advice, but it had taken a while for it to sink in with Quinn. When he'd first started working clean-and-gathers, he knew his task was to just hand over whatever he found out and move on. Curiosity was discouraged. But it had been frustrating. There were always so many unanswered questions.

'What the fuck do you want to know more for?' Durrie had asked him one time when Quinn wanted to keep probing after a particular assignment was nearly completed.

'It just seems so unfinished,' Quinn said. 'Just once, I'd like to know what it's all about.'

'What it's all about?' Durrie asked. 'Fine. That I can answer. You see this guy here?'

They were in an unpaved alleyway on the south

side of Tijuana, Mexico. It was well after midnight. On the ground only a couple feet in front of them was the body of a man in his late twenties. 'I see him,' Quinn said.

'This guy's a runner. You know, a messenger boy? But he could've just as easily been a cleaner.'

'Like us, you mean?'

'Like *me*. You're just an apprentice. You'll be lucky to live through this year the way you're going.'

'I'm careful,' Quinn said defensively.

'You're not. Worse, you don't even realize it.'

Quinn's face hardened, but he said nothing.

'You want to know what it's all about, Johnny boy?' Durrie continued. He pointed at the corpse on the ground. '*That's* what it's all about. The more you know, the more likely you'll end up like him. We come in, gather whatever information's been requested. Maybe do a little cleanup if necessary. Then get out. That's the job.' Durrie's eyes locked with Quinn's. 'Kill your curiosity, kid. For your own sake. Hell, for mine, too. Because until you're working on your own, I'll be responsible for your fuckups.'

It took nearly getting shot six months later before the lesson sank in. Still, Quinn was never able to completely dampen his thirst to know more. He later realized that despite what Durrie said, curiosity was an important part of the job. He just had to learn how to control it. As he reread his report about Taggert, he knew there was a lot that remained unanswered. Who had started the fire? Why had Jilis been there? And who the hell was Taggert anyway? Questions that nagged at him, but ones he probably would never know the answers to.

Otherwise, the information Quinn had been able to gather wasn't much more than what he'd already told Peter over the phone. The only omissions were his stops at the coroner's office and Goose Valley Vacation Rentals. And the most those stops had done was to confirm what little Quinn already knew. The exception being the lung tissue sample, which Quinn had added into his report as something Chief Johnson had mentioned.

It wasn't until he'd put away his computer that he remembered there was one other thing he had neglected to include in the report, the silver-colored bracelet Nate had found at the house. At first Quinn thought it had meant nothing, but in light of finding Jills, maybe he'd been wrong.

Chapter 6

Quinn and Nate separated at LAX, Quinn telling his apprentice to meet him at his house in a couple hours to go over everything. Before that, Quinn wanted to have a nice quiet dinner alone.

He picked up his car, a black BMW M3 convertible, from the VIP lot he had parked it in before he'd left on his vacation. The drive across town took a little longer than he'd planned, but soon enough he arrived at the Taste of Siam restaurant on Sunset Boulevard in Hollywood. It wasn't the most popular Thai restaurant in L.A., nor the biggest, but it was Quinn's favorite. His usual table was open when he arrived, so he took a seat and ordered *pad kee mao* with chicken, choosing as always to wash it down with a Singha beer.

Occasionally, one of the waitresses would stop by to say hello. They would smile and say how good it was to see him again, or ask him why he'd waited so long to come back. And each time he'd thank them and say he'd been out of town, then promise not to be gone so long again.

A couple of years earlier, he'd done a favor for

one of the girls who worked there. Somehow she'd picked up an 'admirer' who convinced himself that she felt the same for him. He took to stalking her, day and night. Once she'd come home to find the man in her kitchen making her dinner. When Quinn heard about what was happening, he had a conversation with the guy and convinced him there were better things to do with his time. There had been no more problems after that.

Though the waitress he'd helped had eventually moved back to Thailand, the rest of the staff hadn't forgotten what Quinn had done. Now they were always glad to see him, and he never had to pay for a meal. That was one of Durrie's rules he had consciously broken. 'Never use your training to help someone on the outside.' The 'outside' being anyone not in the business or directly related to a job. Durrie's theory was that if you did, you could expose a weakness an adversary could exploit.

With that in mind, Taste of Siam was a perk Quinn tried not to take advantage of too often. But it was hard to stay away. The food was always good, and the waitresses were very easy on the eyes.

While he waited for his food, Quinn reached into his pocket and pulled out the bracelet Nate had found in Colorado. As he had noted before, it was basically a ring of metal squares joined together by small, thin, wire hoops that gave the bracelet flexibility. Each square had a different pattern etched on its surface. Now that he had time for a closer look, the designs reminded him of family crests. None, though, were familiar to him. The squares were thick, too, maybe an eighth of an inch from top to bottom, maybe more.

At first he thought they were all solid, but on the one next to the hasp he detected a faint line running along the bottom edge. *Plated?* he wondered. Before he could investigate further, his food arrived. He put the bracelet back in his pocket to study later.

As usual, the food was just what he needed. When he asked for the check, he received a smile and the standard 'No charge.' He laid a twenty down on the table as a tip, then left.

Quinn's job afforded him the ability to live anywhere in the world. And after careful consideration, he had chosen Los Angeles. The location was optimal. Via LAX, he could get almost anywhere in a hurry, essential for his professional life. Then there was the weather. Warm, low humidity. Few bugs. And no snow. Essential for his personal life.

He'd been born in Warroad, Minnesota, a small town on the edge of the Lake of the Woods, a stone's throw from the Canadian border. A couple thousand people on a good day, competing with the heat and mosquitoes in the summer and the cold and snow in the winter. And nearly every one of them counting their blessings that they didn't have to live in the big city.

Everyone, that was, except Quinn. As soon as he could get out, he was gone. California was his home now.

His house in the Hollywood Hills was on a quiet, winding street, high above the chaos of the L.A.

basin. It sat on a half acre of downward-sloping land, and was surrounded by a tall stone wall complete with a steel security gate across the driveway entrance. As he drove up, he noticed Nate standing off to the side, waiting.

That was one thing Nate had going for him, he was never late. Overeager, a little raw, but never late.

Quinn hit the remote button mounted under his dash and waited while the gate rolled aside. As soon as there was enough room, he drove in. He glanced in his rearview mirror to make sure Nate had walked in behind him, then hit the remote again to close the gate.

Quinn got out of his car, then pulled his suitcase out of the trunk. 'Here,' he said. 'Carry this.' He handed the suitcase to Nate, then walked past him and up the steps to the front door.

As he unlocked it and pushed it open, he asked Nate, 'Thirsty?'

'Sure,' Nate said.

'Did you eat?'

Nate shook his head. 'Just dropped my bag off at my place. Had an errand to run.'

'There might be a can of soup in the cupboard. If not, you're out of luck.'

Quinn stepped across the threshold and stopped at the security panel just inside the doorway. He pressed the pad of his left thumb against the touch-screen monitor, then punched in his release code. He and Nate were the only ones the system would recognize.

A moment later he was greeted with a double

beep telling him the system was now on standby. Nate followed him into the house.

Quinn scrolled through a series of menus and reports, checking on the security status of his house. When he was satisfied that all was well, he switched the system to *House Occupied.* Number of people present: *Two*. This allowed the system to remain in an active mode while still accounting for his and Nate's presence.

'So, did you enjoy your Thai food?' Nate asked.

'Thought you said you had an errand?'

'I did.'

'You decided you'd try following me, didn't you?' Quinn asked.

'Just trying to get in a little practice,' Nate said, barely able to contain a smug smile. 'At first I thought you'd made me. You definitely didn't take the most direct route. But then you gave up, and I realized you hadn't seen me after all.'

There was triumph in Nate's voice.

'What's the one thing I've told you about following someone in a large city?'

A bit of Nate's smile disappeared. 'That it's easy to do. Too many cars. Hard to be spotted.'

'Especially at night, right?'

'Right.'

'So how much skill would it have taken to follow me around?'

Nate shrugged. 'Not a lot, I guess.'

'And how skillful would I have to be to have spotted you?'

'You'd have to be the best,' Nate conceded.

'Try following me at three in the morning if you

want me to see how good you are.' Quinn paused. 'Besides, tonight you were always at least three cars behind me. A dark blue Nissan Altima.'

Nate stared at him.

'Arizona plates. I can give you the number if you'd like.' Now it was Quinn's turn to smile. 'How about a drink?'

Nate continued to gape. 'You knew I was there the whole time?'

'Try to keep up with the conversation, all right? What do you want to drink?'

'Eh . . . Scotch and soda?'

Quinn eyed him curiously. 'That's an old man drink. Since when do you have those?'

Nate shook his head. 'Never had one before.'

'Then why would you want to start now?'

'Saw someone have one on TV,' Nate said. 'Thought I'd give it a try.'

'Why don't we save that for your sixtieth birthday. I'll make you a mai tai.'

'Haven't had one of those, either,' Nate said agreeably.

Quinn walked over to the built-in bar near a large stone fireplace on the left side of the living room and began making the drinks. 'What do you think your biggest mistake was?'

'When I was following you?'

'In Colorado. Where did you mess up the most?'

'Oh. I guess going to see the police on my own.'

'That was a close second, I'll give you that. Try something else.'

'That I didn't do as you told me?'

'We'll make that one-B,' Quinn said.

Nate was silent for a moment. 'I'm not sure what you're looking for.'

Quinn emerged from behind the bar carrying two drinks. He walked over to Nate and handed him one. 'What name did you use when you were out there?'

Nate glanced away for a second. 'Nathan Driscoll. And before you even ask, I know. Never use any part of your own name.'

'That's a pretty simple one.'

'I didn't want to get tripped up,' Nate said. 'Besides, I only used my first name.'

'It's enough,' Quinn said, then took a sip of his drink. 'Tripped up in Colorado this morning or killed ten years from now in someplace like St Petersburg because someone ID'd you from the name you used with the chief of police. It's pretty much the same thing, isn't it?' Quinn raised his glass in a mock toast. 'Here's hoping that one never comes back to bite you in the ass.'

When Quinn bought his house, it had been a twelve-hundred-square-foot fixer-upper. By the time he'd finished his renovations, it was more than twice its original size, and little trace of the old structure remained.

The main floor was located at street level. It was a large, open space that stretched nearly the entire length of the house. Through a series of half-walls, bookcases, and furniture, it was divided up into a dining room, living room, study, and kitchen. Only the bathroom was truly private. The three bedrooms and office were all downstairs, below street level, following the slope of the hill.

The house had a warm feel to it, due in part to a large amount of exposed wood. Nate said it reminded him of a rustic farmhouse stuck on the side of a hill. That image cut a little too close to Quinn's farm-boy roots. He preferred equating it to a comfortable mountain cabin.

Quinn carried his drink across the room, then opened the curtains that were drawn across the entire back wall of the house.

'I never get over your view,' Nate said.

The rear of the house was mostly glass. And Nate was right, Quinn's view of the city was spectacular. Lights spread across the L.A. basin as far as the eye could see. Closest to them was the Sunset Strip. Beyond that, Century City, and a little more to the right in the distance was the dark void of the Pacific Ocean.

'This was a good trip for you,' Quinn said. 'If you're smart, you learned a lot.'

Nate was about to take a drink, but stopped instead and lowered his glass. 'I'm smart.'

'Tell me how smart?'

'Never use your real name, first or last,' Nate said. 'Never talk if I've been told not to. Never visit the scene of an operation unless supervised.' He paused for a moment, then added, 'And never show any initiative unless you tell me I should.'

'You're right. You are smart. Someday you can show all the initiative you want. Someday, your life will depend on it. But now?'

'Both our lives depend on what you decided,' Nate said, repeating a maxim Quinn had been drilling into him since Nate's first day on the job.

Before Quinn could say anything further, his cell

phone rang. He glanced at his watch. It was nearly midnight.

Quinn walked over to the end table and picked the phone up from where he'd left it.

'Hello?' he said.

'I need you in D.C.' It was Peter.

'You're working late.'

'Look, we've got a big operation gearing up and it looks like we could use your help. This is top priority.'

'Something to do with our friend in Colorado?'

'At this point, the details are not your concern. You'll be briefed when you arrive. I have you booked on a plane leaving at seven in the morning. I've e-mailed you the details.'

'I think we've missed a step here. I don't actually work for you. You need to ask me first. We call this the job offer.'

'Technically, you're still on the payroll.'

Quinn's eyes narrowed. Peter was referring to his two-week minimum on the Taggert job, of which Quinn had only really used two days. But there was an unwritten rule that the minimum applied only to the specific job he was hired for. Peter was stretching things.

Apparently taking Quinn's silence for acceptance, Peter said, 'I'll see you in the afternoon.' The line went dead.

'What's up?' Nate asked as Quinn put the phone back down.

Quinn told him the basics, the whole time thinking he definitely had to reconsider the working-for-one-client thing.

'You're going, then?' Nate asked.

'Yeah.' Quinn drained his drink. 'I'm going.' He glanced over at Nate, who was smiling at Quinn's annoyance. 'And you're driving me to the airport.'

'Come on,' Nate said, his smile gone. 'I just want to go home and go to bed.'

'Sleep on the couch,' Quinn told him. 'We leave at five a.m.'

Quinn was deep in a world of nothingness when he felt a distant shaking. It was accompanied by a voice. 'Quinn. Wake up.'

Quinn pushed himself up, immediately awake. Nate was leaning down beside him, next to the bed. 'What?' Quinn asked.

'Your security alarm just went off,' Nate said, his voice an urgent whisper. 'I think someone's outside.'

Security alarm? Quinn should have heard it. He had an auxiliary panel right in his room.

Getting out of bed, he went to the panel on the wall. A red light was blinking. It was then he realized the throbbing he felt in his head wasn't throbbing at all. It was the low-level pulsing tone of the alarm. He hadn't slept well in Colorado, and the day of investigating and traveling had been a long one. Now that he was home, he'd fallen asleep so deeply the alarm hadn't even registered on him. *Sloppy, Quinn,* he thought. *Really, really sloppy.*

'Did you check the monitor upstairs?' Quinn asked.

Nate nodded. 'It says, "Rear Fence Breach." I

pulled up the backyard camera, but I didn't see anything. You think it might be a cat or something?'

'Doubtful,' Quinn said. The system had been adjusted to ignore anything so small. 'What time is it?'

'Almost three.'

Quinn needed to go upstairs and check the security monitor himself. He'd been meaning to install an additional screen in his bedroom, but hadn't got around to it yet.

'Are you armed?' Quinn asked.

Nate raised his right hand. In it was a Walther P99 9mm pistol. Quinn's own SIG 9mm was sitting in his safe upstairs in the living room.

Quinn pulled on the pair of black sweatpants he always kept sitting on top of his dresser, then headed for the stairs. When he reached the top, he stopped to listen.

Silence.

The only light in the house came from the muted, flickering television in the living room and from the gibbous moon filtering through the back windows. Otherwise, the entire upper floor was dark.

Quinn padded over to the security panel near the front door and touched the upper right corner of the screen with his left thumb, bringing the monitor to life. The first thing he did was turn the alarm off. Then, in quick succession, he worked through the feeds from the cameras that kept watch over his property. There was no one in the backyard – not by the back fence nor against the house. If someone had hopped the fence, it would be recorded on the system's hard drive. Quinn could go back and review it later if he needed to.

Nate was watching from over his shoulder. 'Maybe it *was* just a cat,' he suggested.

'Maybe.'

Quinn switched to a view of the front, then tapped the monitor again, zooming the camera in for a tight shot of his house. He began a pan from left to right, moving the camera slowly so that he wouldn't miss anything. About two thirds of the way across he stopped and studied the monitor.

'Not a cat,' Quinn said.

An intruder was crouched on the porch below the bathroom window. Nate started to say something, but Quinn held up a finger for quiet. The bathroom was just around the corner from where they were standing. There was a chance, though slight, that they might be overheard. Quinn quickly dialed through the remaining cameras to make sure the intruder was alone. When he was satisfied there was no one else, he returned to the original image. The intruder hadn't moved.

Quinn motioned for Nate to hand over his gun. No need to break out his own pistol, the Walther would do. Nate handed him the weapon.

'Suppressor?' Quinn whispered.

Nate nodded, then hurried over to the couch where his leather jacket was draped over the arm. From a pocket, he extracted a long cylinder. He brought it back to Quinn, who attached it to the barrel of the gun.

Quinn leaned toward Nate. 'Stay here,' he whispered. 'When you hear a single knock on the front door, open it.'

'What if he gets you first?'

Quinn scowled. 'When you hear a single knock on the front door,' he repeated, 'open it.'

Nate nodded. 'Okay.'

Chapter 7

From outside, it appeared that the only exits to Quinn's house were through the front door or the attached three-car garage. But there was another way, hidden on the west side of the building. Quinn thought of it as his 'escape hatch.' It was a small door that blended in almost perfectly with the surrounding wall. Quinn had built it himself, but this was the first time he had needed to use it.

The door swung inward silently on oiled hinges. Quinn paused for a moment, listening. All was quiet. He eased through the opening and into the night.

He crept along the side of the house, stopping just before reaching the front corner. Carefully, he peered around the edge.

The intruder was still on the porch but was no longer kneeling below the bathroom window. He'd moved to the other side of the front door, just below the window to the entrance hall. Since the interior wooden shutters were closed, the intruder couldn't see in.

Quinn was about to step around the corner of the house when his unwanted visitor pulled what looked like a small black box out of a cloth bag at his side. Quinn stopped to watch. The intruder pressed the device gently against the window, where it stuck easily. He then pulled a set of earphones out of his pocket, plugging it into the box. He put one of the earpieces into his left ear.

This guy's not some random burglar, Quinn thought. *He's a pro.*

Quinn had seen the black box before. In fact, he owned one himself. It was an echo box, a listening device that amplified sounds from inside a building when placed against a window. It was held in position against the glass by a quick-release suction device. For the moment, the intruder would be able to hear almost anything that was said inside.

Keeping low, Quinn moved away from the house, over to where his BMW was parked in the driveway. The move didn't get him any closer to the intruder, but it did put Quinn behind the son of a bitch. He checked the Walther to make sure the sound suppressor was firmly attached, then moved toward the house.

The intruder had removed the listening device from his ear and was now pulling something else out of his bag. Quinn moved silently forward, not stopping until he was only six feet away from his uninvited guest.

'Put it down,' Quinn said in a calm, even voice.

The man froze, then lowered his hands. In one was a thin, ropelike substance. Quinn recognized it immediately. Incendiary cord. He wasn't quite sure what the guy had in mind, but there was no mistaking the ultimate objective.

'Drop it,' Quinn said.

The intruder did as he was told.

'Now turn around and stand up. Slowly,' Quinn cautioned. 'Hands in the air.'

The intruder followed Quinn's instructions. The man was about five foot ten and wiry. He couldn't have been more than a hundred and fifty pounds. He was dressed all in black. Even his face, which was smeared with something like grease or shoe polish, was black.

'Five steps,' Quinn said. 'Two away from the window and three toward the front door.'

He watched as the intruder stepped away from his bag and toward the entrance. So far the guy was following orders. Quinn took a step forward, keeping a wary eye on the man. 'Turn around and face the wall,' Quinn said.

When the intruder's back was to him, Quinn shoved the man between the shoulder blades, forcing him hard against the building. Because of the angle, most of the guy's weight was now on his hands, making it nearly impossible for him to make any kind of move on Quinn.

Quinn did a quick body search. The man was carrying a Glock in a shoulder holster, and a seven-inch Ka-Bar fighting knife in a leather sheath on his belt. Quinn took the weapons, then reached over and knocked once on the front door.

Nate opened it instantly. 'I was wondering when the hell you were going to –' He stopped, staring.

'Hands behind you,' Quinn said to the intruder. 'We're going inside.'

* * *

'Kitchen,' Quinn told Nate once the front door was closed again.

Nate led the way. As they passed the living room, Quinn dropped the Glock and the knife on the couch.

The kitchen was a work of art – exposed wood, stainless steel, and a floor covered by light brown tiles imported from Spain. It was almost like one of those kitchens you'd see in a magazine: spacious, functional, with a large island in the center. Off to one side was a breakfast nook, complete with a nineteenth-century wooden table and an eclectic mix of chairs. Nate pulled one of the chairs out from the table, and Quinn pushed the intruder onto it.

'Turn on the light,' Quinn said to Nate.

Nate walked over to the wall and flipped a switch. The light gave Quinn his first chance to get a good look at his prisoner. Even with the black face paint, he wasn't surprised he recognized the man.

'Hello, Gibson,' Quinn said.

'Quinn,' Gibson replied mildly. 'How've you been?'

Quinn pulled a roll of paper towels off a dowel on the counter. 'Here.' He tossed the roll at his captive. 'You can wipe that crap off your face.'

Gibson smiled, but didn't move. The paper towels bounced harmlessly off his lap and onto the floor.

'Your choice,' Quinn said. He retrieved a bottle of water from inside the refrigerator, then returned his attention to Gibson. 'What are you doing here?'

'I was bored.'

'So this was some kind of random house call?'

'Sure. Why not?' Gibson said.

'I didn't realize you knew where I lived.'

'I looked you up in the phone book.'

Quinn smiled, then took a sip of the water. 'Who sent you?'

Gibson snorted. 'Right.'

Quinn calmly raised the Walther and aimed it at Gibson's head. 'Who sent you?'

'You going to kill me, Quinn? That's not like you.'

'One last time. Who sent you?' Quinn repeated.

'Go ahead. Pull the trigger. Kill me, and someone else will do the job.'

Quinn held the gun in place for a moment, then, still smiling, he lowered it, leaving his finger resting on the trigger guard. 'Are you saying there's a contract out on me?'

Gibson shrugged.

'Who's paying the bills?' Quinn asked.

'Like I'd tell you even if I knew. Which I don't. So it doesn't matter, does it?'

Quinn looked at Nate. 'Do you remember the procedure for getting ahold of Peter?'

Nate nodded.

'Call him. My cell's in the living room,' Quinn said. 'See if he can get a pickup team out here. Somebody local. I don't want this asshole hanging around my house any longer than necessary.'

Nate started to turn away when Gibson spoke again. 'I think Peter's probably got his hands full at the moment.'

When Nate hesitated, Quinn said to him, 'Go.' Then he turned back to his prisoner. 'I've never much liked you.'

'I can't see any reason why I'd care,' Gibson said.

'I guess that's probably part of the problem.' Quinn took a long drink from the bottle, then set it on the counter. 'What I hear is that you're sloppy. Apparently that info's right.'

'Fuck you,' Gibson spat.

'You can't even handle an easy solo job.'

Gibson's brow furrowed. 'I know what I'm doing.'

'Really?' Quinn asked. 'If you're so good, why was I able to catch you?'

'I've been at this almost as long as you have. I'd have been dead long ago if I didn't know what I was doing.'

'Given the circumstances, I'd call that dumb luck.'

Quinn could hear Nate talking to someone on the phone in the other room. A moment later, Nate was back.

'Well?' Quinn asked.

Nate looked at Gibson, then at Quinn. 'Peter couldn't come to the phone.'

'Told you,' Gibson said. He was smiling now.

Quinn turned back to his prisoner. 'Did I ask you a question?'

Gibson shrugged.

'Then shut up.' Quinn looked at Nate. 'Who did you talk to?'

'Misty.' She was Peter's main assistant.

'Did you tell her what we needed?'

'I tried to, but she cut me off.'

'So no one's coming?' Quinn asked.

Nate shook his head.

Quinn closed his eyes for a moment in thought.

When he opened them, he handed the pistol to Nate. 'Don't let him move,' he said. 'If he does, shoot him.'

Nate had left the phone on the arm of the couch. Quinn picked it up and hit Redial. Fifteen seconds later, Misty answered. 'Yes?'

'It's Quinn.'

'He doesn't have time right now, Quinn. Things are a bit crazy here.'

'Things are a bit crazy here, too,' Quinn said.

He could hear her sigh on the other end. 'What's the problem?'

'You mean, other than someone trying to kill me?'

'You, too?'

'What do you mean "you, too"?'

'Hold on,' she said quickly. 'Let me see if I can get Peter.'

It was almost a full minute before Peter came on the line. Without preamble, he asked, 'What happened?'

'I just found Martin Gibson lurking outside my front door. And it wasn't a social call.'

'Where is he now?' Peter asked.

'In my kitchen.'

'Is he dead?'

'No,' Quinn said.

'That's something at least.'

'Jesus Christ, Peter. Who would want to kill me?' Quinn asked.

'It's not just you,' Peter said. 'Others have received visitors tonight, also. Unfortunately, most of them . . .'

Peter let the sentence hang.

'Others?' Quinn said. 'Is there a pattern?'

Peter seemed to hesitate, then said, 'They appear to be hitting only members of the Office.'

'No other agency?'

Another pause. 'No.'

Quinn suddenly went cold. 'A disruption?'

'We don't know anything yet,' Peter said, but there was doubt in his voice.

'Who's behind it?'

'If I wasn't talking to you, I might be able to get a few answers.' Peter took a deep breath. 'Even if I did know something, this is an Office matter. It's our business, not –'

There was a loud noise from the kitchen, followed immediately by the spit of a bullet passing through a suppressor. A second later Quinn heard the unmistakable sound of flesh hitting flesh. He dropped the phone and grabbed Gibson's weapons off the couch.

'Nate?' he called out.

No answer.

Quinn hurried toward the kitchen, using the partial wall that divided the two rooms as cover. He was only a few feet away when a bullet slammed into the wall just behind him.

Without thinking, he dove to the floor. A second later two more bullets raced over his head. Remaining on his belly, he snaked his way to the edge of the wall and peered into the kitchen. Nate was there, on the floor. The chair Gibson had been sitting in was on top of him. From where Quinn was, he couldn't tell if his apprentice was still breathing or not. He looked left, then right. Gibson was gone.

Staying low, Quinn turned around and headed back into the living room. This time his only cover was his leather couch. He stopped for a moment and listened intently.

Nothing.

Wherever Gibson had gone, it wasn't far. And though Gibson had Nate's gun, Quinn had both a Glock and a knife. He also knew the layout of his house better than anyone. He knew all the hiding places, all the exits. Gibson had only experienced the walk from the front door to the kitchen. Every move he might make would be a guess.

Outside, the moon had moved below one of the nearby ridges. The only illumination now came from the flicker of the television and the light that was still on in the kitchen.

Quinn ventured a peek around the side of the couch. Nothing seemed out of the ordinary. He scanned the room a second time just to be sure. This time his eyes paused on the leather recliner that sat facing the couch about ten feet away. Something wasn't quite right. It was the shadow cast by the stuffed chair. As it changed with the flickering of the light from the TV, there were moments when the shadow seemed larger than it should have been.

He watched it for a moment, almost dismissing it as an optical illusion. Then the shadow moved.

Quinn eased out from behind the couch into the living room. As he approached the recliner his ears picked up the sound of breathing – slight, but definitely real.

He raised his gun.

'Stand up,' Quinn said.

Gibson leaned around the side of the chair and fired. The bullet went wide, but only by inches. Quinn pulled the trigger on the Glock. A roar filled the room, followed almost instantly by the smell of expended gunpowder. The shot pierced the chair nearly dead-center.

'You son of a bitch,' Gibson hissed, pain lacing his voice.

'Enough?' Quinn asked. 'Throw down the gun and come out slowly.'

Gibson stood up slowly, his left arm dangling uselessly at his side.

'Now put the gun down,' Quinn said.

For a second he thought Gibson was going to comply. Suddenly the assassin pushed back from the chair, the gun in his right hand moving quickly upward, pointing toward Quinn.

But Quinn was ready. He pulled his trigger first.

By the time Gibson slammed against the window, he was already dead. The bulletproof glass reverberated with the weight of the failed assassin's body, but didn't break.

Quinn ran back into the kitchen. The chair still lay on top of Nate's body. Quinn quickly pushed it off and put a hand on his apprentice's neck. He could feel a pulse, steady and strong. Quinn could also now see Nate's chest expand and contract. A quick visual check revealed no entry or exit wounds along his back, and no pool of blood gathering on the floor beneath him.

Quinn leaned down to Nate's left ear. 'Nate,' he said.

There was no response.

'Nate. Wake up.'

A low moan escaped from Nate's mouth. A moment later his eyelids fluttered.

'Take it easy,' Quinn said. 'Are you hit?'

Both eyes opened slowly. 'Quinn?' he said, his mouth pressed against the floor, slurring his speech.

'Are you hit?' Quinn repeated.

'I don't think so.'

'Maybe you should check.'

Nate closed his eyes again. With effort, he rolled over onto his back. 'Fuck,' he called out, wincing.

'What?' Quinn asked.

Nate rubbed the side of his face. 'He hit me in the jaw.'

There was a red patch on the side of Nate's face, but otherwise he appeared unmarked.

Quinn stood up. 'You might want to put some ice on that.'

Quinn walked back into the living room. The phone was still on the couch where he'd dropped it. He picked it up and was about to dial for help when he heard a muffled voice on the other end.

'Quinn?' It was Peter.

'You're still there?'

'What's going on?'

'Gibson got loose.'

'And?'

'He's dead.'

Peter didn't answer right away. 'It would have been better if you'd taken Gibson alive.'

'Well, shucks. I wish you'd told me that sooner. Or maybe I should have told him to wait a moment while I checked with you.'

'Give me the details,' Peter said.

Quinn took a breath, then filled him in.

'You need help with removal?' Peter asked.

'I'll take care of it.' Quinn paused. 'Are you going to tell me what's going on now?'

The line went quiet for a moment, then, 'We're not sure.'

'You realize I'm not coming to D.C., don't you?'

'It's not a good idea now, anyway. I think you should probably just get lost.'

'Is that an official directive?'

'Let's just call it officially unofficial,' Peter said. 'Make yourself scarce. I don't care where. In fact, I don't want to know.'

'The son of a bitch knew where I lived,' Quinn said, more to himself than to Peter.

'More reason to get out of there. Whoever's behind this might try for you again. And if you stay where they can find you, they might not miss next time. But it's your choice.'

'My choice,' Quinn said. 'Right.' He hung up the phone.

Quinn stared for several moments out the back window into the Los Angeles night. Peter was right. If it indeed was a disruption, then disappearing was the only option.

'Nate,' Quinn called toward the kitchen.

Nate, legs unsteady, weaved into the room, falling more than sitting onto the couch. 'What?'

'I hope you haven't unpacked.'

Chapter 8

Quinn and Nate entered the Tom Bradley International Terminal at LAX just before 10 a.m. As they made their way through the Saturday morning crowds, Quinn had to constantly fight an urge to look over his shoulder. He had little doubt there was someone somewhere at the airport looking for them. Or if not both of them, at least him. He knew he had to maintain the delicate balance between being aware of his surroundings and trying not to draw any attention to himself. Frontline op agents could do this in their sleep, but Quinn – especially since he had Nate with him – had to work at it.

Having Nate stay in L.A. had been an option, but not a good one. Whoever wanted Quinn dead had to know he had an apprentice. So leaving Nate behind would have meant setting him up as a target. If Nate had a bit more experience, maybe they could have tried splitting up. But he was only four months in on an apprenticeship that would last anywhere from three to four years. Four months was nothing. Nate wasn't even close to being prepared to handle this kind of situation. Unlike

Quinn, he had come into the business straight out of college, a recommendation of a friend. If Quinn left him, he might as well just tie Nate to a chair in the middle of his living room and put a big welcome mat at his feet. The end result would be the same.

There had been no choice. Nate had to go with him until things calmed down.

They paused in front of a departure monitor. Quinn pretended to check the display, just another traveler on a holiday. Casually, he looked at his watch, then glanced around as if he were waiting for someone. His gaze never stopped on anyone in particular, and after a couple of sweeps, he decided they were still alone.

'So?' Nate asked.

'What?' Quinn said.

Nate nodded at the departure monitors. 'Which flight are we taking?'

'Give me your passport.'

Nate pulled a blue-covered booklet from his pocket and handed it over. It was one of twenty they carried between them, all fake. Each was top quality, made by a guy Quinn knew who worked out of a shop on the Venice Beach boardwalk.

Dozens of international airlines were set up in Bradley Terminal. Usually they would have had the choice of the whole world. But this wasn't a usual day, and until Quinn heard otherwise, he had to assume most of the world wasn't safe. He needed to select a destination no one would expect them to go to.

Europe was out. As was anywhere in the States

or Canada. Latin America was an option, but not a great one. Too many spooks, too many chances someone might spot him. Russia, Australia, China, Japan – all lousy choices. There really was only one answer. He looked around until he spotted what he was looking for.

'Okay. Let's go,' he said.

'Not even a hint?' Nate asked.

Quinn ignored the question as he headed off through the crowd. It took them less than two minutes to reach the business- and first-class passenger line for Thai Airways.

'All right,' Nate said, smiling.

'Not one more word until we're on the plane, understand?'

'Yeah. Sure. Not a word.'

When their turn came, Quinn gave Nate a warning look before approaching the counter.

'How can I help you?' the ticket agent said. She was an Asian woman about thirty years old.

'I'm wondering if there are any seats left on the 12:05 flight to Bangkok?'

'No business class, sir,' she said. 'But there are still a couple available in first class.'

'Perfect,' he said with a smile. 'Two, please.'

'The seats are not together. Is that all right?' she asked.

'No problem,' Quinn said.

'May I have your passports?'

Quinn handed her the two passports, then smiled again. She looked at them, then punched several keys on the keyboard of her computer terminal. 'How would you like to pay, Mr. Hayden?'

Quinn held passports in many names. Louis Hayden was the one he'd chosen for this trip, it having the benefit of being an identity he'd never used previously. Nate was traveling under the name Raymond James. 'Credit card,' he said, removing from his wallet one of the several he had with the Hayden alias on it.

After he paid, the woman busied herself at her computer arranging their tickets. Quinn casually scanned the terminal again. It didn't take him long to identify two suspicious types near the front entrance. They were big guys, both dressed in dark gray business suits. They seemed to be paying particularly close attention to the people coming into the building. Surprisingly, Nate seemed to have noticed them, too. He looked at Quinn, trying but failing to hide his concern. Quinn shrugged and gave him a quick smile.

'Here you are,' the agent said. She set the tickets and passports on the top of the counter. 'Any luggage?'

Quinn shook his head. 'Just our carry-ons.'

She smiled in approval, no doubt guessing they were seasoned travelers. 'Enjoy your flight.'

'Thank you,' he said. 'We will.'

Quinn eased his chair back, then glanced out the window at the Pacific Ocean, thirty thousand feet below. It was the first time in nearly twelve hours he wasn't doing anything. Physically, he was exhausted.

Nate was across the cabin, three rows back. Quinn had offered him a sleeping pill before they boarded, and apparently it had worked quickly. Nate's head lolled to the side, his eyes closed.

Quinn let his mind drift, trying not to think of anything at all. He needed to unwind and relax. More than anything, he knew he needed to sleep. But his mind kept replaying the events of the last twelve hours: Gibson on his porch, Peter on the phone, Nate on the floor, and –

A flight attendant touched him on the shoulder. 'Pad Thai or chicken curry with rice?' she asked.

Quinn glanced at his watch and was surprised to find several hours had already passed. Sometime during his mental storm he must have actually dozed off. 'Pad Thai,' he said.

'And to drink?'

'Just water.'

As he ate his food he forced himself to concentrate on trying to figure out who Gibson might have been working for, and why they had targeted Quinn.

He had searched Gibson's body thoroughly before turning it over to the local disposal guy. He hadn't expected to discover anything useful, and he'd been right. Other than the tools of the trade in his bag, the only thing Gibson had on him was three hundred dollars in cash.

It was a pretty fair guess that whoever had hired him had deep pockets, enough to fund a small-scale, one-night war on the Office. How many agents had they gone after? Five? Six? A dozen? More? Whatever the number, from the sound of things, Quinn getting the upper hand on Gibson appeared to be the exception. Others, apparently, hadn't been so lucky.

A disruption, Quinn thought.

That someone had attempted to pull one off was hard to believe. Yet it looked like it had happened. And, more surprisingly, it seemed to have been successful.

It was mind-blowing, really. A disruption almost *never* worked. The idea behind it was to cause as much chaos as possible within a particular agency. There were many reasons why: to cover up something that was happening, to cover up something that was going to happen, to foul up an ongoing operation, to get rid of an annoying competitor, or simply to take down somebody else's organization entirely for no particular reason at all. You heard about them when you first started out in the business. About the theory. About the attempts to pull them off in the past, all but a very few unsuccessful. And finally you heard about how no one tried them anymore. History was against success.

Apparently, someone hadn't been paying attention when that lesson had been taught.

Once his tray had been removed, Quinn leaned his chair back as far as it would go. His thoughts were taking him nowhere, and his lack of sleep wasn't helping. He closed his eyes, hoping his mind would settle down and allow him the rest he needed. But his thoughts took one final turn back to the core question.

Why him? He wasn't a member of the Office. He was only a freelancer. He should have been exempt, right?

As sleep began to take hold of him, an answer

started drifting toward the surface. Nothing fully formed. More of a hunch, really.

Taggert.

Somewhere between Los Angeles, a brief stop in Osaka, and landing in Bangkok, they lost Sunday. Travel to Asia from the States was always painful that way, the international date line exacting its toll for daring to travel nearly halfway around the world.

Quinn and Nate were only in Thailand a few hours before they caught a connecting flight out of the country. Nate seemed both disappointed and confused when Quinn said their trip wasn't over. But to his credit, he kept his questions to himself. The second flight was a short trip, but it took them a million miles from everywhere else.

After the plane landed and began taxiing to the terminal, a flight attendant's voice came over the public address system. 'Thai Airways would like to welcome you to Ho Chi Minh City.'

It was midmorning in Vietnam, and the heat was rippling off the tarmac. There were a few clouds in the distance, but otherwise the sky was clear. Quinn looked around the interior of the cabin. Several people were already pulling out bags and purses from under the seats where they'd been stowed. Quinn was content to sit quietly and wait.

Before he left home, he'd cleaned out his safe, taking everything except his gun. In addition to his laptop computer, he had a dozen passports: American, Canadian, Swiss, Finnish, German, Russian – each in a different name. Plus corresponding sets of credit cards, ten thousand U.S.

dollars in cash, a two-gigabyte flash memory stick on which was stored hundreds of contacts and other information, and a notebook filled with pages and pages of visas for various countries around the world. All the sensitive material was stored in a false hard-plastic lining in his suitcase. If he was ever asked to start up his laptop at a security checkpoint, the desktop that would appear would look like that of a typical businessman. Charts and graphics and spreadsheets, all very serious-looking but none important enough to draw undue attention.

He'd inserted Vietnamese visas into both his and Nate's passports in the lavatory of their previous flight just before landing in Bangkok. He'd used a palm-sized stamping kit to apply the appropriate dates, then studied his forgeries to make sure everything looked correct.

The ploy had worked in Bangkok, where they had to show a valid Vietnamese visa in order to pick up their tickets. But that had just been a Thai Airways employee. Now that they were in Ho Chi Minh City, they had to deal with the Vietnamese themselves.

Quinn put his passport in his shirt pocket and pulled his bag out of the storage bin above his seat. With Nate right behind him, he joined the line of passengers making their way off the plane.

'You've gotta be kidding me,' Nate said just loud enough for Quinn to hear as they reached the exit.

There was no covered ramp on the other side of the door leading into the terminal. Instead, passengers disembarked the old-fashioned way, via a wheel-up staircase.

Quinn gave his apprentice a quick, hard look.

'Sorry,' Nate said.

Without another word, they made their way down the ramp, then proceeded to walk across the tarmac to customs. Quinn made sure they inserted themselves into the middle of the pack of departing passengers.

'They won't ask,' Quinn said, 'but if they do, we're here on business. Researching investment opportunities. I'll do the talking, though. You just look serious. Businesslike.'

The terminal building reminded Quinn of a large warehouse. It was old and dingy, cavernous, with mold growing on the walls. There was none of the polish or amenities of Western airports.

Inside, the first thing they came to was passport control. Though there were several stations set up, only two were open, and the lines were long. To be safe, Quinn chose the one with the more bored-looking official. As they neared, he slipped twenty U.S. dollars, a tidy sum in Vietnam, into his passport next to his visa.

He looked over his shoulder at Nate. 'We can only go up one at a time,' he said. 'Try not to say anything. Not even hello. If there's a problem, just motion for me to come back and I'll take care of it.'

'Okay,' Nate said, his voice less confident than Quinn would have liked.

The woman ahead of them finished, and Quinn walked up to the desk. He placed his passport on the counter and held the cover down until the official took it from him. The man opened the passport, glanced up at Quinn, then quickly slipped the twenty into his own pocket. Grabbing a rubber stamp, he pushed it into an inkpad and stamped one of the pages in Quinn's passport. When he finished, he put the booklet back on the counter without a word. Quinn nodded politely as he retrieved it, then moved on.

He stopped twenty feet away, pretending to search for something in one of his pockets. He looked back as Nate handed his passport to the official. The man seemed to be taking a lot more time than he had with Quinn.

Nate glanced at his mentor, a trace of nervousness in his eyes. But a moment later, the official stamped the booklet and put it back on the counter.

Next was customs, but that was even easier. Nate went first, taking less than a minute to get his bag checked. Quinn's turn went just as quickly.

The humidity of the Vietnamese morning, even in January, was stifling. Sweat had begun to form on Quinn's brow the moment he stepped off the plane, and now his shirt was plastered to his back.

Just outside the terminal's front exit was a waist-high fence that ran parallel to the plate-glass windows of the building, creating a walkway about ten feet wide. Not your typical airport exit, but it was easy to see why it was necessary. On the other side of the fence were hundreds and hundreds of people, standing five and six deep. They were pushing and shoving each other, trying to get closer to the front. They shouted as each new passenger exited the terminal, calling out to them with offers of sodas and water and fruit and taxi rides.

At the end of the fence, the path opened onto a

parking lot. There were still many people about, but not nearly as many as lined the gauntlet Quinn and Nate had just come down. A young boy approached them – dark hair, big smile, clothes clean but worn.

'Bag,' the boy said in heavily accented English. He pointed to Quinn's suitcase. 'I help.'

'That's okay,' Quinn replied. 'I got it.'

But the boy either was ignoring him or didn't understand. He reached for the bag. Quinn moved it out of the boy's range. 'I said no.'

Undaunted, the boy quickly changed tactics, turning his attention to Quinn's traveling companion. Before Nate even realized what was going on, the boy had a hand firmly latched to the handle of his bag.

'Hey,' Nate said, trying to pull the bag away.

'I help. I help,' the boy said.

'I don't need your help.'

'Mister. No problem. I help.'

Nate pulled on his bag again. 'Come on. Let go.'

But the boy held on tight. Quinn watch the tug-of-war for a moment longer, then reached into his pocket and pulled out a dollar bill.

'Kid,' Quinn said.

Both Nate and the boy looked over. Quinn held out the dollar. The boy's eyes brightened. He reached out to grab it with his free hand. Before he could, Quinn pulled it back.

'No help,' Quinn said, nodding at the bag, 'and I give to you. Okay?'

The boy let go of the bag immediately. 'Okay. No help.'

This time when he reached out, Quinn gave it to him. Having received his fee, the boy headed off in search of his next mark.

'Thanks,' Nate said.

'You owe me a dollar,' Quinn told him.

A dozen taxis were parked nearby. Several of the drivers were calling out to them, trying to get their attention. Quinn chose the nearest one, and soon the two of them were settled in the back seat, their bags on the seat between them.

'Hello, hello, hello,' the driver said as he got behind the wheel. He was an older guy, short and skinny. 'American?'

'Canadian,' Quinn said.

The driver grinned. 'Welcome, Vietnam. Where go?'

'Rex Hotel,' Quinn said.

Chapter 9

Quinn checked them into adjacent rooms at the Rex Hotel. As they headed upstairs in the elevator, Nate said, 'I think I could sleep for a whole day.'

'But you're not going to,' Quinn told him.

'What?'

Quinn took in a long breath, reminding himself that Nate was still raw, and still had much to learn. 'It's barely noon,' he said. 'You go to sleep now, you'll never adjust to the new time. Meet me downstairs in thirty. We'll go for a walk, get a look at the area.'

The elevator door opened, and they stepped out onto their floor.

'You're joking, right?' Nate said.

Quinn turned to Nate and looked him straight in the eye. 'Do you understand what's going on here?'

Nate was about to respond, but Quinn's glare stopped him.

'This is it,' Quinn said. 'This is what you signed up for. You wanted to get into the game, so here you are. Everything up to the point where Gibson tried to break your jaw was just theory. Not anymore. Understand?'

Nate stared at Quinn, then gave him the slightest of nods.

'This is the real thing,' Quinn went on. 'This is dealing with jet lag. This is blending in with the locals. This is watching your back every goddamn second of the day because if you don't, you're dead. Do you get it now?'

'I get it,' Nate said, his voice barely above a whisper.

Quinn looked at him a moment longer, then started back down the hall. 'The lobby,' he said without turning. 'Thirty minutes.'

Nate was waiting for him downstairs when Quinn exited the elevator a half hour later. They were both wearing a fresh pair of clothes. In Nate's hand was a small silver digital camera. Quinn glanced at it, then raised his eyebrows in question.

'We're obviously not locals,' Nate said. 'People will expect us to carry a camera.'

The corner of Quinn's mouth raised slightly. 'Good,' he said.

Without another word, they headed outside.

According to all the textbooks, Vietnam was a communist country. Though what was communist about Ho Chi Minh City, Quinn couldn't fathom.

Looking around, he was beginning to wonder if anyone other than members of the government had even heard of Karl Marx. Street vendors and shops and restaurants and clubs and salons and hotels and kids running up and down the streets, hocking souvenirs and knockoff copies of Graham Greene's *The Quiet American* – that was the Ho Chi Minh City that greeted Quinn and Nate.

'Postcard . . . You buy . . . Very pretty . . . Look.'

'Mister. Mister. You American?'

'Real lighter. Zippo. From war. Work good.'

'America number one. Spider-Man. Michael Jordan.'

'I hungry. You buy.'

Almost as persistent as the kids on the street were the men on cyclos, bicycle rickshaws. The ones without passengers would slow down as they passed Quinn and Nate and try to get their attention.

'Hello. Tour city. I take you. Two dollars only. Cheap.'

'I know good bar. I get you there fast. Very cheap.'

'Too hot to walk, mister. You ride.'

'You look for girls? I know place. Come, come.'

Quinn had been to Asia many times – Bangkok, Singapore, Hong Kong, Tokyo, Seoul – but things seemed a little more raw here. There was more energy, more of an edge. It felt like a place that was both ancient and just discovering itself at the same time. Temples that had been around for centuries next door to sidewalk restaurants that had been open for only a few days. The Saigon River that had carved out a path through the land long before the first man had ever arrived now played host to would-be entrepreneurs offering boat rides and tours. And children. Everywhere children. Happy, playful, hungry, excited, curious children. He could only imagine what Nate was thinking.

They stopped and bought sodas from a woman who had set up a small hibachi next to a beat-up metal ice chest on a street corner. She was cooking what looked to be either chicken or pork. Quinn declined the offer of a taste. He opened the soda and drank half the can. The afternoon heat and humidity had been draining him ever since he'd left the hotel. Water was what he really wanted, but the cola did fine in a pinch.

Another twenty minutes of exploring was enough.

'Are you hungry?' Quinn asked.

'Very,' Nate said.

There were plenty of sidewalk hibachis, but Quinn still wasn't desperate enough to give them a try. Besides, none provided more than a bit of shade to fight the heat.

They started looking for a 'real' restaurant. A little farther along, Nate spotted a place on a small side road, a block off Hai Ba Trung Street, away from the craziness of the main boulevard. The sign out front identified the restaurant as Mai 99. As they neared, the aroma wafting out the door was more than enough to entice them to enter.

Inside, there were several young women dressed in traditional Vietnamese outfits, flowing colored tunics over white pants. A woman, slightly older than the others, her hair in a bun at the base of her neck, was standing near the entrance. She bowed to them slightly.

'Welcome,' she said. 'Speak English?'

'Yes,' Quinn replied.

'You eat?'

'Yes, please.'

She smiled again, then turned away. 'Come,' she said over her shoulder.

They followed the woman to a table close to the bar. She pulled out a chair and gestured for Quinn to sit, then she moved around to the other side and did the same for Nate.

The restaurant had a tropical feel. Bamboo covered the beams in the ceiling, and rattan mats covered the walls. Pictures of beautiful beaches were mounted throughout.

One of the young waitresses, wearing a dark green tunic, approached them. She said something in Vietnamese, realized her mistake, then pantomimed holding a glass in her hand and taking a drink. Quinn got the message.

'Beer,' he said. He pointed at a neon sign behind the bar. 'Tiger beer.' She followed his gesture and nodded.

'Me, too,' Nate said, nodding toward the sign, then pointing at himself.

The waitress smiled as she backed away from the table.

'Can I ask a question?' Nate said once they were alone.

'If you must,' Quinn said.

'Does this happen to you a lot?'

'What?'

'You know. Almost getting killed in your own living room? Having to fly thousands of miles just to hide out?'

'No more than a couple times a year,' Quinn said, face blank.

'Are you serious?'

Quinn smiled, then slipped his hand into his pocket and pulled out the silver bracelet. He had woken up on the plane to Bangkok with the distinct idea that Nate had been right. That the bracelet was part of this whole mess.

'Is that the one I found?' Nate asked.

Ignoring the question, Quinn examined the individual squares again until he found the one with the faint line at its edge. It definitely looked like there was some sort of extra layer. Quinn did a quick check of the nearby squares. None of the others appeared to have this same feature.

He looked around to see if there was anything he could use to slip into the crack and widen it. What he really needed was a penknife, or even a metal nail file. What he found was a pair of chopsticks and a Western-style fork. The tines on the fork were thick and would never work, but the chopsticks held promise. They were made of hard plastic and tapered to a point like a newly sharpened pencil.

He was about to see if he could use one to create a larger gap on the metal square when he noticed a waitress approaching the table. He put the bracelet in his lap and rested his left hand casually over the top of it.

The waitress, a different one from the girl who had taken their drink order, was dressed in a beautiful blue and gold tunic and was carrying two tall glasses of amber beer on a tray in one hand. She had a warm, friendly face and long black hair. As she neared she reached up with her free hand and tucked a loose strand behind her ear. She set their beers on the table, then smiled.

'Are you ready to order?' she asked.

'You speak English?' Nate said.

'Yes,' she said. 'I am sorry. My friend would like to help you, but she speaks only Vietnamese. I hope you understand.'

The new waitress's English was clipped but clear.

'Of course,' Quinn said.

'Would you like to order now?' she asked.

'We would, but we haven't seen a menu yet,' Nate told her.

The woman's eyes widened. 'Oh. I am so sorry. Wait, one moment, please.'

She walked quickly away from the table and soon returned with two menus. She handed one to each of them. Quinn opened his and was surprised to find the descriptions were in English. It didn't always get the language right, but it was close enough. The names of the dishes, though, were in Vietnamese.

'Your clothes are beautiful,' Nate said.

Quinn groaned inwardly, but tried to keep his annoyance from showing.

She glanced down at her tunic. 'This is an *ao dai*,' she said, pronouncing it 'ow zeye.' 'It is traditional.'

'Well, it's very beautiful.'

'Thank you.'

Reluctantly, Nate looked down at the menu. Quinn ordered something called *bun thit nuong*, hoping he'd like it. Nate went with the *com chien thap cam*.

'If you need anything else,' she said, 'my name is Anh. Just ask any of the waitresses, and they will get me.'

'Thanks,' Nate said, his eyes lingering on her as she walked away.

'Rein it in,' Quinn said.

'What are you talking about?'

'On a different day, in a different life, maybe.'

'What?'

'Right now you need to concentrate on staying alive.' Quinn glanced toward the bar area where Anh was talking to another waitress. 'Your new little friend there? She's a distraction.'

'"And distractions get you killed,"' Nate recited from memory. 'The way you think, just breathing will get you killed.'

'Sometimes,' Quinn said.

Nate frowned. 'I was just being polite.'

'That's how it starts.' Quinn returned his attention to the bracelet. 'Let me know when she comes back.'

It took a little bit of work, but the metal was surprisingly soft and soon he was able to widen the gap. He'd been right, it was some sort of plating, or maybe even a cover. He continued working the chopstick into the opening, parting the top layer of metal from the square below. He found he was able to work his way around all four edges of the square, creating flaps, until all he had to do was loosen the few spots where the two metals were still bonded together.

'What the hell?' Nate asked, peering over at him.

'Eyes on the room. Not on what I'm doing,' Quinn snapped.

Quinn set the bracelet on the table, making sure the square he was working on was lying flat. He took in a breath, then let it out halfway. Hands steady, he used one to hold the bracelet in place and the other to guide the chopstick as he used it to separate the lid from the square. With only a little pressure, it peeled off and flipped onto the table.

As he suspected, the square wasn't solid. It was a container. Inside was what appeared to be a piece of glass embedded in some sort of clear rubbery substance. Quinn's first guess was that the substance was there to protect the glass, only it didn't seem to have done its job. The glass was still intact, but fractured. Oddly, though, the protective rubber looked undamaged. *The heat from the fire,* Quinn thought. That's what must have caused the break.

He leaned down to get a better look and quickly realized it wasn't just one piece of glass, but two thin pieces, each of which couldn't have been more than a sixteenth of an inch thick. They looked like a glass sandwich.

Or a microscope slide, he thought.

Reluctantly, he eyed the glass more closely, looking for signs of a smear or a stain caught between the two panes. But the fractured top layer made it impossible to tell.

A stillness settled over Quinn as he placed the metal top back over the capsule. It wasn't going to stay there on its own once he tried to move it, but covering the contents allowed him to start breathing again. He had no idea what was on the slide, but his instincts told him the rubber barrier was more than just a stabilizer for the slide. It was also there to prevent exposure.

'What is it?' Nate asked.

'I'm not sure,' Quinn said.

What the hell have we stumbled into? he thought.

Quinn's immediate instinct was to go so far underground that no matter how hard anyone looked, no one would ever be able to find them. They could just keep out of sight until the whole thing blew over.

He glanced down at the bracelet again.

If the whole thing blows over.

The bill for lunch was surprisingly small: 150,000 dong, about five dollars each for the food and beers. Quinn left double the total on the table, then got up to leave. Nate did the same.

Anh rushed across the room to open the door for them. 'Are you here long?' she asked.

'I'm not sure,' Nate said. He glanced at Quinn.

'Not too long, I imagine,' Quinn said.

Another smile. 'We hope you come back before you leave.'

'Not to worry,' Nate said. 'We'll be back.'

Chapter 10

Upon returning to the Rex Hotel, Quinn picked up a map of the city, then told Nate he was on his own for a while.

'But don't sleep,' Quinn said.

'I won't.'

'I mean it.'

'I said I won't.'

The map wasn't as detailed as Quinn would have liked, but it did show him the street he was looking for. He had initially thought about putting this trip off until the next morning. Get some sleep, be more alert. He had even contemplated putting it off altogether. His instincts told him it was a mistake, but he had come to Vietnam not only because they needed someplace to lie low, but also because they needed help. And after discovering the secret compartment in the bracelet, he knew they needed that help as soon as they could get it.

On the sidewalk outside the Rex, he started for the line of taxis at the curb, but he changed his mind at the last moment and decided to take a cyclo. Just because he had to make the trip didn't mean he had to get there in a hurry.

The driver, a man in his late twenties, didn't speak English, so Quinn pulled a pen out of his pocket and wrote the address of where he wanted to go on the back of the map. The driver looked at it, then smiled and nodded.

Saigon – Quinn couldn't bring himself to keep calling it Ho Chi Minh City – was a madhouse. An honest-to-God, overcrowded, disorganized madhouse. And he loved it. The city radiated with a vibrancy and excitement he'd found in few other places.

The streets were crowded with motorcycles, bicycles – both standard and cyclos – scooters, even the occasional car or truck. While he'd seen similar vehicular menageries elsewhere in Asia, this was the first place he'd seen a family of five riding on a single 50cc motorcycle.

That wasn't the only sight that caught his attention. There were also the large three-wheeled bikes that had been converted into what amounted to small trucks. A large flat surface was built onto the front halves of the bikes. This allowed drivers to carry anything from cages of chickens, to stacks of old tires, to boxes and tins of God knew what. The merchandise was piled high and wide, seemingly obscuring the driver's view.

Another thing he noticed, something more typical of many third-world countries, was that traffic signs were more like suggestions than actual law. There were cops around, but as long as the traffic kept moving, they seemed content to let things be.

The cyclo driver took him through a particularly crowded section of town. Vendors lined the streets, selling everything from live animals to firecrackers to pots and pans. It was an assault on Quinn's senses. The odor, in particular, was overwhelming. Fish and sweat and trash mixed with the sweetness of flowers and fruit and baking bread.

The cyclo driver leaned forward and said, 'Cholon.' Quinn recognized the name from one of the brochures in his hotel room. It was essentially the Chinatown of Saigon.

After they had been traveling for twenty minutes, the driver turned the cyclo onto a less trafficked side street and pulled up in the middle of the block next to a long, two-story building.

'Is this it?' Quinn asked, forgetting momentarily that the driver wouldn't understand him. Realizing his mistake, he pointed at the address on the map.

The driver smiled widely and nodded at the building. '*Ici*,' he said.

'*Parlez-vous français?*' Quinn asked.

'*Un peu, monsieur.*'

Quinn reached into his pocket. '*Combien?*' he asked.

'Two dollar,' the driver said in English.

The moment Quinn climbed off the cyclo, it began to rain. He ran down the cracked sidewalk and found cover in the recess of the building's doorway just as the initial sprinkles turned into a downpour. He opened the door and went inside.

There was a reception desk at the far end of the lobby. A young woman, Vietnamese but dressed in

Western clothing, was sitting behind it, looking in his direction. Quinn put on a smile and walked over. 'Do you speak English?' he asked.

'Of course,' she said. 'How may I help you?'

'I'm not sure if I'm in the right place,' he said.

'Who are you looking for?'

'The Tri-Continent Relief Agency.'

She smiled. 'You are in the right place. Second floor, on your left. Room 214. Would you like me to show you?'

Quinn shook his head. 'Thanks. I should be able to find it.'

'You are welcome.'

Quinn took the stairs to the right of the desk. When he reached the second floor, he turned left and walked down the hall until he came to room 214.

The door was solid wood. Mounted in its center was a brass plaque engraved with the words in English: *Tri-Continent Relief Agency, Ho Chi Minh City Branch.* Below it, in smaller type, was a Vietnamese translation.

Quinn paused before knocking. He was standing at the edge of the proverbial point of no return. Until his hand actually made contact with the door, he could still just turn around and go back to the hotel. Call the whole thing off.

He took a deep breath, then raised his hand and knocked.

A moment later the door opened revealing a short, middle-aged Vietnamese man. He looked at Quinn expectantly.

'Tri-Continent Relief Agency?' Quinn asked.

The man smiled. 'Please, come in.'

He moved out of the way so Quinn could enter. The room was not large. In fact, Quinn realized, it was about the same size as his hotel room at the Rex. An old wooden desk sat against one wall, piled high with folders and papers. More piles, of books and magazines, lined most of the remaining wall space. Opposite the entrance, several windows looked out onto the now gloomy day.

A door on the right, apparently leading to an adjacent room, was partially closed. Quinn thought he could hear music playing from just beyond it. It sounded like Edith Piaf.

'My name is Mr. Vo,' the man said. 'How may I help you?'

'Is Director Zhang in?'

'She is. May I give her your name?'

'Tell her it's Quinn.'

The man waited for more, but when it became obvious that Quinn had nothing else to add, the man turned and walked into the other room.

Quinn stepped over to a large bulletin board hanging on one of the walls. It was covered with dozens of notices and advisories. He quickly scanned several of the notes. They were all communications about localized disasters throughout Southeast Asia.

He was reading about an upcoming meeting to discuss regional health issues when he paused. He didn't hear her come into the room, but he felt her presence nonetheless. Slowly, he turned around. Standing in the doorway to the adjacent room was a petite Asian woman.

They looked at each other for several moments, neither seeming able to move. Finally, Quinn smiled.

'Hello, Orlando,' he said.

She shook her head, then began walking toward the main door. 'Not here,' she said.

Orlando, known in Vietnam as Director Keira Zhang, led Quinn back outside. The rain had all but stopped as she led him down several blocks to a small park, saying nothing the entire time. On the walk over and without trying to be too obvious, Quinn took in every inch of her.

She had changed little since the last time he'd seen her, four years earlier. The usual red highlights in her shoulder-length dark hair were gone. And she was wearing a pair of narrow glasses framed by translucent blue plastic; that was new. But otherwise, she was the same. Skin the color of bleached pine, and smooth except for a small worry line just above the bridge of her nose when she frowned. She was small, barely five feet tall, and could pass for anything from Japanese to Chinese to Filipino or even Vietnamese or Malaysian. In truth her mother had been Korean and her father half Thai, half Irish American. Quinn was one of the few people who knew this.

She had been his friend, his confidant, his colleague as they both started from nothing, then gained experience in the business. She had been there for him when times were rough, and he had tried to be there for her in return. But he wasn't as good at it as she was, hence the reason they hadn't talked in four years.

There was another reason, too. One of self-preservation. Being near her made him want something he could never have. He didn't need that kind of mental torture. Orlando was off-limits. Always was. And, he knew deep down, always would be.

By the time they finally found a quiet spot in the park, the sky was once again clearing.

'How did you know where to find me?' she asked. There was still no smile, no how-are-you-doing, not even a simple hello. Of course, the last time they had talked, they had agreed never to see each other again. That had been about the only thing they had agreed on that day.

'Do you really need to ask that question?' he asked. 'The relief agency is a nice cover.'

'It's not a cover,' she said quickly.

He arched an eyebrow. 'Not completely, anyway,' he said. Aiding others in need was something hard-wired into who Orlando was. He'd learned as much within a day of first meeting her. So it wasn't surprising that even after she had dropped out of contact and moved to a place where she could keep a low profile, she still found a way to help where she could.

'Why are you here?' she asked.

'I thought I'd surprise you.'

She stared at him.

'I take it, it worked,' he said.

She remained silent.

Quinn glanced at the ground, then looked at her. 'I need your help.'

'Fuck you.'

'Someone's trying to have me killed,' he said.

'I don't care.' Her face remained blank. No trace of sympathy anywhere.

'Maybe not. But I do.'

'Then get someone else to help you, and leave me alone. You promised you wouldn't come looking for me. But I see now you're a liar.'

'I wouldn't be here unless I had nowhere else to go.'

She shook her head, her eyes never leaving his. 'Not my problem.'

'I need your help,' Quinn said.

'Too bad. You're not getting it. End of discussion.'

She turned and started walking away.

She was nearly out of the park when he called out, 'If I could bring him back, I would.'

She slowed momentarily. Quinn thought for a second she might turn back, but instead, she picked up her pace and continued walking away.

When Orlando left her office a few minutes after five that afternoon on an old black Vespa scooter, Quinn was ready for her. He had hired a young guy with a beat-up motorcycle to drive him wherever he wanted to go. The guy spoke enough English for Quinn to get across the idea there was someone he wanted to follow. As Quinn had hoped, his driver – he said his name was Dat – assumed Quinn's interest in Orlando was romantic or at least sexual, so he was happy to comply.

Dat almost seemed like a pro. He never got very close, but he never lost sight of Orlando, either. It helped that her pace was unhurried, driving neither too fast nor too slow. They followed her through Cholon, then north for a while before turning east.

But soon Quinn began to feel anxious. It was too easy. So it was almost a relief when, ten minutes later, Orlando took a quick right turn. The move was sudden, unexpected. The move of someone who knew she was being followed.

Dat may have been good, but he was mismatched. Nonetheless, Quinn urged his driver on even as Orlando rapidly worked her way through the city.

Finally, Orlando turned right at yet another street. As soon as Quinn and Dat had followed her around the corner, they realized the Vespa was no longer in front of them. For half a second, Quinn thought they'd lost her. But then he spotted her. She was parked at the curb, her foot on the ground holding her scooter in position.

'Stop,' Quinn said.

Dat had obviously seen her, too. He quickly slowed, then pulled up behind the Vespa. Quinn dismounted the bike and handed Dat a ten-dollar bill. The boy grinned broadly.

'You want me wait?' Dat asked.

Quinn shook his head. 'Thanks for your help.'

'Sure, no problem. You need more, you call me.'

Dat pulled several scraps of paper out of his pocket and handed one to Quinn. There was a phone number on it. Quinn smiled and put it in his own pocket.

As Dat drove away, Quinn walked over to the Vespa, stopping when he was a few feet away. Orlando's face was as expressionless as it had been in the park. She stared at him for a moment, then glanced past him, at the building they were in front of. Quinn followed her gaze.

The Rex Hotel. She'd figured out where he'd been staying.

'You've been busy since we talked,' Quinn said.

'Why did Gibson try to kill you?' she asked.

'Whoa. You've been *very* busy.'

'Answer my question.'

'I don't know.'

'What happened to the Office?'

'Same answer,' he said.

'You can do better.'

'Disruption.'

She gave a short, derisive laugh. 'No such thing.'

'That's what I used to think.'

They were silent for several seconds. Around them the world continued to move on: taxis picking up and dropping off passengers at the hotel, street vendors trying to attract the attention of the passing pedestrians, people heading either to work or to home or out for a night on the town. But for the moment, Quinn and Orlando were in their own little capsule, aware of the world but momentarily not part of it.

'Why did you come to me?' she finally asked.

He paused before answering. 'Two reasons,' he said. 'This is the last place anyone would ever look for me. And I needed to find someone I could trust, someone who could help me.'

'What about your friends?'

Again he took a moment before answering. 'I don't exactly have a long list to choose from.'

'You didn't come alone,' she said. Not a question, but a statement.

'Nate,' Quinn said. 'My apprentice. If I'd left him, he'd probably be dead by now.'

She took a deep breath, and, for the first time, her face softened, if only just a little. 'Same old Quinn, then.'

Quinn shrugged.

She looked at him, then shook her head. 'Son of a bitch,' she said under her breath. 'Get on before I change my mind.'

Quinn wanted to smile, but he kept his face neutral and climbed onto the back of the Vespa.

She took him to her apartment. It was a large, Western-style place in an area occupied by many foreign workers. She didn't offer him a tour. Quinn knew he was still on probation, so the living room was all he had to judge things by. It was a comfortable space, with a long, overstuffed couch and two matching brown chairs. Nearly every inch of wall space was lined with bookcases crammed full of texts. On one shelf he recognized a brushed-metal container. It was the only thing in the room he'd seen before, but he made no mention of it.

She told him to take a seat on the couch, then disappeared into another room for a moment before returning with two bottles of water.

'Tell me,' Orlando said as she handed him a bottle, then sat in one of the chairs. 'Everything.'

So Quinn did. He left nothing out; there was no reason to. If he was going to get her help, she'd need to know it all anyway.

It took almost an hour. When he was through, she said, 'Sounds like you've been having fun.'

'Yeah. A real joyride,' he said.

'And you think it's all connected? Colorado, the Office, Gibson, the disruption?'

'Absolutely.'

'Do you have the bracelet with you?' she asked.

Quinn reached into his pocket and gently pulled out a small plastic bag that had been secured with a couple of rubber bands.

He started to hand it to her, but she told him to wait. She got up and walked into the hallway that led to the rest of the apartment. When she returned, she was carrying two sets of rubber gloves. She offered one set to Quinn.

'I think it's safe,' he said, but he took the gloves anyway.

Once Orlando had hers on, she reached out and took the plastic bag from Quinn. Slowly she removed the rubber band and opened the package. From inside, she carefully removed the bracelet.

'Not real silver,' she said.

'No,' Quinn agreed.

'These designs are interesting.'

'They looked familiar to me. Not like I'd seen these exact designs before, but something similar.'

'They're German,' Orlando said. 'Old heraldry from three, maybe four hundred years ago.'

'You sure?'

She glanced at him for a moment, then looked back at the bracelet. 'Yes. I'm sure.' She examined the designs on the bracelet for a few more seconds, stopping on a square that had been partially damaged by the fire.

'Is this some sort of inscription?' she asked.

'What?'

She held the bracelet out to him, pointing at a spot on the half-burnt surface of the square. At first he didn't see anything, but then she turned it slightly so that the light caught the spot she was talking about. There was a thin line toward the bottom of the square, running along the edge. It was blackened by soot that had lodged in the grooves, helping it to blend in with the rest of the tarnished metal. Quinn couldn't remember seeing it before, but if he had, he'd probably thought it was just a scratch. Now that he looked closer, though, he knew Orlando's instincts were correct. It wasn't a scratch, but writing of some sort. Only it was so small, they'd need a magnifying glass or possibly even a microscope to read it.

'Maybe it's just the artist's mark,' Quinn suggested.

'Could be,' Orlando said, clearly not buying that explanation. She took the bracelet back from him, then turned her attention to the square near the hasp. Quinn had used another rubber band to keep the two pieces together. 'I assume this is the container?'

'Yes.'

Again, she carefully unwound the rubber band. Once it was off, she removed the top of the square, revealing the glass beneath. She looked at it for almost five minutes before she finally said something.

'You're right. I think it's a slide for a microscope.'

'Do you know anyone who could check it?' Quinn asked. 'Someone you can trust?'

'The damage to the slide might make things difficult. If the sample itself has been compromised, they may not be able to get a fix on it.'

'So you do have someone.'

She didn't answer him right away. Instead she stared down at the slide. 'I have someone. But I have to send it out. They're not local.'

'It won't do me any good just sitting in my pocket,' Quinn said.

Orlando rewrapped the square, then put the bracelet back in the bag and rewound the rubber band around it. 'I'll get it out first thing in the morning.'

'Thanks,' he said. 'See if they can check that inscription, too.'

Orlando said nothing, but the look she gave him said, *Do you think I'm an idiot? Of course I'll have them check.*

Quinn suddenly had the urge to yawn. He tried to stifle it, but was only half successful. It was just a little after 7:30 p.m., but his body wasn't going to let him stay awake much longer. He was beginning to feel a second yawn coming on when he heard a noise from deeper in the apartment. 'What was that?' he asked, sitting up, alert.

Orlando turned and called out, 'Trinh?'

A moment later a young Vietnamese woman appeared in the doorway leading toward the rest of the apartment. Orlando said something to her in Vietnamese. The girl responded, then disappeared the way she had come.

'Housekeeper?' Quinn asked.

'Of a sort.' Orlando stood up, then looked down

at Quinn for a moment, apparently contemplating something. 'Come on,' she finally said.

She led him into the hallway, stopping at a door halfway down. It was partially closed, so she pushed it open. The room was dimly lit. Trinh was there, sitting in a chair, mending a shirt. She looked up and bowed slightly as Orlando and Quinn entered, then returned to her work.

It took Quinn's eyes a moment longer to fully adjust to the low light. When they did, he noticed something he should have realized was there from the beginning. To the girl's left, on a small bed, low to the floor, was a sleeping child.

Orlando walked across the room and knelt down next to the bed. She kissed the child lightly on the forehead, then stood and led Quinn back into the hallway.

'What's he doing here?' Quinn asked.

'He's my son,' Orlando said.

'Yeah, I know. But I thought he was with your aunt in San Francisco.'

'My aunt is getting too old to care for him. Her health isn't what it should be.'

'Is it safe, though? To have him with you?'

She was silent for a moment. Then said, 'He's all I have left.'

Chapter 11

Quinn awoke before the sun. Reaching over to the nightstand, he felt around until he found his watch. Four-thirty a.m.

Sighing, he rolled onto his back. After several minutes of staring into the darkness, he tried closing his eyes again, hoping that maybe he could eke out a little more sleep. But the rest of his body wasn't cooperating. His day had begun, whether he liked it or not.

He reached back over to the nightstand, flipped on the lamp, then got out of bed. The tile floor was cool but not uncomfortable. On the dresser opposite the foot of his bed was a television. He grabbed the remote control off the nightstand next to the lamp and turned the TV on. The business report was running on CNN International. Though Tuesday morning was imminent here in Vietnam, the New York Stock Exchange had just rung its closing bell on Monday afternoon. A financial reporter was running through a list of numbers, but Quinn paid little attention. He didn't play the market. Too risky.

He retrieved his computer, his text pager, and the flash memory stick from his bag on the floor. The stick was attached to an otherwise empty key ring. His everyday keys were in his BMW back in L.A., stowed in a safe compartment few would ever be able to find.

He sat down at a table next to the bed. He opened his computer and turned it on.

The previous evening, before he'd fallen asleep, he'd spent twenty minutes reading *Native Speaker* by Chang-rae Lee. As he read, the lights in his room had dimmed three times. It made him leery of the electrical system in the building, so he'd decided to run his computer off battery power for now. It wasn't a problem. The laptop had a full charge and could run for several hours.

Quinn slipped the memory stick into a port on the side of the computer. The first thing he did was access an encoded document containing information he'd been compiling over the years. The document was a list of locations and bank accounts, a blueprint of potential hideaways and cash deposits that were available to him if needed. He didn't know how long they could stay in Vietnam, so he had to be ready just in case they had to move. From the list, he chose three potential backup destinations.

He closed the document, then opened his modem software. After entering his personal code, he clicked the button labeled 'Connect,' and was promptly greeted with an error message: `<Modem not properly configured.>`

Quinn's pager doubled as a wireless, high-speed

satellite modem. He turned it over, unhinged a tiny cover in the upper left corner, slid it away, and exposed three small buttons. Using a ballpoint pen, he pushed the middle button, then the one on the left. He flipped the pager back over and opened the cover so he could view the display screen.

<Searching . . . > blinked on and off for several seconds. Then it was replaced by <Acquiring Signal> blinking more rapidly than the first message. Finally <Secure Link> held steady on the screen.

Returning his attention to the computer, he signed on and went directly to his e-mail.

There were a dozen messages waiting for him. The first he opened was from Orlando, sent only a few hours earlier.

Call me when you wake up. - O.

Obviously she didn't expect him to be up quite as early as he was. *If I called her now, she might never speak to me again.* He couldn't help smiling as the thought passed through his mind. But it wasn't just the thought that had made him smile, he realized; it was seeing her again, talking to her. It was actually being close enough to reach out and touch her if he wanted. Strike that. He did want to, but his conscience wouldn't let him.

On the television, the business report was replaced by the world news – a report about the recently elected president of Serbia. A reformer, apparently. Reaching out, the reporter said, to his country's former enemies in an attempt to heal old wounds with a promise to send both civilian and governmental representatives to some upcoming European Union conference on the Balkans.

Quinn picked up the TV remote and lowered the volume, then looked back at the computer screen. Of all Quinn's messages, Orlando's was the only one sent directly to his main e-mail address. Everyone else sent their correspondence to Quinn via dummy accounts that would then electronically forward the messages through a series of circuitous routes to his main e-mail hub. There was a note from his father. A joke, and not a very funny one, about ice fishing and polar bears. Another was from his mother, hinting that she needed help around the house, mentioning three times how useless his father was. It was an old complaint.

He sent them each a quick e-mail, telling them he was on another business trip and would call when he got back home. They thought he was a private consultant in the banking industry, with clients all over the world. It was his standard cover story, though embellished somewhat for his parents.

Six of the nine remaining messages were from other freelancers Quinn had hired at one time or another, all checking in, looking for work.

That wasn't unusual at all. People were always keeping in touch with Quinn, in case anything came up. Recently he'd been receiving more messages than usual, averaging at least one a day. Things had been quiet for several months, so everyone was anxious to make some cash. It was a kind of espionage recession. Quinn blamed it on more and more organizations and state-run agencies trying to do things 'in-house' to hold down costs. But that would eventually change. The old adage 'You get what you pay for' would come into play soon enough.

What was unusual, though, was that the last of these looking-for-work e-mails was sent two days ago, about the time Quinn was making his way out of L.A. Since then, no you-got-a-gig-for-me inquiries from anyone. Had word gotten out about his 'situation'? That would explain why the e-mails had stopped. Still, it seemed unusual. Though rumor and gossip were as fast-spreading in Quinn's world as in any other subculture, the halt in any communication had been *too* fast and abrupt. No way word of his new situation could have traveled through the normal channels in that amount of time. Someone wanted word to get out, and had likely helped in its propagation. Of course, the lack of e-mails could have been a coincidence, but Quinn doubted it.

He frowned. It was the disruption again. It looked like the sons of bitches who'd included him on the target list had taken the extra precaution of making sure everyone knew about it, effectively cutting off his contacts and making him persona non grata. He was still having a hard time connecting the dots that put him on that list. According to Peter, he was the only non–Office staffer targeted. But that didn't make sense.

If he were an ops guy, okay, he could have seen himself being thrown in with the rest. Ops guys were subject to being removed. Even freelance ops. It was an occupational hazard. But Quinn was a behind-the-scenes player. An investigator, an assessor, a perception arranger, even an occasional setup man. In other words, a *dry* cleaner. An *independent* dry cleaner. No killings, no exchanges, no face-to-face meetings. No wet work at all.

Though he couldn't figure out exactly what the connection was, it must have had something to do with this business in Colorado. A guy named Taggert who'd been turned into a chunk of charcoal, and Jills, who'd come to the end of her career years before she planned. Perhaps whoever had done this thought Quinn had learned something necessitating his removal. If Peter had called someone else in to do the job, Quinn would have probably still been sitting on the beach on Maui enjoying his vacation, and the other guy would be the one scrambling for his life. Or, more likely, would be dead already.

Quinn looked at the three messages still unread. The first was from Chief Johnson, a copy of the Allyson Police Department's report on the Farnham fire. Quinn perused it quickly and didn't notice anything unusual. If need be, he could come back to it and read it more thoroughly later. The second was the e-mail Peter had sent him with flight information to D.C. prior to the disruption.

He didn't recognize the sender's address on the final message, but that wasn't unusual. The message had been sent only six hours earlier. He opened it.

Xavier,
Peter has asked I get in touch with you. There is a project that needs your help. Pls reply upon receipt.
P4J

Quinn sat back, mildly surprised. Maybe not all his contacts had dried up. Xavier was a cover name he sometimes used for e-mail communications, but not anytime recently. And P4J was the identifier of a middleman in Europe named Duke. The last time they had worked together had been two years ago. A simple gig. Quinn had successfully pre-bugged a meeting so Duke would have a record of what went down. A painless operation.

Still, Quinn was glad to be finished. There was something slimy about Duke. Maybe it was the phony accent he cultivated, or maybe it was the three-hundred-plus pounds he carried on his barely five-foot ten-inch frame. Whatever it was, he was the kind of guy Quinn never felt comfortable around.

The message was intriguing, though. 'Peter has asked I get in touch with you.' What did that mean? Was the Office back in business? It didn't seem likely. Maybe Duke was just fishing and was using Peter's name as bait. If that was the case, Duke was even stupider than Quinn thought.

Quinn picked up his phone and punched in the number for Peter. He let it ring ten times before hanging up. The fact that no one answered was perhaps not unexpected, given what had been happening, but it was certainly unusual. A bright neon sign in the front of his mind was flashing, *Proceed with caution.*

Returning to Duke's e-mail, he checked the routing to see what address it had initially been sent to. Nothing unusual there, either. It had gone to an anonymous ID at Microsoft Quinn had set up years before. He kept it active as a fallback in case any of his old clients wanted to get ahold of him. Old clients like Duke.

Quinn clicked his tongue against the roof of his mouth, thinking. He could either wait until he was able to get through to Peter or he could try and extract some more information from Duke. Cautiously, of course.

He clicked the Reply button.

Interested. Need details. X.

Quinn included instructions as to where Duke could securely upload any sensitive information, then hit the Send button. His computer would automatically reroute his reply so that it was delivered from the same address Duke had sent his message to.

Outside, the sky was beginning to lighten with the coming sunrise. The humidity was already inching toward a barely tolerable level, and Quinn was starting to feel sticky. It would be another hour at least before he could call Orlando. Plenty of time for a shower.

For years, Quinn's and Orlando's lives had paralleled each other's. While he was four years older, they had both gotten their start in the business at around the same time, Quinn as a clean-and-gather apprentice to Durrie and Orlando as a research specialist with Abraham Delger, Durrie's sometime friend, sometime partner.

Quinn had been a rookie cop, working in

Phoenix, Arizona. He had been assigned to crowd control on a murder investigation, but as usual, his curiosity got the better of him. He did a little digging on his own time and ended up stumbling across some information that should have remained buried.

He traced the killer back to a hotel in Mesa, then was able to find a picture of the man on the hotel security tapes. For the next few days, he spent hours searching through mug books and criminal databases trying to match the face with a name. When he finally did, he took the information to the detective in charge of the investigation. That earned him a quick trip to the chief's office, where he was told that he was operating outside his area of assignment. That if it happened again, he would be demoted to parking duty. That was on a Tuesday.

On Wednesday, he was called in again. With little explanation, he was told his services would no longer be needed. Even the union rep was there, nodding his head in agreement with the chief.

'They were going to kill you. You realize that, right?' Durrie said to him months later. 'The Office had you fired, then arranged for someone to deal with you.'

'Right,' Quinn said, thinking his mentor was just trying to scare him. He was still new to the business then, naive to the ways of the world he'd been brought into.

'Believe me or not, Johnny. It's up to you. But you found out too much, too quickly. You were a problem that needed to go away. That's how it's done here.' Durrie paused. 'Remember that job interview in Houston? The one where they were going to fly you out?'

Quinn nodded, brow furrowed.

'What if I told you there was no job?' Durrie said.

'What?'

'I'm just telling you, if I hadn't shown an interest in you, you'd have been dead. Of course, if you hadn't been too smart for your own good, I wouldn't have cared about you one way or the other.'

Quinn remembered how Durrie's revelation had sobered him. It was at that point things started to become more real for him.

As for Orlando, she had been plucked from the ranks of a computer trade school in San Diego – a hacker who was constantly riding the probation list. She, like Quinn, had been curious about things most people left alone.

Because their mentors tended to work together a lot, and since they were both new to the business, it was natural that Quinn and Orlando would form a bond of friendship. What was more surprising was that Durrie and Orlando would form their own kind of bond. Years later, when Quinn was a successful solo operative, and Durrie's own career had taken a bit of a downturn, things for all three of them changed.

When Quinn was just an apprentice, Durrie was the most buttoned-up person in the business. But not later. At some point in the years after Quinn struck out on his own, Durrie lost focus. Quinn heard about all sorts of things: jobs Durrie worked on that didn't go as planned, assignments where things were missed, and more times than not the need for extra work to keep events suppressed.

It wasn't from Orlando that he heard these things. It was from Peter at the Office, who was forced more and more to hire Quinn instead of Durrie.

Orlando was quiet at first, telling Quinn nothing when he called. But eventually she told him about Durrie's growing anger and frustration. At first she thought it was just with work, his lost jobs, his less-than-stellar performances. Not that he ever talked about how his work went; she just knew him too well not to be able to read between the lines. But as his slide continued, she realized it was more than work. It was as if he were mad at life itself. And when his anger turned to depression, it seemed almost a natural progression.

When Quinn called Orlando and told her he had a project he was thinking about offering Durrie a job on, she had told him she thought it was a great idea. She said she'd even encourage Durrie to go. And when Durrie said yes, Quinn assumed Orlando's influence had helped.

The job should have been a simple one. But somewhere along the way, it turned ugly. A gunman had been hidden in the warehouse they'd been sent to. Even then, they should have gotten away unhurt. Durrie, though, entered the building before they'd done a proper assessment. Quinn had tried to stop him, but his mentor just scoffed.

Thirty seconds later, gunfire broke out. Even as Quinn dove for cover, he could see Durrie jerk from the impact of several bullets.

Quinn knew it was too late even before he reached

Durrie. Durrie's clothes were drenched in blood, and though Quinn searched frantically, he could find no pulse. Stunned, Quinn knelt next to Durrie's body. His mentor was dead. *Orlando,* he thought. *How am I going to tell her?* Guilt over what he could have done to save Durrie collided with the realization that it didn't matter. There was nothing he could –

Something hard hit him in the back of the head. His vision collapsed into a narrow tunnel.

Then everything went black.

The job was a bust. When Quinn awoke, he was in the passenger seat of their van. Ortega, the man Quinn had hired to drive and act as backup, was behind the wheel. In back, Durrie's body lay on the floor. When they reached their medical contact's office, Ortega looked into the back of the van.

'What do you want me to do with him?' he asked Quinn.

Quinn paused, then said, 'The usual. But bring me back the ashes.'

It was several hours before Ortega returned, finding Quinn in a small, makeshift hospital room in the back of the office. He set a cardboard box on the end table next to Quinn's bed and removed a brushed-metal urn from inside.

'It was all they had on short notice,' he said.

'It's fine,' Quinn told him.

This was the way it was in their business. Even when one of their own died, the cleanup had to continue. The only difference was instead of dumping the contents of the urn, Quinn had saved Durrie's ashes for Orlando.

But when he first went to Orlando's house, he couldn't find her. She had already heard the news and had disappeared. By the time he located her, ten months had passed and the son none of them knew she'd been pregnant with at the time had already been born. This had been in San Francisco, at her aunt's house. At first Orlando refused to see him. Even when she finally relented, she wouldn't let him in the door.

'You were there,' Orlando said, accusing Quinn not only with her words but also with the anger radiating from every inch of her. 'You should have protected him. Now my son will never know his father.'

It was unnecessary, really. Though Quinn knew there was little he could have done to keep his old mentor alive, he had already judged himself guilty of playing a large part in Durrie's death.

Still, he tried to talk to her, to make her understand he felt as bad as she did. But she didn't want to listen. She wouldn't even take the urn from him.

'Leave me alone,' she had said. 'I don't ever want to talk to you again.'

And because she was the only one in his whole life he found it difficult to say no to, he'd said, 'Okay.'

She shut the door. He stood there for several minutes hoping she'd return. Finally, he set the urn on the doorstep and walked away. Numb and hollow.

Chapter 12

Quinn and Nate met in the lobby again at noon.

'You look like shit,' Quinn said as soon as Nate arrived. 'Didn't you sleep?'

Dark bags hung under Nate's eyes. And while he had shaved, there were definitely a couple of spots he'd missed.

'I did what you told me,' Nate said. 'Stayed awake as long as I could. But by eight I was done. Then at midnight, my eyes popped open and I couldn't get back to sleep until seven this morning. Of course, that only lasted until you called me.' He eyed Quinn. 'Thanks.'

'No problem.'

Neither said anything for several seconds.

'I thought you said something about getting lunch,' Nate said.

'I did.'

'Is someone going to bring it to us here?' Nate grinned.

Quinn rolled his eyes, then turned his attention to the front entrance. He watched as people came and went from the hotel. Vietnamese,

Europeans, Americans, men, women, even a few children. When Orlando entered, Quinn looked at Nate.

'Time to go,' he said. He started walking toward the exit.

Nate, who had also been watching the door, seemed caught off guard by Quinn's sudden movement. He was still two steps behind when Quinn stopped next to Orlando.

'So this is the albatross,' Orlando said, looking at Nate.

'This is him,' Quinn confirmed.

'What the hell does that mean?' Nate asked.

Orlando held out her hand. 'Nice to meet you, Al.'

'It's Nate, actually,' Nate said as they shook.

'Whatever,' she said.

Nate looked at Quinn, then back to Orlando. 'And you are. . . . ?'

'This is Orlando,' Quinn said. 'She's an old friend.'

He started walking toward the door, Orlando in step beside him.

'Wait.' Nate rushed to catch up, then, smiling, he added, 'I didn't know you had any friends.'

Quinn led them through the front entrance to the sidewalk outside, ignoring Nate's comment.

'So,' Orlando said. 'Where to?'

'Thought we'd find someplace close by,' Quinn replied.

'Um . . . I know a place,' Nate said.

Quinn shot him a look.

'Really?' Orlando said. 'Where?'

* * *

The taxi ride to Mai 99 only took a few minutes.

The same woman who had greeted Quinn and Nate the previous evening was there again. She smiled broadly, obviously recognizing them, then showed all three to a table. She set menus in front of them before returning to her place near the door.

'So, you come here often, do you?' Orlando asked.

Nate smiled.

A few minutes later, Anh approached their table.

'Welcome back,' she said to Quinn, then to Nate, 'Hello, Raymond.'

'Hi, Anh,' Nate said.

Her smile grew after he said her name. 'Do you need some more time, or would you like to order now?' she asked.

'I think we're ready,' Quinn said, his voice flat.

They gave her their orders.

'It's good to see you again,' Anh said, smiling. 'I will be back with your drinks in a moment.'

As she walked away, Orlando said, 'Pretty. Is she why we're here?'

'Something you want to tell me?' Quinn said to Nate.

'You told me to stay awake, so I came back here for dinner,' Nate said. 'What? At least I didn't use my real name.'

Quinn started to open his mouth, then closed it, saying nothing. A few moments later, Anh brought them their drinks, beers for the men and a bottle of water for Orlando.

After taking a sip, Quinn looked over at Orlando. 'Update?'

'It's not much,' she said. 'The Office is shut tight. Deleon, Collins, Markewicz, Costello, Holton, Dyke. As far as I can tell, they're all dead.'

'Damn,' Nate muttered.

Quinn couldn't help sharing Nate's surprise. Orlando had just named the six top ops agents at the Office.

'Those were the only names I could confirm, but they weren't the only ones.'

'Durrie once said that no matter how you got into the business,' Quinn said, 'there are only a couple ways out. Death is just the most likely.'

He frowned. It was worse than he'd thought.

'What about the disruption?' he finally asked. 'Any claims of responsibility?'

'Not yet.' Orlando looked at him, then added, 'Maybe you should just let it go. You can stay here for a couple of weeks. By then it should be okay to go home.'

'Someone wants me dead,' he said. He took in a deep breath, then blew it out. 'I need to find out who.'

Orlando nodded slightly. He knew it was the same thing she would have done.

No one said anything for several seconds.

'What exactly does that mean?' Nate asked quietly.

'The truth?' Quinn said as he raised his bottle again.

'Yes.'

Quinn took a drink, then set the beer back down. He turned so he was looking directly at Nate. 'It means you have a choice to make. One, you stay here. Hide out like Orlando said. In two or three weeks, you go home. I'll give you whatever cash you need. But when you get there, you're going to have to find a new job. This life you started by working for me will be done.'

'And my other choice is to stay with you,' Nate said.

Quinn shook his head. 'It's more than that. It's doing everything I say. It's not questioning anything. Even then you might be dead before the end of the week.'

A tense silence descended over the table. Orlando looked as if she were about to say something, but Quinn shook his head.

'So?' Quinn asked, once he sensed he'd given Nate enough time.

'I'll stay with you,' Nate replied.

Quinn waited for more, but none was forthcoming. 'You're sure?'

'I'm sure.'

'Impressive,' Orlando said after Nate had excused himself to use the bathroom.

'He probably made the wrong choice,' Quinn said.

'I'll bet he's throwing up in the toilet right now.'

Quinn chuckled, but quickly grew somber. 'Peter contacted me,' he told her.

'Really?' There was a look of both surprise and caution on her face.

'Not directly.' He told her about the e-mail from Duke. 'But I haven't been able to get through to Peter to confirm.'

'What do you think?'

He shook his head. 'I'm not sure.'

She poked at her food for a moment, then said, 'Did Duke say what the job is?'

'No.'

'Did he at least say where?'

Quinn shook his head. 'Since I couldn't get ahold of Peter, I e-mailed Duke for more information. No replies yet.'

Orlando's face scrunched, the worry line above the bridge of her nose in full display. 'Does he still work out of Berlin?'

'As far as I know.' Even as he answered her, he could feel the hair on the back of his neck begin to stand on end. 'Germany,' he said. 'The symbols on the bracelet.'

'Probably means nothing. You said you didn't tell Peter about it.'

'Right. Makes it a little more interesting, though.' He hesitated for a moment, almost deciding to say nothing, but instead he went ahead and threw it out. 'Are you up to doing a little more research for me?'

The air grew heavy between them. Several seconds passed without a word. When Quinn did finally speak, his voice was low, almost like a whisper. 'There was a point right before Durrie and I left the hotel for the op when I could have told him to stay. Ortega and I could have done it without him.'

Orlando stared at the table, immobile, like she wasn't even listening.

'I remember thinking at the time,' Quinn said,

'for maybe a split second, that he wasn't ready. But I didn't say anything. He was my mentor. He was Durrie.'

'He wouldn't have listened to you even if you had said something.' Orlando's voice was a barely audible whisper.

Quinn remained silent, waiting.

'He just couldn't keep it together anymore. There would be weeks when everything was fine. He was the old Durrie. The one I'd fallen in love with. Then suddenly he'd pull back, a depression overtaking him. He'd lock himself in his office for days. Sometimes he'd disappear completely. For a week, maybe two. You remember that job in Mexico City, right?'

Of course he did. He and Orlando had gone down together. Durrie had said he was unavailable. Because of the need to keep a low profile, Quinn and Orlando had shared a room. When Durrie found out, he didn't yell or demand that they take separate rooms; he simply withdrew.

'When I got home, he accused you and me of sleeping together,' she said. 'It took me a week to convince him that nothing happened. Eventually he even apologized, saying he knew I would never do that to him.'

'Why did you stay with him?' Quinn asked, the words escaping his mouth before he even realized it.

She looked at him. Her eyes were drawn and tired, the memories pulling at her. 'I'd been with him almost five years at that point. I wasn't going to just leave him. He needed me.'

'Sorry,' Quinn said. 'I didn't mean anything by it.'

There was quiet for several moments.

When Orlando finally looked up at him, she said, 'I wanted to blame you. I wanted to hate you. For a while I did. When you came to see me in San Francisco, you were lucky I didn't kill you.'

'What changed?'

She eyed him for a moment. 'Time.' She paused. 'I knew what he was like there at the end. I just didn't want to believe it. Don't misunderstand me. I'm still pissed off. At you. But also at me. And most of all at him. I wonder sometimes if he'd lived long enough to know about Garrett, if that might have changed him. You know, given him something to hold on to.'

'I'm sorry,' Quinn said.

'So am I.'

'So you'll help me then?'

She let out a short, derisive laugh, but when she looked at him, there was just the hint of a playful smirk on her face. 'You paying me for this?'

Quinn laughed. 'No.'

The smirk grew wider, then quickly disappeared. 'What do you need?'

Quinn sighed inwardly. For a second there it was almost like the old Orlando was back. *Just give it a little time,* he thought.

'I need to know what Gibson's been up to,' he said. 'Who he's been working for. What jobs he's done lately. See if there is anything that can tie him to Taggert somehow.'

'Okay, but he was probably just a one-time hire,' Orlando said. 'That's the kind of thing Gibson loves to do.' She paused, then corrected herself. '*Loved* to do.'

'Check anyway. All right?'

She looked away for a moment before answering. 'I can do that,' she finally said.

As they were getting up to leave, Nate said, 'Anh's offered to give me a tour of the city.'

'Is that right?' Quinn said, not sounding surprised. 'When is this supposed to happen?'

'Eh . . . now, if you think it's okay.'

'Do you think it's okay?'

'Quinn, let him go,' Orlando said.

Quinn chose to ignore her. 'You remember the rule of attachments,' Quinn said to his apprentice.

'Don't have any,' Nate said.

'Close enough.'

'I won't forget.'

Quinn gave him a single, terse nod.

'Thanks,' Nate said. He gave them both a smile, then headed over to the bar, where Anh was waiting.

'He'll be fine,' Orlando said as she and Quinn left the restaurant. 'Quit acting like his dad.'

'He's my responsibility right now.'

'You know who you're starting to sound like?' she asked.

He knew exactly who she meant. Durrie.

'Go to hell.'

As they climbed into a taxi for the ride back to the Rex, Orlando said, 'Do you mind if we make a stop first?'

'No problem,' Quinn said.

She gave directions to the taxi driver and soon

they were on their way. After ten minutes, they pulled up to the curb in front of a large pagoda. Orlando paid the driver, and they got out.

'A temple?' Quinn asked.

Orlando simply nodded, then led the way up the steps and inside.

The central room was vast, lit mainly by sunlight entering through the large, open doors that surrounded most of the building. But once inside, the light was quickly diffused by a layer of smoke that hung in the air. Quinn couldn't immediately see the source, but he could smell it. Incense. Spicy and sweet. The aroma inviting him in, relaxing him, soothing him.

Orlando led him toward the altar in the center of the room. It was at least twenty feet across, and nearly the same high. In the middle was a life-size statue of the Buddha.

But instead of stopping in front, Orlando walked around and behind the altar. Quinn followed. In the back, there were over a dozen people praying before a second, smaller altar. Again, there was the Buddha, this one the size of a small child. Lining the front of the altar were several round pots of sand, each stuffed with dozens of incense sticks. Many were withered and used, while others glowed as thin spirals of smoke rose from their tips toward the ceiling like ethereal tails pointed at heaven, only to dissipate and become just another part of the perpetual haze.

Surrounding the Buddha statue were shelves lined with photographs of the recently and not-so-recently departed. Orlando found a spot to the far left, then kneeled and began to pray. Instead of bowing her head, her eyes were glued to one of the pictures on the shelves. Quinn, careful not to disturb her, moved around until he had a better view of what she was looking at.

It was a picture of a man. But unlike the other photos, the man was Caucasian. The glass covering the image was so dirty with smoke residue from the constantly burning incense, most people probably didn't even notice.

As Quinn stared at the picture, a surge of conflicting emotions churned inside him. The picture was of Durrie. It was probably taken only a few years before his death. Durrie's hair was almost as gray as it had been on the job that had gotten him killed, but he was smiling and he seemed relaxed.

Quinn tore his eyes away and went back outside before Orlando finished praying. He bought a soda from an old man who'd set up shop at the bottom of the steps, then found a bit of shade near the base of the stairs.

He tried not to think about how the picture of Durrie had affected him. But there was no ignoring it. Guilt. Sadness. Hatred. Hatred for a man who had deserted a son he never knew. Hatred for a man who had taught Quinn how to survive and thrive, and yet was unable to follow his own lessons. But most of all, hatred for a man who had left Orlando heartbroken, damaged, and alone.

A short time later, his soda still unopened, Orlando rejoined him.

'Thank you,' she said.

'How often do you come?' he asked.

She looked up at him. 'Every day.'

Quinn wanted to say, *He doesn't deserve it,* or even better, *He doesn't deserve you.* Instead, he handed her the soda, then walked to the curb and hailed a taxi.

Chapter 13

There were two new e-mail messages waiting for Quinn when he arrived back at his hotel room. The first was from Duke.

```
Files uploaded as requested.
Pls respond earliest.
P4J
```

The second was from Peter.

```
Call me.
```

Before calling Peter, Quinn navigated through cyberspace until he arrived at the location where he'd instructed Duke to upload the information. It took less than thirty seconds to retrieve the file. As the download proceeded, the computer automatically ran the file through a series of virus protection programs. Once Quinn was satisfied nothing nasty was waiting for him, he disconnected the link.

As he expected, the document was a job brief.

According to the information, Duke needed Quinn's help in monitoring some unusual activities going on in Berlin. What those unusual activities were, Duke didn't specify. Though the brief did say a combination of audio, video, and direct observation methods would probably be needed at several locations throughout the city.

Duke still wasn't sure who was behind the activities, but his best guess was JLK, a big player in the German underworld. If that was true, it could also mean the involvement of English, Spanish, or Russian undesirables.

How JLK fit into Peter's problems was even less clear. Had the Office done something to piss the Germans off? If they had, Quinn hadn't heard about it. Of course, as Peter was fond of pointing out, Office business was not Quinn's business.

Quinn reached for his phone.

'Problems?' Peter asked.

Quinn stood at the window of his hotel room looking down on the square below, his phone pressed against his ear. 'Other than the fact that I had to kill someone in my own living room and make an unscheduled trip out of town? No. Everything's fine.'

'I didn't realize killing people was something you were interested in.'

'It's not,' Quinn said.

'Might open some new opportunities for you.'

'I'm not looking for new opportunities.' Quinn paused. 'Duke contacted me.'

'Good. When are you leaving?'

'Who said I was going anywhere?'

Peter was silent for a moment. 'I need you to do this for me.'

'I thought you were the one who told me to disappear,' Quinn said.

'Duke has evidence that the activity he's seeing could be tied into the disruption. Into the attempt on your life.'

'Could be, Peter. Not *is*.'

Again silence. 'It's the best lead we've had.'

'Okay. Then send someone else.'

'I don't have anyone else. You're it.'

'And if I say no?' Quinn asked.

'Then Duke does it on his own. Which we both know means he'll screw it up.'

'I guess you do have a problem.'

'Jesus, Quinn. If he's right, this might be the only chance we get to find out who's behind the attack. I need you to do this. I'm asking you as a favor to me.'

'I don't do favors.'

'When you were first on your own, I hired you when no one else would even give you a chance,' Peter said, a layer of anger underlying his words. 'I've made you a wealthy man. You owe me this much.'

Quinn closed his eyes. He could argue that Peter had continued to hire him because Quinn was the best at what he did, and that any wealth was a result of his talents. But Peter was right about giving Quinn his start, albeit at Durrie's prodding. It just pissed Quinn off that he was playing that card.

'If I do go, you're going to pay me for this,' Quinn finally said.

'I thought you might be interested in doing this gratis,' Peter said.

'That just cost you double.'

'Fine,' Peter said, as if he had expected it.

'I'm going to need a team, too.'

'Just get your resources together and get your ass to Berlin.'

The line went dead.

Quinn stared out the window for several minutes before he returned to his computer and woke it up. He opened the last e-mail from Duke, then hit Reply and wrote:

```
I'll be there. Will advise when
you should expect me. Have
talked to Peter and told him I
will need a full team. I'll put
together prior to arrival. Need
confirmation of payment when I
get there. No shit hotels this
time, okay?
Xavier.
```

Quinn blind-copied Peter and Orlando on the message.

'You didn't want to check with me first?' Orlando asked, irritated.

Quinn was still in his hotel room. Orlando had called him not ten minutes after he sent the e-mail to Duke.

'Hold on,' he said into his phone. 'I'm not asking you to come. I don't *want* you to come. I just need somebody else to know what's going on.'

'Sometimes you're a real asshole, Quinn.'

'What the hell does that mean?'

'You can't do this alone,' she said.

'No kidding.' He was the irritated one now. 'I've got Nate. I just need one more person.'

'Yeah. A tech.'

'So I'll find a tech. There's plenty of them around.'

The line was silent for a moment.

'I'm only going because Peter has no one else,' Quinn said.

'Right.'

'What's that mean?'

'It means maybe that's one reason,' she said.

She was more right than he was willing to admit, so he changed the subject. 'Have you got anything new for me?'

She paused. 'Not yet.'

'Then let's meet later tonight.'

'I won't have anything for you until the morning.'

'Okay. We'll meet for breakfast,' he said. 'Your place? Seven-thirty?'

'Can we make it nine?' she asked.

'Nate and I are going to have to fly out sometime tomorrow. So earlier is better.'

'Okay. Fine,' she said, obviously not happy about it. Quinn was about to say goodbye when Orlando added, 'I'll also check around. See who's available.'

'You don't have to do that,' he said.

'Yeah. I know.'

When Nate finally checked in, Quinn tasked him with picking up some supplies they would need for the next leg of their journey. Quinn then set himself in front of his computer with two goals in mind.

First, he hoped to find someone to help him in Berlin, and second, he wanted to see if he could discover something that might help him figure out who wanted him dead. Unfortunately, he had no luck on either account.

When he finally gave up, night had fallen over Saigon. His legs ached and his eyes were strained from staring at the computer screen. Not surprisingly, he felt the need to get out of his room and clear his head.

He called Nate to see if he wanted to get a drink, but there was no answer. *Probably off with his temporary girlfriend,* Quinn thought.

If Orlando hadn't stopped him, Quinn probably would have clamped down a little harder on Nate. No matter what, they were going to have to have another chat about relationships when this was all over.

But for the time being, it looked like he was on his own, so he headed out. In front of the hotel, he flagged down a taxi, then had to stop two more before finding a driver who spoke English. 'Where to, mister?' the cabby asked as Quinn climbed in.

'A bar,' Quinn said.

'You look for girls? I know place.'

'No. Just somewhere to relax.'

'Okay, okay. No problem.'

The cab took off.

The first place the cabby took him looked like such a dump from the outside, Quinn didn't even get out of the car. The next place wasn't much better. Still, Quinn didn't want to waste the whole night in the back of a cab.

The driver must have registered Quinn's hesitation. 'No, no. Not here,' the driver said. 'I know better. Close to hotel. You like.'

They drove for fifteen minutes, then pulled up in front of another building. This one was on a darkened street a couple of blocks from the Saigon River. There were a dozen people standing outside, clustered around the front door. A mix of Vietnamese and foreigners. All were well dressed.

'Apocalypse Now,' the driver said. 'Very popular.'

As Quinn got out, he noticed two more cabs pull up. Out of the first climbed a young Vietnamese couple. Out of the other came three boisterous Caucasian men. By their accents, Quinn identified them as Australians. At least the cabby appeared to be right about one thing: Apocalypse Now was a popular place.

There was a bouncer at the door, but he let Quinn in without a word. Being a foreigner meant money.

Inside, the place was packed, seventy percent Vietnamese, the rest a mix of other nationalities, but mostly Caucasian men. Music blared from somewhere, a song by the Gorillaz from a few years back, 'Clint Eastwood.' There were tables and an open area for dancing. Quinn began working his way through the crowd toward the bar.

He was halfway there when someone placed a hand on his shoulder. Quinn turned.

'You speak English?' It was a young guy, white. Judging by his accent, either German or Dutch. The guy's eyelids were heavy. Quinn guessed he'd been drinking for a while.

'Yeah?' Quinn answered.

'American, huh?'

Quinn said nothing.

'You need anything, man?'

Quinn shook his head. 'I'm fine.'

'Hash? Opium? I think I got some X left, too.' The guy began digging into a pocket.

'I'm fine,' Quinn repeated. He headed toward the bar.

'All right,' the drug dealer called out. 'You need something, you know where I am.'

Quinn ordered a rum and Coke. Drink in hand, he turned back to study the room, unsatisfied. This wasn't the scene he needed. What he wanted, he realized, was to be doing exactly what Nate was probably doing – sitting at the Mai 99 restaurant, drinking a Tiger beer and talking to the waitresses. That was Quinn's comfort zone. A less intense atmosphere. Casual flirtation with women he didn't know well. Relationships that would go nowhere. Nights spent alone back in his room. With a book. With the TV. With his computer. But with no warmth beside him. It was easier that way.

To his left, another foreigner, maybe six foot two and solidly built, was talking to a tiny Vietnamese woman. Girl, really. She couldn't have been more than eighteen years old. Quinn couldn't hear what they were saying over the loud music, but he got the idea that a business deal was being discussed.

A moment later the woman kissed the man on the cheek, then walked off. The man straightened, a smirk on his face, then noticed Quinn looking his way.

'How's it going, mate?' the man said. Australian. Quinn recognized him as one of the guys who'd arrived just after he had.

'Fine,' Quinn said.

'Didya get a load of her?'

Quinn nodded but said nothing.

'A real pro, that,' the man said. 'Wanted a hundred fifty U.S. Hell, I could go to Phnom Penh and find a real looker who'd stay with me all week for less than a hundred and fifty. She'll be back though. Unless she finds a newbie not clued into the local pricing structure.'

Quinn shook his head sympathetically. It wasn't a conversation he had any real interest in. 'Where you from?' the man asked.

'Canada,' Quinn said. 'Vancouver.'

'To the Queen, then.' The man raised his beer, and Quinn tapped it with his own glass. 'Leo Tucker,' the Aussie said. 'That's me.'

'Tony Johnson.'

'Here on business, Tony?'

Quinn nodded. 'You?'

'Nah. Just checking out the action. The ladies here are fucking gorgeous, but they're pricing themselves out of business. You here for long?'

'Leaving in the morning.'

'Too bad,' Tucker said. 'There's a private party tomorrow night. Hoping it'll salvage my trip. A friend's throwing it. Should be a lot of fun. Plenty of women to go around.'

Quinn professed his disappointment, then, feigning fatigue, he made his escape. As he stepped outside, he felt a momentary sense of relief. But it didn't last long. Standing just outside the door was the drug dealer from inside. There was no one else around. Even the bouncer seemed to have disappeared. Quinn's senses went on alert.

'Where you going, American?' the dealer asked.

'Home,' Quinn said.

'It's early. Party's just starting. You want some pot?'

Quinn shook his head. 'No, thanks.'

There was a cab parked a block up the street. He began walking toward it.

But before he got very far, the dealer ran up and grabbed Quinn's arm. Quinn turned, glaring.

'Hold on,' the dealer said. Metal flashed in his hand. A knife. 'Let's you and me go for a walk. Okay?'

Quinn turned quickly, grabbing the man's arm with both hands and shoving him backward until he was pinned against the outside wall of the club.

The dealer cursed in surprise, obviously not expecting Quinn to react so quickly.

Quinn held on tight to the hand holding the knife. He knew he couldn't let go. If he did, he'd end up on the sidewalk cut, bleeding, maybe even dead.

The dealer knew this, too. He began to punch at Quinn with his empty hand while trying to pull free the one holding the knife. Quinn rolled into him, offering only his back to the man's blows. The dealer's breaths quickened, each huff more vocal than the last as his frustration grew.

Quinn twisted the man's wrist, trying to make him drop the knife. But the dealer's grip was strong.

Changing tactics, Quinn pulled away slightly, then slammed himself back into the man's chest. He did it again. And again. The third time, he knocked the breath out of the dealer. Surprisingly, the asshole still wouldn't let go of the knife.

As the man gasped for air, Quinn quickly looked around. There was an old pipe, maybe four inches thick, running up the side of the building only a few feet away. Quinn pulled the dealer toward it, then smashed the man's wrist against the pipe over and over again.

Suddenly there was a crack and the man cried out in pain. The knife clattered to the ground. Quinn found it with his foot and kicked it as far away as possible before he let go of the man. He needn't have bothered. The dealer slipped down the wall until he was sitting on the ground, cradling his arm in his lap.

'You son of a bitch,' the man said.

Quinn leaned down, grabbed the man by the hair, and pushed his head back until their eyes locked.

'When someone tells you no,' Quinn said, 'you should listen.'

He let go of the man's hair, then stood back up.

'What the hell?' a voice called out in English.

Footsteps. It was Leo Tucker. 'You all right, mate?' Tucker asked when he reached Quinn.

'I'm fine.'

Tucker looked down at the writhing drug dealer on the ground. 'Who the hell is he?'

'I don't know.'

'I saw him take a swing at you.' Tucker nodded in admiration. 'Good move.'

'He's high. It wasn't hard.'

In the distance, they could hear the sound of sirens.

'Christ,' Tucker said. 'The last thing you need is to be messing with the police. Come on.'

Tucker started toward a cab that had just pulled up. Quinn had no desire to get involved with the local authorities, so he followed. Tucker opened the door for him.

'Thanks,' Quinn said. 'I owe you.'

'Just get in,' Tucker said.

Quinn ducked inside.

'You're going to have to scoot over,' Tucker said, leaning through the doorway.

'I appreciate your help, but I've got it from here.'

Then Quinn saw the pistol in Tucker's hand. The Australian smiled, and Quinn slid over.

Chapter 14

Tucker said something in Vietnamese to the cab driver, then settled back and gave Quinn another smile. 'Cheer up, mate. We'll get our business done, then you can be on your way.'

'And what business would that be?' Quinn asked.

Tucker said nothing.

Quinn shrugged as if to say he didn't really care what the answer was. In many ways, that was true. Survival was his main objective now. He couldn't afford to believe Tucker would just let him go after their 'business' was done. But until the opportunity to escape presented itself, he knew he'd have to play along.

They rode in silence. Without looking at his watch, Quinn guessed it was a little before 10 p.m. As the cab moved through the city, he marked the path in his mind. A hotel here, a bamboo scaffolding there, a three-tiered pagoda, a blue lantern hung in a window. Though he was in a part of the city he had never been before, he knew, given the opportunity, he would be able to make it back to familiar ground.

After about ten minutes, they entered an area that looked primarily residential, not just apartment buildings, but a few homes, too. Tucker leaned forward and said something to the driver, who nodded, then turned at the next street. The houses here were different – larger, better kept. Two blocks later, the cab stopped beside a large white wall. At the left end of the wall was a gate. In front of it stood two Vietnamese men. They eyed the cab suspiciously as it came to a halt. From the way they stood, Quinn knew they were armed.

Tucker handed the cabby some cash. 'We're here,' he said to Quinn.

Quinn opened the door and got out. One of the men at the gate took a step toward him, his face taut and expressionless. But as soon as Tucker emerged, the man relaxed.

'What now?' Quinn asked.

'We go in for a chat.' Tucker nodded toward the gate. 'You first.'

Before they passed through, one of the two men searched Quinn, patting him down. The guard came up with a roll of Vietnamese dong and Quinn's folded-up map of the city. He handed the items to Tucker. Quinn was grateful he'd given himself the night off and left the tools of his trade in his room. But the map was a problem. On one side was written the address of Orlando's office. He needed to get it back.

Once the search was complete, the other man pulled the gate open just enough to allow Quinn and Tucker to walk through. Behind the wall was a large, white, two-story house surrounded by a well-tended garden. Lights were on in several of the windows. From one drifted the sounds of music – Ennio Morricone's soundtrack to *The Mission,* if Quinn wasn't mistaken.

As they neared the house the front door opened. A large, muscular man stood in the threshold. Like Tucker, he was Caucasian, although not quite as pasty as the Australian. Maybe a little Latin blood, Quinn decided. Or maybe just more time in the sun.

'This is Perry,' Tucker said to Quinn. 'Perry's in charge of making sure nothing gets broken around here.'

'Does that include me?' Quinn asked.

Tucker laughed.

Perry, unsmiling, moved out of the way so they could enter. Once inside, Quinn felt like he had stepped out of Vietnam and directly into an English country manor. Beyond the entryway was a large living room filled with dark antique furniture. On closer inspection it actually seemed more French than English. It was the paintings on the walls that gave it the English feel – paintings of hunting dogs, game birds, and horses, but none of people.

'Your place?' Quinn asked Tucker. 'It's a little nineteenth century, isn't it?'

'That way.' Tucker pointed to a hallway at the far end of the living room.

Quinn shrugged. As he walked in the direction Tucker had indicated, he carefully noted everything he could use to aid him if needed. There were several objects in the living room that would make for good blunt instruments: a vase, a fist-sized brass sculpture of a sleeping dog, a glass ashtray. But none were in his direct path.

Once in the hallway, Tucker directed Quinn to open the first door on the left. Inside was a bookcase-lined den. A large desk faced the door, dominating the space. Behind the desk sat a man, another Caucasian. He wore a dark blue dress shirt and looked to be in his early sixties – mainly due to his silver, close-cropped hair. He stood as Quinn and Tucker came in.

'Please,' the man said, gesturing to two chairs in front of the desk. 'Have a seat.'

Quinn took the chair to the right, and Tucker took the one to the left. The man behind the desk waited until they were settled before he sat back down.

'Can I get you something?' the man asked Quinn. His accent had a Mid-Atlantic cast to it. 'Water, perhaps? Or a soft drink? I'm afraid we've no alcohol here.'

'I'm fine,' Quinn said.

There was a pitcher of water and four glasses on one side of the desk. The man reached over and filled three of the glasses. He set one in front of Quinn and one in front of Tucker, taking the third for himself. 'Just in case you get thirsty.'

'Thanks,' Quinn said, leaving the glass untouched.

'Well then. I guess we should get started.' The man paused for a moment. 'Leo,' he said to Tucker. 'Where's Art? Wasn't he with you?'

'Seeking medical attention, I'd guess.' Tucker looked over at Quinn. 'Our boy here did a number on him outside Apocalypse Now.'

The older man frowned. 'Dreadful place. Too loud, too many undesirables. I suppose I should find out if he'll be all right.'

'He'll be fine,' Tucker said. 'Looked like a broken arm.'

'Wrist,' Quinn corrected.

'That'll take a while to heal,' the older man said.

'Who are you?' Quinn asked.

The man laughed. 'I should have introduced myself sooner. I apologize. My name's Piper.'

'As in Pied?' Quinn asked.

'As in Mister,' Piper responded.

The name tickled something in the back of Quinn's mind. He was sure Piper wasn't someone he'd worked with before – Quinn would have remembered him instantly if that were the case. But the name was familiar.

'Now why don't you tell us who *you* are,' Piper said.

Quinn shrugged. 'Sure. The name's Tony Johnson.'

Piper laughed again. 'You don't look like a Johnson to me. Do you think he looks like a Johnson, Leo?'

'Not to me, he doesn't.'

'Leo was the one who spotted you,' Piper said, returning his attention to Quinn. 'He's pretty good at faces. He was at the airport checking the new arrivals yesterday. Something he does for me most mornings. And there you were.'

'There he was,' Tucker agreed.

'The famous Jonathan Quinn,' Piper said.

Quinn didn't flinch. 'And you just decided to have me over for . . . a glass of water?'

'Just a chat,' Piper said. 'Consider the water a gift.'

'What do you want?'

'That depends.'

'On what?'

Piper smiled. 'Did you know there's a price on your head?'

'That doesn't surprise me,' Quinn said calmly. 'How much am I going for these days?'

'Not enough to make me shoot you on the spot, but enough to make me curious. Leo, what was the amount?'

'Twenty-five thousand U.S.,' Leo said.

Piper looked back at Quinn. 'You see. Curiosity money, really. Not worth my trouble.'

Quinn leaned back in his chair, then said, 'So who wants me dead?'

'Good question,' Piper said. 'There was no name attached to the . . . request. I was hoping you might know.'

Quinn shrugged. 'I guess we're all in the dark.'

'Curious how only you are mentioned,' Piper said. 'I guess your friend isn't as important.'

'Friend?' Quinn asked, suddenly tense.

'You weren't alone when you arrived,' Piper said. 'A young man? Tucker tells me he had some trouble with one of the local kids.'

If they had noted Quinn's arrival, of course they would have made Nate, too.

'A colleague, perhaps?' Piper asked.

'Could be I just met him on the plane,' Quinn said.

Tucker snorted. 'Right,' he said, laughing.

Piper pulled something out of a drawer in the desk and set it on the blotter in front of him. It was a photo of Quinn and Nate standing outside the Rex Hotel. Piper turned it so that Quinn was looking at it right-side-up, then tapped the picture several times.

'I haven't been able to ID him yet, but my instinct tells me he works for you.'

Quinn smiled.

'What are the two of you doing here?' Piper asked.

Quinn glanced down at his left hand as he ran his thumb over the pads of his fingers. 'What's the play here?' he said, looking up. 'Are we waiting for someone? When he shows up, maybe he takes me on a ride into the countryside? He comes back. I don't.'

Tucker laughed again. 'Pal, you really must be having a bad week.'

Piper leaned back, his eyes studying Quinn. 'As you can probably guess, my business here is very sensitive. What I don't want is for the two months I've had to spend in this hellhole to be blown by someone like you. So you see why I'm curious about your intentions. That is the only *play* I care about.'

'Then we don't have a problem,' Quinn said. 'Until Romeo here picked me up at the bar, I didn't even know you were in town.'

'And why should I believe you?' Piper asked.

'I don't care if you believe me or not.'

'You should,' Tucker said.

'No,' Quinn said. 'I shouldn't. You think I'm here to foul up your gig and want to take care of me now or someone out there wants the money and shoots me in the back of the head tomorrow, what's the difference? Believe me or don't. Just choose one and let's move on.'

When no one said anything, Quinn pushed himself off his chair. 'Thanks for the talk, but I've got things to do.'

Tucker jumped up a moment after Quinn, but Piper remained seated.

'Which one of you is going to call me a cab?' Quinn asked.

Finally, Piper stood up, a smile growing on his face. 'It would be best if you left Vietnam.'

'Is tomorrow too soon?' Quinn asked.

'It'll do.' Piper laughed quietly. 'A piece of advice.'

Quinn said nothing.

'Get yourself a new partner. He's very sloppy. Leo followed him most of the day without ever being spotted. Clothing shops, a couple of cosmetic stalls, some T-shirt stands.'

Leo shrugged. 'When I left him, he was eating dinner at a restaurant off Hai Ba Trung.'

'If you're really leaving tomorrow, I think we can live with that,' Piper said. 'But don't push it. Twenty-five thousand dollars isn't enough for me to get involved. But I can't speak for Leo here. Or even Art. He may feel the money should be his in exchange for the pain you've caused him. If you're still here the day after tomorrow, I can't guarantee your safety.'

'No hard feelings, I hope?' Tucker asked. He held out his hand.

Reluctantly, Quinn shook it. 'Can I get my money back now?' he asked.

‘What? Oh, right.’ Tucker pulled the cash and map out of his pocket and handed everything to Quinn, who then slipped it all into his pocket. ‘I’ll walk you out,’ Tucker said. ‘Make sure you get that cab.’

They turned for the door.

‘Mr. Quinn,’ Piper said. Quinn looked back. ‘I don’t know for a fact who’s put up the reward, but that doesn’t mean I don’t hear rumors.’

‘What’s the rumor?’ Quinn asked.

A pause. Then Piper said, ‘Borko.’

‘Borko?’

Piper nodded. ‘He’s no friend of mine, and by your reaction, he’s not one of yours either. I’d be careful if I were you.’

Quinn stood motionless for a moment, absorbing this new information, then nodded and left.

Chapter 15

It was during the cab ride back to the hotel that Piper's identity finally clicked in Quinn's mind. Reuben Piper. He could be no one else. Durrie's first partner, long before Quinn had joined the business. Durrie had seldom spoken of Piper, but occasionally a story would come out. Quinn could recall few details. The pairing had ended badly, though. That much he did remember.

The cab dropped Quinn off in front of the Rex at 11:30 p.m. Technically, it was after the citywide 11:00 p.m. curfew, but the streets were still busy, and Quinn had noticed several restaurants and clubs still open during the drive back. His mind spinning, the last thing he wanted to do was to go up to his room, yet the idea of returning to a club did not appeal to him. He considered for a moment walking over to Mai 99, but opted in the end for the rooftop bar at the Rex.

As he took a sip from a glass of Tiger beer, he couldn't help but consider the ramifications of his encounter with Piper. Quinn had thought he was coming to a safe haven in Vietnam. Instead he and

Nate had been spotted the moment they'd stepped off the plane. And as if that little bit of news needed an extra kicker, Piper's revelation that Borko might be involved in the disruption was disturbing to say the least.

About the only positive that came out of the impromptu meeting was what Piper had not said. There'd been no mention of Orlando at all. If Piper had known she was also here, he wouldn't have let Quinn go so easily. It was bad enough having Quinn in town, but two top-level agents in Saigon at the same time? Two agents who not only knew each other, but had worked extensively together in the past? It would have been too much. But apparently their paths had not crossed in the couple of months Piper had been there.

Quinn's thoughts returned to Borko. He was a problem, and not just a small one. It was like going to the dentist for a cleaning and being told you had to have multiple root canals right away, Quinn thought, then quickly changed his mind. *More like going to the dentist and being told all your teeth have to be pulled out.*

Still, Quinn had to admit, Borko's involvement made a certain amount of sense. Undertaking a disruption was a huge task, one that usually wasn't worth the risk. But Borko's organization was the Sex Pistols of the intelligence world, willing to do things that few of their competitors would touch. The strategy both helped and hurt Borko. Most clients wouldn't deal with him. But occasionally an unconventional need would arise, and that's when he'd get a call.

While Quinn's path had crossed that of the Serbian's organization only once, it was enough. No matter how hard he tried, the memory of that job was something he could never forget.

It had been six years earlier in Toronto.

It started off like a lot of his jobs did, with Quinn crammed in the back of a van, staring at a rack of monitors mounted temporarily against the wall. This time the images on the screens were different angles of a work area in a City of Toronto vehicle maintenance facility. He wasn't the only one watching. Two other guys were shoehorned in there with him.

'What's that? Eight shots?'

'Nine,' Quinn said.

Dan Skyler, the one who asked the question, was sitting to Quinn's right. He was a local guy Quinn had hired for the gig, a disposal specialist among other things, though Quinn wasn't planning on tapping into that part of Skyler's talents.

When the job had been offered to him, it had been characterized as being straightforward. Keep an eye on things as the exchange went down, then go in after everyone was gone and sanitize the scene – remove any trace of their presences: tire tracks, fingerprints, footprints, things moved out of place, any physical evidence at all that might lead someone to pick up the trail of the asset. If someone had later been able to trace the asset to the exchange location, it needed to be a dead end. Quinn liked to think of it as a water job. Like in a movie, where someone would run into a creek and use the water to cover his tracks and wash away any scent he might leave behind. Quinn's job was to be the creek.

Only based on the scene in front of them, it was going to take more than just a creek to clean things up. Skyler's specialty was going to be needed after all.

To Quinn's left was Joseph Glaze. He was with the client, a group called V12, there to monitor Quinn's work and communicate back to his superiors when everything was done. Not a situation Quinn was particularly fond of, but it sometimes came with the job.

'Jesus Christ,' Glaze said, his eyes wide. 'We need to do something.'

He started to push himself up out of his chair, but Quinn reached over and grabbed Glaze's shoulder.

'Hold on,' Quinn said.

'But –'

'It's not our job.'

Reluctantly, Glaze sat back down.

For nearly a minute, all was quiet on the display screens. No noise, no movement. Quinn took a slow, deep breath as he scanned the monitors. What was supposed to have been a simple asset transfer had turned into a massacre. The floor of the garage was becoming stained by something more than motor fluids.

'I count three down,' Quinn said.

'That's the whole transfer team,' Glaze said. He leaned forward for a closer look. 'Where's the asset?'

They scanned the monitors for several seconds.

'There she is,' Skyler said, pointing at one of the screens.

Quinn looked over. The asset was half hidden in a shadow cast by a stack of steel drums. As Quinn watched, her right foot moved a few inches.

'She's still alive,' he said.

'Are you sure?' Skyler asked.

Quinn nodded.

'We've got to do something,' Glaze said.

'You want to tell me what?' Quinn asked.

'We can't just sit here.'

'Yes, we can.'

'We've got movement,' Skyler said.

Four men were moving into frame on the wide shot. Each was dressed in dark clothing, and all were carrying identical weapons – Heckler and Koch G36K assault rifles. Those were not the weapons V12's team had been equipped with.

The four men moved cautiously across the floor, the barrels of their guns sweeping the areas in front of them. As they reached the first of the bodies lying on the floor, one of the men pushed it with his foot. There was no reaction. The second body yielded the same results. But the last moaned as the foot was jammed into his side. Without hesitating, one of the armed men pointed his G36K at the man's head and pulled the trigger.

As they rounded the stack of drums, their rifles suddenly tightened against their shoulders, barrels pointed at the asset.

'Secure,' one of the gunmen called out. 'She's unarmed.' Then, more quietly, said, 'Get up. Slowly.'

The asset rose to her feet. The gunman who had spoken motioned for her to move forward. As she stepped out of the shadow, she appeared to be cradling her right arm. Blood soaked her sleeve, but otherwise she appeared uninjured.

'Who's that?' Quinn asked. Movement had caused him to look at the monitor on the far right.

From the same direction the four gunmen had entered, a fifth man appeared. This one was different from the others. He was wearing an expensive-looking gray suit, and unlike his friends, he wasn't carrying a rifle. But there was a bulge at the small of his back, under his jacket. So he wasn't completely unarmed. He was tall and thin; Quinn guessed maybe six foot three, and 170 pounds. His dark brown hair was long, falling just below his shoulders in waves and curls that made his head appear larger than it was. Though there was no smile on his face, Quinn sensed an air of satisfaction surrounding him. No, it was more than that – an air of superiority, of extreme confidence in every step he took.

'I think we need to get out of here,' Glaze said.

'What are you talking about?' Skyler asked.

'We need to leave,' Glaze said. 'Now.'

'A minute ago you were ready to rush in there and help,' Quinn said.

'I was wrong.' Glaze started to rise again. This time instead of heading toward the back door, he was turning toward the front of the van.

'Hold on,' Quinn said. 'We're not going anywhere.'

'Don't you know who that is?' Glaze stared at the other two, eyes blazing. 'That's Borko.'

There was a moment of silence as Quinn and Skyler looked back at the screen.

'No shit?' Skyler said.

Quinn stared intently. He'd only seen pictures of Borko before, none very good. The man in the garage certainly could have been the Serb. He fit the description.

'How do you know?' Quinn asked.

Glaze stared down at Quinn. 'Because I worked with him before, that's how,' he said, as if daring Quinn to challenge him. 'Last year. We used him on a job. I met him at the setup meeting. He didn't do what we asked. People died who shouldn't have died. But he didn't care. I don't think he cares about anything.'

Glaze couldn't fake the fear that radiated from his words. There was little chance he was lying. Quinn looked at the screen again.

Borko was one fucked-up son of a bitch. Not everyone in the business knew who he was, but Quinn had heard stories from several very reliable sources. Borko reportedly cut his teeth as one of the late Slobodan Milosevic's ethnic-cleansing experts. He was even said to be a member of the *Sluzba drzavne bezbednosti* – Milosevic's malevolent state security service – getting his start in the early 1990s infiltrating university student groups to help quell an uprising that threatened to topple the regime.

He should have been arrested years ago. He should have stood trial for crimes against humanity in the World Court in The Hague. He should have been killed a thousand times over, but he hadn't been.

In fact, he'd simply disappeared when the war ended, his name never appearing on any wanted list. A few years later he resurfaced, this time as the head of his own little organization. For a price, he and his team were available to do people's dirty work. The only limitation on projects they would accept was the price clients were willing to pay.

'Don't you get it?' Glaze said. 'He's going to come after us next.'

'No,' Quinn said. 'He isn't.'

'What the fuck are you talking about?' Glaze said. 'He's going to kill us.'

Quinn looked up at Glaze, his gaze steady but calm. Finally, the look in Glaze's eyes changed from fear to dawning understanding. Slowly, he sat back down.

'If he knew we were here,' Glaze began, 'he'd already have come after us, right? Before he went inside.'

'Exactly,' Quinn said.

'You're sure?' Glaze asked.

'I'm sure.'

They returned their attention to the screens. Two of Borko's men had escorted the asset into the center of the room. She didn't even try hiding her fear; Quinn could clearly see it on her face. What was happening wasn't part of the plan that had been laid out to her. V12 was just supposed to transfer her to a team from SCG, who in turn would have been responsible for getting her safely out of the country. That was the service her friends had paid for. That was what the asset had been expecting.

Borko approached the woman.

‘Are you Karina Sanchez?’ he asked.

‘I don’t know who that is,’ she said much too quickly.

Borko smiled, then casually removed his pistol from under his jacket and slapped the woman across the face with its barrel. Her knees buckled, and she fell to the floor. When she looked up, blood began seeping out of the new cut on her cheek.

‘Are you Karina Sanchez?’ Borko asked again.

Before she could answer, a noise came from the side of the room. It was a door opening. Borko’s gunmen whipped around, their rifles pointed at the source.

Quinn’s eyes jumped to the monitor with the best view. Two men had just entered the building. They were talking at first, two friends arriving early to work. One was carrying a cup of coffee, while the other held a toolbox.

The moment they saw Borko and his men, the man with the coffee dropped his cup and bolted for the door. A bullet took off the back of his head before he could escape. His friend watched, frozen to the spot where he stood. As he turned his eyes back toward the center of the room, he was greeted with the barrels of four guns pointed at him.

‘Hey, it’s cool,’ the man said. ‘Listen, I don’t care what you’re doing. Just let me go and I’ll keep my mouth shut.’

Borko reached down and lifted the asset back to her feet, then looked at the new arrival. ‘Why don’t you come over here for a moment?’

The man hesitated. ‘I think it might be better if I just leave.’

'You a mechanic? This where you work?' Borko asked.

The man nodded.

'You're a little early, aren't you?'

'Just picking up a little overtime,' the man said. 'That's all. I'll come back later, okay?'

'Bring him over,' Borko said to his team.

One of the men approached the mechanic, his gun pointed at the man's head. 'Move,' the gunman said.

The mechanic did as he was told, stopping when he was only a few feet away from Borko.

'You can put that down,' Borko said, glancing at the toolbox.

The man seemed to suddenly remember he was carrying something, then quickly set the box down on the floor. 'I swear, you let me go, I'll forget I ever saw you.'

But Borko had stopped listening. His attention was back on the asset.

'Miss Sanchez, the person who paid me to find you is not very happy that you decided to find employment elsewhere. As you can imagine, he is not anxious for others in his organization to follow your lead. So he has asked me to make sure you let the others know you made a mistake.'

Borko nodded once. Two of his men quickly shouldered their rifles and grabbed the mechanic by the arms. Once he was secure, Borko kneeled down next to the toolbox and opened it.

'What do you carry in here?' Borko asked. Before the man could reply, Borko reached into the box and pulled something out. 'This will be fine.'

As he stood up, Quinn could see a long, thin screwdriver in the Serb's hand. Borko looked back at the woman.

'Don't worry. I am not actually expecting you to make any kind of speech. There are many ways to deliver a message. Perhaps you'd like to get a preview of what your message will look like.'

Borko turned to the mechanic, the screwdriver held tightly in his hand.

'What the fuck?' the man said. 'Come on. I ain't done nothing. Please.'

The Serb put his free hand on the man's shoulder, smiled, then jabbed the screwdriver deep into the man's abdomen.

The mechanic cried out in agony and started to double over. But the gunmen held him up so Borko could pull the tool out. Borko waited a moment, then shoved it in again, this time on the other side.

The mechanic vomited, his breakfast barely missing Borko's shoes. Borko once again removed the screwdriver. This time he held the bloody weapon in front of the asset's face.

'You see, one more time and he'll probably pass out,' he said. 'He won't be dead yet, but he will miss all the fun. This method is effective, but most of the damage is on the inside. Outside? Only a couple of small holes. Not very dramatic. To be an effective message, there has to be a more dramatic presentation.'

Without warning, he lashed out with the screw-driver, slashing its blade across the mechanic's face, detaching part of the man's cheek. He did it again and again and again. Face, neck, shoulders, chest.

Finally he plunged the weapon upward under the man's rib cage, undoubtedly aiming for the heart.

Within seconds, the mechanic was dead.

As the gunmen let the body slump to the floor, Borko pulled his makeshift weapon out and turned back to the asset, smiling.

'So, Miss Sanchez, are you ready?'

He raised the bloody screwdriver again.

After Borko and his team cleared out, Quinn told Skyler to get behind the wheel, but not to start the engine yet. Quinn glanced at his watch, then fixed his eyes on the monitor displaying the wide shot of the carnage. Each minute that passed was agony to Quinn. The chance that another civilian – perhaps a security guard, or another city worker arriving early – would enter the room and find the massacre increased with each moment Quinn continued to hold their position. But he'd been well trained, and understood that caution was one of the most important parts of the job.

The wait paid off. After nearly fifteen minutes someone stepped out from the shadows of one of the trucks. It was Borko himself, armed now with one of the G36K rifles. He appeared to be alone. *Does the son of a bitch think he could take on an entire rescue team by himself?* Quinn thought, then paused. *He probably does, and probably could.*

The Serb walked around for a moment, gave each body a shove, then exited the building.

Another fifteen minutes passed. Quinn wanted to wait longer, but knew they couldn't chance it. Finally, he said, 'Now.'

Skyler started the engine and pulled out.

'Don't rush,' Quinn reminded him. 'Nice and easy. Like a routine you do every day.'

Per their plan, Skyler didn't drive directly to the entrance of the garage. Instead he drove a route that took him around several buildings in the immediate vicinity, checking for Borko and his men.

They found no sign of them.

'What about SCG?' Glaze asked. 'We were transferring her to them. Their guys have to be here somewhere.'

Quinn shook his head. 'Their guys never made it.'

As Skyler drove toward the garage, Quinn handed Glaze two pairs of gloves. One pair was the lightweight rubber kind doctors used. The other was also rubber, only heavy duty – janitor gloves, extra tough. He and Skyler had similar sets.

'What are these for?' Glaze said.

'You're going to have to help us,' Quinn said. 'Gloves on at all times. Surgical first, then the others over the top. Only take the thick ones off if you need to do detailed work. But be careful. No prints. You get a tear, you let me know. I'll get you another pair.'

Quinn could still see the fear in the other man's eyes. But to Glaze's credit, he didn't protest.

'One more thing. When we're inside, I do the talking. No comments. No unnecessary noise. If you have a question, okay. But think it through first and keep it brief. Understand?'

'I understand.' Glaze's voice was a dry whisper.

At the garage, Quinn entered first, slipping in through the back door and making a quick search of the facility. Except for the bodies, they were alone.

Despite not expecting any casualties, Quinn had come prepared with plenty of plastic sheeting. He, Skyler, and Glaze were able to get the bodies wrapped quickly, securing each package with duct tape, then loaded them into the back of the van. It was a tight fit, but they were able to get them all in. All, that is, except the civilian shot while running for the door.

'Not yet,' Quinn said when the other two moved to wrap the man up.

Instead, he had them turn their attention to the blood on the cement. While Skyler and Glaze mopped up the excess fluids, Quinn searched the garage. He found several bags of absorbent sand, probably used to soak up motor oil spills. Quinn brought one of the bags over to where the murders had occurred.

As Skyler and Glaze finished, Quinn poured sand over the wet spots on the concrete to draw out as much of the blood as possible. He knew there would be a stain, but the plan he had in mind would deal with that.

While the sand did its work, Quinn and his team did a detailed search of the room, collecting all the brass left over from the gunfire. When they were done, Quinn stood still for a moment, taking in the room.

'Toolbox,' he said to Skyler.

Skyler immediately walked over and picked up the abandoned box, then set it by the door so they'd take it with them when they left. They had already found the screwdriver. Borko had conveniently left it shoved up one of the asset's nostrils.

To Glaze, Quinn said, 'Scoop up the sand. I notice a box of heavy-duty trash bags under the workbench. If you don't fill them too much, they should be able to hold everything. When you're done, get the wet-dry vacuum from the van to make sure you get it all.'

'What about him?' Skyler said, nodding toward the dead mechanic by the door.

'We leave him here,' Quinn said. 'There's spray paint in the kit in the back of the van. Tag a few of the vehicles, some of the walls.'

They would make it look like an act of vandalism gone bad. To cover the bloodstains, Quinn would open one of the fifty-gallon drums of used motor oil, letting it spill over the entire floor. Hide one crime scene with another. And at least this way, one family would have some kind of closure.

Quinn gave the room one final look before they left. It was a good job, and, surprisingly, it had gone quickly. Only eighteen minutes by his watch. But it wasn't their handiwork that stuck in his mind as he climbed into the van. It was Borko and that goddamn screwdriver.

Karma was something Quinn was pretty sure existed. Only in his mind it wasn't perfect. Some people got away with some pretty bad shit. If Borko's karma ever came back at him, it was going to be hellish. And for just a moment, Quinn was not opposed to exacting some of the payment himself.

'Have you ever dealt with anything like that before?' Glaze asked as they drove away.

'It's what we do,' Quinn said.

'Are they all like that?'

'I've seen worse,' Quinn lied.

Quinn ordered another beer. It was nearing midnight, and the Saigon evening had finally turned pleasant. Still warm, but the humidity had dropped to bearable levels. There were about a dozen or so other people spread out across the rooftop dining area. But at the bar there was only Quinn and the bartender.

Quinn took a deep drink from the bottle before setting it down on the counter. It had been six years since that incident in Toronto, yet Quinn had still never encountered another incident as brutal.

Borko.

Shit.

He raised his beer to his lips and finished it off.

'Another,' he said to the bartender.

Chapter 16

The next morning there was another message from Duke.

Xavier,
We're on. Need you in Berlin by Sunday. You are registered as Donald Bragg at the Dorint Hotel Am Gendarmenmarkt. Contact information and update after you arrive. Advise any arrangements I need to make for your team.
P4J

Quinn sent Duke a confirmation.

'We're definitely leaving today,' Quinn said.

He and Nate were sitting with Orlando at the table in her dining room eating *pho* – Vietnamese soup – that Trinh had made. Quinn had already filled both of them in on his meeting with Piper, leaving out only the part about Leo Tucker tailing Nate. Though Orlando was aware Piper and his team were in Ho Chi Minh City, she was pleased to hear they weren't aware of her.

Quinn turned his attention to the job in Berlin. 'Were you able to find anyone for me?'

'I don't want you to argue with me about this,' Orlando said, her eyes locking on his. 'It makes the most sense.'

'No,' Quinn said, realizing where she was headed.

'I'm the logical choice. There's going to be a lot of surveillance going on. That means a ton of data that needs to be processed and analyzed. That's what I do. I'm the best and you know it.' She paused. 'There's no choice here, Quinn. You need me. And I'm coming.'

'We can do this without you,' he said. 'There are others who can handle it.'

She stood, picking up her empty bowl of soup. 'I've already got my ticket,' she said. 'I leave tomorrow.'

Nate looked down at his bowl of pho as if it had suddenly become the most important thing in the world.

'Dammit!' Quinn said. He stood and followed her into the kitchen. 'I said I don't need you.'

'My son will be fine while I'm gone.'

'I didn't say anything about him,' Quinn said.

She set the empty bowl in the sink, then looked at Quinn for a moment. 'But it's what you're worried about.'

Quinn took a deep breath. She was at least partially right. But it was more than just her son that concerned him.

Orlando returned to the living room. Again, Quinn followed.

As she sat back down she said, 'Remember that Indian restaurant near Oranienburger Strasse?'

'What are you talking about?' Quinn asked.

'It was just north of the Mitte.'

Quinn closed his eyes for a moment as his mind switched gears. 'Amit? Amid? Something like that?'

'Amirit,' she said. 'We'll meet there at nine p.m. Saturday.'

'Orlando –'

'Quinn, don't. Just tell me you'll meet me there.'

He didn't bother masking his irritation. 'I'm not going to be happy about it.'

'Good. You shouldn't be,' she said. 'Today I'll work on getting all the equipment arranged. Any special requests?'

Quinn took a deep breath, then thought for a moment. 'A surveillance kit. Weapons. We'll need video taps, too.'

'How many?'

'I don't know,' Quinn said. 'At least fifteen to be safe.'

She looked over at Nate. 'What do you use?'

Nate looked up seconds later, confused by the silence. 'What? Are you talking to me?'

'What kind of gun?'

'I have a Walther back home.'

She frowned. 'A Glock would be better. Lightweight. Single-action. Easy to use.'

'I've never had any problems with the Walther.'

'A Glock would be better.'

A hesitation, then he said, 'Okay.'

Orlando wasn't writing any of it down, but Quinn

had no doubt she would remember. She asked, 'Is that it?'

'If you have any time, a little info on what Borko's been up to lately could be useful.'

'Don't press your luck,' she said.

'What kind of name is Borko?' Nate asked.

'That's a stupid question,' Quinn said.

Nate looked momentarily stung, then his eyes narrowed in thought. 'Okay,' he said. 'Should I be worried about him?'

'That's better. And the answer is yes,' Quinn said.

'He led a group of Bosnian Serbs during the war,' Orlando added. 'They were particularly adept at ethnic cleansing.'

'Great,' Nate said, not looking happy.

Quinn turned to Orlando. 'So how about it?'

'I'm going to have to bring in some outside help on this,' she told him.

'Your paranoid friend?'

'Not paranoid. Just cautious. He's already helping us with the slide, anyway.'

Orlando's contact went by the name 'the Mole.' Quinn had never talked to him. For all he knew, the Mole was some college geek playing spy out of his dorm room. Given his choice of a code name, Quinn wouldn't have been too surprised if that was true. 'Just don't run up a big tab. Okay?'

'Mama?'

The child's voice came from behind Quinn. He turned.

Garrett, Orlando's son, was standing near the entrance to the dining room. Awake, he looked even more Caucasian than he had when he was sleeping.

'Garrett,' Orlando said as she stood up.

'I heard loud talk,' the boy said in English. 'Are you mad?'

'No, honey. Everything's fine. Come and say hello to Jonathan and Nate.'

The boy approached cautiously, then stuck out his hand. 'Hello, Mr. Jonathan. Hello, Mr. Nate.'

Quinn squatted down to the boy's level to shake hands. 'Good morning, Garrett,' Quinn said.

'Are you a friend of Mama's?'

'Yes. I am.'

Garrett turned to Nate. 'What about you?'

Nate nodded his head. 'Sure. I'm her friend.'

'Do you want to watch a movie with me?' Garrett asked. He looked up at his mom. 'Can we watch *Increbidolls*?'

'We'd love to,' Quinn said. 'But we have to leave.'

Garrett frowned, disappointed.

'Maybe next time,' Orlando said. 'But you can watch it in my room, okay?'

'Okay,' Garrett said, brightening.

Quinn put a hand gently on Garrett's shoulder. 'It was a pleasure meeting you. You take it easy, okay?'

'Yes, sir.'

Quinn looked at Orlando. 'I don't want you to come.'

She looked back at him. 'Neither do I,' she said. 'I'll see you in Berlin.' She pulled Garrett to her and mussed his hair.

Her son smiled. 'Mama, stop.'

Back in his hotel room, Quinn gathered the few things he'd unpacked and threw them back in his bag. The new clothes and other items Nate had picked up had already been split between them and put in each of their bags. He then met up with Nate downstairs so they could make their flight arrangements.

'There are several airlines that fly out of Ho Chi Minh City,' the woman at the desk told them. 'Thai Airways. And Air France, of course. Their office is just across the street, next to the Hotel Continental.'

Quinn thanked her, then headed for the exit with Nate in tow. While Thai Airways was one of his favorite ways to fly, Air France sounded like the better bet. They should be able to make it all the way to Europe with minimal trouble. And if they could go through France, even better. A couple of Caucasian passengers carrying European passports and arriving on a European airline would draw little attention.

The woman at the counter of the Air France office informed Quinn that there was a flight leaving that evening for Bangkok, where he could connect on a flight to Paris. 'Are there any seats available?' Quinn asked.

'How many tickets do you need?' She looked Vietnamese and spoke English with a French accent.

'Two,' Quinn said.

'That shouldn't be a problem. May I see your passports?'

Five minutes later, they had their tickets.

Quinn allowed Nate a final meal at Mai 99, but didn't let him go alone. Of course, Anh was there.

In a way, he envied the distraction she had provided Nate. There were times when Quinn longed for a similar tangent, a little time when he could forget the shit his life had become. In reality the few women he had gotten even remotely close to had only served as ultimately unsuccessful attempts at self-deception, none ever completely helping him forget the fact he wanted to be with someone else. They basically ended up being only bridges from one point to another. Nothing more. An emotional connection, something deeper that could have lasted more than a few months or even a year, eluded him.

He tried to convince himself it was his line of work that made things difficult.

'Getting hooked on one woman is the last thing you want to do,' Durrie had told him when Quinn once casually mentioned he'd met a woman he liked. 'She becomes your weak spot. And once you have a weak spot, you're through. Fuck around all you want. There's pussy everywhere. Just don't get hung up on just one. It'll get you killed. Understand?'

Ironic, given Durrie's own entanglement with Orlando, but it had stuck with Quinn. He even turned it into a kind of mantra, using it as an excuse for why he had to live his life alone. But deep inside, in the part of his mind he always tried to ignore, he knew the truth. He knew the reason why his relationships didn't work. It had nothing to do with his mentor's advice.

Unfortunately, there was nothing he could do about it. He had made a promise, and to act on his true feelings would mean breaking that promise.

It didn't matter that Durrie was dead. Quinn had given his word to avoid getting involved with her.

'You're her best friend,' Durrie had said. It was a week before the operation that took him down. He had asked Quinn to fly down to San Diego to discuss the upcoming gig. 'If she needs anything, and I'm not there to help, you make sure she gets it.'

'You know I will,' Quinn said.

'By helping, I don't mean moving in. You get me?'

Quinn froze momentarily. 'I –'

'Shut up,' Durrie said. 'I'm not stupid. I know you love her, Johnny. But she'll always be mine. Understand?'

The only thing Quinn could do was nod. Durrie was a shit to the end. He knew Quinn too well. He knew when Quinn made a promise, he'd keep it. Even a promise to a dead man.

He'd kept the promise, too. Even in the years he and Orlando had not talked, he'd kept tabs on her. Paying others to go to wherever she was living, checking that everything was okay. But he never went himself. He feared he wouldn't be able to stay away from her if he did.

After Quinn finished his dinner and drank the last of his Tiger beer, he slipped Nate five hundred dollars under the table.

'What's this for?' Nate asked.

'Put it under your plate when we leave.'

Nate still stared at him, not getting it.

'It's a tip.'

'This is not a tip,' Nate said.

'Think of it this way,' Quinn said. 'You may not ever see her again, but she'll never forget you.'

'I thought the idea was always to be forgettable,' Nate said.

Quinn stood up, gave Nate a half smile, then turned for the door.

Chapter 17

They separated in Bangkok, Quinn sticking with Air France headed to Paris, while Nate flew British Airways to London, transferring to a British Midland flight across the Channel.

Quinn was waiting for him near the gate when he arrived, and was happy to see Nate had followed his directions. Gone were the jeans and short-sleeved shirts he had been wearing in Vietnam. They had been replaced by a sharp-looking dark blue business suit, white shirt, and matching patterned tie. Gone, also, was the slightly unkempt brown hair. Now he was sporting a slicked-down, side-parted hairdo. The gel he used had darkened the shade of his hair considerably.

'Well done,' Quinn said as he fell into step next to his apprentice.

'Thanks,' Nate said. 'I had, like, fifteen minutes in London to change, goop up, and catch my flight. I probably had some of that crap still on my hand when I gave the attendant my ticket.'

'Really?' Quinn asked, suddenly concerned.

'No, Dad. Not really,' Nate said. 'I like your glasses.'

'You can have them when I'm through.'

'I don't like them that much.'

Like Nate, Quinn had also changed his appearance. The glasses were black framed, narrow and stylish. He, too, wore a suit, only his was black and the shirt beneath a dark shade of gray. But unlike Nate, he'd had more time to deal with his hair. He'd shaved it close, leaving little more than a quarter inch all the way around.

'We're on the five p.m. to Berlin,' Quinn said. 'Lufthansa.'

As they moved on, Quinn sensed the mood of his apprentice changing, becoming tenser. Until now, they had been playing a game of hide-and-seek. But Berlin was a real job, real work, and, undoubtedly, real danger. And the memory of Gibson couldn't be far from Nate's mind.

'Pop quiz,' Quinn said.

'I'm sorry?'

'In *The Odessa File*, tell me what Jon Voigt's character did right at the printer's shop.'

'Um . . .' Nate blinked. 'He took the gun.'

'Right. And what did he do wrong after breaking into Roschmann's mansion?'

'Easy. He didn't shut the door behind him. But he did get away with it.'

'True. But if you're in the same position?'

'I close the door. Every time.'

'Good,' Quinn said. 'Nothing to worry about, then.'

In Europe, unlike Vietnam where even in January it seemed like summer, winter had taken a firm hold. The temperature upon their arrival in Berlin was hovering just below zero degrees centigrade, immediately bringing back memories of Colorado to Quinn.

Tegel Airport was not a large facility by international standards, but it was light-years beyond Tan Son Nhat International Airport in Ho Chi Minh City. Tegel had the amenities most international travelers expected: restaurants, bars, bookstores, souvenir shops, information booths. The terminal at Tan Son Nhat had been nothing more than a distribution warehouse that moved people from street to plane or plane to street.

Quinn paused as he disembarked the flight, letting his mind shift gears. He was in Germany now, a country he was familiar with. The Germans spoke a language that he spoke as well as a native. It was almost like being home again. That is, if you liked living in a place where you had to be constantly on guard. Dozens of organizations had field offices in Berlin, so you never knew who might be in town. And while he had initially thought Vietnam would have been the safest place on the planet for him and Nate – a reality that was shattered by Tucker and Piper – he knew Germany was quite likely the most dangerous.

His guard up, Quinn led his apprentice from the gate through the terminal to the main exit. He'd been to Berlin more times than he could count, and he'd used Tegel Airport on many of those occasions. So when they stepped outside into the cloudy, cold night, he instantly knew to turn left and walk toward the end of the building. There they found a row of waiting beige taxis. Like most German cabs, they were all Mercedes.

'Guten Tag,' the driver said as his new passengers climbed in.

Quinn nodded. *'Guten Tag.'*

The taxi took them across town to the Four Seasons Hotel on Charlottenstrasse, kitty-corner to the Gendarmenmarkt and across a side street from the Dorint Hotel. The Dorint was the hotel in which Duke had arranged for Quinn to stay, but Quinn wasn't expected until Sunday. He'd purposely arrived early so that he could get a feel for what might be going on without any interference or bias from Duke. By the time they'd checked in and been shown to their suite, it was just after 8:00 p.m. on Friday night.

Their accommodations had two bedrooms. Quinn took the one on the left, set his bag on the bed, then headed into the bathroom and took a steaming hot shower.

When he reentered the living room thirty minutes later, he found himself alone.

'Nate?' he called.

There was no answer.

He walked over to the other bedroom. The door was partially open. Looking inside, he found Nate sprawled across the bed, jacket off, but otherwise still fully dressed. His breathing was slow and deep, rhythmic. Quinn closed the door and returned to the living room. It was late enough. Barely. No sense in waking him up.

After ordering dinner from room service, Quinn retrieved his computer and set it up on the desk.

It didn't take long before he was online. As he hoped, there was a message from Orlando, sent several hours earlier:

Flt. confirmed. We're on for dinner.

Good news. I've heard from more than one source you're no longer hot property. Should be safe for you to walk the streets again. But I'd be careful. Everyone might not have gotten the update yet.

Now Borko. Dropped out of sight. No one I've talked to has had contact with his organization for six weeks +. Makes me think he's involved. More, but I'll tell you when I get there.

As for the slide, my friend says it's a mess. Could take days, or more. Looks to be a tissue sample. Says almost zero chance of any exposure.

BTW, things at the Office still shit.

Arriving early p.m. in Berlin. Will see you at nine. I hope

`you got me a room. I'm not sleeping on your floor. O.`

If anyone was going to sleep on the floor, it would be Nate. But there'd be plenty of room for both once Quinn moved over to the Dorint. The Four Seasons suite would be a perfect base for Orlando to set up her gear.

Quinn logged off his e-mail more relieved than he expected by the news about the slide.

As exhausted as he was from the travel, he still had a little while before he would allow himself to go to sleep, so he opened his web browser and brought up a search engine. He typed in 'Robert Taggert' and was rewarded with nearly ten pages of hits. Apparently it was a common name. He found one mention of a Robert Taggert from the eighteenth century. There was also one who served in the Army of the Republic during the American Civil War. Quinn quickly discarded any links to Taggerts who were either dead or too young to be the man who'd been consumed by the fire in Colorado. This narrowed his list considerably.

Quinn's Taggert had probably been in his fifties. This impression was backed up by the photocopy of the driver's license Ann Henderson had given him. To be safe, Quinn decided to give himself a ten-year window, considered for a second, then adjusted it to a range of men between forty-eight and sixty-five years old. The list condensed again, leaving only twenty-five relevant links.

Seven referred to the same Robert Taggert, a business administration professor at Clemson

University. Two more led Quinn to an East Lansing, Michigan, man who was protesting the local development of a shopping mall. Twelve links were to different locations of a chain of auto service establishments in Kentucky owned by a Robert Taggert. And the final four were articles, each of which mentioned a different Robert Taggert.

A knock on the door interrupted Quinn. Room service had arrived with his dinner. As the server set the tray on the table next to his computer, Quinn pulled out five euros from his pocket. He tipped the man, who smiled politely, then left.

Quinn sat back down at the table and took a bite of his steak before returning his attention to his computer. With a little more searching, he was able to find pictures of five of the matches: the professor, the Michigan protester, the auto service king, and two others. None even came close to matching the picture Quinn had. There were no pictures available of the other two, but after reading the articles, he doubted either was the man he was looking for.

It was what he'd expected when he'd begun: no records of *his* Taggert. That left two possibilities. The first was that Taggert had never done anything to get his name on the Internet. Quinn found that highly unlikely. The second, however, that Robert Taggert wasn't the real name of the guy who had died in Colorado, made more sense.

Removing the Taggert name as a variable, Quinn spent the next hour searching for any missing persons who matched Taggert's description and fit the time frame. There were a few, and he made a note of each. He'd give the info to Orlando after she arrived and let her take a crack at it.

After another forty-five minutes of surfing the net, Quinn disconnected the link and put his computer into sleep mode. He got up and stretched. His body, screwed up by all his recent travel, didn't know which end was up. Most of his dinner remained untouched. He was tempted to just crawl into bed and go to sleep, but instead he plopped down on the couch and grabbed his phone.

'Where are you?' Peter asked as soon as he came on the line.

'En route,' Quinn said into his cell phone.

'You're not in Berlin yet?'

'Duke said he didn't need me until Sunday.'

'Really?' Peter said. 'I guess that makes sense.'

'Why?'

'Duke got word to me that there's some sort of meeting going down next week. He has evidence it might have something to do with our . . . situation. He's trying to get a fix on its location. Once he does, you'll go in, bug it, then see if he's right.'

'Do you know who's involved?' Quinn asked.

'Still no word.'

Quinn considered sharing the name Piper had told him, but decided not to. Best to be sure before throwing gas on a fire. 'I heard the contract on me has been canceled.'

'I heard that, too,' Peter said. 'Lucky you.'

'I take it things aren't going well there?'

Silence on the other end.

'Who'd they get?' Quinn asked.

'Pretty much the whole first string. Every ops team has had damage.'

'How many dead?'

'Seven for sure. Three more we can't get ahold of. Another three in the hospital. And a fourth at home nursing a concussion.'

'What about there in the District?' Quinn asked.

'Things have been quiet for days now,' Peter told him. 'But I'm not doing a lot of walking around in the open.'

'How many other operations have you been able to get going?'

'You're kidding, right?' Peter asked. 'The only thing I have even partially going is the thing with you and Duke; otherwise I've got no one available to me. My ability to mount even a simple field operation is gone. They didn't need to get any of us here in D.C. They've already put us out of business. For the short run, anyway.'

'Only staff members,' Quinn said, more to himself than to Peter.

'You were probably thrown into this by mistake,' Peter said. 'It doesn't matter. You're not marked anymore.'

Neither of them spoke for a moment, then Peter said, 'Call me when you get there.'

Quinn spent most of Saturday familiarizing Nate with Berlin. The city had an excellent public transportation network, the jewels of which were the U-bahn and S-bahn train systems. In effect, the U-bahn was the subway, while the S-bahn was an aboveground service. Of course, there were times when the U-bahn traveled aboveground and the S-bahn below. Apparently even the great German planners weren't always perfect.

They rode the trains for hours, getting off on occasion to check out some of Quinn's old hang-outs. They never went inside anywhere Quinn thought he might be recognized, but it was good to see that most of his former 'safe' locations were still intact. He almost passed checking on Der Goldene Krug, but in the end they made the stop, albeit only looking at it from across the street. Quinn was tempted more than he had been at any other location to go in for a drink. But in the end, he led Nate back to the U-bahn station.

Temptation was one thing, but stupidity was something else entirely.

'Please tell me you're kidding,' Nate said.

'I told you to dress warm,' Quinn told him.

'I did.'

They were standing in a darkened alcove that served as an entrance to an old stone office building. It was about half a block away and across the street from Amirit, where Quinn was to meet with Orlando. The air was particularly cold that evening. The forecast had called for temperatures dipping as low as minus five degrees centigrade. Nate was wearing a long London Fog jacket over a bulky sweater. On his head was a dark stocking cap. He held a steaming cup of coffee in one hand, while the other was jammed into a jacket pocket.

'We shouldn't be more than an hour and a half,'

Quinn said. 'If you see anything suspicious, I mean anything, you text me 911 immediately.'

Nate pulled his hand out of his pocket. He was holding a cell phone. 'I just have to hit Send.'

'All right then.' Quinn started to turn away, then looked back. 'Stomp around every once in a while. Quietly. It'll slow down the frostbite.'

When Quinn entered Amirit, he found Orlando already waiting for him at a table across the room against the wall. She had chosen the chair that allowed her a direct view of the front door. Quinn walked over and sat in the empty seat across from her. Almost immediately, the waiter approached. Quinn ordered a *Hefeweizen* while Orlando said she wasn't sure yet. Nearly as quickly, the man was gone.

'Pleasant trip?' Quinn asked.

'As far as I know,' she said. 'I slept the whole way.'

'Where's your stuff?'

Quinn heard a dull thud from under the table. Glancing down, he saw a brown duffel bag between Orlando's feet.

'I'm traveling light,' she said.

'Anybody follow you?'

She stared at him. 'Yeah,' she said. 'He's sitting at the table behind you. Would you like me to introduce you?'

Quinn smiled. 'A simple no would have been fine.'

'Do you really think I'd be here if someone had tailed me?'

'So you did check, then,' he said.

'You can be really annoying sometimes, you know that?' she said. 'Where's Nate?'

‘Keeping watch.’

‘You left him outside?’

Quinn shrugged. ‘It’s good for him.’

The waiter returned with Quinn’s beer before either of them could say anything else.

‘Would you like to order now?’ he asked.

Orlando chose the lamb curry and a glass of cabernet sauvignon. Quinn ordered the chicken Madras and some garlic naan. By unspoken agreement, they engaged in small talk until the food arrived.

Their meals were served in copper-colored bowls, the aroma of curry, lamb, and garlic preceding the delivery by several seconds. Once the food was on the table, Quinn pushed the one containing the chicken Madras toward Orlando.

‘Try it,’ he said.

She took a spoonful and put it over some of the rice on her plate, then took a bite. The look of satisfaction on her face said it all. They ate in silence for several minutes.

‘Anything new I need to know about?’ Orlando finally asked.

‘Not from Duke,’ Quinn said. He took a sip of beer. ‘But I did talk to Peter last night. Apparently Duke’s onto some sort of meeting. Peter wants us to bug it and check it out.’

Quinn broke off a piece of naan and dipped it in his sauce before popping it in his mouth.

‘What do you think?’ Orlando asked. ‘Are these the guys?’

‘I don’t know. It could be nothing.’ Quinn reached for another piece of naan.

'But if it is them?'

Quinn didn't answer.

On Sunday at 1:45 p.m., Quinn left the Four Seasons through the exit on Friedrichstrasse, then took the U-bahn across town to Charlottenburg. There he grabbed a cab and rode it basically back to the point where he'd begun, exiting in front of the Dorint Hotel. It may have been overkill, but there was always the possibility someone could have discovered what Duke was up to and, in turn, learned about Quinn's arrival. If that was the case, he didn't want anyone to realize Orlando and Nate were set up right next door.

As an additional precaution, Orlando was stationed in the square across the street from the Dorint, keeping him briefed via a micro–radio transmitter and receiver she'd brought with her. The receiver fit comfortably in Quinn's ear and was invisible to the casual inspection. The microphone was no bigger than a button and was affixed to the inside of his collar. Nate, similarly wired up, sat in the small hotel lobby, glancing at a magazine and pretending to wait for someone.

Quinn's check-in went quickly and efficiently. His room was prepaid, and all was ready for him. He asked if he had any messages, but there were none. The room was on the sixth floor. Another suite, though considerably smaller than the one at the Four Seasons. Quinn half expected to find an envelope with instructions waiting for him when he entered, but nothing was there.

He put his suitcase on the double bed, then took

a seat on the couch in the living room. He switched on the TV and found that there were only two channels in English, CNN International and BBC World. According to the brochure on the coffee table, there was an additional pay movie channel in English, this month featuring a Stanley Kubrick retrospective including *2001: A Space Odyssey* and *Full Metal Jacket*.

He flipped on the news first and caught the end of a report about a bus driver strike in France, then the beginning of a report about the upcoming Balkan conference sponsored by the European Union president, Gunnar Van Vooren. Uninterested, Quinn switched over to the movie channel and found himself in the middle of the space station scene of *2001*.

'Taxi,' Orlando said in his ear. 'Two men, suits. No luggage, but one is carrying a briefcase.' It was the third time she'd informed him of an arrival in front of the hotel. 'They're going inside.'

'Got 'em,' Nate said a few seconds later. 'They've bypassed the front desk and are heading for the elevators.'

Several minutes later, Quinn heard footsteps in the hall outside. They stopped in front of the entrance to his room. For nearly thirty seconds, nothing happened. Then something was slipped under his door. Immediately Quinn could hear the footsteps receding down the hallway.

'Looks like I've just had a visitor,' Quinn said.

'They're there now?' Orlando asked.

'No. But they left me something.'

He approached the door. On the floor was a manila envelope, not very thick. On the outside, in red, was a large X. Quinn shook his head. Sometimes he wondered if the people he worked with got their training out of Ian Fleming novels.

'They just came back out the elevator,' Nate whispered. 'Could it hurt these guys to maybe smile a bit?'

'They're grabbing a cab,' Orlando said in his ear.

'Did you get pictures?' Quinn asked.

'Of course.'

Quinn picked up the envelope and carried it back to a desk along the wall behind the couch. He used a letter opener from the desk drawer to slice open the top, then carefully slipped out the contents. Five pieces of paper. The top two were maps of Berlin; one focused on the Mitte, where the Dorint was located, and the other on the area known as Neukölln. One of the other pages was a wire-transfer confirmation of payment into one of Quinn's many accounts, something he had already confirmed on his own earlier that morning. Another was a detailed brief of the operation. The final page was a reduced-down copy of blueprints to a building. Presumably it was the location of the upcoming meeting.

Quinn skimmed through the documents until he found what he was looking for. 'Looks like Duke's found out more about that meeting. He thinks it's happening on Tuesday night.'

'Thinks?'

' "Meeting Tuesday night, ninety percent," ' Quinn read. 'In a building in Neukölln.'

'Any ID on the players yet?' Orlando asked.

'Only a partial. RBO out of South Africa. But even that's uncertain.'

'Odd.'

'Yeah. I know.'

'Any mention of Borko?' Orlando asked.

Quinn scanned the brief. 'Nothing.'

'Maybe Piper's information was wrong.'

'Maybe,' Quinn said, voice neutral. He read a little more to himself. 'Duke wants to do a drive-by with me this afternoon.'

'When?'

'In an hour.'

'Can I go back inside now?' she asked. 'I'm freezing my ass off out here.'

'Yeah. When you get to the suite, download the pictures, and e-mail them to me. I'd like to take a look at them before I meet Duke.'

'You don't want to come over to see them? Maybe bring me a king-size cup of coffee?'

Quinn smiled to himself. The cold Berlin winter seemed to be thawing Orlando out. 'Just e-mail them. Nate'll bring you a cup.'

'I hate you,' she said.

'So you've told me before.'

Chapter 18

Duke arrived in front of the Dorint Hotel ten minutes late in a Mercedes C320 sedan.

'Quinn, so good to see you,' Duke said as Quinn climbed in.

'You haven't changed at all,' Quinn said, smiling. That was the truth, too. Duke had not lost a pound since the last time Quinn had worked with him.

Duke just laughed, then put the car into gear and pulled away from the curb. 'Any troubles?' he asked.

'No,' Quinn said.

'Did you have to travel far?'

'How can you live in this kind of weather?' Quinn asked, ignoring the question.

Once again Duke's laughter filled the car.

Tuesday's meeting was apparently going to take place in an old, unused waterworks building in the Neukölln district of Berlin. The building was on a cobbled street only a block long named Schandauer Strasse. The water plant was on the east side, in the middle of the block. Duke parked his Mercedes at the end of the street, then handed Quinn a pair of compact binoculars so he could take a better look at the structure.

'Are there any guards?' Quinn asked before looking through the binoculars.

Duke smiled. 'One in front and one in back,' he said. His accent seemed thicker than it had been two years before, sounding Czech or something similar. They were speaking in English. Quinn suspected it was actually Duke's native tongue. 'The one in front, he is usually sitting in car on street near gate.'

Quinn raised the binoculars to his eyes and took a look. Sure enough, there was a man sitting in a beat-up Volvo near the entrance to the water plant. It looked like he was reading a newspaper.

'No one inside?' Quinn asked.

'Not as far as I have been able to determine,' Duke replied, then shrugged. 'But who knows?'

The property was surrounded by a six-foot-high wrought-iron fence. Duke told him the driveway gate was latched in the middle and swung inward rather than out. The building itself was four stories high, excluding an attic, and was taller than it was wide. The façade was a mix of dark red bricks and concrete. Spaced approximately every three feet were tall, narrow sets of windows that ran vertically up the side of the building. The windows were framed in blue-painted metal.

Duke told him when he got close enough he'd be able to see gouges in the exterior where bullets and shrapnel had struck the building in the last days before Berlin fell at the end of the Second World War.

'Don't let bricks fool you,' Duke said. 'Underneath, concrete reinforced walls. Half a meter thick.'

'What's the layout?' Quinn asked. He'd studied the blueprints, but he was hoping Duke could give him a few more details.

Duke pointed across the street to the southwest corner of the building. 'There,' he said. 'The entrance is just around that side. Inside, the front two thirds is open space that stops just below attic. Four stories high, approximately twenty meters long by twenty meters wide.'

'That's a lot of room.'

'Used to hold machinery, but it's all gone now,' Duke told him. 'In back there is stairway along south side. On each floor are two rooms. A small room, six meters by eight meters. And a large room, ten meters by twenty.'

'Are they all in use?'

'I do not think so. Maybe just ones on first and second floors.' Duke paused. 'Excuse me, I forget you are American. Second and third floors.'

In Europe, the ground floor was the ground floor and the first floor was one flight up. But Quinn had already made the adjustment. 'Is that it?' Quinn asked.

'Attic,' Duke said. 'A large space. Goes over entire building. But my guess is it is empty, not being used. I would not advise going up there. I was inside building one time many years ago. But even then the floor of attic was quite unstable. If you fall through, it is long way down.'

'And the basement?' Quinn asked.

Duke shook his head. 'I never went down there,' he said.

The blueprints had shown only a large open area in the basement. Nothing more. 'When can I get inside?'

'Tonight would be best, if you are ready. The closer we get to time of meet, the more difficult, I think. Yes?'

'Good,' Quinn said. 'That's what I was thinking. How do I get in?'

Duke smiled, then reached into his pocket, a process that took a lot of effort. When he pulled his hand back out, he was holding a shiny silver key.

'For front door,' Duke said. 'Lucky Berlin is my home now. I know everyone.' Duke chuckled. 'Is your team in place?'

'Yes.'

'May I ask who they are?'

'I'll take that key now,' Quinn said.

Duke handed the key to Quinn. 'How will you get around the guards without causing concern?'

'You don't need to worry about that.'

Quinn raised the binoculars to his eyes again and took another look at the building. When he was through, he handed them back to Duke.

'You have seen enough?' Duke asked.

Quinn looked at the building a moment longer, then nodded. 'For now.'

Quinn had Duke drop him off in Charlottenburg on the pretense that he had a few things to pick up before visiting the water plant that evening.

Instead, he made his way to the U-bahn station and caught the U7 east. He got off at Berliner Strasse, checking as he did to see if anyone had decided to join him. No one had.

He switched to the U9, taking it north to Kurfürstendamm, where he got off in the same manner. Still there was no one suspicious. He went up to street level and inserted himself into the crowds on Ku'damm for nearly a half hour. He pretended to window-shop, all the while keeping an eye on his back trail. Finally, when he was confident he was alone, he caught a taxi back to the Mitte. He had the driver drop him off two blocks from the Four Seasons, then made the rest of the way to Orlando's suite on foot.

He let himself in with the key he'd kept. As he entered, Nate jumped up from the couch where he'd apparently been watching the TV. Immediately his apprentice grabbed the remote and turned the volume down. Orlando, on the other hand, was hunched over her computer, her attention firmly on the screen.

'How did it go?' she asked without looking up.

Quinn gave them a quick rundown.

'Still no direct connection to the disruption of the Office, though,' he said.

'Did he have anything else?'

Quinn shook his head. 'Not really. He said while the Office was never mentioned by name, he felt certain it was what all the noise was about. He said he "had a feeling."'

'No mention of Borko?' Nate asked.

'Nothing. I didn't ask either. Borko scares a lot

of people, and I was afraid Duke might suddenly disappear on us. Like it or not, we need him right now.' There was a bottle of water on the coffee table near Nate. Quinn pointed at it. 'You drinking that?'

Nate picked it up and tossed it to him.

'So what do you think?' she asked.

Quinn shrugged. 'It's probably better than an even chance this is a dead end. But we don't have much else to go on.' He opened the bottle and took a sip. 'Learn anything?'

She hit a couple keys on the keyboard. 'Yes. But it's not what I was expecting.'

Quinn waited.

'Word is, the reason Borko was out of touch for the past month and a half was that he was recovering.'

'From what?'

'A bullet in the shoulder and another in his hip. He was doing a job for the Syrians. Apparently it didn't go well.'

'Who shot him?' Quinn asked.

'I don't know. But I do know it took place in Rome. Zeus was on cleanup. He said he barely had time to get Borko out of there before the local cops showed up.'

'You talked to Zeus?'

'Uh-huh. But that's all he'd give me,' she said. 'He claimed he didn't know who Borko was meeting.'

'It was an exchange?' Quinn wandered over to the window and peered outside. Dark clouds were gathering over the city. Snow was forecast for later that evening. 'You sure it wasn't just an ordinary hit?'

'You mean with Borko as the target?'

'Him or his contact.'

'Zeus said it was a straight exchange. He doesn't know why it went bad.'

'And Borko was working for the Syrians?'

'According to Zeus.'

Quinn looked back at Orlando. 'Do you believe him?'

She hesitated, then shook her head.

'What do you think happened?' he asked.

'Nothing.'

'Nothing?'

'I did a little more checking,' Orlando said. 'There are no police reports in Rome even hinting that something like what Zeus described went down that night. If the cops almost caught them, there should have been something.'

'You don't think the operation in Rome ever happened.'

'No,' she said. 'I don't.'

Quinn glanced back out the window. 'Interesting. So Zeus is lying.'

Orlando nodded.

'But why?' Quinn asked.

'To create a smokescreen?' she offered. 'Provide a way for Borko to get out of the spotlight so he could concentrate on the bigger picture?'

'Like taking out the Office,' Quinn said.

Orlando frowned, then shook her head. 'It's weak.'

Quinn sighed in agreement. 'It would be a hell of a lot easier if someone just claimed responsibility.'

'That'd take all the fun out of it, though,' Orlando said.

Quinn took another drink of water, then set the bottle on the side table next to the couch. 'All right. Borko's still a suspect, but we'll remain open to other possibilities.'

'Right,' Orlando said.

'But if it is Borko, there's something else that's missing.'

'You mean motive?' Nate asked.

'No,' Quinn said. 'The only motive he needs is money. It's more a question of who's paying the bills. Borko's strictly a hired gun.'

Orlando hesitated. 'I might know the answer to that.'

'Tell me,' Quinn said.

'I've found a couple references of Borko being involved with Dahl.'

'Dahl?' Quinn said. 'That name sounds familiar.'

'Yeah,' she said. 'That's what I was thinking, so I did a little digging. Apparently he's been around since the late eighties. A fringe player. Haven't been able to talk to anyone who's worked with him, but I'm still checking. I get the impression he's now fronting a lot of Borko's work.'

'Another winner.' Quinn closed his eyes in thought. 'What a mess.'

'I could be wrong.'

Quinn let out a humorless laugh. 'Okay. We concentrate on Duke's lead first. Maybe it's Borko. Maybe it's somebody else. Maybe it's this Dahl guy. Hopefully, no matter what, it'll clear things up. If not, and Borko's not involved in this meeting, we'll go after him directly.'

Orlando nodded.

'Nate. You're with me tonight,' Quinn said.

'Okay,' Nate said.

Quinn looked at Orlando. 'You'll keep tabs on us by radio from here. I can let you know if I find anything useful.'

'Lucky me,' she said.

Chapter 19

It was a quarter after ten. Schandauer Strasse was quiet and dark. The only illumination came from a few security lamps attached to apartment buildings farther down the block. There were no streetlights.

Cars lined either side of the road, leaving no place to park, but Quinn and Nate didn't need one. A taxi had dropped them off several blocks away, near the city administrative building on Karl Marx Strasse. They were dressed warmly, in dark clothes. On Quinn's back was a black backpack. Heavy, but manageable.

'You want me to go over it again?' Quinn asked as they walked down the cobblestone sidewalk toward Schandauer Strasse.

Nate shook his head. 'I keep out of sight, watch the street, let you know if there's anything unusual. Right?'

'Not just unusual,' Quinn said. 'Anything. Got it?'

'I got it.'

A couple of hours earlier it had begun to snow. Lightly at first, but it had increased steadily until it was falling at a rate of nearly an inch an hour.

Quinn guessed by morning there probably would be over a foot on the ground.

At the corner of Schandauer Strasse, they paused to study the water plant. Like most of the rest of the buildings on the street, it was dark.

'There,' Quinn said, speaking in a low voice. 'The Ford parked near the gate.'

The Volvo that had been there that afternoon was gone. In its place was a Ford sedan. Quinn could just make out the shape of a person sitting in the driver's seat.

'I see him,' Nate said.

'Are you in yet?' Orlando's voice sounded in Quinn's ear.

'We're at the end of the street,' Quinn said.

'Tell me what you see,' Orlando said.

Quinn scanned the street. 'Schandauer Strasse. It's cobbled. Just wide enough for cars to park on both sides of the street and still have two-way traffic. Quiet. The water plant is half a block away. To the right, there's a three-story building. Looks like it's used for offices. To the left a smaller building. Brick. There's a Ford sedan with a guard in it parked where the other car had been this afternoon.'

'What about the water plant?'

'Just like I described it to you this afternoon. Only dark now.'

'Anything else?'

'Other than it's cold and wet and snowing and I should still be on Maui?'

'Yeah.'

'Nothing,' Quinn said.

* * *

Quinn and Nate made their way carefully along the row of parked cars until they came to the back of the Ford. They waited a moment to be sure they hadn't been noticed, then Quinn reached up and attached a small ball of a putty-like substance to the bottom corner of the rear passenger-side window. When activated by heat, it would work its way around the rubber weather strip lining the window and enter the interior of the car as an odorless gas. Within moments, whoever was inside would be knocked out for up to two hours.

Quinn waited a moment to be sure the putty was staying in place, then retrieved a small plastic packet from his coat. He carefully opened it and removed a thin, mesh fabric pad. He placed this directly over the compound on the window, careful to cover the putty completely, then took several steps back.

They watched as the ball began to reduce in size, the pad not only heating it but also directing the gas to go into the car instead of out onto the street. When it was done, Quinn looked at his watch and waited a full three minutes before nodding to Nate.

'He's out,' Nate said, after he'd peeked into the front of the car. 'That stuff's cool.'

'Are you ready?' Quinn asked, all business.

Nate nodded.

Quinn put a hand on Nate's back. 'Remember –'

'To tell you everything,' Nate finished.

'Good man.' Quinn made a final scan of the street. All was quiet. 'Okay, into position.'

Nate nodded, then moved across the street to a spot they had determined prior to arriving. Quinn checked the guard one last time. The man's head was tilted back against the seat, his mouth half open. Quinn glanced down at the sentry's chest to make sure the man was breathing. He was.

After giving Nate a quick wave, Quinn moved over to the fence. He quickly scanned the street and the water plant for signs of another sentry. There was no one.

After taking a deep breath, Quinn pulled himself over the fence and dropped down on the other side. He found himself on a short driveway that ran in front of the building and around to the south end, where the door was.

In the left-hand pocket of his jacket was the key Duke had given him and a small but powerful flash-light. Quinn removed the key but left the flashlight. For the moment there was enough residual light to see what he was doing. As he neared the door the silence that had enveloped the street was replaced by a muffled, low-level hum. It took him a second before he realized it was coming from inside the building.

He slipped the key into the lock and turned it. The lock was a little sticky, but it appeared to be old, so that wasn't surprising. After he heard the latch click, he slowly pulled the door open. There was no light coming from inside. He took a deep breath, then stepped into the building and closed the door behind him.

He was instantly enveloped by total darkness. He remained motionless for several moments, listening. Other than the loud hum, there was no other noise. He shoved the key back in his pocket, pulled out the flashlight, and turned it on. A quick sweep of the beam revealed he was alone.

'Nate, how's the street?' Quinn asked.

'Freezing,' Nate said, then added, 'all quiet.'

'You should be used to the cold by now,' Orlando said.

'I seem to remember you not being too happy when you had to stand in front of the Dorint,' Nate said.

'I was just faking it,' she said. 'Thought it might make you feel better.'

'Enough,' Quinn said. 'In case anyone's interested, I'm in.'

He aimed the light at the front of the building and began to make a more thorough investigation of his new surroundings. It didn't take long to discover why it was so dark inside. Wooden baffles had been erected over the inside of the windows and were secured firmly to the walls. As an added precaution, thick cloth strips had been affixed to where each baffle met the wall, guaranteeing no light from outside could seep in.

To the side of the door was a steel reinforced panel. The panel was mounted on tracks and could easily slide in front of the entrance, effectively sealing off the room.

He uttered aloud, 'What the hell do they need that for?'

'What're you talking about?' Orlando asked.

He described the baffled windows and the security door to her. 'Everything looks recently installed.'

He noticed there was a distinct odor in the room, too. Not offensive. In fact, quite the opposite. Clean, almost antiseptic. But not like a hospital. The antiseptic smell of a hospital was tinged with medicine and death. This smell was the clean of a room thoroughly disinfected, scrubbed from top to bottom and then wiped down with an abundance of ammonia.

'What do you think it means?' she asked after Quinn described the odor to her.

'I don't know.'

'Tell me about the rest of the room.'

He pointed the flashlight toward the ceiling. 'The room's big all right. Just like Duke said. Cavernous. Maybe seventy feet to the ceiling.'

'What's that noise?' Orlando asked.

Slowly, so he wouldn't miss anything important, he swung the flashlight around to his right.

'What the hell?' he said.

'What did you find?'

'I'm not sure,' he told her. 'Give me a few minutes.'

At first Quinn wasn't sure what he was looking at. The object took up over half the length of the room, side to side, and almost reached the ceiling. It was a giant sphere, not unlike a hot-air balloon, except it seemed to be sitting on a black pedestal. From where Quinn stood near the front door, it looked like the sphere was made of a thick white fabric. Maybe canvas. The black pedestal, a wide ring around the bottom of the sphere, looked to be about seven feet high. Unlike the sphere, it appeared to be made of something solid – metal, wood, or hard plastic. He wouldn't know for sure until he took a closer look. The whole thing made Quinn think of a giant golf ball sitting on a black tee.

He moved the flashlight across the object. A quarter of the way around to the left was a solid-looking scaffolding tower. Up one side of the tower ran a metal staircase. Quinn followed it with his light. It ended at a platform that was then connected to the sphere by a fifteen-foot-long canvas tunnel.

Interesting, Quinn thought.

As he played the flashlight over the tower again, he noticed something else. There was an elevator running up through the center of the structure.

Quinn's next thought was that the whole thing was some sort of makeshift containment unit, perhaps for the transfer of hazardous materials. *Or,* unable to keep the image of the glass slide out of his mind, *something biological.*

He took a few steps into the room. Whatever was making the noise was coming from deeper in the room, toward the back. He moved farther into the room to get a better angle, then shone his light past the sphere in the direction of the noise.

It looked like an air pump. That made sense. Something had to keep the sphere from collapsing in on itself. He relaxed for a moment, relieved. The pump would be pushing air into the sphere, inflating it. The pressure needed to keep the sphere from collapsing had to be greater than the pressure outside, which would be an unsuitable arrangement when working with dangerous materials. To be effective that way, the pressure in the sphere would have to be less than the surrounding room, preventing the unintentional release of anything nasty, and the structure itself would have to have something other than the air supporting it.

Without going inside, there was no telling its purpose. Perhaps it had nothing to do with the meeting. Then again, perhaps it did. Quinn would have to bug it, just in case.

'Well?' Orlando said.

'I'm still not sure,' Quinn told her.

'You've got to give me more than that.'

'Why don't I just show you?' he said.

He pulled the backpack off his shoulders and set it on the ground. From inside he took out two objects. One was tiny and black, and the other was a rectangular box about the size of a candy bar. He put them both on the ground, then set the flashlight on top of the backpack, pointing it in front of him so he could use it as a work light. That done, he picked up the smaller object, turned it over and found a small number etched into the object's base. 'Camera 17,' he told Orlando.

'You'll need to power up the signal booster,' she told him.

'Hold on.' He picked up the rectangular box, the booster, and flipped a tiny switch on its side. He felt a slight vibration as the booster came to life.

Five seconds later, Orlando said, 'I've got signal.'

Quinn set the booster on the ground next to his backpack. 'How much light do you need?'

'Is there any seeping into the room?'

'Not that I can tell.'

'Point your flashlight in the general direction of what you want to show me. That should be enough.'

The camera's night vision was top of the line.

Orlando would have settled for nothing less. Quinn turned his backpack so that the flashlight was pointing toward the sphere. He then stood up and began a sweep of the room with the camera.

'What the hell is that?' Orlando asked.

He was aiming the lens at the sphere. 'I don't know. There's a staircase and an elevator over here.' He pointed the camera toward the scaffolding. 'At the top it looks like that tunnel thing is some sort of entrance.'

'Duke didn't tell you about this?'

'He said he hadn't been in the building for several years. Probably doesn't even know it's here.'

'I'm not sure I like this,' Orlando said. 'Maybe we should call it off. See if we can find a little more information first.'

Quinn paused a moment before answering. 'No,' he said. 'I'm here. We'll do this now.'

He panned the camera over the sphere, giving Orlando a longer look.

'How many cameras did you give me?' Quinn asked.

'Twenty,' she said.

Five more than he'd asked for. 'Okay. I think I can cover most of this room with just seven.' Quinn had worked it out in his mind ahead of time, but now he was going to have to make an adjustment. 'I haven't had a look at the rest of the place yet, but based on the blueprints, let's say another eight for the back offices. That leaves five. One for outside the front door of the building. One for around back to cover the door there. One for directly across the street, and two for either end of the block. Shit, that's all of them.' He thought for a moment. 'Okay, maybe only seven for the rest of the building. That'll give me one I can put inside the sphere.'

'You're not going inside there,' Orlando said, surprised.

'If I get the feeling something's wrong, I'll just turn around and back out, okay?'

'That sounds like a great plan,' she replied, not hiding her displeasure.

'Glad you like it.'

It took him an hour to place the cameras throughout the building. Each was paired with a microphone that was really no more than a tiny disk attached to a piece of adhesive. As long as it was placed within ten feet of the camera, audio could also be picked up.

Seven cameras were still one shy for covering the two rooms per floor on the four floors in the back of the building, but there wasn't much he could do about that. He hid the booster in the attic, jamming it between the rafters where it would be hard to find. Duke had been right. The floor of the attic was definitely weak. More than once Quinn was worried that he might crash through.

When he was done, he headed back downstairs. There were six cameras left in his bag when he returned to the front room, five for outside the building and one for inside the sphere. Quinn walked over to the metal staircase that led up to the platform.

As he mounted it Orlando asked, 'Do you think you can make a little more noise?' She was undoubtedly watching him from one of the cameras he'd placed around the large room earlier. The stairs, though sturdy, were loose in their fittings. No matter how quietly Quinn tried to move, they clanked with every step.

He came to the short platform at the top of the stairs. Ahead of him was the entrance to what he'd started to think of as the air lock. Now that he was close to it, he could see that the material surrounding the sphere and the tube wasn't made from simple canvas. It was thicker and had an almost rubbery look to it.

The entrance to the tube was through a hard plastic doorway mounted in an equally sturdy frame. There didn't appear to be any lock. Quinn turned the knob and opened the door. 'I'm going into the tunnel,' he told Orlando.

Flashlight in hand, he stepped into the tube and shut the door behind him.

The inside was lined with a dark opaque material. As a test, he switched off his flashlight. He held his hand up in front of his face, but couldn't see it.

He switched the flashlight back on and proceeded forward along a narrow metal platform. Glancing at the ceiling of the tube, he realized there was something there he hadn't noticed before. Something colored the same matte black as that of the material that lined the tube. Not only was it on the ceiling, but it also covered the walls. Quinn took a step closer for a better look.

Thin rods, he realized. Made of some sort of sturdy yet flexible material that could bend with the shape of the structure. They formed a series of triangles that covered the whole inside of the tube. A geodesic skeleton of some sort?

Quinn continued moving forward. At the far end was another door similar to the one he had just passed through. As he approached it, a green light set into the door frame at eye level came on. The light was about the size of a half-dollar. He guessed it must have been triggered by a motion sensor.

'I'm going into the sphere itself now,' Quinn said. He reached for the handle and opened the door. There was a rush of air as he carefully stepped over the threshold. Once inside, he pushed the door closed behind him.

Almost immediately, his ears popped. It only took a moment for the meaning to register on him. His ears had *popped*. Not only that, but the rush of air when he entered, hadn't it been moving in *with* him? He turned back to the door and opened it again. There was another rush of air, not as strong as before, but definitely moving *into* the sphere from the tube.

Quinn closed the door again, then played the light along the inside surface of the sphere. It was identical to that of the tube: black opaque material, and the same metal skeletal structure. It all added up to one thing. The air pressure in the sphere *was* lower than that outside.

'Jesus Christ,' he muttered.

'What's wrong?'

He told Orlando what he'd found.

'Okay, don't panic,' she said.

'I'm not panicking.' He took a deep breath.

His original instinct had been correct. The place was a classic bio-secure zone. Quinn turned around, putting his back to the door and shining his light toward the center of the space. The platform he was standing on extended out another ten feet. At the other end of the platform was a door to a structure that looked like a large square box. It was what he had expected to find. A stand-alone containment room. Undoubtedly the pressure inside it was even lower than that in the sphere. It would be the place in which the real work was done.

Peeking over the edge of the platform, Quinn could see the whole thing was sitting on an elaborate metal scaffolding tower that plunged downward into the bowels of the sphere. He allowed himself to relax a little. If there were deadly bio-agents inside the containment room, he should still be safe where he was.

They had been looking for a link to the disruption, but what they'd found was a link to the deaths in Colorado. The bracelet. The slide and now this? It was too much to ignore. And though he didn't have the proof yet, Quinn was sure it all tied into the disruption.

'Take some pictures of the setup here. I want to send them to Peter when I get back, okay?'

Orlando didn't answer. Quinn tapped the receiver in his ear. 'Orlando, did you hear me?'

Still nothing. 'Nate, are you there?'

The only thing Quinn heard was his own breathing. There was a prickling sensation at the back of his neck. 'Orlando?'

Silence.

'Orlando?'

No response.

Then he heard something. Not over his receiver, but from somewhere beyond the walls of the sphere. It was the clank of metal on metal.

Someone was coming up the scaffolding stairs.

Chapter 20

Quinn looked left, then right. But he already knew what he'd find. The only way out was the way he'd come in. *It's a goddamn trap,* he thought. *And I'm right where they want me.*

'Son of a bitch,' he said under his breath.

Outside, the sound of steps moving up the stairs continued. Soon they'd reach the platform and the tunnel that led into the sphere. Had Quinn been anywhere else in the building, he would have had multiple opportunities for escape. But standing where he was, his options were severely limited.

He stopped himself. There was one possibility. There had been a door in the housing at the bottom of the sphere. He wasn't sure if he could get there from where he was, but trying was better than just standing there and waiting for them to arrive.

Quinn hurried across the platform toward the door to the containment room, stopping and kneeling down just before he reached it. He looked over the edge of the narrow walkway into the space below.

The crisscrossing scaffolding structure he'd

glanced at moments earlier led down into the darkness at the bottom of the sphere. It would be easy to climb down. He quickly pointed his flashlight at the very bottom, and though it was hard to tell for sure, there appeared to be some kind of hatch on the floor. His best guess was that it led down into the circular base structure where the other door was located.

Potential escape was there, but he'd never make it in time. He'd be spotted by whoever was coming up the stairs before he was even halfway down.

He looked under the platform again.

Okay. Escape might be impossible, he thought. *But what if –*

The clanging of the metal steps ceased.

There was no more time to think. Quinn stowed his flashlight and quickly lowered himself over the edge of the platform. Moving as silently as he could, he maneuvered his body underneath it.

He paused for a fraction of a second to get his bearings, then worked his way across the scaffolding, using it like a kid's jungle gym. When he was directly under the center of the bio-containment room, he stopped.

He could feel the sweat beading on his brow, and his breaths were coming in short, silent bursts. But he knew just hanging from the center of the room wasn't enough.

He pulled his feet up and secured them on top of one of the crossbars, tucking himself horizontally against the bottom of the room. He wasn't invisible, but it was the closest he could get to it.

He heard the door to the sphere open. There was a rush of air, followed by the sound of two people stepping through the opening and onto the platform. A pause, followed by a low voice, then a flicker of brightness. The new arrivals were scanning the space with a flashlight. Quinn could see the reflection of the beam as it occasionally slipped below the level of the platform and glinted off the scaffolding.

After several moments, the footsteps continued across the platform, to the door of the lab. There was a sucking sound as the door was opened and air moved from one space to another. A moment later the door shut.

Quinn's left calf had begun to cramp. He chanced moving his leg to relieve the pressure and had just found a more comfortable position when the door to the lab opened again. Then: 'One, this is Matz. The sphere is empty.'

The voice spoke German, clear and distinct. Matz was apparently talking into a radio. It was also obvious by the unhampered sound of his voice that he was not wearing any protective gear over his face. To Quinn it meant the lab wasn't hot yet. He would have felt a sense of relief if he hadn't been hanging dozens of feet above the ground wondering how long it would be before a bullet pierced his skull.

The radio crackled with static, then a voice, also in German but not with a native accent, said, 'You checked everywhere?'

'Yes,' Matz replied. 'There is no one here but us.'

'Underneath?' the voice asked.

Another pause. Then Matz said, 'We're checking now.'

Quinn tensed. There was nothing he could do except remain perfectly still. He couldn't even grab his gun without upsetting his balance.

Suddenly, the flashlight beam swung over the edge of the platform. There was a thump, and Quinn guessed that one of the men was kneeling down so he could get a better look below. The beam of light flashed across the scaffolding close to Quinn as it traveled down toward the bottom of the sphere. Once there, it moved slowly across the floor, taking in every inch.

'I don't see anything,' a voice said. Not Matz this time, but his partner.

'Are you sure?' Matz asked.

'You want to look?'

'One, this is Matz. There's no one below.'

'He has to be in the building somewhere,' the voice on the radio said, his irritation coming through clearly. 'He hasn't come outside yet.'

'Maybe his partner warned him,' Matz offered.

'Not a chance. Get out of there and go out back in case the others are able to flush him out.'

'Understood.'

Quinn listened as the two men walked across the platform above him and exited the sphere.

Quinn remained hanging under the platform, as still as possible, for what he guessed to be about thirty minutes. Eyes closed, his breathing even, he silently recited the lyrics to the songs on *Changes One,* David Bowie's first greatest-hits album.

Halfway through 'John, I'm Only Dancing,' his leg cramped again. He flexed his foot back and forth, easing the pressure on his calf. But neither Bowie nor the pain in his leg could clear his mind.

The operation had really gone to shit.

It's the disruption all over again, he thought. Only this time, it was obvious who had set them up.

Duke.

'Fuck conspiracy theories,' Durrie had said. 'The obvious is right ninety-nine percent of the time.'

From the moment Duke had sent Quinn the e-mail, it had been a setup. The only reason he hadn't been taken out the minute Duke had him in his car was that they wanted to get Quinn's entire team.

Quinn's eyes narrowed. Did that mean Peter was involved in the deception, too? After all, he was the one who had pushed Quinn to come to Berlin. Taking it a step further, could that then mean Peter was involved in the disruption of his own organization?

A chill passed through Quinn, but he couldn't bring himself to fully believe it. Whatever the truth was, he wasn't going to figure it out hanging here. He'd waited long enough. It was time to move.

The interior of the sphere was in complete darkness, but he couldn't chance using his flashlight. He eased himself down the scaffolding by touch, careful to transfer his weight from one point to the next slowly, cutting down on any unnecessary noise. Finally, his feet touched bottom.

No longer able to minimize the risk, he pulled out his flashlight. Before turning it on, he put his hand over the lens to better control the beam. Once he flipped the switch, his palm glowed a reddish yellow.

He played the light across the floor. Black hard plastic, molded to fit the bottom of the sphere. He was standing on top of the pedestal he'd seen from the outside. That put him approximately seven feet above actual ground level.

Off to his right was something that looked like a submarine hatch. It was set into the floor and hinged to lift upward. The only thing missing was a handle to open it. Instead, there were two buttons set into the center of the door. One red, one green.

Quinn pushed the green button. For half a second, nothing happened. Then the seal on the door released and Quinn was able to pull it open. Again, air rushed past him into the sphere.

He leaned over the opening and shone his light inside. The space was tiny, just enough for one person to stand comfortably. Mounted to one wall was a ladder. On the wall opposite was a door, and set into the frame next to the door was a colored light, shining red.

Quinn lowered himself through the opening and onto the ladder, then climbed down. He tried the lower door, but as he expected, it didn't open. He reached up and pulled the hatch closed. There were buttons on the inside that matched those on the outside. He pushed the red button and heard the hatch reseal. As he turned around, the red light beside the lower door turned green. If he was right, this time the door would open.

He was right.

* * *

Quinn stepped through the door and found himself in a circular room. Only two objects broke up the curved walls: the air-lock shaft he'd just exited, and a door about a quarter of the way around to his left. It had to be the same door he'd seen from the outside.

As he walked toward it he stumbled over something on the floor. He brought his flashlight around to see what had caused his misstep.

It was a concrete lip about four inches high. It surrounded a large rectangular pit in the floor. As he shone his light into the hole, he realized it was a stairway leading downward into blackness.

The basement. They had constructed the sphere over its entrance.

Screw the pedestal door, he thought. Here was a potentially better way out. There had to be some sort of exit down there. If he used the door in the pedestal, he'd be stepping into the main room of the water plant. Who knew who'd be standing there waiting for him?

He was about to start down the steps when he heard a now familiar clank. Someone was coming up the outside staircase again. Apparently they hadn't been satisfied with their previous check.

Quinn scrambled quickly downward. There was a door at the bottom made of metal, but it was old, and locked.

Quinn removed the set of lock picks from his backpack. He found what he needed and made quick work of the door. Above him he could hear men climbing below the platform, heading for the air lock to the circular room.

Quinn turned off his flashlight. He didn't know what was on the other side of this door, and he didn't need his light making him an easy target. He eased the door open, then slipped into the basement.

Quinn paused, listening carefully to make sure he was alone. Once he was convinced, he relocked the door from the inside. He returned the picks to his backpack, then turned on the flashlight again.

He was in a large space, half the length of the building above, stretching from the midpoint of the water plant to the front end. There were several metal cabinets lining the far wall. Four sturdy white plastic tables sat in the middle of the room. Under each table were large bins, also plastic. There was another hum coming from somewhere nearby. Not like the hum of the air pumps upstairs. This was deeper in tone and not as loud.

Quinn's instincts told him to check the bins and cabinets and find out what was inside. It might be information that could prove valuable. But he stopped himself. At the moment, staying alive and free was more important.

He continued his scan. At first, there didn't appear to be any other exit. It took him a second pass before he picked out a door set in the wall to his left. The door was painted the same beige color as the rest of the room, and had a latch that lay flush with the surface, making it nearly invisible. He walked over to it. There was no locking mechanism, so he pulled it open and stepped through.

Another dark room, this one noticeably colder

than the one he'd just come from. He closed the door behind him and looked around. In the far corner was the faintest trace of light.

Quinn smiled. It was a window.

As he began walking toward it, he moved the flashlight from left to right. Long worktables were scattered around. To his right was what appeared to be a large refrigerating unit. It was the source of the new humming sound. He stopped and took a longer look at it.

The refrigeration unit was of the walk-in variety. It would have looked more appropriate sitting in the basement of a butcher shop than a decommissioned water facility.

Quinn knew he had to get out of the building, but he couldn't help wanting to take a look inside. This time his desire to investigate overrode his desire to flee.

He grabbed the handle on the unit's door and gave it a pull. At first it wouldn't open. Then he saw a steel pin was preventing the latch from releasing. He removed the pin, and the door opened easily.

Freezing air flowed over him. The unit hadn't been set to just cold but *damn* cold. Freezer cold.

Quinn stood in the doorway and moved the beam of his flashlight around the inside of the refrigerator. He estimated that it was about eight feet deep by five feet across. Against the walls on either side were heavy-duty storage racks. Each had four wide metal shelves. All empty. Even so, it made for a cramped space.

He was beginning to close it back up when he

heard a noise coming from the other part of the basement. He glanced at the door between the rooms, almost expecting it to burst open and let in a flood of armed men. But it remained shut.

He closed the refrigerator door and replaced the pin so nothing would look suspicious. From where he stood he could see the window in the far corner of the room. It was high up on the wall, just above the outside ground level.

The freedom of the German night beckoned him. He turned and looked back at the door that separated him from the people in the other room. He couldn't chance it.

Dammit! he thought. *This is really starting to piss me off.*

Quinn jammed himself into the space between the ceiling and the top of the refrigerator, as far back against the wall as he could. In his right hand he held the SIG Sauer Orlando had picked up for him. Attached to the end of the barrel was a suppressor. The last thing he wanted to do was use the weapon, but if they found him, he wasn't going to go easily.

Half a minute later, the door to the outer room opened. It was followed immediately by the sound of several people entering. Flashlight beams darted from wall to wall, covering every inch of the space. All, that is, except the place Quinn hid.

Quinn counted footsteps. Four men. The sounds of movements stopped after a few moments.

'See?' It was Matz, the one who'd first come into the sphere looking for Quinn. 'I told you. He didn't come down here.'

'Then where is he?' a second man asked. It was the voice from the radio, in person now. Matz had referred to him as 'One.' But now that Quinn heard the voice without static, it sounded very familiar.

'Perhaps he got by the guards upstairs?' Matz suggested. 'Made it outside without anyone seeing?'

'You think that's possible?' One asked.

'I don't know. But he's obviously not down here. The basement door was still locked. If he didn't get away, then he must still be upstairs somewhere. You did say he was good.'

'I asked for professionals and Duke gives me morons.'

Quinn's lips pressed hard against each other. Duke, again.

Silence. 'What about in there?' One asked.

'The cold storage?'

'Yes.'

Their footsteps approached the refrigeration unit and stopped near the door. 'There's a safety pin that acts as a lock. It's still in place. If he was inside, he couldn't have put it back in.'

One finally said, 'Let's go.'

Quinn listened as the men left the room. He heard the door close, but he didn't move. Something wasn't right.

Finally after several minutes, he heard the shuffling of feet. Then a door opened, and the man who had been waiting behind departed.

Quinn remained still for a moment longer, his mind racing.

It was the lingerer. The voice from the radio. The

person Matz had called One. The man Piper had warned him about.

A man he'd last seen in Toronto.

Borko.

Chapter 21

It was nearly one in the morning by the time Quinn finally made his way out of the building. Borko had left guards, but as the Serbian himself had admitted, Duke's men were morons. Quinn had little difficulty sneaking through their surveillance.

Quinn caught the last train heading north out of the Rathaus Neukölln station, the U7. There were only a handful of other passengers aboard. For a while he just rode, his mind racing. He knew he had to get to the emergency rendezvous point, but he was having a hard time processing everything that had just gone down.

Borko had gotten the better of him, no denying that. Quinn had been lulled into believing he was in control. But it was Borko who had been in control all along. And even though Quinn had actually gotten away, Borko was still in control.

The Serbian wasn't an idiot. If they'd been able to grab Orlando and Nate, they wouldn't have killed them yet. Borko would know as long as the two of them were still breathing, they would be insurance in case he had any problems with Quinn.

Quinn got off at the Bismarck Strasse. Back at street level, he hailed a cab and took it to Ku'damm. While he sat in the back, he removed a small square of purple paper from his backpack. It was a sticker, one of a dozen he was carrying. Orlando and Nate had matching sets, only Orlando's stickers were gray and Nate's were black. Dark colors were chosen because they would draw less attention and could easily go unnoticed.

Quinn had the cab driver drop him off two blocks from the ruins of the Kaiser Wilhelm *Gedächtniskirche,* the Kaiser Wilhelm Memorial Church. During the day, it was the most popular tourist site in the city. As one of the few remaining bombed-out structures from World War II left standing, it served as a memory of what had happened and could never be allowed to happen again. But at the late hour Quinn arrived, it was all but deserted.

An indoor shopping mall sat just to the southeast of the monument. There was an outside stairway leading down from the street to the lower level of the mall. When he was sure he was not being watched, Quinn descended the steps.

If possible, the air seemed even colder the lower he went. It was worse than Colorado, he realized. More like nights in the dead of winter from his childhood near the Canadian border.

Halfway down on the right side, he attached his purple square to the edge of the handrail. He had been hoping to find squares from Orlando and Nate, but his was the first. He tried not to think about what that might mean. In the morning he'd return to check again. Surely their markers would be there then.

In the meantime, he needed a place to sleep. Returning to the Dorint or the Four Seasons was out of the question. For that matter, it was probably a good idea for the moment to avoid all hotels.

That really left him only one choice.

Reluctantly, he went back up the stairs and hailed another cab.

'Pilsner, bitte,' Quinn said, as he took an empty stool at the end of the bar inside Der Goldene Krug.

The bartender was a short, thin man with a full mustache and a three-day growth of beard. He filled a glass from the tap and put it in front of Quinn. *'Zwei euro.'*

Quinn started to pull some coins out of his pocket when a voice stopped him.

'*Nein,* Max.'

The bartender looked over his shoulder at a woman who had just emerged from a back room. 'It's on the house, okay?' she continued in German.

Max shrugged, then moved away to help someone else.

The woman, a brunette with an hourglass figure who looked much younger than she probably was, walked along the bar until she was standing just behind Quinn. She tapped the shoulder of the man who was sitting on the stool next to him, and motioned him to move elsewhere. The customer was about to protest until he realized who wanted his seat. Without a word, he picked up his beer and moved to a table in the corner of the room.

The woman took the abandoned stool. 'Max. The usual.' The bartender nodded. The woman turned to Quinn. 'Hello, Jonathan.'

'How are you, Sophie?'

'Still in the same place I was the last time I saw you,' she said. 'Nothing has changed. I have my regulars. They pay my bills.'

Max approached them from the other side of the bar and placed a Pink Squirrel in front of Sophie. She nodded thanks as he moved away. She took a sip, then set the glass back down on the bar. 'Business?' she asked.

'I'm sorry?'

'Business? Is that why you're here?'

'In Berlin?'

'In my bar.'

'Yes,' he said. 'To both.'

'Good. Because if you said you were here to just see me, I'd tell you to get the hell out.' Her tone was casual, almost light.

Quinn smiled slightly.

'It's been, what? Two years?' she asked.

'Something like that.'

'What are you doing here?'

He watched her as she took another drink. 'I need a place to stay.'

'Tonight?' she asked.

'Yes. Tonight.' He paused, then added, 'Maybe tomorrow, too.'

'What do you think my husband will say?'

'You're not married.'

'The hell I'm not.'

'The hell you are.'

She seemed about to say something more, then started to laugh. 'You're still an asshole, you know that?'

'Yeah,' Quinn said. 'So I've heard.'

It wasn't until after 3 a.m. when Sophie and Max were able to chase the last of the customers out. Quinn nursed his beer in the corner of the room as they cleaned up. Finally Max left for home, and Sophie led Quinn upstairs. Her apartment was a two-bedroom flat above the bar. There were two ways to get upstairs. The first was a separate entrance out front off the street, and the second was up a staircase located next to the storage room at the back of the bar.

Pausing at the upper landing, Sophie dug her keys out of her pants pocket. She unlocked the door to the apartment and led Quinn inside. As she closed the door, her hand brushed against his arm, then she leaned forward, her lips suddenly on his.

His first reaction was to pull away. This wasn't what he wanted. He just needed someplace to sleep. Someplace no one would find him.

Besides, the relationship they'd had, a relationship that had lasted only a few months two years earlier, had been just another one of Quinn's failed attempts to connect with somebody. He had only come to her because there was no one else he could turn to.

But instead of pulling away, he felt his lips loosening, becoming soft. Before he knew it, his hands were on her back, pulling her to him, caressing her, undoing the buttons on her blouse. His need for her – no, not for her, for human contact – suddenly consuming him, controlling him.

He pulled the garment off her shoulders, following its downward motion with his mouth until his lips found her left breast. He remembered her nipples, short and erect, were the most sensitive areas on her body. He ran his tongue slowly around them but not touching them, teasing her. Even as he was doing this, her hands were undressing him.

Soon there was a pile of clothes on the floor. Quinn moved Sophie to the couch, where he continued to explore her body, inch by inch. His mouth, his tongue, searching, kissing, caressing. All the while the scent of her, a mix of beer and sweat and lavender perfume, filling him with memories of their past.

'Now,' she said in his ear, her voice a low whisper. 'Fuck me now.'

They enjoyed a second, slower round in the bedroom. Later, after they were finished, Sophie got up to get a glass of water. When she returned, she had a grin on her face. 'You've been practicing,' she said.

'Occasionally,' he said, trying to keep the regret out of his voice.

'Here.' She handed him the glass. 'And don't worry.'

'About what?'

'You look like someone who's afraid the woman you've just slept with is going to say she loves you.' She snorted. 'Don't worry. I don't. Nothing has changed, okay? Just two old friends who haven't seen each other in a while.'

'So that was your way of saying hello?' Quinn asked.

'If you stay here tomorrow,' she continued, 'you'll have to do this again. Consider it rent.'

He smiled weakly, but said nothing. He took a drink of water, then handed the glass back to her. Sophie promptly finished it off and set the empty glass on the nightstand. After she climbed into bed, Quinn pulled the comforter over them.

'It's good to see you,' she said.

'It's good to see you, too,' he replied. Not quite a lie, not quite the truth.

She turned on her side, her back to him, so she could spoon into his chest. He draped an arm over her, his hand resting lightly on her stomach. He remembered this was the way she liked to sleep. As proof, only a few moments later, she was out. But Quinn wasn't so lucky.

Even when he did finally nod off, he was never far from the surface. And what dreams he had were a mix of Orlando and Nate. Dead. Dying. Tortured. All of it while he stood by, letting it happen.

Chapter 22

Quinn awoke four hours later. It was morning and the bedroom was lit by the weak winter sun. Beside him, Sophie lay on her side, covered by the down comforter. If her habits were the same as before, she wouldn't stir for hours.

He found his clothes in the living room where they'd been dropped the night before. As he pulled them on, he took a look around the room. Little had changed in Sophie's apartment during the time he'd been away. The pictures, the cracks in the walls, the overstuffed armchair, everything seemed the same as it had been that first night she'd brought him here, long ago.

He'd met Sophie between projects. His short vacation, as he had called it at first, had turned into a two-month affair. Even then, he didn't know why he stayed. He had liked Sophie, and enjoyed her company. But there wasn't much more. The only reason he could come up with was he'd been alone for a long time prior to her. Not one of the most stellar reasons for starting a relationship, but an all too common one for Quinn.

It was at the Saturday morning outdoor antiques market near the Tiergarten S-bahn station when he first saw her. Sophie had come there with friends, and Quinn, alone, had followed them for a while, until Sophie stopped by herself at a stall selling old books.

They'd fallen into conversation easily. He used his standard cover, claiming to be a bank consultant helping one of his international clients with a business deal in Berlin. She didn't probe further – few people ever did. Banking was one of those professions that, unless one was in it, was an accepted enigma. Still, if he ever did stumble across somebody who did know the business, he was educated enough to talk a good game.

Within the first week, he'd moved out of his hotel and into her apartment. They had spent hours and hours making love. Many times, after their passion had been sated, she'd lead him through the dining area next to her kitchen, then out the window onto a short expanse of roof at the back of the building. She had turned the area into a makeshift patio. There was a wooden table, a few mismatched chairs, and several ceramic pots filled with tomato plants. 'My farm,' she called it. For hours they'd sit in the chairs and drink wine or beer and stare at the stars, talking about nothing at all.

But after a while Durrie's rule of romantic entanglements kicked in, and Quinn was gone, leaving one morning while she was sleeping, a short note his only goodbye.

Now, as Quinn slipped on his shoes, he couldn't help thinking he was doing it again. He paused for a moment, listening to see if she might have woken up. But the only noise from the bedroom was the breathing of a woman fully asleep.

Quinn picked up his backpack and opened the door.

Ku'damm was already crowded by the time he returned. He moved smoothly through the mixed groups of tourists and locals, his mission urgent but his pace relaxed. When he checked the staircase handrail at the mall, though, his was still the only marker. He added a second square near the first, letting his team know he was still safe, then melded back into the crowd walking into the mall.

For the moment, his only assets were those he carried in his backpack: his phone, the SIG Sauer and three additional magazines, six remaining miniature cameras, a portable monitor to check the camera angles as he was setting them up the night before, his set of IDs, a knife, his lock picks set, a small first-aid kit, and a pair of lightweight binoculars with limited night vision. Money wouldn't be a problem. He had plenty of accounts under names no one knew but him and were therefore untraceable.

What he didn't have was his computer. An annoyance, but not the end of the world. No one but Quinn would ever be able to access any of the data on his hard drive. It would simply purge itself if anyone tried. Most of what the machine contained was backed up on disks in L.A. anyway. What information he did need was on the flash memory stick in his pocket. If he needed to access it, he could buy computer time at dozens of places all over the city.

His most immediate need was clothes. He found a department store and picked up enough items to last him a couple of days. He paid for his items in cash, then changed in the store's bathroom. Once he was ready, he went in search of a pay phone.

'Could you connect me to Herr MacDonald's room, please?'

Quinn was standing in a phone booth outside a bakery, not far from where he'd purchased his clothes. His cell phone was in his backpack. Until he bought a new charging unit, he needed to preserve the phone's battery as long as he could.

'I'm sorry, sir,' a male voice said. 'Herr MacDonald checked out this morning.'

'Danke,' Quinn said. He hung up.

He took a deep breath. MacDonald had been the name he'd used to check into the Four Seasons. Even if Orlando had ditched the room as a precaution, she wouldn't have checked out. It only confirmed what he'd already expected. Borko had somehow traced their encrypted communications signal back to the hotel while Quinn was in the water plant. Quinn had to assume they'd taken Orlando in the process.

A call to the Dorint Hotel yielded the same results.

There was a tap on the door behind him. Quinn glanced over his shoulder. An impatient-looking teenage girl stared at him through the glass.

Quinn nodded, then opened the door and stepped out.

Finding Orlando and Nate was now his top priority. And as he walked away, he knew exactly where to start.

Duke had been operating out of Berlin for a long time. Too long, actually. And that was good because he'd done things. Stupid things. Things smart people in the business didn't do no matter how long they lived somewhere. Duke wasn't that smart. Just lucky.

Quinn sat in the driver's seat of a Volvo station wagon he'd stolen a half hour earlier in Ku'damm. He was parked across the street from a nightclub on Kaiser Friedrich Strasse. It was early yet, and the club didn't open for several hours. But there was already plenty of activity: cases of alcohol being delivered, windows being cleaned, sidewalks being swept.

It was Duke's place. He probably thought of it as a cover, but to Quinn it was a liability. 'Always keep a low profile,' Durrie had said. 'Don't be flashy. Flashy gets you killed. You can make enough money in this business that you don't have to throw it around. Are you listening to me?'

Quinn had listened. But apparently no one had taken the time to make Duke understand. Because, as he did every morning, Duke pulled up in front of the club in the same Mercedes sedan he'd driven Quinn around in the day before.

Duke was alone. His arrogance his downfall. A 'Berlin is my town, nobody can get to me here' kind of attitude. *Stupid,* Quinn thought.

His purpose for coming to the club this early

was to check the receipts from the night before. Quinn knew this from the last time he'd worked with the man. Back then Duke had bragged about his businesses, how he liked to start each day knowing exactly what was going on. And how, specifically, he would begin with an 11 a.m. stop at La Maison du Chat – the not so subtle name for his club.

Patterns. Idiotic, thoughtless patterns.

Quinn watched the big man get out of his car and waddle into the club. Twenty minutes later, Duke reappeared at the door, smiling. He turned and said something to someone inside before lumbering back to his car.

As Duke started his Mercedes and pulled away from the curb, Quinn started the Volvo. He waited until the Mercedes was half a block away, then made a U-turn to follow.

They drove across town, stopping finally in front of a jewelry store. Again Quinn waited while Duke went inside. This errand didn't take nearly as long. Apparently, the receipts here were less than desired. There was no smile on Duke's face as he returned to his car.

They spent two hours going from business to business. Duke may not have been very smart when it came to the intelligence game, but he obviously knew how to diversify his interests. He seemed to have his hand in a little bit of everything: a nightclub, several jewelry stores, some restaurants, an accounting office, a promotions company, over a dozen magazine kiosks. Still, even if all were moneymakers, none would have paid him as much as brokering a single good undercover job. Of course, from Duke's point of view, at least none of these other ventures could get him killed.

Just after 2:00 p.m., the Mercedes turned down a residential street and stopped near the end of the block in front of an apartment building. This was a new twist. Quinn had no idea if it was where Duke lived or just another source of cash, but he was getting tired of simply following the man around. And unlike any of the other stops, this one might provide an opportunity for a private conversation.

Quinn removed his gun, suppressor, knife, and set of lock picks from his backpack. He put all but the gun into the pockets of his jacket. After Duke exited his car, Quinn got out of the Volvo and slipped the gun under his waistband at the small of his back.

The building Duke had parked in front of was an old five-story structure that needed a new coat of paint. The other buildings on the street weren't in much better shape. There was a short staircase that led up from the sidewalk to a faded blue door.

Quinn closed the gap as Duke labored up the stairs. When Duke entered the building, Quinn jogged up the steps and grabbed the door just before it closed.

He froze in position and listened carefully to make sure Duke hadn't heard him. There were footsteps, slow and natural. Not the rushing footsteps of someone who thought he was in danger. Quinn waited until they faded, then opened the door and slipped inside.

He found himself in a dingy entrance hall. A bicycle was chained to a metal pipe running up the side of the wall and into the ceiling. To Quinn's left were a series of battered, built-in mailboxes. In front of him was another door that led into the main part of the building. The door was propped open, a brick holding it in place. By the look of things, the door appeared to have been in that position for years. Beyond it was a staircase leading up and to the right, and a hallway that jogged around the stairs heading back toward the rear of the building.

Quinn passed through the open doorway, stopping at the base of the stairs. The air inside smelled of mold and food and urine. The place was just a few notches above uninhabitable. Duke wouldn't have lived in this building. He had to be here for something else.

Using the staircase as cover, Quinn leaned around the banister and looked down the hall expecting to see Duke, but it was deserted. There was a faint whining sound coming from down the hallway, though. Moving cautiously to investigate, he found the cause halfway down in a small alcove.

An elevator.

A moment later the whining stopped abruptly. Duke had apparently arrived at his destination. Unfortunately, there was no indicator to show Quinn which floor he had stopped on. But the building wasn't that high, and unlike Duke, Quinn had no problem with exercise. He returned to the stairs and mounted them in search of his former client.

* * *

Quinn found Duke on the fourth floor knocking on a door halfway down the hall. Staying in the shadows of the stairwell, Quinn waited.

The door opened, and an elderly woman stuck her head out. 'Frau Russ,' Duke said. *'Ich müss mit Ihnen reden.'*

'Ja, Herr Reimers,' she said. *'Einen Moment, bitte.'*

The woman disappeared back into the room, leaving the door ajar. Quinn moved silently into the hall. As he neared Duke, he pretended to reach into his pocket as if searching for something, tilting his head down to help conceal his identity. Duke glanced at him, then returned his attention to the old woman's apartment.

As Quinn was about to pass the fat man, he stopped. It took Duke a moment to realize that something was up. As he turned, Quinn smiled.

'*Guten tag,* Herr Reimers,' Quinn said.

Chapter 23

Quinn shoved Duke through the door and into the apartment. Once they were both inside, Quinn kicked the door closed. The old woman appeared in a doorway to the right.

'Was ist los?' she asked.

Duke stumbled against an old cloth-covered chair. He turned and looked back at Quinn, then started to push himself up.

'Don't move,' Quinn said to Duke. He shot a glance at the woman. *'Was ist hinter dieser Tür?'* he asked her, nodding toward a door on the other side of the room.

'Wer sind Sie?' she demanded.

Quinn glared at Duke. 'What's behind that door?' he asked in English.

'It's a bathroom,' Duke said.

Quinn looked at the woman and told her in German to go into the bathroom. She didn't move. To Duke, Quinn said, 'Maybe she'll listen to you. Tell her if she doesn't, I'll shoot her.'

'What's the problem here?' Duke asked.

'*Tell* her.'

Duke turned to the old woman. 'Frau Russ. *Bitte gehen Sie in's Bad, während wir uns unterhalten.'*

This time the woman did as ordered. Quinn watched as she entered the bathroom and shut the door, then he turned and looked down at Duke.

'Get up,' Quinn said.

Duke pushed himself against the chair and found his footing. 'What's going on, Quinn? What's wrong?'

Quinn scoffed, but said nothing.

'I'm confused. Please, you're scaring me.'

'Good,' Quinn said. 'Let's cut through all the you-don't-know-what-I'm-here-for bullshit. All right?'

Duke's hand suddenly shot under his jacket, but Quinn was already in motion, slipping his knife out of his pocket and into his right hand. He grabbed Duke by the hair with his left hand as he pressed the blade against the fat man's neck. 'Not a good idea.'

Duke stiffened.

'Now. Slowly,' Quinn continued. 'Hands to the side.'

Duke started to speak, but Quinn said, 'Quiet.'

Duke moved his hands away from his jacket.

Quinn let go of Duke's hair, then moved his free hand to the spot Duke had been reaching for. From under the jacket, he pulled out a pistol. A Glock.

Quinn transferred the gun into the pocket of his coat. 'Anything else?'

'No,' Duke said.

Quinn increased the pressure on the knife. 'No,' Duke repeated. 'Nothing.'

'In the chair,' Quinn ordered.

He pulled the knife back and let Duke sit back down in the old chair. Sweat beaded on the fat man's brow. In front of the chair was a coffee table. Quinn pushed a stack of magazines off it and onto the floor, then he took a seat on the edge. 'Who are you working for?'

'None of your business.'

Quinn brandished the knife. 'You see, that's just stupid. I'm a little pissed off right now. My self-control isn't exactly running at full strength.'

'Borko,' Duke said quickly.

'Only Borko?'

Duke eyed the blade nervously. 'He's been my only contact.'

'Not Dahl?'

'The name doesn't mean anything to me.'

'God, I hate it when you lie.'

'I'm not,' Duke said. Quinn inched the knife closer. 'Okay, okay. I've heard the name, all right? He called Borko once when I was meeting with him. That's all.'

Quinn stared without saying anything.

'I swear, that's it.'

'Then let's talk about the water plant. What's it being used for?'

'You think they would tell me?' Duke asked. 'Borko wouldn't even let me in the building.'

'I have a hard time believing that. Borko isn't based here. He needs a local guy. Someone who knows the city and can make things happen.' Quinn pointed the knife at Duke. 'That's you. So don't fucking tell me it isn't.'

‘I’m a nobody, Quinn. A hired hand. Like you. That’s all,’ he said, his accent all but gone. ‘Borko doesn’t tell me anything. Sure, I got the property for them, but that’s it. What they’re doing, I haven’t a clue.’

‘Think really hard. Maybe you’re forgetting something. Something Borko might not have told you directly. Maybe something you overheard or even figured out on your own.’

Duke didn’t say anything, but the look in his eyes told Quinn he knew more.

‘What is it?’ Quinn asked.

Duke hesitated, then said, ‘It’s just a guess.’

‘Then guess.’

‘They needed the Office out of the way. I don’t know why. Borko handled that. I think he worked with someone on the inside.’

‘Who?’ Quinn asked. ‘Was it Peter?’

Duke said nothing.

‘Fine,’ Quinn said. ‘But why take me out? I don’t even work for the Office.’

Duke hesitated.

‘What?’ Quinn asked.

‘You were a special request.’

‘Special request? You mean I was singled out?’

‘That’s all I heard, okay? It’s all I know.’

Quinn let the meaning of Duke’s words sink in. A special request? Could that be true? Even if it was, it did little to explain what was going on.

‘What are they up to?’ Quinn asked.

‘I already answered that,’ Duke said.

In one quick, fluid motion, Quinn flicked the blade against Duke’s ear. Blood began running down the fat man's neck. 'What the fuck?' he said as he put a hand over the wound to staunch the flow.

'What's the job?' Quinn asked again.

'I told you, I –'

The knife started to move again.

Duke raised his hands, palms outward. 'Wait. All right. I overheard something. But it didn't make sense to me.'

'What?'

'Just some initials,' Duke said. He closed his eyes, as if straining to remember.

'What initials?'

'Give me a second!' Duke's voice rose in frustration. 'It was "I" something. ICME . . . ICUT. No, not IC. IO . . . IOMP. That's it. IOMP.'

'What's that mean?' Quinn asked.

'How should I know?'

'You're lying,' Quinn said, knowing Duke was holding something back. 'What does it mean?'

'I don't know.'

'Then what do you know?'

The fat man looked down but didn't answer.

'What?' Quinn demanded.

'Just a name. I've never heard it before.'

'What was it?'

'Campobello.'

Quinn's eyes narrowed, the connection immediately made in his own mind. 'There has to be more,' he said.

'No,' Duke said. 'Nothing.' Quinn moved the knife a fraction of an inch. 'I swear,' Duke said. 'It's all I heard.'

'You're a lot of help, aren't you?'

'I'm telling you everything I know.'

'I doubt that,' Quinn said. 'Where can I find Borko?'

'I've never met him in the same place twice,' Duke said. 'He calls. We meet. A restaurant. A bar. Whatever. I don't have a clue where he might be staying. Your best bet is the water plant. He must go there sometime.'

Quinn had already thought of that. He stared at Duke until the fat man looked away. 'Just one more thing. How much did they pay you to set us up?'

Duke stammered. 'I . . . I didn't . . . they . . .'

'How much? Ten thousand a head? Twenty? I hope you were getting at least twenty-five K for me. That's what they offered Gibson.'

Duke's lips were pressed tightly together.

'Where's my team?'

Duke shook his head. 'I don't know.'

'You're lying.'

'I'm *not*,' Duke pleaded.

'I don't believe you,' Quinn said. He pulled Duke's pistol out of his pocket.

'What are you going to do with that?' Duke asked.

'The same thing you tried to do to us.'

Quinn aimed the gun at Duke's forehead and pulled the trigger.

Chapter 24

Quinn made several stops that afternoon, purchasing tools he needed for the task ahead. He also checked the handrail in Ku'damm, but it was still devoid of any sign of Nate or Orlando. He knew he should assume the worst, but he wasn't ready to do it yet. Eventually he found a café just south of Tiergarten where he ate an early dinner and waited for the sun to go down.

As he sat nursing a cup of coffee, Quinn thought about his conversation with Duke. IOMP. Maybe it was nothing. Duke might have made it up on the spot to keep Quinn from killing him. If so, it was just another example of Duke's bad judgment. But if it meant something, Quinn couldn't afford to ignore it. He searched his memories for any kind of connection, but couldn't come up with one.

It was the other tidbit Duke had dropped that had clicked for him. *Campobello*. It had been the city listed on Robert Taggert's driver's license. Campobello, Nevada. Still, its ultimate meaning eluded him.

Then again, maybe none of it mattered, he thought. Did he really care what Borko was up to? Was there any reason he needed to know?

Only if it helped him find Orlando and Nate, he decided. Otherwise he didn't care.

Once night had fallen, Quinn caught a taxi and returned to Neukölln. He told his driver he couldn't remember the exact address of the building he needed to go to, but that he knew it was on Wildenbruchstrasse somewhere east of Sonnenalle.

As they drove through the city, Quinn closed his eyes to focus on the job ahead. He tried to go over his plan step-by-step, but instead his mind filled with images of Orlando and Nate dead, their bodies dumped in some dark corner of the city. When he opened his eyes again, they were in Neukölln. He leaned forward and instructed the cabby to drive slowly so that they wouldn't miss his destination.

As the taxi passed the south end of Schandauer Strasse, Quinn checked the street for surveillance. He easily picked out the spotters at each end of the block. One was sitting in the back of an Audi at the curb. The other one was hiding in the shadows of the entrance to an apartment building.

Quinn assumed there were more. Borko wouldn't take chances, especially not with Quinn still loose. There had to be at least one camera, maybe two. And probably one more guy on the street near the entrance to the water plant. Approaching the building unnoticed from the front would be all but impossible.

Quinn kept up the charade for two more blocks. Just beyond the canal, he picked out a random building and had the taxi driver drop him off.

The mission for tonight was simple: reenter the water plant, look for signs of Orlando and Nate, set up surveillance so he could keep tabs on what was going on inside, and get out.

Prior to leaving for the plant, Quinn had checked the signals from the original cameras he had put in place the previous night, the night of the trap. All he got was static. Borko's men had undoubtedly removed the equipment not long after Quinn had made his escape. But the locations those cameras had been in were no longer as critical to Quinn. Where he wanted to put the cameras now was in the two locations he hadn't been able to that first night. In the basement, and in the sphere. These were the focal points of Borko's operation, the most likely spots from which Quinn could learn anything useful.

The storm from the night before had moved on and had been replaced by a mass of frigid air. Quinn pulled the collar of his jacket up around his neck, trying unsuccessfully to ignore the cold.

He made his way back across the bridge spanning the canal, then turned right on Weigandufer. On one side of the street was the man-made river, and on the other side a row of apartment buildings, each between six and eight stories high. Quinn walked down the sidewalk, casually scanning the buildings. Near the middle of the block, he found what he was looking for.

The entrance to the mustard yellow building

was up a short flight of steps. It was a way in, but a bit more public than he wanted. All he really needed to do was get to the other side.

The better option was to the left of the entrance, at street level. It was a tunnel through the structure, an opening built to allow cars to drive through to a parking lot in the back. There were two large wooden doors attached to either side of the opening. Since it was still early in the evening, the doors were open, allowing residents easier access in and out.

Quinn walked through the opening as if he belonged. He stopped at the back end of the tunnel and surveyed the parking lot. It was not large, just room enough for ten cars and a few motorcycles. There were two floodlights mounted at either end of the lot. The bulb in the one at the far back corner was flickering, and would need to be replaced soon. At the rear of the property, behind the lot, was a row of trees. Beyond the trees was an open field. And at the other end of the field, the water plant.

Quinn stepped out from the shadows of the tunnel, intent on crossing the lot and reaching the cover of the trees. But he only got a few feet when he heard the groan of rusted hinges. A door was opening to his right. He glanced over and saw a man stepping out of the building into the parking lot.

Quinn ducked down behind one of the cars. Carefully, he peeked through the car's windows. The guy looked to be in his late fifties, tired and overweight. Quinn watched as the man held the door open, and a medium-sized dog, a mutt, ran outside.

The man shut the door, then lit a cigarette.

While he smoked, the dog sniffed around the lot, stopping once to pee. As the mutt neared Quinn's position it stopped suddenly, nose in the air. Quinn cursed silently, bracing himself to make a quick escape back through the tunnel to the street. Only instead of barking, the dog came over and began to lick Quinn's hand.

The man with the cigarette took a few steps into the lot. 'Charlie?' he called.

But Charlie seemed to have taken a liking to his new friend. Quinn gently tried to push the dog away, but Charlie wouldn't move. Quinn glanced over the side of the car again. The dog's owner had taken a few more steps away from the door. He took a final puff on his cigarette, then flicked it to the ground and stamped it out.

Looking up again, he called out, 'Charlie!'

This time the dog's ears pricked up.

'Bei Fuss.'

The dog began backing away from Quinn, then paused.

'Charlie!'

The dog gave Quinn one last look, then ran off to join his master.

The man walked back over to the apartment building and opened the door. A few seconds later, he and the dog disappeared inside. Quinn waited to make sure they were gone, then stood and jogged across the lot.

A chain-link fence separated the row of trees at the back of the parking lot from the field. Quinn grabbed the fence and gave it a gentle shake. He could climb over it, but since it was so loose there was no way he could do it quietly. There had to be at least one of Borko's men stationed at the rear of the water plant. The noise of the fence would betray Quinn before he could even reach the top. Going over was out.

Quinn searched along the fence looking for a different option. He knew he could just cut through the fence, but that kind of handiwork was not likely to go unnoticed. The last thing he needed was for anyone to know he'd been there.

The metal fence post seemed like the most logical point of attack. He pulled a pair of wire cutters out of his backpack, then began removing the wire loops that held the lower edge of the fence to the post.

The task turned out to be harder than he expected. To mask the sound, he had to coordinate his cuts with the noise of cars passing on the nearby street. And the snow wasn't helping, either. He had to carefully move enough away from the bottom of the fence so he had a clear path. It took him five minutes to get through the fence and onto the other side.

The field was lit by hints of light filtering between buildings and through the trees from Schandauer Strasse beyond. It wasn't that large of a space, only two hundred feet from right to left, and another hundred or so feet to the buildings on the other side. The ground itself was covered with a thick layer of new snow. Off to one side lay a pile of large metal pipes, undoubtedly left over from when the plant was still operating.

Quinn focused his attention on the back of the building, looking for movement or any sign the place was being guarded. After a moment, he spotted something. It had been subtle, a simple adjustment of position. A muscle cramp maybe, or an itch that needed to be scratched. Whatever had caused it, a shadow had moved, unknowingly exposing a sentry near the left corner of the plant.

Keeping low, Quinn moved to his right, toward the stack of unused pipes. The pile was over five feet high, providing him the perfect cover as he turned and headed up the field. His biggest concern was the snow itself. The cold air had begun to freeze the top layer, creating a natural alarm system. Each step he took had to be carefully executed so that the crunch made by his foot as it broke the surface was minimal.

After working his way around the end of the pile, Quinn made his way south until he was only twenty feet from the basement window he'd escaped through the night before. He crept over to it, pausing to make sure he hadn't been spotted. When he was confident he was still in the clear, he turned his attention to the window.

Faint light spilled through it. Quinn cautiously peered inside. A single work lamp glowed weakly in the corner opposite the window. Quinn quickly scanned the rest of the room, looking for any signs of movement. All seemed to be quiet, but to his left, the refrigerating unit created a blind spot someone could have been standing in.

The window was hinged at the top and swung outward. Quinn grabbed the bottom of the frame and pulled the window toward him just a little, testing to see if it was still unlocked. It was.

He removed his gun and made sure the suppressor was properly connected. Slowly, he swung the window open, then waited to see if there was any reaction from inside. Still nothing. With his gun pointed toward the blind spot, he slipped partially through the open window, head-first, for a better look.

Though there was still a small portion of the room he couldn't see, it appeared as if no one else were there. Not wasting any time, he pulled himself out, turned, and dropped feetfirst through the opening, shutting the window behind him.

Only the hum of the refrigerating unit greeted him.

A more detailed survey of the room revealed there were some changes since the previous evening. Several hard plastic travel cases now sat on the worktables. He walked over to see what they contained, but they were all empty. Perhaps the contents had been moved to the large refrigerator, he thought.

Quinn stepped over to the unit and was surprised to find the simple safety pin had been replaced by a heavy-duty padlock. He considered picking it, but decided against it. He already had a lot to do, and he couldn't spare the time.

Quinn turned and walked to the door that led into the second basement room. Pausing, he listened.

Silence. He took a deep breath, then opened the door.

This room didn't look the same as the night before, either. The worktables were now covered with tools and boxes and equipment. Quinn crossed the room, noting everything, but making no guesses as to the purpose of it all. He paused by one of the metal cabinets near the door and opened it. The cabinet was full of medical supplies: bandages, tape, scissors, medicine. In a second, larger cabinet hung several heavy-duty biohazard suits. They were white, and made from some sort of nonporous material. On the floor of the cabinet were several identical boxes. Quinn picked one up and opened it. Inside was a full-face mask wrapped in a plastic bag. They looked as if they'd fit snuggly into the facial opening on the biohazard suits.

Quinn opened a third cabinet. No biohazard suits in this one. Instead there were air tanks mounted in backpack-like harnesses. Quinn checked the gauge on each. While most were empty, two of the tanks were nearly full.

He removed his backpack and set it on a worktable. From inside, he extracted one of the six remaining cameras. There were several different frequencies on which the cameras could broadcast. The choice of frequency was made via a tiny dial located at the back of the camera. He turned it, choosing a different frequency from the one he'd used before. It would allow him to see what was going on, without tipping off Borko and his team. The only limitation was the distance from which he could monitor the cameras. Without another booster, he would have to stay within a mile to see anything. Less than that if he wanted to make sure the picture was clear.

Quinn mounted cameras in both rooms of the basement. When he was done, he picked up his backpack and headed toward the staircase that led up into the base of the sphere.

Just before the door, he stopped himself. After a moment's hesitation, he returned to the cabinets. He put down his bag, opened up the larger cabinet, and donned one of the biohazard suits. He then picked out a face mask and grabbed one of the full tanks from the second cabinet.

The outfit would serve two purposes. The first would be to protect him from anything deadly that might be floating around. The second to act as a disguise in case he was spotted.

Quinn removed the four remaining cameras from his backpack and transferred them to the plastic bag the mask had been in. He was about to place his gun in with them when he realized that it would be useless. While the bio-suit's gloves were flexible, they were just thick enough so that none of his fingers would be able to slip over the trigger. Reluctantly, he stuffed the gun back into his backpack, and stowed the bag in the cabinet.

Quinn clung to the scaffolding just below the platform in the center of the sphere, the same spot he'd hung from the night before while Borko's men searched for him on the platform above. He attached one of the remaining cameras to the pipes, aiming it downward so he would be able to observe anyone going into or out of the air lock on the floor of the sphere.

As he was checking to be sure the camera was securely in place, he heard voices above him. It sounded like two men had just exited the containment room and were now on the platform heading to the outside air lock. Unfortunately, he wasn't close enough to make out what they were saying. He contented himself with waiting silently until they were gone.

Once all was clear, Quinn worked his way across the scaffolding to the edge of the platform, then pulled himself up and onto it. His first stop was the exit leading to the air lock. He paused, listening at the door to be certain no one was inside. More silence.

Quinn pulled out another camera and placed it above the door. He adjusted it so that it pointed across the platform toward the bio-containment room. As he had hoped, the black casing of the camera blended in well with the black covering of the sphere. Someone would have to really be looking for it to notice it. Satisfied, he then adhered the tiny strip of adhesive with the embedded microphone just above the door entrance.

He walked quietly back across the platform, stopping in front of the entrance to the containment room. Stretching as high as he could, he was just able to put a camera on top of the room, aiming back at the air-lock entrance. Now he had all the doors covered.

It was time to turn his attention to the interior of the containment room. He studied the entrance. If he'd guessed correctly, beyond it would be another double-door air-lock system.

Still, he hesitated. If they'd gone operational in the last twenty-four hours, there was no telling what might be stored on the other side of the air lock.

He gave himself a mental nudge, counted to three, then pulled the door open. There was no rush of air this time. The two men who had just passed through had equalized the pressure in the air lock to that of the interior of the sphere.

Quinn peered inside.

He was right, a small chamber, big enough for two people at most, then another door with a bright red light set into the jamb at eye level at the other end. Quinn entered, then pulled the door shut. Above him, a light came on, a single fixture recessed into the ceiling.

For a moment, nothing happened. Then, with a barely audible click, the red light next to the interior door switched to green, while the light on the door he'd just passed through turned red.

Quinn took a deep breath, then opened the interior door. As he expected, air moved with him as he stepped over the threshold.

The center room was dark. He tried shutting the door, thinking it might also have an automated light system, but nothing came on. He opened the door again, allowing the light from the chamber to spill into the room until he located a switch just to the left of the door. He flipped it on, then let the door swing closed.

The room was cramped but deserted. Along the wall to his left were a series of chest-high mini-refrigerators. Stainless steel and brand-new. Quinn opened the nearest refrigerator. It was running, but empty.

Shutting the door, he continued his inspection of the room. Along the wall opposite the refrigerators was a long stainless-steel table. Everything looked newly assembled, like a showroom. All that was needed were whatever supplies and instruments were necessary to make the room operational.

In the center was another table. On it were two large transparent cases, made of either plastic or glass, Quinn wasn't sure which. Inset on the front face of each box were two holes that allowed access to a set of rubberized gloves attached to the inside of the box. The gloves would let someone standing in front of the box work on items inside without actually touching them. Quinn had seen a setup like this before. It had been on the Discovery Channel, a documentary about the Centers for Disease Control. They were safety cabinets, designed specifically for the manipulation of dangerous microorganisms. Older models, Quinn seemed to remember. But still highly effective.

'Shit,' he said.

Back in the basement, Quinn removed the bio-suit and stored it in its cabinet. He retrieved his backpack, pulled out his gun, and tucked it in his waistband. He then donned the pack and exited the basement using the same window he'd entered through.

'Halt.'

Quinn whipped around, his gun quickly moving

back into his hand. The voice had come from behind him to the right and very near. Quinn saw the shadow of a man. Without hesitating he pulled his trigger.

There was the spit of a bullet passing through the suppressor, followed almost immediately by a thump as the sentry's body hit the ground. Quinn hurried toward the guard, his gun held in front of him. But it was unnecessary. The man was dead.

From around the side of the building came the sound of running footsteps. Quinn searched the sentry's body quickly for the dead man's gun. He found a Glock with its own suppressor in the man's right hand. Quinn grabbed the gun, then watched the side of the building intently.

Seconds later another man came around the corner. Quinn fired the Glock so that the bullet would come close to the new man but not hit him.

The man retreated quickly back around the corner, then called out, 'Rolf, it's me!'

Quinn let off another shot, and the man returned fire. That was what Quinn was waiting for. He let off one more shot, then dropped the Glock near the dead man's hand. He sprinted back along the wall until he was a safe distance away, hidden in the shadows.

The second guard fired his gun two more times, then waited. When there was no return fire, the guard called out again. 'Rolf?'

A second voice joined the first. 'What is it?'

'Rolf just shot at me.'

'Are you sure?' the second voice asked.

Quinn didn't wait to hear the rest. Soon enough

they would discover that Rolf was dead, and if Quinn was right, they'd assume that Rolf was the one who had shot first. It was a trick Durrie had taught Quinn, but this was the first time he'd ever used it.

The activity surrounding the dead guard created a large, temporary hole in the building's security. Quinn saw no one else as he made his escape.

Chapter 25

Having little choice, Quinn knew he'd have to return to Sophie's for one more night. On the way, he stopped once more in Ku'damm.

In the low light of the stairwell, he almost didn't see it. It didn't help that he had been prepping himself to find nothing. A mind often sees what it expects. When he did see it, he had to rub his finger over it to be sure that it was really there.

A gray square, affixed to the handrail next to his.

Orlando.

She was alive, and she was free. Quinn had to force himself to breathe again. Carefully he removed another purple square from his bag and placed it halfway on top of the gray one. If all went according to plan, they would meet up at 10:00 a.m. the next morning.

'When?' Sophie asked.

'In the morning,' Quinn said.

He expected her to ask him why he was leaving

or where he was going, or even what he'd been thinking coming back to her in the first place. But she didn't.

'Unless you want me to leave now.'

A sly smile crossed her face. 'What I want?' she said. She began to grind her hips against him. 'What I want is more of this.'

Quinn awoke early again the next morning, collected his things, and left before Sophie stirred. Even though he had told her he might return, coming back for a second night had been taking a big chance. He told himself it would be the last time, though. He couldn't tempt fate for a third night.

He took a taxi to Potsdamer Platz, where he was able to buy a breakfast sandwich in the lower level of the mall. Upstairs were the typical stores one would expect to find. Quinn first located a Saturn store, a franchise specializing in electronics, and purchased a charging unit for his phone. Next he went down one level and found a shop where he picked up a few more shirts before venturing back outside.

He spent thirty minutes making sure he wasn't being watched, then made his way into the S-bahn station and down to the northbound S2 platform. He almost expected to find her standing there on the platform when he arrived. But though there were over a dozen people waiting for the next train, Orlando wasn't one of them.

Quinn took up a position at one end near an exit tunnel. He checked his watch. It was 10:05 a.m.

She was late. Three minutes later a new train arrived. As the doors opened, a group of elementary-age children and their outnumbered adult supervisors disembarked. The noise level on the platform increased exponentially.

Quinn scanned the handful of other passengers who also got off. Still no Orlando. There were a few chaotic moments as arriving passengers headed for the exit and departing passengers made their way onto the train. Then suddenly the train was gone, and the platform was quiet and empty.

No, not completely empty, Quinn noted. Someone was leaning against the wall at the far end. By the way the person stood, Quinn immediately thought female, though she was bundled up in a way that made it difficult to confirm.

She was looking in Quinn's direction, so he began walking toward her. As he neared he noticed a red and black checkered scarf wrapped around her face in a way that left only her eyes exposed. Her Asian eyes.

If he hadn't been so well trained, he would have broken into a large smile of relief. Instead he made no indication that he had recognized her. He kept walking, heading toward a staircase that would take him back up to ground level, without giving her a second glance.

Even with the training, it took all of his willpower not to turn and make sure she was following him. But the Berlin train system was covered by cameras, and while it was highly unlikely Borko would have the resources to check them all, it was safer to assume he did. The last thing Quinn wanted was for Borko to know they'd found each other.

Once he was outside, he allowed himself to be consumed by the morning crowd. A moment later, she was beside him.

'Nate?' she asked, her voice partially muffled by the scarf across her mouth.

'No sign yet,' Quinn said. 'Are you okay?'

'A couple scrapes. Nothing serious.'

They walked past a mother pushing her baby in a stroller, then an elderly couple weighed down with plastic shopping bags.

'What took you so long to check in?' Quinn asked.

'Not sure you've noticed this, but I don't exactly blend into the crowd here,' she said. 'I couldn't get there the night we were blown. So I found someplace safe and stayed there. No way I was going to show my face in the daytime, so yesterday was out. At least until after dark. That's when I found out you were still alive.'

'It's daytime now.'

'Yeah, I'm not too happy about being out here. Come on,' she said. 'I've got us a room at the Mandola Suites.'

'What?' Quinn stopped, and looked straight at her for the first time. 'Hotels are the first place Borko will look.'

'We have to stay someplace, don't we?' she asked.

'What if someone already made you when you checked in?'

She shook her head. 'No chance. I did it all by phone. Had a messenger pick up the key and bring it to me at Friedrichstrasse Station. As far as he knew, I was just someone's assistant. Yours, I guess.' She reached into her pocket and pulled out an electronic keycard.

As far as hotels went, the Mandola Suites was an excellent choice, especially given their situation. It had been designed with the long-term guest in mind. There were several private entrances, which meant guests never had to pass through the lobby. Each room was also equipped with a kitchen. And, best yet, it was right there in Potsdamer Platz. Their room was on the fifth floor, and had a view of Leipziger Strasse. Unfortunately, Orlando had only been able to secure a one-bedroom suite, so Quinn would have to camp out on the couch.

As they shed themselves of their winter cover, Quinn noticed a bruise near Orlando's ear, high on her cheek.

'Ashtray,' she said after he pointed it out.

'You fell on it, or it fell on you?'

'The guy who threw it was aiming for the back of my head, but I turned at the last moment.'

Quinn stared at her, waiting for more.

Orlando sat down on the couch. 'They must have keyed into our signal somehow. They knew where you were. From that they must have got a fix on me. Probably surprised the hell out of them I was right next door to where you were staying.'

'Then why didn't they get you?' Quinn asked.

'When you were in the sphere and our signal got jammed, I knew I only had a few seconds,' she said. 'I grabbed my gun, got behind the couch, and aimed for the door. I think their timing must have been a little off. They probably wanted to cut our communication and break in at the same moment.' She shrugged. 'It's how I would have planned it.'

Quinn nodded in agreement. It's how he would have planned it, too.

'There were three of them,' she went on. 'I got the first one as he came in. The second as he ran toward the bedroom. It was the last who gave me the most problems.'

'He was the one with the ashtray?'

She nodded. 'But he won't be throwing anything else soon. After that, I didn't want to wait to see if anyone else was coming, so I grabbed what I could and got out of there.' She nodded at him. 'Your turn.'

Quinn told her about his escape from the sphere, his conversation with Duke, and his subsequent return to the sphere the previous night.

'So are you intentionally trying to make me look like a slacker?' she asked.

'I wasn't exactly going to point it out.'

'Your sensitivity is touching,' she said. 'What about Nate?'

Quinn's mouth tensed. 'He should have checked in by now.'

'He's not going to.'

'I know.'

Orlando looked at him for a moment. 'We'll find him,' she said.

Quinn nodded, but said nothing. He only hoped his apprentice was still alive when they did.

He thought for a moment, then pulled his cell phone out of his pocket. 'I think it's time I had a real talk with Peter.'

'Yeah. Have fun with that.' She got up and walked into the bedroom.

As Quinn turned on his phone and dialed Peter's number, he could hear the shower being turned on in the other room.

A moment later, Misty answered. 'It's Quinn,' he said.

Silence on the other end.

'Misty?' he asked.

'Sorry,' she said, sounding shaken. 'It's just . . . we heard you were dead.'

'When was this supposed to have happened?'

'Two nights ago,' she said. 'In Berlin.'

'I don't feel dead.'

'Thank God for that. I assume you want to speak to Peter.'

'Please.'

Within seconds Peter was on the line. 'Holy Christ, Quinn. What the hell's going on?'

'You tell me.'

'Borko's bragging that he took you and your whole team out. He seems to know you were working for me.'

'Really? Tell me, who are *you* working for, Peter?'

'What's that supposed to mean?'

'The job with Duke was a setup,' Quinn said. 'Turns out he was in deep with Borko. I know. Shocking, isn't it?' he said, his voice flat. 'But you want to hear something even more interesting? He told me Borko was responsible for the disruption. And that he'd had inside help. You're the one who really wanted me to work with Duke. You begged me. Now it turns out Duke was working for Borko.

And Borko was the one who took out the Office. See where I'm going with this?'

'Fuck you. Fuck you for even thinking what you're thinking,' Peter said. 'You're saying I was in on something that killed several close friends of mine? You think I would have done that?' He paused. 'Fuck you.'

'You're the one who wanted me here.'

'I had *nothing* to do with what happened. As far as I knew, Duke was just helping us out. How was I supposed to know otherwise? I can't even leave my goddamn office. And I've got no one out there but you.'

Quinn paused. As much as it looked like Peter was involved, it just didn't seem right. He'd known Peter for a long time, and despite the man's faults, the head of the Office had never turned on one of his assets. So Quinn was inclined to believe him. But that didn't mean he'd make it easy for Peter. 'If it wasn't you, then who was it? Maybe you need to take a hard look at your employee situation. How's morale?'

'Go to hell,' Peter said. 'Everyone's clean here.'

'How can you know that?'

'I just do. All right?'

'If you say so.'

'What's your situation?' Peter asked.

Quinn took a breath. 'Nate's missing.'

'You think he's dead?'

Quinn hesitated, then said, 'No. I think they've got him.'

'Using him as insurance?'

'That would be my guess.'

'They get anyone else?' Peter asked.

'No.'

'Who else are you working with?'

'That is not something you need to know.'

'I'm just trying to help.'

'Really?' Quinn said. 'That's good to hear, because I need some information.'

'What kind of information?'

'Anything relevant. Taggert. Jills.' Quinn paused. 'The Office's involvement. You've got to tell me everything.'

'What's that have to do with anything?'

'The disruption and the job in Colorado are tied together,' Quinn said. 'Come on. You've got to realize that.'

'I don't know what's going on.'

'Don't fuck with me, Peter. I've heard too many I-don't-knows lately. Tell me what's going on.'

'There's nothing to tell,' Peter said.

Quinn clenched his teeth. 'You're not doing a lot to win my trust.'

'Do you know for sure Borko was behind the disruption?'

'I'm sure enough,' Quinn said. 'His operation here leads me to believe he's tied into Taggert, too. Peter, we're wasting time.'

'I can't tell you.'

Quinn took a deep breath. 'Let me throw another name at you,' Quinn said. 'Dahl.'

'Dahl?' Peter was obviously surprised. 'Where did you hear that? Did Gibson say something to you?'

Quinn paused. 'Why would Gibson have said anything?'

It was Peter's turn to go silent. When he finally did speak, his voice was laced with barely controlled anger. 'At each . . . incident of the disruption, there was a message. We didn't realize there was a pattern until yesterday. Each message was the same. A white business card stuffed into the victim's throat, far enough back so they couldn't be found without an autopsy.'

'You did autopsies?' Quinn asked. That wouldn't have been procedure. The cause of death would have been pretty obvious.

'We didn't,' Peter replied. 'But the local authorities got to one of our casualties before we could. Their M.E. found the card. Once we knew about it, we went back and checked the others.'

'What was the message?'

'It was only a single word. "Dahl." The son of a bitch wanted us to know who did it.'

'Gibson didn't have a card,' Quinn said.

'Maybe he got rid of it before you got him.'

'Not a chance.' It bothered Quinn that the attack on him deviated from the others in this way. Duke's words came back to him: *You were a special request.* 'Is he somebody you crossed before?'

'I . . . don't know.' Peter sounded truly stumped. 'He's been around awhile, but as far as I can determine, we've never worked with him.' A pause. 'But I want him now. Find him and I'll give you triple bonus.'

'Then I need your help.'

Quinn could hear Peter exhale on the other side of the line. 'Okay. But I need to check something out first,' Peter said.

'Are you kidding?'

'I'll get back to you.'

Before Quinn could say anything else, the line went dead.

As soon as Orlando emerged from the bedroom, Quinn said, 'I want to contact your friend. See if he's found anything out yet.'

Her hair was damp and she was wearing one of the white robes the Mandola provided. 'The Mole? I don't have his number. He changes it every day.'

'Then how do you get ahold of him?'

'E-mail first, then he sends me the number.'

'Okay. We'll find a computer.'

She sighed wearily. As she turned to walk back into the bedroom, she said, 'Okay.'

'Wait,' Quinn told her. 'How much did you sleep last night?'

She looked back at him. 'Enough.'

'How much?'

'Maybe an hour.'

'Curled up in a ball in some doorway?'

'Something like that.'

'You stay here. I'll contact him,' Quinn said.

'He may not talk to you.'

'I'll be very persuasive. What's the e-mail address?'

She gave it to him. 'You'll need the code, too. If he actually answers your message, you won't be able to understand anything without it.'

Quinn found an Internet café on Ku'damm called Easy Everything. He paid in advance for an hour of time, then sat down at one of the machines in the back of the store, where there would be less chance of someone looking over his shoulder.

He logged on to the computer and used its browser to access one of the many services that provided free e-mail addresses. It took him less than three minutes to sign up for a new identity. Composing the short message to the Mole took longer.

```
You're doing an appraisal for
me. A bracelet I picked up in
Colorado. O said I should
contact you directly about
authenticity. Can we talk?
JQ.
```

He clicked on Send. Now it was just a matter of waiting. While leaving the window with the mailbox open, Quinn brought up a new window to access the website of a printing firm based in Chelsea, Massachusetts. Using a back door he'd secretly placed on their server, he routed himself to a paper supply company in Baltimore, Maryland, and from there into the computers at the Government Services Administration, the GSA, in Washington, D.C. Now it was a simple matter of skipping over to the FBI's system, using channels Orlando had set up long ago.

Once he was in, Quinn spent thirty minutes going over the list of potential missing persons that could be Taggert. He was even able to cross half of them off his list.

Before he went further, Quinn opened another window, and used it to access MapQuest for the

U.S. He typed 'Campobello, Nevada' in the appropriate field, then hit Return. He was greeted with a map for Campobello, South Carolina. He tried again, but got the same results.

He switched from Mapquest to Google. For his next task, a simple search engine would be enough. He typed 'Campobello, Nevada' into the subject line, then clicked on Search.

Within seconds, he was presented with a list of over ten thousand hits, but none of them were for a Campobello, Nevada. The hits had keyed in on either the word 'Campobello' or the word 'Nevada' but not both. He scrolled through the first couple of pages. In Italy there was a city named Campobello di Mazara on the island of Pantelleria. Italy also produced a product line called Campobello Riserva Olive Oil & Balsamic Vinegar. Probably from the same region.

In Canada there was a Campobello Island, where Franklin Roosevelt had had a summer retreat. There was a Campobello's Pizzeria in St. Louis, and a Campobello Lodge at the Bar-N-Ranch in West Yellowstone. But no Campobello, Nevada.

Quinn rolled his shoulders back, stretching. He moved his head from side to side and was greeted with a loud pop as his upper vertebrae realigned.

Since Campobello didn't seem to be getting him anywhere, he decided to check if he'd received any e-mail yet. He brought the window forward and clicked the Refresh button.

There was one message. He clicked on the link to open it.

501587331861xc2

All right, Quinn thought.

He went to a park nearby. The sun was shining, and the temperatures had risen a bit. But it was still cold, so there were few other people about.

Quinn pulled his phone out of his pocket. He used the code Orlando had given him to extract a phone number from the Mole's message, then punched the number into his phone. The other end rang once before someone picked up. There was no greeting, just silence broken by the faint sound of breathing.

'This is Quinn.'

'How do I . . . know?' The voice was flat, electronic, and seemed to pause unnaturally at odd moments. Quinn guessed that it was being run through some sort of digital filter to disguise the speaker's identity.

'You don't,' Quinn answered truthfully. 'How do I know you are who I think you are?'

'You don't.'

Quinn said, 'Have you figured out what was on the slide in the bracelet?'

There was a long silence. 'Like I said before, how do . . . I know you are . . . really Quinn?'

'You don't, dammit. You're going to have to trust me.'

'Trust,' the voice said, 'is not something . . . I do.'

'You trust Orlando, and she trusted me enough to tell me how to get in touch with you.'

'Perhaps you got it out of . . . her through . . . other means.'

'Oh for God's sake,' Quinn said. 'Either you believe me or you don't.'

'Where is she?'

'Safe.'

'You've . . . seen her recently?'

'About an hour ago.'

More silence. 'There was word she . . . was dead.'

'There was word I was dead, too.'

'So you've heard.'

'Can we get on to why I called?'

There was movement on the other side of the phone. The Mole undoubtedly shifting position.

'The slide was . . . very damaged . . . it . . . is taking us some . . . time . . . maybe in a . . . few days . . . I'll e-mail you . . . when to call me.'

'Wait,' Quinn said, sensing the Mole was about to hang up. 'What about the inscription on the bracelet?'

'It also . . . is providing a challenge.'

'So you don't have anything yet?'

'Not . . . yet.'

Quinn had been hoping for a little news, something that would at least put them on the right track. 'Okay,' Quinn said. 'I have another request.'

'What,' the voice said, 'do you want?'

Quinn told him.

Chapter 26

Somewhere an alarm was ringing, not a bedside alarm, but something more robust. More urgent. Quinn opened his eyes. It took him a moment to reorient himself. The bed he was lying on was harder and narrower than he was used to. And he was on his side; that wasn't normal. Then he remembered. He wasn't on a bed at all. He was sleeping on the couch in the suite at the Mandola.

He lifted his head and glanced at the digital clock sitting on the end table: 3:43 a.m.

'What's that noise?'

Quinn looked toward the voice. Orlando was standing in the doorway to the bedroom, an oversized T-shirt and a pair of sweatpants serving as her pajamas.

Quinn sat up, focusing his attention on the alarm. It wasn't coming from inside the hotel room, but rather from the hallway beyond.

'Fire alarm,' he said, suddenly alert.

He pushed himself off the couch and walked quickly toward the front door. As he did so, he sniffed the air, trying to detect any smoke. The air seemed as fresh as it had been when he'd gone to sleep. He placed a hand on the door.

'It's still cool,' he said.

In the hallway beyond, Quinn could hear people running and calling to each other over the drone of the alarm. It was the panicked sound of people who had been ripped from their sleep into a dangerous situation.

'This doesn't feel right,' Orlando said.

'Get dressed,' Quinn said. He'd had the same thought as she did. 'And grab your stuff.'

His own clothes were draped over a chair near the couch. He pulled them on in record time. He then stuffed his new purchases into his backpack, pulled on his coat, and threw his bag over his shoulders, cinching it tight.

Moments later Orlando, now dressed, rejoined him in the living room. Quinn crossed back to the door and listened again. The alarm was still clanging loudly, but the sounds of movement and voices in the hallway were gone. He hesitated. There were only two possibilities. Either the fire was real or it wasn't. And if it wasn't, that meant this was a flush. Quinn wouldn't even consider the possibility that it was just a false alarm. That would be too much of a coincidence. And believing in coincidences, like indulging in curiosity, was just one more thing on a long list of items that could get you killed.

So if this was a flush, that meant Borko suspected Quinn and Orlando were in the building but didn't know where. Fire or flush, it didn't matter. The solution was the same. Get out.

Quinn undid the deadbolt, then eased the door

open. Only a crack at first, just enough to peer outside.

'It's empty,' he said.

He pulled off his backpack, unzipped the flap, and retrieved the Glock he'd taken off of Duke.

'Here,' he said, handing the gun to Orlando.

She released the magazine and checked to see if it was loaded.

'I'm down a round,' she said.

Quinn pulled one of the spare mags for the SIG from his bag, and released one of the 9mm rounds.

'Catch,' he said as he tossed it to her.

He returned the mag to his bag, then slipped the bag over his shoulders. From his jacket pocket, he pulled out his own weapon.

Gun in hand, he gave Orlando a quick nod, then opened the door all the way and stepped into the hall. No smoke, no smell of smoke, no sign of fire at all. Only the two of them in the otherwise empty corridor.

There were two stairways, one at each end of the floor. Quinn had examined each soon after they'd arrived. The one to his left, the west stairwell, went from the top floor to ground level. The one to his right went all the way up to the roof.

Quinn motioned toward his right, then headed down the hallway; Orlando trailed right behind him, watching their back. Once inside the stairwell, they paused and listened for a moment. Someone else was on the stairs, maybe two people. They were several floors below, but Quinn couldn't tell whether they were going up or down.

Quinn and Orlando went up.

The entrance to the roof was located three floors above their room. It took them only forty-five seconds to get there. Again, they paused, listening.

Steps. Perhaps four floors below, definitely heading in their direction.

'Hotel security?' Orlando whispered.

'Maybe,' Quinn said. But they both knew they couldn't take that chance.

A sign on the door to the roof warned that an alarm would sound if it was opened. Quinn guessed it couldn't be any worse than the alarm that was still ringing throughout the hotel. He pushed the door open, and, as promised, a second alarm went off. But it was merely an electronic bleep that could barely be heard above the din of the fire alarm.

Once outside, Quinn pushed the door shut behind them and looked around. The roof was a large flat space with vents and pipes sticking up here and there.

To their right was Leipziger Strasse. Quinn hurried over to the edge of the roof and peered down. Three fire trucks were parked in front of the hotel. Not far away, dozens of people were huddled together, trying to stay warm. A moment later Orlando was at his side.

'Who are they?' she asked, pointing to a group of three men standing off to one side.

Unlike most of the guests, the men were fully dressed in warm, dark clothing. Two of them seemed to be watching the building. The third was talking on a cell phone. They could have been with the fire department or hotel security. But where were their uniforms?

'Whoever they are, I don't think they're looking for a fire,' Quinn said. 'Come on.'

He stuffed his gun into the pocket of his jacket, then headed to the east end of the roof. Unfortunately, the Mandola was a stand-alone building and didn't butt up against any other structure. But the top floor of the hotel did boast luxury suites with open-air patios only ten feet below the roof. It was something.

'You first,' Quinn said.

Without a word, Orlando slipped over the edge and dropped to the patio below. As soon as she had scrambled out of the way, Quinn climbed up onto the elevated lip that surrounded the edge of the roof. He was just beginning to lower himself over the side when a voice called out, *'Stop!'*

Quinn let go.

His feet landed on the tiled deck of one of the patios, barely missing a chaise lounge. His pursuer was seconds behind him and knew exactly where he'd come down.

'He saw me,' Quinn whispered.

But it was unnecessary. Orlando was already on the move. She quickly climbed over the dividing wall onto the patio of the suite to Quinn's left.

Quinn was closer to the one on the right. So he climbed onto the wall at the edge of the patio, then tight-roped his way onto the next deck. He got down and ducked out of sight just as a dark form appeared over the edge of the roof.

Quinn watched the form from his hiding place against the wall that separated the patios of the suites. The man was speaking into a phone.

'I don't know,' the man was saying in German. 'He went over the side, but I don't see him.'

Quinn's pursuer removed the phone from his ear and slipped it into a pocket. He leaned over the edge, peering intently at the patio beneath him. As he did so, a faint light from the street illuminated his features. Quinn placed him almost immediately. He was one of the two men in the photograph Orlando had taken, the photo of the men who'd put the information from Duke under Quinn's door at the Dorint.

Above Quinn, Borko's man swung his legs over the edge of the roof. He dropped down onto nearly the same spot where Quinn had landed. The wall that separated the patios ran diagonally from the retaining wall at the edge of the building up to the roof. Good for cover, but it also now blocked Quinn's view of the man.

Quinn checked to be sure the suppressor was firmly attached to his gun.

There was a patio chair only a few feet away. Quinn reached over and gave it a push, then pressed himself tightly against the dividing wall as the chair scraped loudly across the tile.

Almost instantly he heard the man's steps rushing toward the dividing wall. A moment later the man's head popped over the top. He was looking deep into the recesses of the patio. Quinn crouched directly below him, unseen, gun in hand.

The man jumped up on the retaining wall, his left hand grabbing the diagonal wall between the suites to keep his balance. To his right was a drop of nine stories.

'You can stop now,' Quinn said in German.

His pursuer started to whip around, a gun in his free hand. 'I'll kill you before you have a chance,' Quinn said.

The man stopped, still gripping the dividing wall with his left hand.

'Drop your gun,' Quinn ordered.

The man remained motionless.

'Do it,' Orlando said.

The man jerked his head in her direction, nearly losing his balance in the process. She was standing only a few feet away from him on the patio they had all jumped down on.

'Careful,' she said. 'It's a long way down.'

The man looked from her back to Quinn, a rueful smile on his face. 'So you found each other,' he said.

'The gun,' Quinn said.

The man opened his hand and allowed the pistol to fall over the edge of the building toward the sidewalk below. So this one wasn't one of Duke's incompetent recruits. He was obviously a pro.

'Am I staying up here?' the man asked coolly. 'Or may I come down?'

'You can relax right where you are,' Quinn told him. 'For the moment.'

'Now what? We just wait here until my friends arrive?'

'So they can kill us?' Quinn asked. 'I don't think so.'

'Why would we kill you? Those were not our instructions.'

'Right,' Orlando said.

'You don't believe me?' The man started to reach into his pocket.

'Don't,' Quinn said.

'I'm just getting my phone.'

Quinn thought about it for a moment. Then he nodded. 'Slowly.'

'*Bleiben Sie dran,*' the man said into the phone. He held the instrument out to Quinn.

'Toss it to me,' Quinn said.

The man did so.

'What?' Quinn said into the telephone.

'Quinn?'

There was no mistaking the voice. 'Hello, Borko.'

'I understand you are entertaining a friend of mine,' Borko said.

'And I believe you have one of mine. Where is he?'

'How should I know?'

Quinn hit the end-call button and tossed the phone back to the man, who just barely managed to keep it from flying past him over the side of the building. 'I'm not interested in playing games.'

Immediately the phone rang. Before Quinn could stop him, the man answered, then held the phone out again. 'He wants to talk.'

'Tell him to go to hell.'

The man repeated Quinn's instructions. He listened for a moment, nodding, then looked at Quinn. 'He says to tell you Nate is still alive.'

When Quinn had the phone again, he said, 'Make it fast.'

'What Gregory just told you is true,' Borko said. 'Your friend Nate is one of my guests.'

'Then let him go.'

'Turn yourself in to us, and I will.'

'Why don't I believe you?'

Borko didn't reply immediately. 'You know,' he said, breaking the silence. 'You are a very talented individual. You've really surprised me.'

'Sorry I haven't made myself an easier target.'

'That's good. You are a challenge. Too bad we aren't working together.'

'That will never happen.'

'Never?'

'Believe it,' Quinn said. 'Let Nate go.'

'Are you going to let Gregory bring you in?'

'You know I'm not.'

'Then I think I might keep him for a little while longer. Until I'm sure you won't be a problem.' Borko paused. 'If you won't turn yourself in, my advice to you is to get out of town. Forget about your friend. If that happens, once I am finished here, he will be free to go where he wants.'

'And my advice to you is to go fuck yourself.'

There was silence. Then Borko said, 'If you need a little more motivation to leave us alone, you should have your girlfriend call home.'

'What the hell does that mean?' Quinn asked, unable to keep himself from glancing at Orlando.

But there was no answer. Borko had already hung up.

As Quinn closed the phone, he thought he heard something on the roof above them. Footsteps, still distant but getting closer.

Gregory smiled at Quinn. 'We seem to have company.'

Gregory's hand moved quickly to his side. Suddenly there was a knife in his hand. Quinn wasn't sure whose bullet hit Gregory first, his or Orlando's. With a look of surprise, Borko's man sailed backward over the edge, arcing upward first, then plummeting into the darkness below.

Chapter 27

They moved through the suite, down the main hallway, and into the west stairwell. There they took the stairs down to the first floor, one floor above ground level. Slipping into the corridor, Quinn spotted four firemen at the far end of the hallway. He motioned for Orlando to wait in the stairwell, then he strode toward the men.

'Who are you?' one of them called out in German, challenging him. They were all roughly the same size, within an inch or two of Quinn's own height, and fully outfitted in fire gear.

'What have you found?' Quinn said, sounding like it was his right to ask.

Another of the firemen spoke up. 'Nothing.'

'It could be a false alarm,' Quinn said. 'But we need to be certain, yes? Two of you come with me. The other two keep looking to make sure you haven't missed anyone.'

'Who are you?' the first one asked again.

'Criminal Investigations. Whoever pulled that alarm did it deliberately. I need to find him and find out why. I suggest we get moving.'

'Yes, sir. Absolutely,' the first fireman said. 'I will stay with you.'

'So will I,' the man next to him said.

The other two moved off down the hallway. Quinn led the volunteers back to the west stairwell.

Quinn and Orlando discarded the firemen's gear behind the IMAX theater at Potsdamer Platz. The outfits would undoubtedly be found and reunited with their owners once the men explained how they got knocked out and stripped of their clothes.

The gear had provided Quinn and Orlando with the perfect cover. And even though the outfit Orlando wore was several sizes too big, no one had noticed a couple more firemen walking out of the Mandola.

They walked nearly a mile before Quinn felt it was safe to hail a taxi. 'Where can I take you?' the driver asked, once they had climbed into the back.

'Neukölln,' Quinn said.

They found a vacant store on Karl Marx Strasse, less than a mile from the water plant on Schandauer Strasse. Using his lock picks, Quinn was able to open the back door.

'No one's been here for a while,' Orlando said.

She was right, Quinn noted. There was a fine layer of dust over everything, disturbed only by the footprints they had created when they entered.

Quinn passed through the short hallway into the modest showroom that made up the front half of the store. It was occupied only by a few empty display cases and a cardboard box full of trash. The windows were covered with white paint, preventing anyone outside from looking in.

Suddenly a dim light came on from somewhere behind him.

'Did you do that?' Quinn called out.

'In here,' Orlando said from the back of the building.

Quinn retraced his steps and found her in a room off the hallway. There was a single low-wattage bulb glowing from a fixture in the ceiling. Orlando flipped a switch and the light went off. Another flip and it was back on.

'It's the only one that works,' she said.

The room they were in had once served as either a storage room or a large office. It was at least fifteen feet across and ten wide.

'We can set up in here,' she said. 'Get a few sleeping bags, maybe some air mattresses. Just like home.'

The mention of home made Quinn pause.

'On the other side of the hall there's a bathroom,' Orlando went on. 'I checked the water. It's still running. It's only cold, though.'

'Orlando,' Quinn said.

She looked over at him. 'What?'

He glanced at the floor, buying himself an additional moment to collect his thoughts. 'Borko said something to me,' he began. 'It's probably just a bluff.'

She was staring at him now, her eyes unblinking. 'What did he say?'

'He said if we needed any more reason to back down, I should tell you to . . .' Quinn paused.

'What? Tell me what?'

'Tell you to call home.'

Her gaze passed through him for a moment, her face blank. When she took a step toward him, her movement was so sudden it surprised Quinn.

'Give me your phone,' she said.

'He was probably lying.'

She reached for his jacket, grabbing at one of his pockets. 'Give it to me!'

'Wait,' he said, pushing her back. 'It's not there. I'll get it for you.'

He pulled off his backpack, set it on the floor, and kneeled beside it. From one of the smaller zippered pouches he removed his phone. Before he could even move, she grabbed it out of his hand.

Within seconds she had it open and a number already punched in. She waited with the phone pressed against her ear for nearly a minute, then disconnected the call and input another number. This time someone answered.

She spoke rapidly in Vietnamese, and though Quinn couldn't understand what was being said, he could tell by the rising anxiety in her voice that it couldn't be good. When she finally finished, the hand holding the phone fell to her side and her eyes closed.

'Tell me,' Quinn said.

She opened her mouth, but instead of speaking she sucked in a convulsive breath. When she opened her eyes, they were watery but no tears escaped.

'What is it?' he asked.

She tried to speak, her mouth moving, but nothing coming out. Her body began to shake, and the tears finally began to stream down her cheeks.

'Garrett,' she finally said, her voice a forced whisper. 'He's gone.'

It took a while, but Quinn finally got the whole story. It was Mr. Vo, Orlando's assistant at the relief agency, she'd talked to. Apparently he had tried calling Orlando several times, but because her phone was one of the items she'd left during her escape, he hadn't been able to reach her. Trinh, the nanny, was in the hospital. Mr. Vo said she had been beaten badly. A concussion, broken leg, cuts, and bruises. No one knew exactly what had happened. Trinh had been in and out of consciousness, then had been drugged to allow her body to heal. What she had been able to say was that it had been at least two men – one Asian and one Caucasian. It had been in a park while Garrett played. When she awoke, she was in the hospital and Garrett was gone.

The only clue came in the form of a simple business card slipped carefully into Trinh's pocket as she lay bleeding on the grass. Like those left on the victims of the disruption, there was but a single word on it. Instead of pronouncing the word, Mr. Vo had carefully spelled it out so that he wouldn't get it wrong. 'D-a-h-l,' he had said.

Quinn's head began to spin as he processed this. Dahl? In Vietnam? Why? And was it even possible? The idea was almost too bizarre to accept. But the card was proof. Just as with the disruption, he wanted them to know who was responsible.

'We have to find Borko,' Orlando said. 'Right now. We'll force him to take us to Dahl.'

'We don't even know if Dahl is in Germany,' Quinn said.

'I don't care. We have to go. We have to find Garrett.' She was frantic now, her eyes darting around the room. Her body moved from side to side, her hands touching her arms, her shoulders, her face. But her feet remained rooted to the floor, paralyzed with indecision.

Quinn took a deep breath, hoping she would do the same. He needed her to calm down and think more rationally. He tried to put a hand on her shoulder, but she shook it off. 'We will find him,' he said, keeping his voice soft and even. 'But think it through. It's not even dawn yet. We don't know where Borko is, or even what Dahl looks like.'

'We can't just sit here.'

'Yes,' Quinn said. 'We can.' This time he put a hand on each of her shoulders and held on as she attempted to remove them. 'Orlando, we have to be smart about this. Rushing will hurt more than help. That's probably what they're hoping for anyway.'

'No,' she said, trying to twist away from him. 'They have my son!'

He pulled her to him, putting his arms around her and holding her tight as she fought him. Slowly, she began to stop pulling away. She leaned her head against his chest. There was no sobbing, though, just the deep, rapid breathing of panic and anger.

'Listen to me,' Quinn said. 'Gathering information, then operating from a position of strength. This is what we do.'

She looked up at him. 'You just want us to do nothing and wait?'

'Wait, yes. Do nothing?' He shook his head. 'No way.'

Neither of them said anything for over a minute. Finally, Orlando pushed herself away from him. But it was gentler; the fight had temporarily gone from her.

'God knows what they're doing to Garrett right now,' she said. 'We should get help. You can use your contacts at the Agency.'

'They won't do anything to him,' Quinn said. 'Garrett's too valuable. They'll only do anything if Dahl thinks we're becoming too much of a problem. That's why we can't call anyone. You know that. Garrett's best chance is with us. No one else.'

Her shoulders sagged, and he knew she realized he was right.

'I promise,' he said, 'the moment an opportunity to get Garrett comes up, one where we have a chance of succeeding, we'll take it. Until then we do things step-by-step. Okay?'

She didn't answer.

Quinn reached into his backpack and pulled out the small first-aid kit he carried. It was no more than a cloth bag with a zipper on top, about the size of an average eyeglass case. From inside he removed a small packet, opened it, and dumped two pills into his palm – sleeping pills. He held them out to her. 'I want you to take these.'

Her eyes narrowed, and she shook her head. 'No.'

'Take them,' Quinn said. 'You're not going to be able to help your son unless you're sharp. And you won't be sharp unless you get some sleep.'

'I said no.'

'Orlando. Please. He needs your help, and I need your help. But not when you're like this.'

'I don't want to,' she said, but her voice was low, not fighting him, just telling him.

'I know,' he said, still holding the pills out to her.

Finally she reached out and took them from his hand. She stared at them and then, without saying anything else, put them in her mouth and dry-swallowed them.

'We'll get him back. I swear to you we will.'

Without a word, she turned away and moved over to the wall, then sat down with her back against it. From inside her coat she pulled out something small and rectangular. She held it in her hand, staring at it until her eyes finally closed.

Once she was asleep, Quinn sat on the floor beside her. He looked over to see what she held so tightly in her hand. It was a plastic wallet insert, the kind that would hold several pictures. It was starting to slip out of her hand, so he gingerly picked it up with the intention of setting it on the floor beside her. Instead, he glanced down at the photo she'd been looking at. Garrett. He could have guessed as much. Most of the other pictures in the miniature album were of Garrett, too. Only the last one was different. A cropped image of the same photo sitting on the altar in Vietnam. Durrie.

Feeling like he was trespassing, he set the pictures on the floor.

To get his mind on something else, he pulled the remote viewing monitor from his backpack, setting it on his lap. The device wasn't much bigger than a typical hardback book, and only a half-inch thick. On the upper portion of the flat front surface was a color screen that provided sharp detail. Below the screen was a keypad, not unlike that of an accountant's calculator. The pad allowed its user to switch rapidly from one camera position to another. It also had an internal hard drive that would allow for several hours of multi-camera recording. There were two data ports for external devices to be connected, a built-in speaker, and a place to plug in a set of headphones.

Since his current position was well within the one-mile signal radius of the cameras, he expected to have no problem receiving an image. He turned the monitor on, then removed the set of Sennheiser earphones that went with it from his backpack. He plugged them into the audio slot and fit the earpieces into his ears.

Outside it was dark. The winter sun was still hours away from rising. Quinn shuffled through the views coming from the six cameras. Everything looked quiet. Exactly what he expected at this early hour. He turned the monitor off and set it on the ground.

His eyes grew heavy, and as he was falling asleep a thought grew in his mind, one that would shape his dreams over the next few hours.

What if I can't keep my promise?

By 10 a.m., Quinn was awake again, studying the monitor. Orlando, still asleep, had slumped onto her side. There was activity in the water plant now. Two men were moving through the sphere into the bio-containment room. They were wearing biohazard suits. Each was carrying a hard plastic case, about the size of a typical carry-on suitcase. Quinn recognized them as the cases he had seen sitting open in the basement room containing the refrigerator.

Once the men were in the center room, they set the cases on the stainless-steel counter. The taller of the two men went over and opened the door of the refrigerator nearest the room's entrance, while the other opened his case. The first man then returned to the counter and opened his own case. They began removing small cardboard boxes from inside and setting them on the table. It didn't take long. There were only a total of eight boxes.

They then took turns carrying the boxes one by one from the table to the refrigerator. It was all done very slowly, and very methodically.

On the second-to-last trip, one of the men stumbled. It wasn't much. There was no danger of spilling the contents of the box. Still, the other man rushed over and took the box from his companion's grasp. He quickly carried it back to the table and opened it. Leaning down for a closer look, he appeared to be checking that everything inside was all right.

After a moment, the man seemed to relax. Apparently everything was as it should be. As he was closing the box again, Quinn caught a glimpse of something inside. Balls or pellets or something similar. They were white.

The men put the two remaining boxes in the refrigerator, then closed the plastic cases they'd arrived with and stowed them under the counter. Their job seemingly finished, they departed.

Quinn waited another hour to see if anything else was going to happen. But the room remained empty.

'Coffee?' Quinn asked when Orlando finally stirred and sat up.

There was a market a couple of blocks away. Quinn had chanced leaving Orlando alone and had gone to get a few supplies. He'd also purchased two large cups of coffee to go from a kiosk inside the store.

'Sure,' she said, without much enthusiasm.

He handed her a cup. Once she'd taken a drink, he asked, 'How do you feel?'

'How do you think I feel?' She noticed the monitor sitting on the floor. 'You see anything?'

'Yeah,' he said, then told her about the two men and their activities in the containment room.

She was quiet for several seconds. 'What could this possibly have to do with Garrett? They don't really need him as insurance against us. That's what Nate's for, right?'

She was right, Quinn knew. Nate was all the insurance they should have needed. Taking Garrett had been overkill. More than overkill, it didn't make sense. Too much work would be involved in pulling it off.

'How did they know?' she asked.

Because I went to Vietnam, Quinn thought, unable to actually say the words.

But Orlando wasn't an idiot – she'd already made

the connection. 'Piper tipped him off, didn't he? Somehow he knew I was there and he tipped Dahl off.'

Quinn nodded. It was the same conclusion he'd come to. Piper wasn't as clean as he made himself out to be. Maybe he was working for Dahl directly. Maybe he and his team had followed Quinn to Vietnam. There was no telling what Piper had lied about. Except for Borko. But even that revelation hadn't made a difference in the end. If anything, it had lent credibility to Duke's job offer, sweetening the trap.

'I'm sorry.' Quinn wanted to say more, but couldn't find the words.

'Don't,' she said as she closed her eyes. 'I made a choice to come here. I should have stayed home. I should have protected him.'

If he wanted to, he could have continued the argument. Saying it was his fault Piper had found her in the first place. Then she would have found some other excuse for blaming herself, and they would go around once more.

Quinn took a step back. 'I need to check a few things out,' he said. 'Will you be all right here?'

'I can't just do nothing.'

'I'm not asking you to do nothing.' He picked the monitor up off the floor and handed it to her. He then motioned to the corner where he'd put the bag containing the items he'd bought at the store. 'If the power is getting low, there's some stuff in that bag you can use to rig a line down from the light socket. Otherwise, I need you to watch.'

* * *

Quinn was able to buy some computer time at the Berlin Hotel, then logged on to the e-mail account he'd created the day before. As he had hoped, there was a message from the Mole.

36.241.10

Keeping himself on the move, he took a cab to KaDeWe. It was Berlin's largest department store, and, with the exception of Harrods in London, the largest in all of Europe. It was located near the Kaiser Wilhelm Memorial Church. He took a table in the café, then used the code the Mole had sent him to adjust the previous phone number to a new one.

'It's Quinn,' he said once the connection was made. 'What have you got?'

'Taggert,' the Mole said.

'You know who he is?' Quinn asked.

'There's still a question of payment.'

Quinn scowled. 'How much?'

'My standard fee . . . is five K per request . . . you've . . . made two requests . . . that's ten thousand . . . U.S.'

'I'm good for it.'

'Not if you're dead,' the Mole said.

'I'll wire you the money. E-mail me your information.'

'When?'

'As soon as I get your info.'

There was a brief silence from the other end of the line. 'A viral biologist by the name of . . . Henry Jansen has been MIA for months . . . he fits the description . . . of your . . . victim in Colorado.'

'Maybe,' Quinn said. 'But that fire was only two weeks ago.'

'I can't help you with . . . your time line . . . but the . . . maiden name of his paternal grandmother . . . was Roberts . . . you want . . . to guess the maiden name of his . . . maternal grandmother?'

'Taggert?'

'Well done.'

'Any way you can get me a picture?'

'Sending the e-mail now.'

'And the other matter?' Quinn asked.

'The International Organization . . . of Medical Professionals.'

'IOMP,' Quinn said, impressed.

'They are . . . about to hold their annual . . . convention.'

'Where?'

'Berlin,' said the Mole.

Of course, Quinn thought. *Where else would it be?*

'I have another request for you,' Quinn said. 'And before you say anything, I'll include the additional payment in the wire transfer.'

'Go on.'

Quinn told him about the abduction of Garrett. 'See if you can find any signs of Orlando's son. He may have been taken out of Vietnam. If so, somebody must have seen something. Hell, maybe you can figure out why Dahl would want him in the first place.'

'I will . . . try.' The Mole paused. 'The inscription.'

'You figured it out?'

'Most . . . it is an FTP address . . .' A file transfer

protocol site. 'The inscription . . . includes the user . . . name . . . but the password has . . . been destroyed.'

'Have you tried to hack in?'

'Of course . . . but the security is . . . unusually tight.'

'Text message me the information,' Quinn said.

'Hold.'

A few seconds later, Quinn's phone beeped. Message received.

'Got it,' Quinn said. 'What about the slide? Is it a tissue sample?'

'Yes . . . damaged.'

'By the fire?'

'Not the . . . fire . . . by something from . . . the inside.'

Quinn sucked in a breath.

'There is . . . still uncertainty about the actual . . . identity of what . . . caused it to happen . . . it is complicated . . . we should . . . have that maybe by . . . tomorrow . . . but I can . . . tell you one thing.'

'What?'

'It is a virus.'

Chapter 28

Quinn found Internet access at a small coffee shop a couple of blocks from KaDeWe. The Mole's promised picture of Henry Jansen was waiting for him. Quinn recognized the face in the picture immediately. Taggert and Jansen were indeed the same man. He spent the next fifteen minutes trying to get into the FTP site. He attempted variations on 'Taggert' and 'Jansen' and 'virus.' He typed in the birthday that had been listed on his driver's license, and '215 Yancy Lane' – the address of the house Taggert had stayed at in Colorado before it had burned down with him inside. He even tried 'Campobello,' thinking for a moment that had to be it. But nothing worked.

Outside again, he called Peter.

'You either help now, or we're done,' Quinn said.

'Is that a threat?' Peter asked.

'Absolutely.'

Peter didn't say anything for a moment. 'Do you remember four years ago?' he asked. 'Montevideo.'

'Ramos,' Quinn said.

Ramos was a local politician who'd run afoul of

a drug cartel. It was apparently in someone's interests to help him out, so the Office was hired to assassinate the head of the cartel. Quinn made a few bodies disappear when things didn't go as planned. 'What about it?' Quinn asked.

'Your contact on the operation.'

Quinn thought for a moment. 'Burroughs. Some kind of Agency or NSA guy, wasn't he?'

'Something like that.'

'So?'

'He'll have some answers for you,' Peter said.

'Where do I find him?'

'He's working out of NATO headquarters.'

That gave Quinn pause. 'In Brussels?'

'Yes,' said Peter.

'Maybe you're just trying to set me up again,' Quinn said. 'Couldn't get me in Berlin, you're taking another shot.'

'That's up to you to decide.'

'Will you still be here when I get back?' Quinn asked.

He had returned to the abandoned store in Neukölln, stopping on the way to purchase a couple of sleeping bags, blow-up mattresses, and two lightweight folding chairs. Orlando was in the room where they'd spent the night, sitting on the floor and staring intently at the portable monitor. He told her about what the Mole had learned. He then wrote down the FTP site address and the user name on a piece of paper, in case she had the chance – or more accurately the inclination – to try her hand at getting in. Finally, he recounted his conversation with Peter.

'Will you?' he repeated.

'You're kidding, right?' she said. 'If I learn something that will help me get Garrett back, I'm not staying.'

'Even if it made more sense for us to act together?'

Her eyes turned steely. 'We're talking about my son,' she said. 'Don't you understand that? The moment there's even a hint of where he is, I'm gone.'

Quinn crouched down and put a hand on her knee. 'I do understand. I'm just saying he has a better chance if we go after him together.'

She stood up and started to walk out of the room.

'Orlando,' he said.

She stopped, but didn't turn to look at him.

'Just wait here for me.'

Her breathing became deep and angry, but she didn't say no.

He rented a car and drove southwest out of Berlin into the German countryside. The recent snowstorm had created a landscape of white, but the roads were clear and traffic was moving quickly.

As he drove, he worked out his plan for Brussels. No way Quinn could approach Burroughs directly. Though they'd worked on the same team in South America, Burroughs had made his contempt for freelancers clear. He was an arrogant asshole who seemed to think his position with the government made him somehow better than the 'barely necessary scum' he was forced to associate with.

Then there was the whole Peter issue. If he'd gone bad, Quinn could be walking into another trap. So simply calling Burroughs ahead to set up a meeting was out.

But that was fine. There were ways around the problem.

After midnight, Quinn left the car in a parking garage in downtown Frankfurt. He hailed a taxi and had it take him to a hotel near the airport. Prior to going to his room, he used the twenty-four-hour business center on the hotel's first floor to check his e-mail.

Quinn accessed his primary e-mail account. There was only one message in the in-box. There were two files attached, both jpegs. He clicked to open the first one.

His eyes narrowed, and his jaw tensed.

It was a picture of Nate. He was sitting in a metal chair, tied in place. His face was battered, his eyes half open. Propped up on his lap was a copy of the *International Herald*. It was that morning's edition. An old technique, but still effective. It was proof of life, conveying that, as of that morning, Nate was still alive.

Afraid of what the second file might reveal, but knowing he had to look, he opened it. It was a picture of Garrett. But unlike Nate, the boy appeared unharmed. The image was a profile shot of Garrett sitting on a carpeted floor, eyes glued to a cartoon playing on a large TV. The room he was in was not familiar to Quinn. It was definitely not taken in one of the rooms at Orlando's apartment. In fact, it didn't look like Vietnam at all.

Beyond Garrett was a window, its curtain pulled open. Through it, Quinn could see another building not far away. The roof of the neighboring building was covered with snow. And then there was the sky. Heavy, gray, and cloudy. If Quinn were to venture a guess, a particularly German sky.

But maybe that's what the sender wanted him to think. Faking a picture these days was easy. Give a halfway decent computer artist a copy of Photoshop and he could have put Garrett almost anywhere.

Of course it wasn't really the setting that mattered. It was the message that both the picture of Garrett and the one of Nate represented: 'Don't fuck with us.'

Still, if the picture hadn't been faked, there was always the possibility someone could narrow down the location. The chances were slim, but it was worth checking. Quinn opened a new message, attached the picture, then wrote:

Yes, this is another request.
Need location in photo.
JQ

He sent it to the Mole, then downloaded each picture to his memory stick.

He caught an 8:00 a.m. flight to Brussels. That was the easy part. Getting to Burroughs was still the challenge. What Quinn needed was a conduit. Someone Burroughs could trust, or if not trust, at least not suspect of doing something out of the ordinary. Quinn knew just the man to help him out.

Finding Kenneth Murray's flat was not difficult. A simple hack job using a computer at an Internet café to break into the NATO personnel records and obtain Murray's home address was all it took.

Quinn located the flat, then found a quiet café and enjoyed a leisurely lunch. Having left his gun in Berlin, he spent an hour in the afternoon securing a firearm from one of his local contacts. Once he was rearmed, there was nothing else to do. So he took a cab to Murray's apartment and let himself in.

It appeared as though Murray were living alone again. His second wife, a Flemish woman named Ingeborg, had left him several years before. Soon after, a Turkish secretary who worked at NATO had moved in. But there was no sign of her presence now.

The flat had a definite male feel. The living room was dominated by a large television. Murray liked sports, that much Quinn remembered. American sports, football and baseball mainly. Along the other walls were shelves and bookcases. Souvenirs of Murray's many postings shared space with rows of books, few of which Murray had probably read. The great philosophers section. The historical section. The sensitive man section. Each designed to impress, whether it be a coworker, a boss, or a date.

Quinn moved into the kitchen. It was neat and organized. Not surprisingly, the refrigerator was all but empty. A bottle of chardonnay, cream for coffee. No food. Murray was one of those types who ate every meal out.

Down the hallway, on the other side of the living room, were two bedrooms. The larger contained a double bed, a black lacquer dresser, and an elaborate stereo cabinet that housed a top-of-the-line audio system.

The other room was a home office complete with desk, computer, printer, and scanner. Murray's private lair and, apparently, a room he never shared with anyone. Neatness here was no longer necessary. Stacks of papers, files, and books everywhere.

Quinn thought about switching on the computer and getting onto the net so he could make another attempt at the FTP site, but there was a good chance someone somewhere monitored Murray's surfing activities. Murray wasn't the most important man at NATO, but he was important enough to draw interest from several different directions.

Quinn returned to the kitchen, poured himself a glass of wine, then carried it into the living room. He found the remote and switched on the TV.

No sense being bored all afternoon, he thought as he settled down in one of Murray's chairs.

Kenneth Murray returned home at ten minutes past eight that evening. His hairline had receded a bit since Quinn had seen him last, but otherwise he was the same old Murray, blessed with one of those faces that blended easily into crowds. Not too tall, not too short. He was the perfect go-between man.

Half an hour earlier, Quinn had turned off the TV. He was sitting in the darkened living room, finishing off a second glass of wine, when the door opened. At first, Murray didn't notice Quinn as he entered the flat and turned on the light. Humming softly to himself, he placed his keys in a ceramic bowl on a stand next to the door, then turned toward his living room.

'Working late?' Quinn asked.

Murray slammed back against the door in surprise. He sucked in air, trying to catch his breath. 'Who the hell are you?'

'It hasn't been that long, has it, Ken?'

Murray's eyes grew wide. 'Quinn.'

'How are you doing?'

On two prior jobs, Murray had served as a secondary contact for Quinn. On each occasion they had met only once: the first time during a soccer game in Ostend, the second time over dinner in a café near Murray's previous apartment. Murray had struck Quinn as the nervous type. All talk when it came to impressing the women, but little substance when it came to any real action.

Somehow he had gotten it into his mind that Quinn killed people for a living. Quinn had decided not to set him straight. Both times they met, Murray had seemed to want to get it over with as quickly as possible.

'What are you doing here?' Murray asked.

‘I thought maybe we could have a chat.’

Murray’s eyes darted toward the kitchen, then toward the back hall. ‘Are you alone?’

‘For the moment.’

The reply did little to ease the tension in Murray’s face. ‘What do you want to talk about?’

Quinn casually stood up. As he did so, Murray backed away a few feet along the wall. ‘Please, Ken. What do you think’s going on here?’ Quinn asked. ‘Do you think I want to hurt you?’

‘I don’t know what you want to do,’ Murray said. ‘But I’m pretty familiar with what you can do.’

‘We’re on the same side, buddy. I just came to talk.’ Quinn nodded toward the couch. ‘Have a seat. I’ll get you a glass of wine. Okay?’

‘I’m fine.’

‘It’ll help you relax.’

Quinn waited until Murray broke away from the wall and sat down. ‘See?’ said Quinn. ‘That wasn’t so hard.’

He walked into the kitchen and pulled the bottle of wine out of the refrigerator. From an overhead cupboard he removed a wineglass and carried it and the bottle into the living room. He sat back down in the chair he’d been in when Murray arrived and poured a generous amount of wine into the glass.

‘Here.’ He held it out to Murray. ‘It’s good. I’ve had some myself.’

Murray took the glass. With only the slightest hesitation, he raised it to his lips and took a big gulp.

‘Better?’ Quinn asked, as he sat back down.

Murray nodded slightly. 'Are you going to tell me what you want now?'

'Just talk.'

'That's it?'

'That depends on the talk.'

Murray took another drink. 'Are you here to kill me?'

'I don't kill people. Not unless I really need to.' Quinn cocked his head. 'Is there a reason I should need to?'

Murray shook his head vigorously. 'No.'

'Okay, then. You've got nothing to worry about.'

Murray relaxed a little more. 'You know,' he said, still with an undertone of nervousness, 'you really scared the shit out of me.'

Quinn remained silent.

'I mean, I thought maybe you were a burglar or something.'

Quinn still said nothing.

'I'm glad you're not.'

'I'm glad I'm not, too.'

'So.' Murray gave him a weak smile. 'What do you need?'

'I'm looking for someone.'

'Who?'

'Somebody who works at NATO. He probably came on recently.'

'What's his name?'

'Burroughs.'

'Mark Burroughs?' Murray asked, eyes widening.

'I take it you know him.'

'I can't help you,' Murray said quickly.

'That's disappointing.'

'Burroughs is into a lot of heavy stuff here. He's untouchable. I've been able to steer clear of him, and I really don't want to change that.'

Quinn leaned close, his face only a few feet from Murray's. 'And I was hoping I wouldn't have to tell anyone about that little incident in Lisbon you told me about.' Reflexively, Murray recoiled. 'Are you going to help me or not?'

Murray closed his eyes. 'Goddamn it, Quinn. Why the hell did you have to pick me?'

Quinn smiled. 'Because I knew I could count on you.'

After several phone calls, Murray learned that Burroughs was having dinner at Duquois, a small upscale restaurant downtown. 'There,' Murray said after he wrote the restaurant's address down and handed it to Quinn. 'Have a nice talk.'

'I think you may have misunderstood something, Ken,' Quinn said. 'You're coming with me.'

'No, I'm not,' Murray said.

Quinn smiled. 'Yes. You are.'

Chapter 29

A taxi dropped Quinn off one street away from Duquois thirty minutes later. He made a two-square-block inspection of the area surrounding the restaurant to be sure there wasn't anyone waiting for him to arrive. All appeared quiet.

Once inside the restaurant, he was shown to a table near the front door. He ordered a glass of mineral water and a stuffed mushroom appetizer. There was no need to look for Burroughs. Quinn had seen him the moment he walked in.

The spook was sitting in the far corner near the back. Quinn noticed that Burroughs's taste in companions hadn't changed. Burroughs liked them tall, he liked them blonde, and he liked them fake. He liked them young, too. Tonight's date couldn't have been more than twenty-four, at least a quarter century younger than Burroughs. The man himself hadn't changed, either. His unnatural tan was still capped by dyed black hair. As usual, he was wearing an expensive, European-tailored suit.

He and his date seemed to be near the end of their

main course. Quinn watched as a busboy approached their table and removed some dishes. A moment later a waiter brought over an unopened bottle of wine. He showed it to Burroughs, who nodded. While the waiter opened the wine, Burroughs returned to his conversation with the woman.

Quinn turned away when he heard the front door to the restaurant open. It was Murray. He stood nervously near the front, waiting to be helped. He started to glance toward Quinn but stopped himself, obviously realizing it wasn't a good idea. A moment later, the maitre d' looked up. Quinn watched as Murray spoke to the man, then they both glanced toward Burroughs.

The maitre d' turned back to Murray and asked a question. Murray replied, then slipped him some euros. This seemed to satisfy the maitre d', as he smiled and pocketed the bills. He held a hand up indicating for Murray to wait, then walked across the restuarant toward Burroughs.

When he reached the table, the maitre d' leaned down and whispered something in Burroughs's ear, pointing back toward Murray. Burroughs looked over, and Murray gave him a little wave. The look on Burroughs's face was not pleasant. He turned his attention to his date, said a few words, then stood up and followed the maitre d' back across the restaurant.

Once the two had passed him, Quinn placed enough money to cover his bill on the table, then rose and followed at a reasonable distance.

'What do you want?' Burroughs asked as soon as he reached Murray.

Quinn continued past them, stopping at the dessert counter and leaning forward to examine the cakes. He was just close enough to hear them.

'I'm Kenneth Murray. Strategic planning.'

'I know who you are,' Burroughs said. 'Why are you interrupting my dinner?'

Murray paused, no doubt uncomfortable that Burroughs knew his identity. 'There's an emergency that needs your attention,' he finally managed to eke out.

'What kind of emergency?'

'I don't know. I was still at the office, so I got volunteered for the run.'

'Why didn't someone just call me?'

'I was told it was too sensitive. It's got to be face-to-face.'

Burroughs seemed to ponder this. 'Okay. We're face-to-face. Give me whatever it is you've brought.'

'I'm not really the messenger. I got volunteered to be the chauffeur,' Murray said, sticking to the script Quinn had worked out for him. 'The information's with the captain in the car. I thought it would be less conspicuous if I came in. You know, instead of someone in a uniform.'

Burroughs scowled. 'Are you parked close by?'

'Across the street.'

'Hold on.' He turned and walked back to his table.

As soon as Burroughs was gone, Quinn looked at Murray, giving him the barest of nods. Murray looked like he was about to crumble.

Quinn glanced over his shoulder and saw that

Burroughs was talking to the blonde, no doubt telling her he'd be back in a few minutes.

That was Quinn's cue to leave.

A few minutes later, Quinn could hear their footsteps on the cobblestones. He was sitting in the passenger seat of Murray's car, back straight, like a good military messenger. He'd had Murray park as far as possible from any streetlights. While he could see them approaching on the sidewalk, they would only be able to make out his shadowy form in the car.

He waited until they were only a few feet away, then opened the door and got out.

'All right, Captain,' Burroughs began. 'I understand you have something for –'Burroughs stopped and stared at Quinn. 'Who the hell are you?' He turned and looked at Murray. 'What's going on here?'

'We've met before,' Quinn said.

Burroughs stiffened. 'We have?' Burroughs's eyes narrowed. 'I do know you, don't I?' he asked. 'Manila?'

'No. Montevideo,' Quinn said.

Burroughs began to nod. 'Ramos.'

'That's right.'

'You're Quinn.'

'Right again.'

'What do you want?'

'Why don't you get in the car? We'll have a little more privacy in there.'

Burroughs took a step backward, his eyes narrowing. 'I don't think so.'

Quinn pulled his gun out of his pocket. 'It may have sounded like it, but it wasn't actually a request.'

* * *

Murray drove around Brussels, while Quinn sat in back with Burroughs. 'They're going to come looking for me soon,' Burroughs said. 'You'll both be in deep shit.'

Quinn looked at him. 'Does it look like I care?'

'What do you want?'

'An exchange of information.'

'I don't deal.'

'Tell me about Robert Taggert.'

Burroughs looked at Quinn with contempt, but there had also been a flicker of what-the-fuck in the spook's eyes. 'Is that name supposed to mean something to me?'

'Try this one then. Henry Jansen?'

This time it was a twitch, just above Burroughs's left eye.

'It's a little confusing,' Quinn said. 'I mean, since they're the same person.'

Burroughs shrugged. 'Okay. If you say so. So what?'

'Jansen was supposed to give you some information,' he said. 'About an operation run by Borko.'

Burroughs stared hard at Quinn, then turned to Murray. 'Stop the car,' he commanded.

Murray, surprised, slammed on the brakes. Burroughs started to reach for the door. 'Hold on,' Quinn said calmly as he raised the gun. 'Ken, just keep driving.'

The car lurched forward as Murray pressed down on the accelerator.

'Stop the fucking car!' Burroughs snapped. Turning to Quinn, he said, 'I don't know what you're playing, but I'm getting out now.'

'Keep driving,' Quinn said. He raised his gun, aiming it at Burroughs's chest. 'If you think I'm kidding around, you're wrong. Some people I care about are in a lot of trouble because of whatever's going on. My personal rules of engagement aren't as strict as they used to be.'

Burroughs clenched his jaw. His fingers were still on the handle of the door. Quinn waited. It was obvious that Burroughs knew something he didn't want to share.

Finally, Burroughs let go of the handle and leaned back into the seat.

'Jansen. Taggert. You're right, okay? They're the same guy,' Burroughs said.

Quinn remained silent.

'And yes. He said he had come into some information that he wanted to pass on to us.'

'Who's us?' Quinn asked, moving the barrel of the gun a fraction of an inch to remind Burroughs it was there.

'The Agency. Who did you think?'

'What did he want to tell you?'

'If we knew that, he wouldn't have had to tell us, would he?'

'So, he never said anything about a biological sample he might have for you?'

'He wasn't specific about what he had.'

'That's all you knew?'

Burroughs hesitated, then said, 'He told us it was something tailored.'

Quinn furrowed his brow. 'What does that mean?'

'That's all he would say. We were meeting so he could give me the details.'

'Tell me about the meeting,' Quinn said.

'We were supposed to meet in Vail. On the slopes.'

'When?'

'The same day as the fire. I was in Vail, but Taggert didn't show up.'

'Didn't you know where he was staying?'

'No. He insisted on making those plans himself. The only thing he allowed us to do was arrange for someone to drive him around.'

'Protection?'

'We insisted.'

'And this chauffeur didn't tell you where he was?'

'She was instructed not to. Taggert was very nervous. We didn't want anything messing up the meet.'

She? 'Jills,' Quinn said.

'That's right. You were the one who found her, weren't you?'

Quinn stared at Burroughs for a moment, eyes narrowing. 'What's the Office's role in this?'

Burroughs seemed to gauge how much he wanted to say. 'I tell you this, and you have to tell me everything you know.'

'I did say this was an exchange, didn't I?'

Burroughs nodded. 'But you haven't shared anything with me yet.'

'You're right,' Quinn said. 'I haven't.'

'Quinn?' Murray said from the front seat.

'What?' Quinn asked.

'You told me to keep a lookout for anything unusual.'

'What is it?'

'I think we're being followed.'

Quinn swiveled around in his seat to look out

the back window. There were several cars behind them. 'Which one?' he asked.

'The sedan. Directly behind us.'

A dark Ford was two car lengths back. 'You're sure?' Quinn asked.

'I've made a couple of turns. He's staying right with us.'

'Do it again,' Quinn said. 'A quick turn at the next block. No signal.'

Quinn watched out the back window as Murray executed his instructions. The Ford continued to follow them.

'Again,' Quinn ordered. 'Left at the next street.'

The sedan stayed with them. Quinn turned to Burroughs, who had a look of satisfaction on his face. 'I told you they'd come for me.'

'Where the hell did they come from?' Murray asked.

'The blonde,' Quinn said. 'She works for you, doesn't she?'

Burroughs smiled but said nothing.

'The girl?' Murray asked.

'She probably saw us drive off with our friend here and called it in.'

'Sorry,' Burroughs said. 'It looks like we're done.'

'Lose them,' Quinn ordered Murray.

'Are you kidding?' Murray whined. 'You've already got me in deep enough shit as it is.'

'That's right, Ken,' Burroughs said. 'Don't make it worse.'

Quinn turned back to Burroughs. 'Keep quiet.'

'Fuck you,' Burroughs said. 'Ken, pull over, and I'll make sure they understand you did this against your will.'

Quinn lowered the angle of his gun and pulled the trigger.

Burroughs screamed in pain as the bullet tore through his right foot. It was all the message Murray needed. He pressed the accelerator to the floor.

Chapter 30

Quinn knew he had very little time left. He turned back to Burroughs. The man was still hunched over in pain, clutching his wounded foot.

Quinn shoved him back against the seat and glowered at him. 'You smug asshole. Believe it or not, until a few minutes ago I wasn't your enemy.' He thrust the barrel of the gun against Burroughs's right shoulder. 'This won't kill you either. But it'll hurt like hell.'

Burroughs raised a bloody hand defensively.

'This is no longer an exchange,' Quinn said. 'This is a one-way flow of information. From you to me. Got it?'

Burroughs nodded.

'Why was the Office called in?'

Grimacing, Burroughs said, 'Taggert was not considered a completely credible source. He'd cried wolf before. If something went wrong, we didn't want it boomeranging back to us. So they were running the protection.'

'Jills was working for the Office?'

'Yes.'

Something else Peter was keeping from him.

'What was Taggert up to?' Quinn asked. Burroughs's eyes darted toward the back window. 'Your friends are still there, if that's what you're wondering. Just talk.'

'He'd been working undercover. On his own.'

'A freelancer?'

'More of a lone wolf.'

'Doing what?'

'Research.'

'What kind of research?' Quinn asked.

'Biological research is what he said. He was a virologist by training.'

'So he was working with the people who were doing the . . . tailoring?'

'That's what he said.'

'And Borko was running things?'

'No,' Burroughs said. 'Jansen claimed Borko was just the muscle.'

'Then who?'

'Some guy named Dahl.'

'He must have told you more,' Quinn said. 'What is it? Smallpox? Ebola?'

'No, no,' Burroughs said. 'Neither of those. He told us that much ahead of time. Still, we weren't very inclined to believe him. Then he said he had tangible proof. That's why we gave him the meeting. But whatever proof he thought he had burnt with him in the fire.'

Or maybe not, Quinn thought, an image of the bracelet in his mind.

'It doesn't matter,' Burroughs continued.

'Why?'

'He was single-source. There was no other corroborating evidence,' Burroughs said. 'I already told you, Jansen was unreliable. All he wanted was the cash.'

Quinn let out a short, bitter laugh. 'You didn't believe him.'

'He'd made a lot out of nothing before. There was no reason why he wasn't doing it again. Besides, he told us Borko was involved. Our sources confirmed Borko has been out of commission for over a month.'

Quinn couldn't believe what he was hearing. 'But what about the murder? What about the disruption at the Office?'

'Just an interagency spat. Jansen got caught in the wrong place at the wrong time.'

'And that's what you believe?'

Burroughs was a bit slow to answer. 'Yes.'

'You're an idiot,' Quinn said. He looked out the back window. There were cars behind them, but he couldn't pick out the sedan. 'Did you lose them?' he asked Murray.

'I don't know,' Murray said. 'I think they're still back there, just not so close.'

'You're doing great. Let's see if you can put a little more distance between us.'

'Fuck,' Murray said. 'I'm a dead man.'

'I'll take care of it,' Quinn said. 'You'll be fine.'

'How the hell are you going to take care of it?' Murray asked, glancing back at Quinn.

'You'll just have to trust me.'

'So, what?' Murray asked. 'We drive around all night?'

'You're going to drop me off first,' Quinn said. 'After that, you might want to take a little vacation. A week should do it.'

'You son of a bitch,' Murray said.

'I can't help you if I'm in jail,' Quinn said.

'You'll never make it,' Burroughs said, his voice weak.

'Really?' Quinn asked. 'You better hope I do.' He peered through the windshield. 'Take that next right. Then at the next street right again.'

Murray did as Quinn ordered. As soon as they made the second turn, Quinn said, 'Over to the curb. *Now.*'

Murray pulled to the curb and jammed on the brakes. Quinn threw open the door. 'Don't worry,' he said as he climbed out.

'Fuck you,' Murray said.

Instead of flying directly out of Brussels, he drove to Amsterdam, where he caught the 7:20 a.m. KLM flight to Hamburg. There he took a train to Berlin, getting off at the Zoologischer Garten station. He made his way down through the station to the eastbound U2 platform, where he only had to wait a few minutes for the next train. He didn't take a direct route back. Instead he switched trains often, every time checking to make sure he wasn't being tailed. As far as he could tell, he wasn't.

He made it back to Neukölln by 1:30 p.m. The sidewalks on Karl Marx Strasse were filled with shoppers taking advantage of the relatively warm day. Quinn bought a couple of bratwurst sandwiches and two cans of Coke, then made his way back to the store on Karl Marx Strasse.

He almost expected Orlando to be gone, the store truly and completely abandoned. But when he opened the door and stepped inside, he could feel her standing beside him before he even saw her.

'I could have killed you,' she said.

He slowly turned to her. She was holding the Glock in her hand, pointing toward the floor at Quinn's feet. Her eyes were red, her face drawn and ashen. Quinn wondered if she'd slept at all while he was gone.

'Where the hell have you been?' she asked.

'Brussels,' he said. 'I told you that's where I was going.'

'I thought you'd be back yesterday.' Her red eyes flashed in anger.

'It took me a little longer than I'd hoped.'

He walked past her into the other room and sat down. From the bag, he pulled out one of the sandwiches. Orlando followed him in a moment later. He held the bag out to her.

'I've got one for you, too.'

She walked over to him, ignoring the bag. 'You should have called me.'

Quinn almost snapped back at her. But he held himself back. 'I'm sorry,' he said. 'You're right, I should have called.' He raised the bag a little. 'Take the sandwich.'

For a moment it looked like she was going to bat it out of his hand. Instead, she finally took the bag and sat cross-legged on the floor in front of him.

As they ate, he told her about his encounter with Burroughs. Orlando made no comments, only nodding on occasion.

'There's something else,' he said after he'd finished telling her about Brussels.

She looked at him expectantly.

'Before I got to Belgium, I received something in my e-mail.'

There was a spark in her eye. 'What?'

'I'll show you.'

He picked the portable monitor off the ground and set it in his lap. From his pocket, he removed his flash memory stick and inserted it into one of the ports on the side of the monitor. As he was doing so, Orlando moved around so she could see the screen, too. It only took him a moment to locate the pictures he'd downloaded in Frankfurt. He opened the one of Nate first.

Orlando drew in a breath at the sight of their injured colleague. 'He's alive,' she said.

'For the moment, he's more valuable that way.'

'I saw there were two files,' she said.

Quinn nodded slowly. Not wanting to, but not knowing any way to avoid it, he closed the picture of Nate and opened the other file.

This time Orlando actually gasped. 'Where is he?' she asked, grabbing at the screen.

'I don't know,' Quinn said. 'The photo might be doctored.'

She pulled the monitor close, her eyes less than a foot away from the image of her son.

'Does the picture look familiar?' Quinn asked. 'I don't mean the setting. Just Garrett's pose.'

'I've never seen it before,' she said, instantly understanding where he was going.

There was the possibility that Dahl's people had taken a photo from Orlando's home and changed the background. If that was the case, that could mean something worse than kidnapping had happened to Garrett, and Dahl had been forced to create the illusion that Garrett was still alive. But if Orlando didn't recognize any part of the photo, perhaps it was actually genuine.

'Where is he?' Orlando asked again. She looked at Quinn. 'Where the hell is he?'

'We'll find him,' Quinn said. 'I promise you.'

She stared at Quinn, her nostrils flaring. She seemed to be waiting for him to say something, but nothing he could think of would help the situation.

Finally, she said, 'I have something you need to see.'

She sat down on the floor next to him and held the monitor so they could both view the screen. She punched a few of the buttons, accessing a specific time on the disk. The screen remained black for a moment as the player located the requested spot. Then the blank screen was replaced by an image of one of the rooms in the basement, the room without the refrigeration unit.

There were four men present. On the tables were several air tanks. As Quinn and Orlando watched, one of the men started up a portable air compressor that was on the floor.

'There.' She pointed at the monitor. To one side of the room, standing alone but watching the others, was a man.

Borko.

The Serb looked nearly unchanged from when Quinn had first seen him in Toronto. The only difference now was that gray hair had started to invade his dark brown mane.

'Hold on,' Orlando said.

She pushed another button, and the action on the monitor began to accelerate. Quinn watched as the men moved from tank to tank, filling those that needed it. Once the operation was complete, they set the tanks on the floor in a row next to one of the cabinets.

'Here,' Orlando said. She punched a button, slowing the picture back to normal speed.

Just as the men were leaving, a phone rang. Borko motioned for the others to continue on, then pulled a black cell phone from his jacket pocket. He looked at the display, then answered the call.

'Borko,' he said into the phone.

He paused, listening to the person on the other end, then started speaking again. But not in Serbian or even German. In English.

'Yes. Yes,' Borko said. 'On schedule. The rest will be here tonight.' He stopped to listen. 'Don't worry. We have forty-eight hours, right? It will be tight, but we will make it.' Another pause. 'No, you don't have to come out. I will come back this evening. Make sure everything has arrived. Tomorrow we put it all together. It will be fine.'

Borko smiled. 'No sign of him or the woman,' the Serbian continued. 'But we have our insurance cards. You sent the files?' A grin. 'That should keep them in check. If they don't give us any more trouble, we can get rid of our guests after the delivery has been made.'

Orlando pressed Pause. 'There's nothing else important,' she said. 'Who do you think he was talking to? Dahl?'

Quinn nodded. 'That would be my guess.'

Quinn glanced down at the frozen image on the screen. Borko was caught in the middle of moving the phone away from his ear. In the background, the door to the room had opened and a man was in the process of stepping inside.

'Press Play,' Quinn said.

Orlando looked at the screen for a moment, her brow furrowed. After a moment, she pressed a button.

Borko slipped his phone into the pocket of his jacket, turning to look at the new arrival as he did so.

'Pause it there,' Quinn said.

The man had walked up and stopped next to Borko. He had sandy brown hair, cut short on the sides, and was a couple inches over six feet tall.

'You know him?' Orlando asked.

Quinn nodded. 'It's Leo Tucker.'

Orlando's eyes widened in surprise. She looked back at the monitor.

'Are you sure?'

'Yes.'

Silence.

'So Piper's group didn't just pass on the information about us,' Orlando said. 'They're actually involved.'

But Quinn didn't answer right away. He almost

kept his thoughts to himself, but he knew he couldn't. 'What if Piper *is* Dahl?' Quinn said.

Orlando started to speak, then stopped herself. He could see the realization dawning on her face as she put the pieces together.

'Of course,' she said, more to herself than to him. She looked up. 'That's it, isn't it? Piper is Dahl.'

'It was more than just bad blood between Piper and Durrie, wasn't it?' Quinn said as he tried to remember the exact circumstances of the split.

'Durrie just thought he was a fool,' Orlando said. 'But for Piper, yeah, there might have been more. Durrie kicked him off a high-profile job for something petty. Durrie said Piper missed an important planning meeting. Durrie said it made them look like amateurs. He badmouthed Piper for months after. It damaged Piper's credibility. Took him years to recover.'

'Right,' Quinn said. 'Only the way he used to tell the story, I think Durrie was just looking for an excuse to break up the partnership. So now that Piper's back in the game, he's in a position to exact a little revenge. Only Durrie's no longer around, so he turns on the only viable targets. The girlfriend and the apprentice. You and me.'

'And Garrett.'

'No,' Quinn said. 'Garrett's a bonus. He may not have even known about Garrett until I led him to you.' Quinn paused, his face hardening. 'Dammit. He made it out like he'd been in Ho Chi Minh City for a long time. But he probably followed me to Vietnam, getting there not long after I did.' He looked at Orlando. 'I led him right to you.'

She turned to him. If she blamed him, she didn't say so. Nor did she say she forgave him either. The look on her face was tense and serious. 'Tell me what you think we should do now,' she said.

He thought for a moment. 'When Borko leaves the plant tonight, we follow him,' he said. 'See if we can arrange a private conversation.'

Orlando nodded. 'Good. If you said anything else, I was going to go alone.'

He wanted to ask her why she didn't just suggest it. Instead, he said, 'Glad we're still on the same team.'

Her smile was not reassuring.

Chapter 31

The argument over who would actually do the following and who would do the spotting was a quick one. Quinn was the better driver and was more physically suited to take on Borko if it came to that. Reluctantly Orlando agreed to be the lookout. But only on the condition that if she could get back to the car quick enough, he would wait for her.

'Thirty seconds,' Quinn had said.

'Forty-five,' she countered.

He sighed. 'That's it, though. If you're not there by then, I'm gone.'

The elementary school directly across Schandauer Strasse from the water plant would have been the perfect place to position Orlando. But there was no easy way to get there, so the roof of the apartment building behind it would have to do.

Once again the early darkness of the northern latitudes proved useful. No one paid attention to two more bundled-up pedestrians walking the half-lit streets. It took Quinn less than fifteen seconds to unlock the front security door of the apartment building. Inside, Orlando spotted the stairwell and led the way up. They passed no one, though when they reached the fourth floor, they could hear people talking in the hallway.

There was a landing at the top of the stairs and beyond it a door that led, Quinn hoped, to the roof. The door looked seldom used. Orlando searched around the jamb, then looked at Quinn. 'I don't see any alarms,' she whispered. 'Shall I?'

Quinn nodded.

She reached down and tried the knob. It turned, but the door didn't open. 'Deadbolt,' she said.

Quinn motioned for her to step aside, then pulled out his pick set. One of the items in the kit was a simple screwdriver. The deadbolt housing had been mounted from the inside of the building, so it was easy to remove the screws and disassemble the mechanism. Once the deadbolt was retracted, Quinn fiddled with the lock, jamming it so that it would no longer work. Then he put everything back together.

The door looked as it had when they'd first arrived, only now the deadbolt was disengaged and could not be reengaged without the help of a locksmith. Chances were it would be months before anyone noticed. Quinn pulled the door open, and he and Orlando exited the stairwell into the cold darkness of the roof.

They headed toward the back of the building, crouching as they neared the raised lip that surrounded the edge of the roof.

Once they reached it, Quinn peeked over the top. Closest to them was the school. Thankfully, it was a one-story structure that only partially blocked the view of Schandauer Strasse itself and not the water plant. Their position was not optimal but acceptable.

'Give me the glasses,' Quinn said.

Orlando handed him the pair of binoculars Quinn had been carrying around in his backpack since the night Nate was taken. The Rigel 2100 binoculars he owned back home turned night into day. The ones he was holding now turned night into twilight. They would have to do.

He scanned the water plant. Most of the front was dark. The only light was from the single-bulb fixture around the side, above the entrance. There were several cars parked out front. By Quinn's count: two Mercedes, a Ford, and a Peugeot. Near the entrance was a dark-colored van. Quinn continued his search until he spotted what he knew was already there. Sentries.

There were half a dozen of them scattered across the property. No doubt there were more on the street. This was a huge ramp-up from what the security had been just days before.

Quinn ducked back down behind the protection of the retaining wall. 'Here,' he said, returning the binoculars to Orlando, then told her what he'd seen.

'Call me the second you see him,' Quinn said.

'I will.'

Quinn started to back away from the edge.

'Forty-five seconds,' she reminded him.

'That's all, though,' he said. He pushed himself up and jogged away.

* * *

Quinn had parked his car directly in front of the apartment building earlier that afternoon when the street was less crowded. Good thing, too. Now the street was packed with cars parked bumper-to-bumper along both sides.

Quinn sat in the front seat wishing he had a cup of hot coffee, but knowing he was probably more comfortable than Orlando at the moment.

It had been a busy afternoon. In addition to stealing the Mercedes he was sitting in, he'd picked up a few other items they might need. Rope, a crowbar, some other tools, even a phone for Orlando. He'd also spent some more time online, which proved to be both beneficial and frustrating. Beneficial, because he was able to discover the location of the IOMP convention office and was even able to register himself for the convention as Dr Richard Kubik, from Topeka, Kansas. He wasn't sure he would need to actually show up, but if he did, having a registration badge would make things much easier.

The only thing that had made him pause was that the convention wasn't scheduled to begin for another week. Borko had indicated his operation was to start within forty-eight hours. There was a time disconnect Quinn couldn't yet reconcile.

Time. The convention. The connection to the Office. The very nature of the biological agent itself. All were questions Quinn had no good answers for.

Maybe the IOMP meetings were merely a cover for the delivery of the biological agent. Maybe it was just a coincidence, and Duke had just been trying to mislead Quinn. Or maybe any of a hundred other scenarios. As for the identity of the disease, the answer was just as elusive. Quinn had been hoping the Mole would have gotten back to him with an answer by now. But there had been no word.

But most frustrating had been his lack of progress with his attempt to get to whatever files had been uploaded to Jansen's FTP server.

He jerked slightly when his phone rang. Orlando's name was on the display. Quinn put the hands-free earpiece in his ear.

'Yes?' Quinn asked.

'Borko's here,' Orlando said.

The way Orlando described it to Quinn, Borko arrived in a blue Porsche and waited outside the gate until one of the guards pulled it open. Then he drove onto the lot and around to the side, parking behind the van, near the building entrance. Borko was the only one to get out of his car. As far as she could tell, he'd arrived alone. Borko entered the building, and that's when she made her call.

A Porsche. *Great,* Quinn thought. If they ended up out on the Autobahn for some reason, there would be no way his Mercedes would be able to keep up.

It was nearly an hour before Orlando called again. 'He just came out.'

Quinn started up the Mercedes, but remained parked at the curb. 'What's he doing?'

'Talking to someone,' she replied. 'They're walking to his car.' A pause. 'I'm coming down now.'

'Wait,' Quinn said. 'We need to know which direction he goes in.'

'He'll leave the same way he arrived.'

'You don't know that.'

Rapid breaths came over the phone, the sounds of someone in motion. 'I'm already on my way,' she insisted.

Quinn cursed to himself as he glanced at his watch, then he said, 'You've got thirty seconds.'

'Forty-five,' she huffed. Quinn guessed she was on the stairs.

'You've already used fifteen.'

He pulled the Mercedes away from the curb and onto the street, double-parking in front of the apartment building.

'Fifteen seconds,' he said.

'I'm almost there.'

'Ten.'

'Wait!'

He glanced at the door. No sign of her.

'Time's up. I'm leaving.'

'Don't!' she yelled.

Suddenly she burst through the front door and ran toward the car. Quinn reached over and pushed open the passenger door. She jumped in and pulled the door shut behind her.

'Go, go, go,' she said. 'Elbestrasse. Right in front of you.'

Quinn pressed down on the accelerator. The Mercedes raced forward toward the end of the block, toward Elbestrasse. When they got to the intersection, Quinn stopped. Elbestrasse was empty.

'Maybe he went the other way,' he said.

'No. This way,' she said.

'Then maybe he already went by and we missed him. Or maybe he hasn't left at all.'

She said nothing.

Quinn scanned the intersecting street in front of them. Elbestrasse was divided in the middle by a row of large trees and additional street parking. It was still empty. He considered their options, but basically it came down to wait or give up.

Suddenly there was the roar of an engine and the reflection of headlights off the road. A moment later a dark blue Porsche Boxster flashed by.

'See. I told you,' Orlando said.

Quinn let out a breath he didn't even realize he'd been holding, then turned left onto Elbestrasse, mere seconds behind Borko.

Chapter 32

Borko raced through the city, seemingly with no destination in mind. He was obviously checking for a tail. Quinn kept his distance, but never lost sight of the Porsche.

After twenty minutes, Borko's driving became less erratic, more focused. Finally, he seemed to have settled on a fixed direction. Which meant only one thing.

He hadn't spotted them.

The Porsche pulled up in front of a run-down hotel in the southern part of Berlin known as Schöneberg. Quinn parked the Mercedes half a block away. After a moment, Borko got out of his car and entered the building.

Once Borko disappeared inside, Quinn and Orlando climbed out of their car. They walked toward the hotel, pausing in the shadows near the entrance. From there, Quinn could see into the lobby.

'Three men inside,' he whispered. 'One of them looks like the night clerk. The other two, definitely not guests.'

'Borko's men?' she asked.

'That would be my guess.'

'But he came alone. That means they were already here.'

Quinn nodded.

'There must be something important inside. Something they need to keep watch over.'

He knew what she was thinking. He knew he should probably say something so she wouldn't get her hopes up too much, but he couldn't bring himself to do it.

'We have two choices,' he said instead. 'Either we continue following Borko when he comes back out and look for a better opportunity to get him alone, or we try to find out what's so special inside.'

'I'm staying,' Orlando said. 'You do what you want.'

Ten minutes later, the hotel door opened. Next came the sound of voices, Borko and another man talking as they stepped outside.

Quinn was hiding next to a car parked on the far side of the Porsche. Orlando was crouched in the shadows at the corner of the building. Quinn risked a peek and saw the two men walking toward Borko's car. The guard stopped at the front of the Porsche and watched as Borko got in. While the guard's attention was occupied, Quinn crept toward the front of the parked car, narrowing the gap between himself and the guard to under ten feet. The Porsche's engine started, then Borko backed it into the street and drove away.

Before the guard could return to the warmth of the hotel, Quinn came up behind him and threw an arm around the guard's neck. Using his free hand, he landed two quick, powerful punches to the man's jaw, knocking him unconscious. He picked up the man's gun and tossed it under a parked car, then dragged the unconscious body into the shadows next to the building.

'Are you sure he's out?' Orlando asked as she emerged from her hiding spot.

'He's out.'

Instead of waiting for the other guard to come and check on his friend, they pulled out their guns and entered the hotel. The remaining guard was standing near the elevators. The moment he spotted them, he reached for the gun in his shoulder holster. But Orlando shot first, hitting the man in the arm. The guard yelled in pain, his gun tumbling out of the holster and onto the floor. Quinn raced forward and punched him in the face. The man fell against the wall, then toppled to the ground.

There was a noise to Quinn's left. He shot a look over at the night clerk who was just picking up the phone. '*Nein,*' Quinn said. 'Come here.'

Reluctantly, the night clerk came from around the corner and approached Quinn.

'You have a room we can lock him in?' Quinn asked in German.

The man nodded.

'Help us.'

Once they had both guards locked in a small office off the lobby, Quinn turned to the clerk. 'What room are they in?' he said, playing his hunch.

'Who?' the clerk asked.

Orlando raised her gun, pointing it at the clerk.

'Third floor. Three-twelve.'

There were no guards outside room 312. 'How many people inside?' Quinn asked.

'Three, I think,' the clerk said.

They reached the door. 'Is there a code?' Quinn asked, his voice a whisper.

'I don't know.'

'Then just knock. Tell them their boss sent up some food.'

The clerk hesitated.

'Do it,' Orlando said, playing up her self-chosen role as the enforcer.

The man knocked. Quinn could hear footsteps approaching from the other side, then, 'Who is it?'

'Herbert,' the clerk said. 'Your boss wanted me to bring you something to eat.'

The door opened. Standing just inside was a man in his mid-twenties.

'It's about fucking time. I'm starv –' He stopped when he saw Quinn. He reached for his gun, but he was too late.

Quinn shoved the clerk across the threshold into the man, crashing them both to the floor and dislodging the pistol in the process. Quinn entered behind them and picked up the gun. Orlando followed next, shutting the door behind her.

A second man jumped up from a chair to Quinn's right. He was starting to grab for his weapon, an Uzi resting on the end table next to him. Quinn shot the man once in the shoulder, knocking him back into the chair.

Quinn and Orlando stood in the middle of the room, guns pointed at the guards.

'Anyone else here?' he asked the injured man. 'Don't fucking lie to me.'

'No one,' the man grunted.

Quinn surveyed the room. In the corner was a bed. Someone was lying on it. Orlando had glanced at the bed, too. Quinn could see it in her face, the disappointment and continued fear. The person on the bed was far too big to be her son.

Quinn finished his sweep of the room. To the left were two doors, side by side. Next to one of them was a heavy-looking dresser with a TV on top.

'Where do those go?' Quinn asked, pointing at the doors.

'Closet and bathroom,' the clerk said from his position on the floor.

Quinn looked back at the man in the chair. 'You carrying anything else?'

The guard hesitated, then pulled up his trouser leg, revealing a Walther PPK in an ankle holster.

'Pull it out slowly and toss it over here,' Quinn ordered.

The man did so.

'What else?' Quinn asked.

The man shook his head. Quinn walked over, grabbed the Uzi off the table, and slung it over his shoulder. He then turned his attention to the person lying on the bed. A Caucasian male, mid-twenties.

Nate.

Quinn looked back at his three captives, then motioned to the closet door. 'Inside. You two in the closet,' he told the guards. 'And you,' he said as he looked at the clerk, 'you can have the bathroom.'

The clerk and the guard on the floor got to their feet and started toward the closed doors.

'You, too,' Orlando said to the injured man.

It took the man a moment to stand up, but he was soon following the other two across the room. The guard who hadn't been shot opened the closet door, and he and his partner squeezed inside the tiny chamber.

Quinn walked over to the door. 'Phones,' he said, holding out his hand.

Once the guards had given him their cell phones and he'd stowed them in his pocket, he closed the door.

The clerk was already in the bathroom, sitting on the toilet lid.

'You got a phone?' Quinn asked.

'No,' the man said.

'Are you sure?' Quinn asked, his eyebrow raised.

'No phone,' the man said quickly. 'It's downstairs, under the counter.'

Quinn shut the door, then with Orlando's help, he dragged the dresser in front of the two doors.

Quinn carried Nate in a fireman's hold across the empty hotel lobby, through the main entrance, and into the night. Orlando raced ahead of them and threw open the back door of the car. Carefully, they placed Nate onto the seat.

'Quinn?' Nate looked up at him, his eyes barely open.

'It's okay,' Quinn said.

Nate began to mumble something else, but his eyes closed and his head fell back.

Quinn shut the door. 'I'm sorry,' he said to Orlando.

'Where are we going to take him?' she asked as if she hadn't heard him.

Quinn was silent for a moment. 'I know a place.'

They climbed back into the car. After Quinn started the car, he turned to Orlando. 'We'll find Garrett, too.'

Her only response was a quick, empty smile.

Sophie was in the doorway to the bar, saying good night to one of her customers, when Quinn drove up and parked at the curb.

'I didn't think you were coming back,' she said after he got out of the Mercedes and came around to the sidewalk.

'I need your help,' he told her.

She took a few steps toward the car, but stopped as Orlando opened the passenger-side door and climbed out.

'Who's she?' Sophie asked.

'A friend,' Quinn said.

He walked to the rear passenger door and opened it. With Orlando's help, he lifted Nate out of the back. 'What's wrong with him?' Sophie asked.

'He's hurt.'

'I can see that. How?'

'It's not important.'

'Did you . . . ?'

'No.'

Nate groaned as Quinn shifted his position to get a better grip.

'I don't understand,' Sophie said. 'What's going on?'

'My friend's been drugged,' Quinn told her.

'And given a beating, too.'

'Yes,' Quinn said. He started for the building, Orlando directly behind him.

'Where do you think you're taking him?' Sophie asked. 'He should be in a hospital.'

'I can't take him to a hospital.'

'Why not?'

'I just can't.' They reached the entrance to her apartment.

'Wait.' Sophie put her hand on Quinn's shoulder. 'I can't do anything for him.'

'You have an extra bed, don't you? That's all I want. Someone else will come to take care of him,' he said.

Sophie didn't move.

'Sophie, please,' Quinn said. 'Open the door.'

She pushed past them and pulled the door open. 'What are you getting me into?'

'Better if you don't know,' Quinn said.

They settled Nate in Sophie's guest room, then Quinn retrieved some water and some towels from the bathroom. He started to use them to clean up Nate's wounds.

'Let me.' Orlando reached for the towel, then nodded toward the door that led back into the living room. 'Your friend out there probably has a few questions,' she said, her voice flat.

Reluctantly, he nodded, then let her take the towel.

He found Sophie sitting at her kitchen table, an open bottle of wine and a tumbler, half full, keeping her company. Her hands were clasped in front of her, almost like she was praying. But her eyes were wide open, staring at them, or, rather, staring through them.

He pulled out the chair opposite her and sat down. A closer inspection of the glass revealed the rim was dry. She had yet to take a drink.

She lifted her eyes to meet his. 'What's going on, Jonathan? Who is he?'

'I told you. He's a friend. A colleague.'

'And the woman?'

'The same.'

'Colleagues both? People you work with?'

He hesitated. 'Yes.'

'This doesn't seem like bank business.' She was referring to his cover.

'Sophie –'

He was interrupted by a loud, short buzz coming from the living room. Sophie looked over her shoulder toward the sound, then turned back to Quinn. 'Someone's at the front door,' she said, surprised.

'It's okay.' Quinn rose and headed for the door that opened to the landing at the top of the stairwell.

'Who is it?' Sophie asked.

'Help,' Quinn said.

Dr. Garber was Quinn's medical contact in Berlin. He had been in the business for a long time and was a specialist at this type of work. A late-night call for immediate assistance at some out-of-the-way location. No notes taken, no records kept. Only the care of the patient, and the exchange of cash. Quinn had called him on the drive over to Sophie's.

The doctor spent half an hour with Nate while Quinn, Orlando, and Sophie sat in the living room, the only noise coming from the TV Sophie had turned on. The two women didn't even look at each other. They seemed to be lost in their own thoughts. As for Orlando, Quinn could almost feel her nervous tension. He knew she wanted to keep moving, keep looking for Garrett. Sophie was not only tense, but seemed confused and scared as well. There were several times Quinn wanted to say something to her, but he always stopped himself. His words would be meaningless, and liable to provoke Sophie more than comfort her. Instead he listened idly to the droning voice of a newscaster reciting the day's news: concerns over a proposed industrial facility in Dresden, preparation for an EU conference in Berlin, and an update on a story about a German tourist killed while on vacation to Central America.

When Dr. Garber finally came out of the guest bedroom, Quinn stood quickly.

'Without doing any real tests, I don't know exactly what they gave him,' the doctor said. 'Something to keep him under control, I'd guess. Not for the pain.'

'Will he be all right?' Quinn asked.

'With some rest,' Garber said, 'he should be able to get around soon. But I wouldn't count on him being one hundred percent for quite a while.

Along with the facial lacerations, one of his ribs is broken. At some point he dislocated his shoulder, too. It's been reset, but there's much tenderness and inflammation around the joint. I have left some medication on the table next to his bed.'

'When can we move him?' Quinn asked.

'Two days,' Garber said.

'Two days?' Sophie shot up. 'He's not staying here two days. Take him to the hospital if he needs so much help.'

'Sophie,' Quinn said evenly, 'I told you that's not possible. I know I'm asking a lot.'

'I don't understand. No hospital? If he's your friend, you would take him there.'

'He's safer here,' Orlando said.

Sophie glared at Orlando. 'You, I don't know who you are. Don't tell me what's safe or not. Don't even talk to me.'

'Sophie –' Quinn started.

'Who is she?' Sophie pointed at Orlando. 'Is she your lover? Is that what this is?'

Quinn took a breath. 'She's not my lover. She's my colleague.'

'I don't believe you.'

'I swear, Sophie. We work together.'

'And your friend in there? You work with him, too?'

'Yes.'

'What kind of work that someone beats your friend up? That you can't take him to the hospital?'

Quinn sighed. 'You have to trust me. I need your help. This is the safest place I could take him.'

Sophie took several deep breaths, each a little longer than the last. Her shoulders started to sag slightly.

'He is really your friend?' she asked, her voice now quiet, almost defeated.

'Yes,' Quinn said.

A pause. 'Two days?' Sophie asked, looking at the doctor.

'No more than that,' he replied.

She was silent for a moment. 'All right. Two days. Then you take him away.'

'Thank you,' Quinn said.

Dr. Garber headed toward the door. 'I'll be back in the afternoon,' he said to Sophie. 'Quinn will give you my number if you need me sooner.'

Sophie looked at Quinn. 'What about you two? Are you leaving, too?'

'Orlando will,' Quinn said. 'I'll stay until morning. But then I have something to do.'

Sophie was silent for several moments. 'Fine,' she said, then turned and walked into her own bedroom, shutting the door behind her.

Chapter 33

The night had been a restless one. Quinn had spent most of it in a wooden chair next to Nate's bed. He wanted to be there if his apprentice woke, but Nate barely stirred. In the morning he reluctantly returned to their makeshift base on Karl Marx Strasse.

'How is he?' Orlando asked. She was sitting on one of the chairs, the monitor on the floor beside her.

Quinn unfolded the other chair and joined her. 'The same.'

She looked at Quinn. There were dark circles around her eyes. 'They're not going to be happy we found him.'

'You're right,' he agreed. 'Did you sleep at all?'

'What if Piper or Borko does something to Garrett now?' she asked, ignoring his question.

'That's the last thing they'll do,' Quinn said. 'He's the only leverage they have over us.'

She took a few deep breaths, then said, 'There's something you should see.'

'What?'

'When I got back here after I left you last night, I checked the cameras in the plant again.'

'And?'

'At some point, someone put a bunch of boxes in the basement. It had to have been while we were following Borko. The boxes weren't there before.'

'Something from the delivery van that was parked at the door?' Quinn asked.

'Could be.'

'Show me.'

She picked the monitor up off the floor and turned it on. The screen flashed to life. There was a view of one of the rooms in the basement.

'Those the boxes?' Quinn asked. There were several of them, some sitting on the worktable and several more on the floor.

'Yeah,' she said. There was hesitation in her voice.

'What?' Quinn asked.

Orlando stared at the monitor.

'What?' Quinn repeated.

'There are only fourteen boxes,' she said.

'So?'

'Last night there were twenty.'

Quinn looked at the monitor. Silently, he counted the boxes. She was right. There were fourteen. 'Are those labels on the boxes?' Quinn asked.

'Yes. But I wasn't able to get in close enough to one to read it.'

'The sphere,' Quinn said.

Orlando switched to a live view inside the containment room. Quinn's eyes grew wide in surprise at the new image.

'I don't think this is good,' Orlando said.

There were four people in the room. All were dressed in bio-containment suits. Two were at the worktable against the wall on the right. On the table was a box that matched those still in the basement, its top open. On the floor were three more boxes, stacked. They looked like they were still sealed. Near the door, almost out of the camera's range, were the last two boxes. These were open and empty.

The other two men were positioned in front of the safety cabinets in the center of the room. One of the men had his arms and hands shoved into the cabinet nearest the door, while the other man looked on.

'What are they doing?' Orlando asked, pointing at the men standing at the worktable.

They were removing the contents of the open box. What they took out looked to be smaller metal boxes in groups of ten, stacked double-wide and held together by shrink-wrap.

Each man lifted a stack out and set it on the table. They then removed the wrapping and placed the smaller boxes side by side on a tray, popping each of them open as they did so. When the tray was full, two stacks' worth of tins, one of the men carried the tray to the center workspace and slipped it through a slot at the bottom end of one of the safety cabinets.

As the man was carrying the tray to the cabinet, Quinn was able to get a glimpse inside the tins. They were empty.

The hatch on the safety cabinet was now closed. The man who had brought the tray over had returned to the boxes at the other table. The man who was at the cabinet had removed his hands from the protective sleeves that allowed him to work inside the unit.

There were several buttons across the bottom of the cabinet. The man pushed one of them, and something in the cabinet moved.

As Quinn and Orlando watched, the bottom of the cabinet slid open. The tray that had been slipped in underneath it rose up. The man put his hands back into the sleeves. On the inside wall of the cabinet was a small shelf, and on the shelf was a container holding what appeared to be dozens of penny-size white pellets. They were rounded so that the middle was thicker than the ends. Quinn knew they had to have been the same ones he'd seen the men stowing in the small refrigerators earlier. The man at the cabinet removed the pellets one by one and placed them in the tins. Each box held six.

'Mints?' Quinn said.

'What?' Orlando asked, but Quinn's attention was fully on the monitor.

It took a while, but when all the tins were full, the man closed the tops on each box. That done, he removed his hands from the sleeves and pushed another button on the case. The tray dropped downward, and the bottom of the cabinet closed above it.

The man then pushed another button. Up from the bottom of the second cabinet came the same tray of tins. When they were securely in place, the second man turned a dial on the cabinet. The entire cabinet instantly filled with a fine mist.

'Is that . . . ?' Orlando left the question hanging.

'Disinfectant?' Quinn asked.

She nodded.

'Something like that, probably,' Quinn said. 'Only a lot stronger than what you can pick up at the market, I'd guess.'

'So the stuff inside the tins . . . ?'

'Is hot,' Quinn finished for her.

Quinn now knew what the delivery device was going to be. An innocent tin of candy. Brilliant. The agent had either been applied to the outside of the mint, or contained inside somehow. Quinn guessed the latter was the more likely. He was also able to surmise something about the biological agent itself. If it was fast-acting, the convention would be shut down and all the participants quarantined, so it couldn't be anything that would show up right away. It had to be something with a long incubation period. Could that have had something to do with the 'tailoring' Taggert had told Burroughs about? And how did it relate to the IOMP convention? That had been Duke's tip.

Quinn paused.

Duke.

'Son of a bitch,' Quinn said.

'What?' Orlando asked.

'I think I know how they're planning on distributing everything.'

'How?'

'Grob Promotions,' Quinn said. 'I should have seen it before.'

'What's Grob Promotions?' she asked.

'Duke owned a company called Grob Promotions,' Quinn said. 'It was one of the stops he made that morning I followed him. At the time I didn't care what they did, because I didn't think it mattered. But it does. When I went online to find out more information about the convention, there was something I read, only it didn't hit me at the time.'

'What?'

'Something like "IOMP Berlin managed by Grob Promotions."' Quinn began pacing the floor in thought. 'If so, that means Grob is handling all the promotion and running of the convention. Including,' he said, looking at Orlando, 'the preparation of gift bags.'

'Gift bags?'

'All of the registered attendees receive complimentary gift bags when they check in. It was on the website. Inside there'll be brochures, convention information, pencils, pens, buttons, and, if I'm right, a tin of mints.'

'You said the convention doesn't start for nearly a week,' she said. 'Why would Borko's deadline be tomorrow? It's too soon.'

She was right, Quinn knew.

'Maybe we're wrong. Maybe the convention isn't ground zero,' she said. 'If that's the case, they could be targeting almost anything.'

Right again.

Quinn looked back at the screen. Work continued in the containment room, but he wasn't really watching anymore. He had a decision to make. A decision, he quickly realized, with only one answer.

'It doesn't matter what the target is,' he said, sounding far more sure of himself than he actually was.

'You're going to try and stop them, aren't you?' she asked.

'I'm going to get Garrett back,' he said. 'And at the moment, the only way I can figure out how to get to Dahl . . . to Piper, is to steal something that's valuable to him.'

'The mints,' she said, her face brightening as she realized his plan. 'We get them, we can trade them for Garrett.'

'Something like that,' he said. It was leverage they sorely needed. He didn't even want to think about what would happen if the candy was distributed.

'We're still going to have to do this alone,' he said. 'If we call anyone in, Piper will find out and he won't hesitate to kill Garrett.' He paused. 'We're it.'

She smiled. 'Good by me.'

From outside, Quinn heard a loud truck pass by the front of the store. There were people on the sidewalk, too. Laughing, talking, arguing. Sharing just another moment in the day. People who, if Quinn did nothing, might not make it to the end of the year.

Orlando's voice suddenly cut through the noisy silence. 'The Mole called right before you came in. He wants you to call him back.'

'Did he say what he wanted?'

'He wouldn't tell me,' she said, an angry tremor in her voice. 'I tried but he said he'd only talk to you.'

Chapter 34

Quinn left the store and headed southeast on Karl Marx Strasse toward Neukölln station. On the way over, he used the number Orlando had given him and called the Mole.

'I received . . . your payment . . . it was more than . . . expected.'

'Consider it an advance on future requests,' Quinn said. 'Orlando said you have some information for me.'

'Something has actually come . . . to us in the last . . . hour . . . concerning the location of . . . Orlando's son.'

'The picture?'

'Not . . . the picture . . . Garrett left . . . Vietnam the day after Orlando did . . . he was with a man . . . Caucasian . . . they flew to Hong Kong . . . but from there no more trace.'

'That's the whole description?'

'The man . . . may have had an . . . accent . . . Australian.'

Tucker, Quinn thought. *Of course.*

'How did he get him out of the country?'

'He claimed he had . . . adopted Garrett . . . he presented all the . . . correct paperwork.'

'Son of a bitch,' Quinn said. Piper had planned things well.

'As for the picture,' the Mole went on. 'There is nothing . . . to tell yet.'

'It *is* faked, then,' Quinn said.

'No . . . we don't . . . believe so.'

Quinn paused, digesting the information. 'But you don't think you can place the location.'

'It is . . . possible . . . there are . . . some geological markers . . . that may help us . . . but I don't think . . . very likely.'

Quinn couldn't remember seeing any markers, geological or otherwise, but if there were, that was something anyway. A chance.

'This isn't why you called me earlier, though, is it?'

'I think perhaps . . . you have . . . made a misjudgment . . . concerning the situation.'

'What misjudgment?'

'The bio-agent,' the Mole said.

'The IOMP convention isn't the target, is it?'

'Then . . . you already know.'

'I wasn't even sure of that,' Quinn said. 'If you know more, tell me.'

There was a long silence.

'It is very . . . ambitious,' the Mole began. 'Remember . . . we only had the . . . damaged tissue . . . sample to work . . . with . . . nerve tissue it . . . turns out . . . still . . . we could only . . . guess.'

'But you know what it is, don't you?'

'We were able . . . to download . . . the documents from the . . . address . . . on the bracelet.'

'You figured out the password?' Quinn said, surprised.

There was a pause. 'Yes.'

'What did you find?'

'Two files . . . a document . . . and a video clip.'

'And?'

'The document . . . contains a breakdown . . . of the virus . . . it helped us to . . . understand why it was . . . not easily categorized . . . it has been tailored.'

'Tailored?'

'The document . . . had a brief note from Jansen . . . shall I read it . . . to you?'

'Okay,' Quinn said, unsure he really wanted to hear.

'"The attached breakdown is what . . . the people paying . . . the bills have . . . dubbed an act of . . . purification,"' the Mole read. '"What they believe . . . their scientists have created is basically . . . a genocide bug . . . designed specifically to . . . affect a targeted . . . population . . . what they could not . . . achieve in war . . . they think they . . . can achieve with this . . . new form of . . . ethnic cleansing."'

The world around Quinn seemed to disappear. The cars, the trucks, the people. He could hear none of them, see none of them.

'These are individuals . . . who . . . think in old ways,' the Mole said, no longer reading. 'Some ancestral fights . . . never seem to end . . . particularly when the . . . objects of their anger . . . share the same land . . . the same water . . . the same air . . .

I would say by the . . . identity of the virus . . . base . . . the level of hatred . . . is extremely harsh.'

'So you do know what the base is?'

'It was difficult to . . . determine that at . . . first because . . . of the alterations . . . but Jansen's documents told us . . . what . . . to look for . . . call it . . . a . . . supervirus . . . resistant to treatment . . . including previous . . . inoculations . . . easy to spread.'

'What is it?'

'Polio,' the Mole said. 'A killer . . . and a maimer . . . all in one.'

Quinn held the phone tightly against his ear. He didn't want to breathe or speak or even think anymore. He wanted to be out, to be far, far away. But running was not an option for him. Garrett needed him.

No, he thought. *Not just Garrett.*

'Who's the target?' he asked.

'Muslims.'

'Arabs,' Quinn said in disbelief.

'No . . . you misunderstand . . . Bosnianks . . . Bosnian Muslims . . .'

Sonofafuckingbitch. 'Borko's a Serb,' Quinn said.

'Yes . . . but an . . . extremist . . . never forget that.'

Quinn's breath caught in his throat. What had he heard on the news? It was while he was waiting at Sophie's, while Dr. Garber examined Nate. There was a gathering, a meeting, something. *What the hell was it?* 'It's not the IOMP convention,' Quinn said as the memory came back to him. 'It's the EU Friendship Conference on the Balkans. It starts –'

'Tomorrow,' the Mole said.

The world that had disappeared a moment ago came rushing back at Quinn. He suddenly felt like he was being watched, that at any second the knowledge he now possessed would get him killed.

'It is . . . worse than you . . . think.'

'What do you mean?'

'Watch . . . the video.'

The idea of creating a disease to kill a specific section of the population made Quinn want to vomit on the spot. It was extremism in the severest of forms. If they were successful, the act would rival what Adolf Hitler had done to the Jews during World War II.

The choice of disease was revealing, too. Polio. Millions would die. And many of those who didn't perish early on would be crippled and eventually have the life squeezed painfully out of them. Gruesome, hideous, atrocious, immoral. No word Quinn could think of seemed strong enough.

The Mole's revelation did clear up one thing, though. Campobello. Quinn should have seen it earlier. Taggert, or rather Jansen, had been trying to deliver the message even after he died. It was right there on his driver's license. Not Campobello, Nevada. Campobello Island. The one off the coast of Maine, where FDR had had a summer home. The same famous home he'd been in when he learned of his own polio diagnosis.

There was a small shopping mall on Karl Marx Strasse, near the north end of Neukölln. Quinn found an American-style burger place on the second floor with a couple of public Internet stations set up in the lobby.

The first thing he did was use the password the Mole had given him to download the video and save it to his memory stick. He resisted the temptation to watch it right away. There were too many people around.

Next, he pulled up a new window. He had a hunch, and he needed to see if he was right.

Within seconds he was on the website for Grob Communications. A link on the left side of the screen led him to a list of upcoming events being serviced to some extent or another by Duke's company. Most of the list comprised names of German organizations holding meetings and conferences. But two others stood out:

International Organization of Medical Professionals

And several items below it:

European Union Friendship Conference for the Balkan States

Quinn clicked on the conference. There were lists of which countries had accepted the invitation to attend and who they were sending as representatives. Grob Communications was organizing several events, including the opening luncheon at the St Martin Hotel the following day – only hours after Borko's deadline for shipment.

All the member nations of the EU would be represented, as well as Russia, Ukraine, and Switzerland. But the stars of the show were Croatia, Slovenia, Macedonia, Serbia, Montenegro, and Bosnia-Herzegovina. Each nation was sending dozens of attendees. By the looks of the list, most were civilians, people in positions of influence. The government officials on the list seemed to be mid-level office holders, probably the people who really got the work done. Quinn noted that the largest delegation by far was from Bosnia.

He sat back, letting it all sink in. After a few moments, he clicked off the Grob Communications website. He sent a final e-mail to the Mole, then went back outside and called Peter.

'Christ, Quinn. What the hell is going on?'

'Have you figured out who your double agent is yet?' Quinn asked.

'I told you. There is no double agent.'

After what Quinn had learned in Brussels, he'd begun to suspect that himself, but he wanted to hear the whole story from Peter. 'Then who fed Borko the info he needed to take you down?'

There was a pause, then Peter said, 'I know you've talked to Burroughs. So you know Jills was working for us.'

'Yeah,' Quinn said. 'Why didn't you just tell me that in the first place?'

'I had clients. Certain trusts that couldn't be broken.'

'Yet you rolled over on Burroughs.'

'I gave you the name of someone you could talk to,' Peter said. 'That's all.'

Quinn shook his head. In Peter's world, he had just been trying to save face. Even in desperation, he'd been unwilling to compromise his integrity. Not because of any moral code, but because doing so might jeopardize future work.

'What about Jills?'

'She wasn't just a one-time hire. She'd started working for me full-time six months ago. Not ops work. She was here with me, working on project planning. I put her on the Taggert job because I trusted her and needed it done right.'

'And you didn't want to waste one of your top guys on such an easy gig,' Quinn guessed.

No answer at first, then, 'That, too.'

'So she knew everything,' Quinn said, connecting the pieces. 'And before they killed her, they made her talk.'

Neither of them spoke for several seconds.

Quinn finally broke the silence. 'Listen to me. You need to do exactly what I say. If you don't hear from me in the next twenty-four hours, shut it all down. Airports, harbors, border crossings. Everything.'

'Why?'

Quinn hung up the phone without another word.

The cab dropped Quinn off a block from Sophie's place. He hadn't intended to come back so soon, but when he called after he'd finished with Peter, Sophie told him Nate had woken up for a while that morning. Quinn couldn't pass up an opportunity to talk to his apprentice and see if he might be able to tell him something that could help.

First, though, he had called Orlando and told her what he'd learned from the Mole. He wanted to leave out the part about Garrett's abduction, but he knew that wasn't an option. Her reaction was several moments of silence followed by a terse 'What are we going to do about it?'

Quinn described the plan that he'd worked up. She hadn't liked it, but she couldn't suggest anything better. They went over a list of things they could need. Though some of the items were unusual, Orlando was confident she could find everything.

As Quinn walked toward Sophie's place, he saw Dr. Garber come out the front door. Quinn jogged to catch up to him. The doctor glanced nervously over his shoulder as Quinn approached. But when he saw that it was Quinn, he slowed his pace.

'Herr Quinn,' the doctor greeted him.

'How is he?'

'As good as possible, after one night. He'll be good as okay soon enough. Until then, he should take it very easy.'

'Thanks,' Quinn said. 'I appreciate everything you've done.'

Quinn was about to turn around and go back to Sophie's place, but something in the doctor's manner made him hesitate.

'I won't be coming back,' the doctor said.

'What? Why?'

'This is too dangerous, even for me. Everyone is looking for you. This morning I had a visitor. Someone I've never met before. But he seemed to know that you and I have worked together in the past. I told him I hadn't heard from you in two years. I'm not sure he was convinced. But he did say if I saw you, I should call him.'

'He gave you a number?'

The doctor reached into his pocket and pulled out a business card. On the back someone had handwritten a telephone number. On the front, professionally printed in black ink, was the name Dahl.

'Here,' he said, handing the card to Quinn. 'This way I won't be tempted.'

Nate's eyes were closed when Quinn entered the guest room. Sophie had barely said a word to him when she had let him in. Now she was busying herself in the kitchen.

The wooden chair was still beside the bed where Quinn had left it. As he sat down, he said, 'Nate?'

Nate's eyelids fluttered, then parted slightly.

'It's Quinn.'

'Quinn?' Nate's voice was a hoarse whisper. 'Where the hell have you been?

He smiled. 'You want something to drink?'

'Water.'

There was a glass of it on the nightstand. Quinn picked it up and held it to Nate's lips. At first Nate only took a sip. But as Quinn started to move the glass away, Nate said he wanted more. By the time he leaned back against the pillow, the glass was nearly empty.

'How're you feeling?' Quinn asked.

'Like someone threw me under a train,' he answered. 'How do I look?'

'I think that's probably a fair assessment.'

'Great,' Nate said, his voice flat. He paused. 'Thanks for coming back for me.'

'I had some time on my hands.'

Nate started to laugh, but ended up wincing in pain.

'You all right?' Quinn asked.

'Sure,' Nate said. 'Never better.'

Quinn said, 'Do you remember much?'

'More than I wish I did.'

Nate told Quinn he had never seen who had taken him out that night at the water plant. He had been standing in position, watching the street for over an hour, then something painful slammed into his right thigh. Needle-like, he said. The next thing he knew, he woke up in the hotel room.

'Sometimes they'd beat me up right there,' Nate said. 'Sometimes they'd take me down the hall to another room. All the furniture had been cleared out. There was a rope hanging down from the ceiling. They'd string me up by my wrists. Ask me questions. Throw a few punches.'

'What did they ask?'

'Questions about you. About Orlando. What you were doing. Where you might hide out. How we were supposed to communicate with each other if the op was blown.'

'You didn't tell them that,' Quinn said.

Nate smiled. 'I told them. I just told them the wrong place.'

Quinn couldn't help but be impressed. This wasn't the Nate he'd come to expect. This Nate was resilient, strong-willed.

'I think when they realized I was new, and they wouldn't get much more out of me, they stopped.'

'You did great, Nate,' Quinn said. 'You kept them away from us. I couldn't have asked for more than that.'

Quinn's phone rang. 'You need some more water?' he asked Nate.

'I'm okay.'

Quinn stood and answered his phone. 'Yes?'

'There's an . . . office building in Charlottenburg . . . on Kaiserdamm,' the Mole said, in response to Quinn's last e-mail. He gave Quinn an address. 'I am told . . . they will . . . be assembling welcome . . . packets there for each . . . of the . . . attendees . . . once they are prepared . . . they . . . will be taken to the . . . luncheon and placed on the tables . . . candied mints . . . are one of . . . the favors to be . . . included.'

'You're confident about this information?' Quinn asked.

'Very,' the Mole said.

Quinn hung up. When he turned back to the bed, Nate was actually sitting up.

'Do you remember any of the people you saw?' Quinn asked him.

'There were mainly two guys.' After Nate described them, Quinn was fairly confident it was the two guards he'd locked in the closet.

'What about Borko?'

'Yes,' Nate said. 'I met him one time.' There was a pause. 'He's not a nice guy.'

'What happened?'

Nate pointed toward his left shoulder, the one that had been dislocated.

'Borko did that?'

'Yeah, but not before I kicked him in the balls.'

'That might have been why he did that,' Quinn suggested.

'Yeah,' Nate said. 'I thought about that later.'

'Did you meet anyone named Dahl?'

Nate hesitated. 'I might have.'

'What do you mean?'

'I was pretty out of it most of the time. A lot of people seemed to come and go.'

'Can you describe any of them?'

Nate thought for a moment. 'There was this one guy, a little older. The others seemed to defer to him.' Nate closed his eyes. 'Sorry, that's not very helpful, is it?'

'It's fine,' Quinn said. 'You did good.'

Chapter 35

Quinn went out to the kitchen. He had hoped to get more out of Nate. Maybe after his apprentice had a little more rest, he'd remember something else. The older guy, though, that could have been Tucker. Or Piper. If it was, it meant the man everyone was calling Dahl was in town. Which could also mean that Garrett was here, too.

'Who are you?' It was Sophie. She had entered the kitchen quietly behind him.

He turned. 'What?'

'You heard me. Who are you?'

'The same person I've been since the day we met.'

'No,' she said. 'The person I met was nothing like you. It was all a lie, wasn't it?'

'Sophie, please.'

'All a lie.'

He looked at her for a moment. 'You would have never believed the truth.'

She scoffed, then sat down at the kitchen table, her back to him. Quinn knew there was more he should say but he just wasn't up to it. There were too many other things he had to focus on. Without another word, he turned and walked back to the bedroom.

'Thanks,' Nate said as Quinn handed him the glass. 'How are we going to –'

Nate's question was cut short by the sound of a muffled buzzer. It was the doorbell. Quinn rushed over to the bedroom door and opened it. Sophie was only a step away from the front door. She stopped before she opened it, turning to Quinn.

'The police are here,' she said, her face hard. 'They called me this morning and asked me to call them if I saw you.'

She pulled the door open and started to step onto the landing at the top of the stairs.

'Sophie. No!' Quinn shouted.

He was too late. Gunfire reverberated up the stairway. Sophie stumbled back against the doorway, several patches of blood growing on her blouse. She looked at Quinn as if she wanted to say something. Then her eyes became unfocused and she collapsed to the floor.

Quinn pulled out his gun and sprinted across the room, stopping just short of the landing where Sophie lay, eyes closed. There was nothing he could do. She was dead.

He pressed himself against the wall beside the door and listened for anyone coming up the stairs. At first there was nothing, then he heard footsteps near the bottom landing. Two seconds later, something heavy struck one of the steps near the top.

Quinn dove behind the couch, landing prone on the floor just as an explosion rocked the building.

As the roar of the blast diminished, Quinn pushed himself to his feet. He rushed back into the guest room. Nate was lifting himself off the bed, his movements slow but determined.

'What the hell was that?' Nate asked.

'Hand grenade,' Quinn said. 'It'll be easier if I carry you.'

'Are you sure you can?'

'I did it last night.'

'Okay,' Nate said.

'Can you hold a gun?'

'I think so.'

Quinn gave Nate his SIG, then he picked him up and heaved him over his left shoulder. Nate let out a grunt of pain. 'Are you all right?' he asked.

'Just get us out of here.'

As they reached the guest room door, they heard something clatter near the apartment entrance. Quinn moved against the wall to protect them from another explosion. But none came. This time there was only a loud pop.

'Hold on tight,' he said.

Quinn rushed through the doorway into the living room. A cloud of gas was hissing out of a soda can-sized canister near the door. Quinn was certain it was more than mere tear gas.

Holding his breath, he raced for the dining room at the back of the apartment. When they reached the dining table, he put Nate down and went over to the window. He hadn't opened that particular window since the summer two years before with Sophie, when it represented a time of pleasure. Now it represented his and Nate's only way out.

He undid the latch and pushed the window open. 'Come on,' he said. 'You first.'

He helped Nate climb through the window and out onto the roof area. Once he was through, Quinn followed him, closing the window behind them.

'That way,' he said, pointing to the right.

The building next door was butted directly against Sophie's building. There was a seven-foot height difference between the two structures, Sophie's building being the lower of the two.

'I don't think I can make it,' Nate said.

'I'll help,' Quinn told him.

At the wall, he created a cradle with his hands. 'Give me your foot. I'll boost you up.'

Nate looked unsure, but did what he asked. 'Okay. On three,' Quinn said. 'One. Two.'

Quinn lifted him upward, pushing Nate until his apprentice was able to get a leg over the top of the wall. When he was out of the way, Quinn jumped up, grabbed the top edge of the wall, and pulled himself over.

Nate was sitting on the roof, arms wrapped around his chest, a grimace of pain on his face. 'Are you okay?' Quinn asked.

Nate nodded.

'We need to keep moving then,' Quinn said, indicating the next building on the block.

He held out his hand and helped Nate back to his feet. Nate leaned heavily against him as they made their way across to the next building. It was only a couple of feet higher than the one they were on, so the transition was less of an effort. Off to the side was a doorway that undoubtedly accessed a set of stairs into the building. Quinn kicked at the latch until the door opened. He motioned for Nate to go inside.

'I'll be right back,' he said.

'Where are you going?' Nate asked.

'I need to take a look.'

Crouching low, he crept to the front edge of the building. There was no raised edge, so he had to lie flat to keep from being seen. He eased forward until he could view the street. There were three cars parked in front of Sophie's place. Standing outside one of the cars was a familiar figure.

Borko.

Chapter 36

They took the U-Bahn, sitting as far away from the other passengers as possible. Quinn had given Nate his coat, but even with the collar flipped up, it couldn't hide the abrasions on Nate's face. Within moments Nate's breathing slowed as he fell asleep.

'We're here,' Quinn said thirty minutes later, gently nudging his apprentice as the train pulled into the station.

The walk from Neukölln bahnhoff to their makeshift headquarters was not far, but they had to stop twice so Nate could rest. The second time, Quinn steered them into the sandwich shop, where he purchased several sandwiches and a large coffee for Nate.

'Here,' he said, handing him the cup.

'I don't want anything.'

'It'll keep you warm.'

They sat at one of the tables until Nate had downed nearly half of the coffee. 'No more,' he said as he set the cup down.

Quinn picked up the container and threw it in the trash. 'Come on.'

★ ★ ★

They reached the store ten minutes later. Orlando wasn't around, but Quinn hadn't expected her to be. The list of items she had to obtain was not an easy order to fill.

'Very cozy,' Nate said from the doorway of the back room.

There were two air mattresses with sleeping bags on the floor of the room. Nate looked at them, then back at Quinn. 'You weren't expecting me?'

'Not this soon,' Quinn said. 'We'll go out for another mattress and sleeping bag after Orlando gets back. You can use mine for now. It's the blue one.'

'I'm not tired.'

Quinn snorted. 'Right. You're going to fall asleep standing there. Lie down.'

Nate smiled. 'Maybe for a few minutes.'

He shuffled over to the sleeping bag and climbed in.

'You warm enough?' Quinn asked.

'I'm fine.' Nate's voice now a soft whisper. After only a moment, his eyelids drooped, then closed.

Orlando returned an hour later.

'Get everything?' Quinn asked.

She nodded. 'Of course.'

He smiled, then told her about his fun-filled afternoon.

'I'm sorry,' she said after he told her about Sophie. She put a hand on his arm. 'Thank God you got Nate out, though.'

'Yeah,' he said, his voice hollow. 'Thank God.'

'It's not your fault,' she said.

'Isn't it?'

She looked up at him, her eyes soft, supportive. After a moment, she said, 'Why don't you show me the video?'

'Okay,' Quinn said. He knew she was trying to get him to refocus and take his mind off Sophie's death. And he was glad for it.

He picked the monitor up off the floor and handed it to her. Stuck in the side port was his memory stick.

'Just hit Play,' he said. 'I've already seen it.'

Orlando cocked her head, apparently expecting him to say something else, but he remained silent. As she looked back at the monitor and pressed Play, Quinn moved so he could look over her shoulder.

The screen was blank for a moment, then up came an image of a man.

'Who is he?' Orlando asked.

'Taggert,' Quinn said. 'Well, Jansen, I guess.'

The shot was tight, from just below Henry Jansen's shoulders to just above his head. The lighting wasn't great. Jansen was only a few shades lighter than the dark background behind him. From the acoustics, Quinn guessed it had been shot in a small room, but there was no way to tell for sure.

Jansen stared at the camera for a moment, then began. 'My name is Dr. Henry Jansen. I'm a research virologist. I have worked around the world for numerous groups, including the World Health Organization and the CDC. I only say this so that you will pay attention to what I have to say. Who I am really isn't important. But the fact that you are watching this means I am not able to give you the following information in person.

'For the past six months, I have been working undercover. This operation I have undertaken on my own. I was contacted by an organization that calls itself HFA. As far as I can tell, they are an extremist Serbian group. I will assume you have already read the document that will be uploaded with this video and know what the HFA plan is. Here are a few more details.

'An American named Dahl was hired to oversee the distribution operation. To be sure it all goes as planned, HFA also enlisted the help of a group run by a fellow Serb named Borko. His primary task, as far as I can figure out, is security.

'HFA is made up of Slobodan Milošević loyalists. I think the fact that he died in prison in the middle of his war crimes trial gave them new energy. They talk of him having been murdered. To them, he has become a martyr to the cause. Milošević believed Bosnia and Herzegovina belonged to a greater Serbia. So what better way to honor him than to finish what he started? HFA feels the removal of the Bosniaks will allow this to happen. They also are now feeling the pressure to move rapidly because of the growing reconciliation movement in Serbia, highlighted by the election of a new, moderate president who has been advocating making amends for past atrocities.

'Because of this, the project has been accelerated. Pressure to produce results has been intense. The HFA leadership is fanatical, and will hear nothing except what they want. The scientific team here tried at first to explain the difficulties of their request. Then one of the researchers turned up dead in his room, and within two days the families of the others received visits from men associated with HFA. No one else was hurt. They didn't need to be. After that, the members of the team only said yes. It didn't matter if the requests were impossible. So the document which you already have represents what HFA has hoped to achieve rather than what the people they've hired have actually achieved. Of course, no one has told HFA that.

'The bracelet in your possession contains a sample of nerve tissue destroyed by the virus in one of the links. I have learned that this virus is to be contained within a small, nonporous pouch that will then be embedded in whatever the final delivery device is. Inside the pouch is a chemical mix that mimics the virus's natural habitat both in composition and temperature. It is designed to keep the virus alive for weeks.'

Jansen paused, his eyes seeming to look directly at Quinn and Orlando. 'This is not polio as we have known it. This virus has been engineered to be far more malignant and destructive.

'What that final delivery device is I have not been told. As I have said, that is a part of the operation Dahl controls. I do know there is little time to waste. I have also not been told when the distribution of the virus is to occur, but my sense is that it will happen sometime in the next month.

'This must not be allowed to happen. The calculated destruction of the Bosniaks is revolting in and of itself. But the task to create such a targeted biological agent is beyond the capacity of those working here. Maybe beyond the capacity of anyone. What I'm saying is the virus they've tailored to attack their intended victims is flawed. Don't misunderstand, it *will* devastate the Bosniaks.

'But what they have really accomplished is to unintentionally engineer a supervirus that won't care which ethnic group a person is in. It could infect anyone, possibly everyone. If released, it *will* create a pandemic unlike any we have ever seen before.

'They must be stopped.'

Jansen reached forward, then suddenly the picture stopped.

It was several seconds before Orlando began breathing again. Quinn's reaction the first time he'd watched the video had been almost the same.

'Do you want to watch it again?' Quinn asked.

'No,' Orlando replied. She sat in the chair Quinn had been in. 'I guess we can assume the mints are the unknown device.'

Quinn nodded. 'The virus packet must be embedded in the middle. Like those mints with the liquid centers.'

She looked up at him. 'It still doesn't matter. Getting Garrett back is still our main goal.'

'Of course,' he said. 'But we can't let them get the virus.'

Orlando looked away. When she spoke, it was so low he almost couldn't hear her. 'I know.'

It was nearly midnight, and Quinn was back inside the water plant. He knew he was pressing his luck by returning, but the job had to be done. Besides, this time he wasn't completely alone.

Orlando was back at their hideout watching the monitor, filling Quinn in. Since they didn't have access to Orlando's communication gear anymore, they improvised by using their cell phones. Quinn's was taped to his arm, the hands-free cable running under his jacket to his ear.

On his back, Quinn carried his backpack. It contained his gun and a few more of Orlando's purchases. The gun was only to be used as a last resort. This mission had to be completed without anyone even suspecting he'd been there.

Orlando talked him through the two basement rooms and into the stairwell that led to the base of the sphere. 'You're clear,' she said.

Quinn climbed the stairs, then opened the hatch that covered the top of the staircase. He stepped into the round room and shut the door. 'I'm going into the air lock now,' Quinn said.

'You should be okay,' Orlando told him. 'The only activity's in the containment room.'

Quinn crossed over to the vertical air-lock tube that led up and into the sphere itself. He pushed the button and waited for the light to turn green. When it did, he entered the tube and shut the door. He then climbed the ladder and reached up to open the hatch above him. 'Wait,' Orlando said. 'Someone just came in from the main air lock.'

Quinn held still.

'Okay,' she said. 'He's gone inside the containment room. Go ahead.'

Quinn opened the hatch. Air from inside the

tube rushed past him into the sphere. Dressed as he was in a black sweater and black pants but no biohazard suit, the artificial wind reminded him how vulnerable he was.

He pulled himself into the sphere, then began scaling the scaffolding. When he reached the top, he positioned himself below the containment room and removed his backpack. Using a pair of Velcro strips, he attached the bag to a pole, then opened it.

The Czech-made Semtex explosive was overkill for the job, but Quinn had to make sure everything in the room above him was destroyed. The bad part was that he'd have to wait to set it off. Several of the boxes of mints had already been carried away. It was possible they weren't even in the building. If Quinn detonated the Semtex now, he might miss those other cases, and, in the process, tip off Dahl and Borko that he was onto them. The destruction of the virus had to be coordinated.

Quinn placed the Semtex at several points along the bottom of the laboratory. He then set a radio-activated detonator at each point. After that, he extracted a small box from the backpack. It was a relay. All they had to do now was trigger the relay with one of the remotes Orlando had obtained, and a signal would be sent out to the detonators. Then *boom.*

Quinn attached the relay to one of the poles, then gave everything a final inspection. Satisfied, he unfastened the strips holding the backpack to the pole and pulled the pack over his shoulders. Now it was only a matter of time.

Chapter 37

Though Quinn's sleep was short, it was the best he'd had in days. It didn't matter that he and his team were holed up in the cold back room of an abandoned store, or that they had to sleep in sleeping bags on blow-up mattresses. It always happened this way. The night before any big operation, Quinn would sleep like the dead.

At 5:30 a.m. his eyes opened. He was fully awake. The first thing he did was check on Nate. His forehead was damp, but not hot. The fever he'd had earlier seemed to have broken. Quinn got up and stepped around the mattresses, working his way out of the room.

He made a quick stop in the bathroom, then went out to the coffee shop just down the street and bought coffee and breakfast rolls. He made one final call to the Mole on the walk back. It was short, this time Quinn doing most of the talking. As he finished the conversation, he passed a news kiosk. On the counter was a stack of the *Berliner Morgenpost*. The headline caught his eye.

'Police Raid Terrorist Cell,' it read in German.

The address of the raided house was Sophie's. She was even mentioned in the article as being a potential member of the organization. He read on:

> One of the suspected terrorists was killed in the gunfight as she tossed a grenade at undercover officers. Extensive damage was done to the structure. Police were forced to fire tear gas canisters to root out the rest of the terrorist cell. According to police sources, at least two others remain at large.

The rest of the story was below the fold, where Quinn couldn't read it. It was all bullshit, of course. But apparently Borko had enough contacts to cover his own tracks.

Quinn returned to the hideout and found the other two still asleep. He set the coffee and food within reach if either of them awoke, then went back into the bathroom.

He stared at his reflection in the mirror for a moment. He hadn't shaved in a couple of days and he was looking pretty scruffy. A plastic shopping bag sat on the floor near the sink. Inside were toothbrushes, toothpaste, a comb, deodorant, a hairbrush, razors and shaving cream, some first-aid stuff.

Quinn pulled out a razor and the cream and gave himself a thorough shave. He wiped away the excess foam, then opened one of the toothbrushes and brushed his teeth. Cleaner now, he turned off the light and returned to the other room.

Orlando was sitting up, drinking coffee. Nate was awake, too, the sleeping bag pulled up around his head. He was peeking out at Quinn through a small opening. 'It's fucking cold,' Nate said, his voice muffled by the bag.

'Have some coffee,' Quinn said.

'Can you just pour it over the top of my sleeping bag?'

'I guess you're feeling better then,' Quinn said.

'Compared to what?'

'Yesterday.'

'I guess.' Nate slowly sat up, letting the bag slide off his head and down to his shoulders. He moved his head slowly from side to side, stretching his neck. 'Definitely better. Yesterday when I woke up, I could barely turn over. I guess this is an improvement.'

'Do you think you're up to this?'

Nate didn't even hesitate. 'I'll be fine.'

'If you can't do it, tell us,' Orlando said, her tone all business.

'Good morning to you, too,' Nate said, turning toward her.

'I'm serious,' she said.

'So am I. I'll be fine.' Nate slowly reached over and picked up the remaining cup of coffee. 'I mean, if you're asking if I can run a mile, then sucker punch someone, I'd have to say no. But I can drive a car.'

'Even with your fucked-up shoulder?' Orlando asked.

'Jesus,' Nate said. 'You need to take a happy pill or something.'

'Nate,' Quinn said quickly.

'No,' Nate countered. He looked at Orlando. 'I

realize this isn't easy for you. I know you wish you found Garrett instead of me. If I were you I'd feel the same way. But I'm here and you need my help to get him back. My shoulder *is* fucked up. I feel like shit. But if I say I can do the job, I'll do it.'

Orlando and Quinn both stared at Nate for a moment. Then Orlando said, 'You could have just said yes.'

Nate's hard expression softened. 'Yes.'

'I'm sorry,' she said.

Nate gave her a smile and waved it off.

'So are we all good now?' Quinn asked. 'Because we need to get a move on.'

Orlando had been able to learn from monitoring conversations at the plant that the transportation of the polio-laced mints was scheduled for 8:30 a.m. Their only chance to take everything out was between the time the mints left the water plant and when they arrived at the building on Kaiserdamm where the welcome packets were being stuffed. A narrow window at best.

Nate unzipped his bag and began to stand up, the whole time wincing in pain.

'There's some aspirin in the bathroom, if you need it,' Quinn said.

Nate looked over at him. 'I may need the whole bottle.'

The information the Mole had given Quinn proved to be accurate. The place where the welcome packets were being prepped was an old stone office building sitting at the corner of a block of similar old stone buildings.

Quinn watched it from the Einstein Coffee Shop on the corner, just down the street. For the past thirty minutes several people had entered the building. The majority were young, probably university students. All were dressed comfortably for several hours of menial work. Quinn pegged them as the hired help who would be filling the packets.

Quinn's phone rang. It was Orlando. 'The van's leaving now.'

For the last hour she had been in position on top of the same apartment building she'd been on two nights before. This time she was watching Borko's goons load the boxes of mints into a white cargo van.

'Is Borko still there?' Quinn asked.

'He left about ten minutes ago.' Orlando's voice came in short bursts. Quinn guessed she was once again making her way down the stairs, this time to Nate, who was sitting behind the wheel of a maroon BMW Quinn had appropriated earlier that morning.

'How many boxes total?' Quinn asked.

'Twenty.'

'All of them, then.'

'Looks like it.'

Twenty boxes, each containing 120 tins, gave Dahl 2,400 miniature biological weapons containers. Multiply that by the 6 mints in each box and the total number of delivery devices was 14,400. There were enough tins so that every attendee could leave with several extras. *Have one now. Take a few home. Share them with your friends.*

'They secured the boxes with a cargo net,' she added.

No doubt to keep the boxes from moving around, Quinn guessed. 'Were they alone?'

'No,' Orlando said. 'Hold on.'

Quinn could hear the sound of a car door opening, then a moment later slamming shut. Orlando said, 'Looks like they're heading toward Karl Marx Strasse.' The words were not for Quinn but Nate.

'Okay,' Orlando said into the phone. 'I'm back. What was the question?'

'Were they alone?'

'No. A silver Mercedes sedan is following. But as far as I can tell, that's it.'

One escort wasn't enough. There had to be more. At the very least, reinforcements would be at the ready at various points along the route if needed.

'You see them yet?' Quinn asked.

'They're about a block ahead of us.'

'Best guess?'

'Route C,' Orlando said, indicating one of the possible directions they had guessed the shipment might take.

'We'll go with that,' Quinn said. 'Call me if anything changes.'

He hung up.

Quinn walked outside to the Porsche he'd picked for his own ride that day. As he climbed into the car and started the engine, he watched a couple of late arrivals hurrying up the steps of the Grob Promotions facility. More college kids, probably just trying to earn a little extra money. Quinn took a deep breath, then pulled away from the curb.

As he drove he connected the hands-free device

to his phone, stuck the earpiece in his ear, and made a call. It took Peter a moment to come to the line. 'This is it,' Quinn said.

'What is it?' Peter asked.

'Just shut up and listen. If things don't go well, in a few hours you'll be getting a call from an associate. If you listen to what he says and do what he tells you, you may still have a chance. But it's not a guarantee.'

Quinn's instructions to the Mole had been even simpler. If Quinn didn't call him by 1:00 p.m. Berlin time, the Mole would tell Peter everything.

'What the hell is going on?'

'I promise, you'll know soon enough.'

'Quinn, I –'

Quinn disconnected the call.

Quinn swung the Porsche onto Kantstrasse, eastbound, then called Orlando. 'Where are you?' Quinn asked.

'Still Route C.'

'Any sign of other escorts?'

'Just the sedan.'

'All right. Give me a five-minute heads-up before you reach the rendezvous point.'

'That won't be long,' Orlando said.

Quinn drove cautiously, trying not to attract attention. By the time he was in position, he still hadn't heard back from Orlando. He found an open spot at the curb and parked, leaving the engine running.

His phone finally rang a minute later.

'Five-minute warning,' Orlando said.

'Status?'

'Everything's the same.'

'They haven't spotted you?'

'No,' Orlando said. 'For someone who can barely move, Nate's pretty good.'

'Don't hang up,' Quinn said.

Quinn pulled his backpack onto his lap. He extracted his SIG Sauer, checked to be sure the magazine was in place, then set the pistol on the passenger seat.

The extra mags were in the backpack. Quinn extracted two of them, slipping them into his pocket. He then set the backpack on the floor in front of the passenger seat.

'Two minutes,' Orlando said. 'They're four blocks away.'

Quinn glanced in the direction from where the shipment would be approaching. Nothing yet. Without looking, he reached back behind his seat and grabbed the Uzi he'd taken from Nate's captors off the floor. He only had the one magazine for the weapon, but its intimidation value would make up for his lack of ammunition.

'Wait a minute,' Orlando said.

'What?'

'They're turning.'

'Which way?' Quinn asked.

'Left,' Orlando said, some of her calm slipping. 'They're going left!'

As Quinn pulled out from the curb, he could hear Nate cursing in the background.

'What is it?' Quinn asked.

'We're blocked off,' Orlando said.

'You've been spotted?'

'No,' she said. 'Just too much traffic.'

'Can you still see them?'

'Hold on.' There was a pause. 'No. They must have turned again. I don't know where they are. Quinn, we've got to find them. We have to get those boxes.' Her voice was emphatic, desperate.

Quinn raced down the road. When he was only a block from where Nate and Orlando had lost the truck, he turned down a side street. His eyes flicked back and forth at every cross street looking for the cargo van. But it wasn't there.

A sense of impending disaster began to creep into his mind, but he quickly pushed it down. They had to get the shipment. There was no choice.

'Scratch the ambush,' Quinn said. 'We have to go to Charlottenburg. To the delivery point.'

'Got it,' Orlando said, then relayed the instructions to Nate.

Quinn made a quick adjustment to his route and was soon heading west toward Charlottenburg.

He tried to stay calm. They could still do this. They *had* to do this.

It was the last possible chance they'd have.

Chapter 38

Quinn retraced his route back to the conference staging building in Charlottenburg, the whole time keeping a lookout for the van. But he never caught sight of it.

'Orlando, where are you?' Quinn asked.

There was a bit of static, then, 'About a mile and a half away.'

With city traffic, that put them several minutes behind Quinn.

'I'm almost there,' Quinn said.

'Are you going to wait for us?'

'No,' Quinn said, without hesitation. 'Just get here fast.'

Ahead was the Einstein Coffee Shop he had been sitting in earlier. As he turned the final corner, his mouth tensed.

'The van's already here,' he said as he pulled the Porsche quickly to the curb and stopped a block away.

'Have they taken any boxes out?' Orlando asked.

'I don't think so. The back's still shut.'

'We're two minutes away.'

'Make it one,' Quinn said.

The van was parked at the curb near the front door of the building. Four people stood near the back. Two of them had the unmistakable look of hired muscle. The other two, a man and a woman, were both younger. Quinn pegged them as two of the hired workers.

There were two sedans parked directly across the street from the van, a dark BMW and a silver Mercedes. Quinn counted three men in each. This was getting more fun by the minute.

He placed his SIG in his lap and rolled down the driver's-side window. At the van, one of the goons had moved over to the doors and was starting to open them. Quinn took a deep breath, then put the car back in gear and gunned the engine. The Porsche jumped away from the curb and began racing down the street toward the cargo van.

The four people standing behind the van looked up almost in unison. The two kids looked on curiously, but the other two immediately rushed around the side of the van looking for cover.

Doors on both sedans flew open. Quinn, gun now in his left hand, aimed the weapon out his open window and let off ten quick shots. The men dove in all directions, unable to return fire. As he squeezed the trigger, Quinn whipped the steering wheel to the right, bringing the Porsche up onto the sidewalk.

The two kids were no longer in sight. Quinn drove the Porsche between the van and the building.

At the last second, he slammed on the brakes, bringing his car to a quick stop.

He threw open his door and jumped out. In one hand he carried his pistol and in the other, the Uzi.

No one had opened fire on him yet. As he had hoped, the contents of the van acted as a makeshift shield. None of them wanted to be the one who destroyed the product.

Quinn headed toward the rear of the van. He needed to get a count of the boxes, make sure they were all still there.

Behind him, something scraped the ground. As he turned he saw a man racing toward him. It was one of the two thugs who had been standing outside. In a single motion, Quinn jumped to his right and unloaded a short burst from the Uzi, before landing hard on the sidewalk.

The man was barely five feet away when the bullets smashed into his chest, whipping him around and spinning him to the ground.

'Give it up. You're not getting out of here,' someone yelled from across the street.

A bullet flew by Quinn, just missing his shoulder. Someone had gotten smart and was shooting under the van. Quinn, ignoring the pain in his side from his fall, pushed himself off the ground and took two quick steps to his left, putting the van's rear wheel between him and Borko's men. The hands-free earpiece to his phone was dangling over his shoulder. He placed it back in his ear.

'Quinn? Are you there?' Orlando asked. 'Quinn?'

'I'm here. I'm okay,' Quinn said.

'We're two blocks away,' Orlando said. 'What's your situation?'

'There are at least six men, probably seven, on the north side of the street.' Quinn's voice was calm. 'They were in a couple of sedans, a BMW and a Mercedes. Don't know if they're still in them now. I'm out of the car, but I've got the van between us. I need you to take those guys out.'

'We're on it,' Orlando said.

'Is that you, Mr. Quinn?' Another voice called to him from across the street. 'You come out now and I'll make sure nothing too bad happens.' A pause. 'Mr. Quinn? You really think you are going to be able to stop this? If you do, you are wrong. You do not start playing smart, in a couple of minutes you are going to be dead.'

Quinn had been silently counting the seconds in his mind. Orlando and Nate should have been here by now. *What the hell was –*

Orlando's voice came over the receiver. 'Cover your ears and duck.'

Quinn immediately curled into a ball, a hand squeezed tightly over each ear.

For a second there was nothing. Then suddenly the air was filled with a loud *whomp.* Quinn could feel his whole body pulse inward, his breath nearly knocked out of him. Thankfully the van protected him from the brunt of the concussion grenade.

'Are you all right?' Orlando asked, still on the phone.

Quinn uncurled himself and stood up. 'I think so. Did it work?'

'Yeah,' Orlando said. 'There were actually eight

of them. But they're all sleeping now. Some more permanently than others.'

Orlando suddenly appeared from around the side of the van, and jogged over to Quinn.

'It was stronger than I expected,' Orlando said.

'Where's Nate?'

'Still in the car.'

'Count the boxes,' Quinn said, nodding toward the back of the van. 'I'm going to see if this thing will still start.'

'Okay.'

Quinn stopped first at the Porsche and retrieved his backpack. At the cab of the van, Quinn threw his stuff inside, then climbed in. It took him less than thirty seconds to find the right wires to hot-wire the vehicle. As he touched them together the engine roared to life.

In the distance, Quinn could hear sirens. They weren't nearly as far away as he would have liked. Soon the street was going to be flooded with police.

'I've got to go,' he yelled toward the back of the van. 'Are you done?'

'They're all here,' Orlando answered.

'Okay,' Quinn said. 'We're back on plan. I'll take the van. You guys run point.'

Something pinged off the hood of the van. Quinn looked out the windshield. Someone was standing at the end of the block pointing a gun at the van. Quinn shifted into drive and hit the gas.

'I'm still in here!' Orlando shouted.

'Hang on,' Quinn yelled back.

They raced down the street. Quinn had no choice but to go in the direction of the man with the gun.

Bullets kept coming, but none had yet to pierce the windshield. The shooter was obviously torn between stopping the van and not putting the cargo in danger. As Quinn got closer he ducked below the dash, keeping the accelerator pressed to the floor.

Another ping, this time off the passenger-side door, followed quickly by two more. Then there was the squeal of brakes and, very near, the wail of a siren.

Quinn looked up. They had passed the building and were in the intersection just beyond. Coming at them from the side was a cop on a motorcycle. The driver had apparently not anticipated the appearance of the van, and was coming at them too fast. At the last second, he turned to the left, laying his bike down in a storm of sparks and screeching metal. The cop rolled off his bike just before it smashed into a light pole, silencing the siren.

Quinn continued to race forward. He was in the middle of a deep breath when there was a bang from the rear of the van. He glanced into the side-view mirror. One of the rear doors, flapping back and forth with the movement of the van.

'Are you all right?' Quinn called out.

'Yeah,' Orlando answered. 'He shot at me as we went by, but it went wide.'

'Didn't want to damage the boxes,' Quinn guessed, then added, 'We almost hit a cop.'

'Yeah. That was kind of hard to miss.'

'Are there any more of them back there?'

'Not yet.'

‘What about Nate?’

There was a pause, then, ‘I don’t see him.’

Quinn turned left at the next intersection. Again, the doors banged against the side of the van.

‘We’ve got to get those shut,’ he said.

‘No shit.’

Ahead the light was turning red. There were two cars in front of him, so there was no way he was going to make it.

‘When I stop up here, you get out and shut them,’ he said.

He halted at the end of the line of waiting cars. From the back, he could hear Orlando jump out and close the doors. A few seconds later, she was opening the passenger-side door and hopping into the seat next to him.

As the light turned green, Quinn moved the van forward with the other cars. But instead of following them through the intersection, he made a right turn onto the less trafficked side street.

‘So that didn’t exactly go as planned,’ Quinn said.

‘I wasn’t going to say anything,’ Orlando told him.

‘But you were thinking it.’

‘I was thinking it.’

For five minutes, they were alone on the road. No pursuers, but no Nate either. Quinn didn’t want to even think about the possibility that Nate had been captured again.

‘I think there’s someone back there,’ Orlando said. She was looking through the side-view mirror mounted to the passenger door.

Quinn looked through the mirror on his side. There were several cars behind them.

'Which one?' he asked.

'The black Mercedes. Three cars back.' She paused, still looking in her mirror. 'The silver one behind it might be with him.'

Quinn moved the van slightly so he could get a better look. 'Okay. I see them. I'll make a couple turns. Keep an eye on them.'

Quinn made a quick left turn.

'Still there,' Orlando said after a moment.

Quinn made another turn, this time to the right. Before Orlando could confirm anything, there was a familiar ping off the side of the van – another warning shot.

'Yeah,' Orlando said. 'They're following us.'

Quinn glanced back at his side mirror. The rear driver's-side window of the black Mercedes was open, and someone was leaning out, a gun in his hand. Quinn immediately swung the van over, blocking the shooter's view.

Ahead, a traffic light was turning from green to yellow. Quinn raced through the intersection just as the light turned red. He checked his mirror and grimaced. Both Mercedes had followed him through the light, ignoring the cross traffic, honking horns, and screeching brakes.

Quinn's only advantage was they wouldn't want the shipment harmed. They were probably instructed to get Quinn to stop the van with minimal damage. Then they could kill whoever was inside.

Another traffic light was turning red. This time

there were several cars between Quinn and the intersection.

'Hold on,' he said.

At the last instant, instead of stopping, he whipped the van around in a U-turn, pulling in front of two cars in the oncoming lanes. There was the loud squeal of tires as one of the cars spun sideways, nearly ramming into the back of the van.

The black sedan was in position to continue the chase. The silver one, at least for the moment, was trapped on the other side of a delivery truck. The black Mercedes swung around, coming up on the driver's side of the van.

'Roll down your window,' Orlando said.

He glanced at her. She was holding the Uzi. Without any further hesitation, he did what she asked.

As soon as the Mercedes came into view, she barked, 'Duck!'

Quinn leaned forward as she unloaded a burst of fire over his head. The bullets sliced into the side of the Mercedes. As soon as she stopped, Quinn popped up again, glancing out at where the other car had been, but it was gone. His eyes flicked to his mirror. The Mercedes was sitting sideways on the far side of the road. All the windows on the side that had been facing the van were shot out. There was no movement from inside.

Quinn could hear more sirens converging on their location, but he saw no flashing lights yet.

'Grab on to something,' he said.

He whipped the steering wheel quickly to the right, turning them onto a narrow side street. He made a left, then two more rights before the sirens began to fade. He started to smile, but then as he looked in his side-view mirror again, his jaw tensed.

The silver sedan was still behind him.

They began a game of cat and mouse, Quinn never quite able to lose them, and the silver Mercedes never quite able to get the drop on him. Nate was still a no-show; that was troubling. Orlando had tried calling him twice, but there had been no answer.

Quinn glanced down at the backpack on the floor between them. Inside was more than enough Semtex to destroy the van and its contents completely. He nodded toward it.

'Hide it between the boxes,' he said.

She looked at him. 'But we don't set it off until we've got Garrett, right?'

'That's the plan. I just don't want to be messing with that stuff later.'

With only a slight hesitation, she reached down and picked up the backpack. She carried it into the back, then unhooked the cargo net holding the boxes in place and pushed open a gap between the containers. Carefully, she placed the bag as close to the center of the pile as she could get. Once the net was resecured, she slipped back into her seat.

'Not until we find my son,' she said, nodding toward the back of the truck.

They found themselves back in the Mitte, driving west on Unter den Linden, near the Brandenburg Gate. Ahead was Tiergarten, Berlin's version of Central Park. In the center was a large traffic roundabout that encircled the Grosser Stern monument, a golden winged angel which looked out over the city from the top of a giant pillar.

Quinn tried to maneuver to the right and take Ebertstrasse toward the Reichstag, but there was too much traffic. He was forced to continue forward, into Tiergarten. To compound his problems, the road had widened into four lanes in each direction. No way he would be able to keep them from pulling up alongside now.

'This might not be the best way to go,' Orlando said.

'Yeah, I know.'

When he looked into his mirror, he saw that the silver Mercedes had been joined by a midnight blue BMW. Whoever owned the car apparently enjoyed his privacy. The windows seemed to be darkly tinted all the way around, including the windshield.

'New arrival,' Quinn said.

Orlando took a look and nodded.

Their only hope was that they could reach the traffic circle before the others did, and use its inherent confusion to their advantage. Quinn pressed the accelerator as far down as it would go and sped forward.

Behind them, their pursuers were driving side by side. It was almost like there was a conversation going on between the cars. Then, when they were halfway through the park, the Mercedes accelerated.

Quinn waited until it was even with his passenger-side door, then he gave the steering wheel a jerk to the right. The driver of the Mercedes slammed on his brakes and swerved out of the way.

Ahead, the Grosser Stern monument drew near. Parked along the side of the road, just before the traffic circle, were several tour buses. Even in winter, the monument would be crawling with tourists.

'He's coming back again,' Orlando said.

Quinn swung the steering wheel again as the Mercedes neared, but the driver had anticipated the move and kept coming.

'Oh crap,' Orlando said.

'What?'

Before she could answer, a bullet slammed into the passenger door. Immediately, a second one shattered the side window, then lodged into the roof just above Quinn's head.

'Dammit!' Orlando yelled. 'I thought you said they'd only fire warning shots.'

'The warning shots would be for me,' he said. 'You're kind of expendable.'

'Then let me drive and you be the expendable one,' she said, taking a deep breath as she finished.

He looked over. Her face was etched with pain.

'Are you hit?' he asked as he swerved to the left, sideswiping an Audi and creating a little distance between himself and the Mercedes.

'It's nothing,' she said, her teeth clenched. Blood was running down her left arm.

'Are you sure?'

'I'm fine. It's just a cut.' She held out the hand of her other arm. 'Give me your gun.'

Quinn gave her his SIG.

'You'll need a new mag, too,' he said as he dug one out of his pocket.

She reloaded the gun, then turned and fired three

shots out her window. The first sailed over the hood of the sedan, but the second and third punctured the side of the car. The Mercedes veered, then straightened out, continuing forward.

As the rear window on the driver's side started rolling down, Orlando fired again. But instead of hitting the open window, the bullets shattered the closed one in front of it, the driver's window. One moment the Mercedes was beside them, a second later it swung violently to the right and slammed into the side of a tourist bus parked at the curb.

'Nice shot,' Quinn said.

The traffic circle was just ahead of them now, six lanes of vehicles, traveling counterclockwise around the monument. As Quinn swung the van into the inner lane and began racing around the circle, he checked his mirrors again. The BMW was still there, content to follow. But about a quarter mile behind it, several police cars raced toward them.

Quinn waited until the monument was between him and the police, then veered off the circle in the direction that would take them north out of town. Hopefully he'd be able to shake the police.

The BMW was another matter.

Chapter 39

As Quinn neared the airport he removed the white business card Dr. Garber had given him. He turned it over so the phone number was visible, then handed it to Orlando.

'Make the call,' he said. 'Whoever answers should be able to get Borko or Dahl.'

Someone answered almost immediately. Once Orlando had hung up, she said, 'We should be getting a call soon.'

Less than thirty seconds later, the phone rang.

'Give it to me,' Quinn said.

Orlando handed it to him. Quinn pushed the connect button and held the phone to his ear. 'Yes?' he said.

'You wanted to talk to me?' It was Borko.

'I'm going to make this fast. We'll give you back the van when you give us the boy.'

'Why would we do that? Soon we will have the van and the boy.'

'Call your friends at the water plant,' Quinn said, then disconnected the call.

He pulled an object that looked like a thick

credit card out of the inside pocket of his jacket. At one end, there were two switches. The first was the safety. Quinn flipped it to the off position. The second was an A/B switch, allowing access to two different channels. Quinn selected channel A. Below the switches was a pad that had been keyed to Quinn's right thumbprint.

'Be careful with that,' Orlando said.

He placed his thumb on the pad. A second later, he was greeted with a barely audible beep.

If everything had worked properly, the sphere in Neukölln had just lit up like a blast furnace. Quinn was certain he'd placed more than enough Semtex to incinerate any residual virus. If he flipped the switch to channel B and thumbed the pad again, it would trigger the explosives in the back of the van. As a precaution, Orlando and Nate had similar triggering devices.

Quinn glanced at the side mirror. There was no outward reaction in the BMW, but almost immediately his phone began ringing again.

'What was the point of that?' Borko said.

'A demonstration. If we don't get Garrett back, alive and unharmed, your building in Neukölln won't be the only thing destroyed. Your call.'

He hung up again.

'You really think it's going to work?' Orlando asked.

His only answer was a nod and a smile. In truth he had hoped to be free and clear when it came time to make the call. Now with the way things were, he just hoped one of them would be able to get out alive.

'Look out!' Orlando said.

Less than a half a block away, a Volvo sedan pulled out from a side street and stopped in their path. Quinn had been paying too much attention to the car behind them and barely had time to react. Pressing down on the accelerator, he turned the wheel so they could swing past the front of the vehicle.

There was the crunch of metal on metal as the front right corner of the van pushed the sedan out of the way, ripping the car's bumper off in the process.

'You're clear,' Orlando said.

Quinn pressed the pedal all the way to the floor.

They drove north through the city, past Tegel Airport, and into the less populated countryside. The BMW was still behind them, as was the bumperless Volvo. Both seemed content to let Quinn lead the way.

There was still no sign of Nate.

'We're going to have to dump this soon,' Quinn said.

He'd been monitoring the gauges on the dashboard. While they had plenty of fuel, the oil pressure had been steadily dropping.

'We can't,' Orlando said. 'We need it.'

'I don't think we're going to have a choice.'

'No!' she yelled. 'We can't. We need it to find Garrett!'

Ahead Quinn noticed a snow-packed road leading into a wooded area. There was a construction sign near the entrance, proclaiming the road off-limits to anyone but employees of Boon Industries.

At the last second, Quinn whipped the van down the road. The Volvo shot past, unable to react in time. But the BMW made the turn, its back end fishtailing as it tried to gain traction on the snowy surface.

'What are you doing?' Orlando asked.

'I'm trying to keep us alive.'

The road wound through a grove of trees before emerging into a clearing. It was a construction site, by the looks of it, not much farther along than the leveling-of-the-ground stage. Work must have been halted when winter rolled in.

Quinn shot across the field. Somewhere there had to be another exit, another way through the construction site. Behind him, the BMW entered the clearing, then stopped, the car's occupants no doubt concerned about an ambush. A moment later, it was joined by the Volvo. It was exactly what Quinn had been hoping they'd do.

He kept driving across the field away from them. The terrain forced him to reduce his speed to only a few miles an hour. His eyes scanned the rapidly approaching trees in front of them.

'What are you looking for?' Orlando asked.

'An exit or a back road.'

They were both quiet for a moment, then Orlando shouted, 'There!'

She pointed at a gap in the trees off to the left. Quinn turned toward it. Almost immediately he realized he'd made a mistake. The ground quickly became uneven and rutted. Quinn jerked the wheel left, then right, then left, then –

A loud thud shook the van as the front passenger tire dipped into an unseen hole about three feet wide, slamming the rubber up against the top of the wheel well. Quinn gunned the engine. The vehicle lurched forward, pulling itself back onto level ground. But the damage was already done. The tire was blown. And from the screeching, it sounded like the axle might be bent.

Quinn cursed under his breath and stopped the van.

'We can't stop here,' Orlando said.

'We don't have a choice,' Quinn said, emphasizing each word. 'The van is done.'

As he turned off the engine he glanced out his side window back toward the other two cars. They were still parked near the entrance to the site, but there was activity now.

The driver of the Volvo was walking over to the other sedan. A window rolled down, and the driver seemed to listen for a moment. A second later he turned and shouted something at the Volvo. The rear passenger doors of the Volvo flew open, and two men jumped out. They ran across the field, not straight for the van, but parallel to it.

'Out, out, out,' Quinn said.

The van had come to a rest at an angle that shielded the passenger side of the vehicle from the BMW and Volvo. Orlando shoved the door open, then slipped outside. Quinn quickly followed her.

As soon as he was outside, Quinn reached into his pocket and retrieved the remote triggering device. He turned the safety off and moved the channel switch to B. To ensure he didn't set the explosives off prematurely, he held the device in his left hand.

Across the field, another car door opened. 'Quinn?'

It was Borko.

'Quinn! Enough already, hey? You had a good run! But give it up, my friend! You have no chance!'

One hundred feet from where they stood, the woods encroached on the clearing. Quinn nodded toward them.

'You first,' he said to Orlando. 'I'll distract them. The moment you're in position, blow the van.'

He could see the hesitation in her eyes. 'We go together,' she said, then held up her gun. 'If we get to cover, we can pick them off. We won't have to set off the explosives.'

'That's not going to work,' Quinn said.

'Dammit, we can at least try.'

Quinn nodded tersely. 'Fine. We'll try. But if it's not working, we blow the van.'

Orlando smiled weakly.

'Quinn, you're finished! Do you understand?' Borko's anger was starting to bleed into his voice, 'Put down your gun and come out where I can see you!'

Keeping the van between them and the sedans, Quinn and Orlando began running toward the woods.

'You would think I'd have lost my patience by now!' Borko continued. 'You have done a great deal of damage! But it is only business! I understand this! Just as I am sure you'll understand I cannot let you get away!'

The trees were only ten yards away now.

'Borko, over here!' another voice called out from Quinn's right. 'They're almost to the woods!'

Quinn glanced over his shoulder. He saw one of Borko's goons circling around the van.

'Run,' he said as he pushed Orlando in front of him.

They sprinted for the trees, Orlando a step ahead of Quinn. The forest was less than fifteen feet away when a sharp, burning pain ripped across Quinn's left thigh, knocking him into Orlando and dropping both of them onto the ground.

'Go!' he yelled at Orlando. It felt like his leg was on fire.

She pulled herself up again and began to run. As she reached the woods, she turned, a look of panic on her face. Immediately he realized what was wrong. She was no longer holding her gun. He could see it on the ground about a body's length in front of him. Too far for him to reach, and too far for her to come back. Yet that looked exactly like what she was about to do.

'No!' Quinn yelled. 'Run!'

A bullet slammed into a tree next to Orlando's head.

'Run!' Quinn yelled again.

This time she listened to him and quickly disappeared into the forest.

Quinn took a deep breath, then reached down to check his wound. He expected to find his leg shredded, but the bullet had only grooved a line across the back of his thigh, never fully entering the muscle.

He could hear the sound of running feet. He was never going to make it to the woods. He had to set off the explosives. Only when he went to push the button, the trigger was no longer in his hand.

'Turn over.' The voice came from only a few feet away. 'Slowly.'

Quinn did as he was told, trying as hard as possible to keep the pain that was screaming at him from showing on his face. As he finally rolled onto his back, he thought he felt something hard under his right arm. His triggering pad. But it was too far up, near his elbow. He couldn't reach it without being noticed.

Borko's man stood just to the side. In his hand was a pistol aimed at Quinn's head.

'I got him!'

Less than a minute later, the BMW rolled to a stop several feet away. Quinn looked over. First the front passenger-side door opened, and the driver from the Volvo got out. Then the back door followed suit, and out stepped Borko.

'The girl?' the Serb asked as he walked over.

'She ran into the woods,' the man who'd shot Quinn replied.

The Serb nodded, then said to the man and his partner who had also approached the van on foot, 'Get her.'

The two immediately headed toward the woods in pursuit of Orlando.

Borko smiled, then turned back to the car. 'The girl is missing,' he called. 'But we'll find her.'

Quinn looked over at the open back door, noticing for the first time that there was someone else in the back seat. So Piper had come along, too, Quinn thought.

The passenger leaned toward the opening. As he did, the morning sunlight fell across the right side of his face. Something wasn't right. The man didn't look like Piper at all.

Quinn all but stopped breathing. It was the shock of the injury causing him to see things. That had to be it.

Slowly, the man swung his legs out of the car, then stood up and walked over to Quinn and Borko. Once he reached them, he stopped and looked down.

'Apparently I taught you well,' the man said, his voice a hoarse croak.

'No,' Quinn said. 'You're dead. I saw you die.'

Durrie, Quinn's mentor, looked down at him and laughed. 'Really? I don't feel particularly dead.' Durrie looked over at the van, his eyes stopping for a moment on the damaged wheel. 'Goddamn it. Thanks for fucking up our transport.'

'We can move the boxes into the cars,' Borko said.

Quinn tried to refocus himself. It took every ounce of concentration to do so. Even then, there was a part of his mind screaming, *It's not him! It's not him!*

He tried to remember what Borko had just said. Something about the boxes. About moving the boxes. *Shit.* If they went into the back of the van, they'd find the explosives. He needed the triggering switch, but it was under his arm. Even if he made a quick move to grab it, Borko would shoot him.

'Put as many of the boxes as you can in the trunk of my car,' Durrie said to the Volvo driver. 'Then you guys can take the rest in your car once the girl's been dealt with.'

'Okay,' the man said.

Quinn watched as the man walked over to the van and opened the back doors.

Borko crouched down next to Quinn. 'You've fucked up our timetable,' he said. 'Some people will have to work very quickly now. That's not going to make them happy.'

The Volvo driver leaned into the van, then stood back up holding two boxes. He carried them over to the BMW. The trunk of the sedan popped open just before he got there.

'Maybe you could give them some mints,' Quinn whispered. 'That should make things better.'

Borko grinned. 'Very good. I was wondering how much you knew. Sadly, I'm afraid the mints would be wasted on them.'

'Because they're not Bosniaks?' Quinn asked.

Borko stiffened. 'How do you know that?'

'Jesus Christ,' Durrie said to Borko. 'It doesn't matter.'

'How did you know that?' Borko repeated, still kneeling next to Quinn.

Two more boxes were placed into the BMW. Quinn added them to his mental tally.

'Borko,' Durrie barked. 'Come on. We don't have time for this shit.'

Reluctantly, Borko stood back up.

Durrie looked down at Quinn. 'I'm going to skip over the how've-ya-been talk, all right? I just don't care. You're dead, Johnny boy. That's all I need to know. Tell your bitch girlfriend when you see her on the other side I'll take good care of Garrett for her.'

Durrie smiled, then pulled a gun out from under his jacket.

'Let me,' Borko said. 'He's killed several members of my team. I owe them his life.'

'You've got to be kidding me,' Durrie said. 'Cut the honor shit.'

'Let me do it,' Borko insisted. 'I'll give you half my share.'

Durrie raised an eyebrow, then laughed. 'If you want it that bad, fine.' Durrie looked down at Quinn. 'I guess I can be bought.' He laughed again, then walked slowly back to the car.

As he neared, the front door opened and out stepped Leo Tucker. Quinn's eyes narrowed. He should have expected him to be here, but seeing him in the flesh made Quinn flush with anger. The Aussie opened the back door for Durrie. As Quinn's mentor got in, the Volvo driver put another two boxes in the trunk.

Six, Quinn thought.

'You guys take the rest,' Durrie yelled toward Borko.

A moment later the BMW was speeding away. As Borko tracked the car, Quinn quickly moved his arm a few inches so that the triggering switch was now under his palm.

As Borko turned back to him, Quinn worked

the switch into his hand, but kept his palm pointed at the ground. He knew he wasn't going to be able to set it off in time to get the BMW. Some of the virus was going to get away.

'Okay. Now we have a little fun,' Borko said. He removed a pistol from a holster under his jacket. It was a SIG P226, just like Quinn's.

'Why didn't Gibson have a card?' Quinn asked. He was trying to buy time as he turned the switch in his hand so his thumbprint would be properly aligned.

Borko's brow creased for a moment, then he smiled. 'You mean at your house? You want to know the truth?' He leaned forward slightly, as if he were passing on a great secret. 'He was supposed to carve Dahl's name in your chest.'

Yeah. That would explain it, Quinn thought as he made sure the safety was off.

'Your plan isn't going to work, you know,' Quinn said. He moved his thumb to the A/B switch. Had he already put it in the B position?

'I don't care what you think. It will work fine.' Borko pulled back on the slide release on his pistol, checking to make sure a bullet was in the chamber.

'I don't mean the fact that your scientists screwed up and your attempt at ethnic genocide would have a wider audience.' *Right side A, left side B. Right? Right side A . . . No.* Left *side A, right side B.*

'Not genocide,' Borko said, raising his gun. 'Pest removal.'

The switch was on the right side. 'Whatever,' Quinn said. He risked a quick glance past Borko at the van, wondering if he was far enough away.

They were almost thirty yards away, and he was lying on the ground. Hopefully it would do some damage to Borko. At the very least it would be enough to knock the Serb to the ground, Quinn thought, give himself a chance to get away. 'That's not why it's not going to work.'

'Really?' Borko said. 'Why isn't it going to work?'

'Unfortunately, you'll probably never know.'

Quinn pressed his thumb against the pad, but nothing happened.

'What the hell is that supposed to mean?'

Quinn pressed again, still nothing. The switch was broken.

'You know what?' Borko asked. 'It doesn't matter. What does matter is –'

Whatever he thought mattered was lost in the explosion that ripped him apart.

Chapter 40

Quinn didn't remember the explosion at first. He did remember hands on his body, pulling things off him, then helping him to stand. He remembered looking for the van, but not finding it. It wasn't anywhere. But he had trouble remembering why any of it should matter.

Then someone slipped an arm under his shoulder.

'Come on,' a voice said, urging him forward.

Why was he having such a hard time walking? His left leg acted like it didn't want to hold him up without the help of his new companion. He looked down and saw a scarf tied around his leg. It was checkered, black and red, and seemed familiar. Where did that come from?

Soon he was surrounded by trees, but his companion kept urging him on deeper into the woods. Quinn could barely keep his eyes open. The journey seemed to take days, weeks even. Finally there was the sound of automobiles, dozens of them. And from somewhere beyond the direction they'd just come from, dozens of sirens screaming out of sync. His companion stopped then, helping Quinn to lean against a tree. Pain began to creep into Quinn's consciousness, and with it returned the awareness of his situation and the realization of what still needed to be done.

Quinn looked over at his companion, at Orlando. All five-feet-nothing of her. She'd been the one to get him to his feet. She'd tied her scarf around his leg. She was the one who led him away from the chaotic debris that had once been the van.

'How long?' he asked.

'Since the explosion?'

Quinn nodded.

She looked at her watch. 'Nine minutes.'

'My switch wasn't working,' Quinn said.

'Mine was.' Orlando pulled a phone out of her pocket. It wasn't the same model she or Quinn had been carrying. She saw him eyeing it. 'Got it off one of the guys who followed me into the woods.'

'Did you take care of them?'

'I wouldn't be here if I didn't.'

He tried to smile, but failed.

Orlando punched a number into the phone, then held it up to her ear.

'Where are you?' she said, then paused. 'You're almost here. A quarter mile at most. Hold on.'

She walked to the edge of the woods and stepped out. She was too far away for Quinn to hear her conversation, but only a few seconds later a car pulled to the side of the road. It was a maroon BMW sedan. *Nate*.

They helped Quinn into the back seat, then climbed into the front – Nate in the driver's seat,

Orlando on the passenger side. Quinn's apprentice pulled the car back onto the road, heading south into the city.

'Just lie down,' Orlando said, looking back. 'We'll get you to a doctor.'

'No,' Quinn said.

Orlando looked back. 'You've probably got a concussion. You need help.'

'No time for a doctor,' Quinn said. 'The St. Martin Hotel. That's where we need to go.'

'Why?' Orlando asked.

'I promised you we'd get Garrett,' Quinn said.

Outside, two police cars rushed past them heading the other way, their emergency lights flashing.

'He's at the St. Martin?' she asked quickly.

'No,' he said. 'That's not what I mean. We have to follow the trail.' When he realized they didn't understand what he meant, he added, 'We didn't get it all.'

'The mints?' she said. 'I blew them all up. Hell, you're lucky I didn't blow you up, too. Some guy must have been standing pretty close to you, because you were wearing parts of him when I found you.'

'Borko,' Quinn said.

'No shit?' Nate said.

Quinn nodded, though Nate couldn't see him. 'But we didn't get all the mints.'

He told them about the transferred boxes.

'Six boxes,' he said when he was done. 'More than enough to get the genocide started. He's got two choices. Dump the boxes, or deliver what he has and still get paid.'

'But why the hotel?' Nate asked. 'You said the

tins were supposed to be part of the welcome packets.'

'Yeah, well, it's too late to get them in the packets now, don't you think?'

'So what? We try to steal the remaining boxes, and still go for the trade-off?' Orlando asked. 'That's pretty weak, don't you think?'

Quinn chose his next words carefully. 'Dahl's the one with the boxes. And Tucker's with him.'

Orlando stared at him. 'Are you sure?'

Quinn nodded. 'They'll know where Garrett is.'

Silence filled the car. Outside, the city once again surrounded them. Nate had to slow the car as traffic began to increase. He shot a quick look at Orlando.

'The St. Martin or Dr. Garber?' he asked.

She didn't even hesitate. 'The hotel.'

Nate pulled up in front of a convenience store, and Orlando ran in. While she was gone, Quinn used the small first-aid kit to dress his wound. After he had the disinfectant and gauze in place, he wrapped an elastic bandage tightly around his thigh several times. He wasn't going to be able to walk perfectly, but the support of the bandage would help a little.

It was only a few minutes before Orlando returned. Once back in the car, she handed a bag to Quinn. Inside was a box of paper napkins and several bottles of water.

'Thanks,' Quinn said.

As Nate got them back on the road, Quinn poured water on several of the napkins, then used them to wipe the blood – Borko's blood, he realized – off his hands and face.

'Your clothes are going to be a problem,' Orlando said.

Quinn looked down. The jacket he was wearing was stained and ripped. Even the shirt underneath hadn't escaped damage. As for his pants, the left leg was soaked with blood from his wound.

'There's a sweater in the duffel bag,' Nate said.

Quinn had already noted the bag on the floor behind the driver's seat. He picked it up and put it on the seat beside him.

'What about pants?' he asked.

Nate shook his head. 'Sorry.'

Quinn removed his jacket and dumped it on the floor. He had to peel the shirt off slowly, as blood had begun to dry on his skin, creating a series of reddish brown lines and circles.

He used more napkins and water to clean off his torso, then opened the duffel bag. The sweater was on top. He removed it and pulled it over his head.

A few minutes later, Nate said, 'There it is.'

Quinn looked out the front window. Two blocks ahead was the St. Martin Hotel. There were police everywhere, and traffic was starting to slow to a crawl.

'Turn here,' Quinn said. 'See if we can get around back.'

'How are we supposed to get in?' Nate asked. 'There's too much security.'

'Just turn,' Quinn said.

Nate turned and drove for a few blocks before turning left again. The traffic was still slow, but it was moving.

'You really think Dahl brought the boxes here?' Nate asked.

'It's his only option,' Quinn said. 'Otherwise the plan is dead.'

'They could take them directly to Bosnia,' Nate countered. 'Maximum effect that way.'

'And the maximum chance HFA would be blamed for the attack. Release the bug here and they can expect a few ancillary outbreaks would occur in Bosniak populations outside of the Balkans. Even if bioterrorism is suspected, the finger would point at a much wider group of potential suspects.'

'But Jansen said the virus won't just infect the Bosniaks,' Nate said.

'*We* know that,' Orlando said. 'But they still think they've created the perfect weapon.'

'Dahl must be getting paid a hell of a lot of money to make this happen,' Nate said.

'I'm sure he is,' Orlando said.

Quinn pulled back slightly. There was more to it than just the money, he knew. He realized he'd been avoiding the subject since Nate had picked them up. But he couldn't avoid it any longer. Only as he started to speak, he couldn't find words to make it sound real. Finally he looked at Orlando. 'Do you still have your pictures of Garrett?'

She looked surprised, one hand unconsciously moving toward the pocket of her coat. 'Yes. Why?'

'Can I see them?'

Still perplexed, she reached into the inside pocket of her jacket and pulled out the small plastic wallet insert. She started to pull one of the pictures out.

'No,' Quinn said. 'Give me the whole thing.'

Reluctantly, she handed it over.

In total, there were three pictures of Garrett: two

recent, the third from when he was a baby. But it was the fourth picture in the miniature album that interested Quinn.

He removed the picture and held it over the seat toward Nate.

'Look at this,' he said.

'Eh . . . I'm driving,' Nate said.

'What are you doing?' Orlando asked.

'Just glance at it,' Quinn said to Nate.

Nate took the picture in his right hand, then held it up near his face, his eyes still on the road. After a moment, he glanced down. But instead of taking a quick look, his eyes remained riveted on the photo.

'That's enough,' Quinn said, tapping him on the shoulder.

'Son of a bitch,' Nate said as he handed the photo back.

'What?' Orlando asked.

'That's him,' Nate said.

'That's who?' Orlando was beginning to sound angry.

'The guy I saw when they had me locked up in that hotel room. The older guy.' Nate looked quickly back at Orlando, then shifted his gaze to the rearview mirror so he could look at Quinn. 'Is that Dahl?'

Quinn held the photo out to Orlando, but she didn't take it. He knew she was well aware who was in the picture.

'I saw him, too,' Quinn said. 'He was in the BMW.'

'That's not possible,' she said, disbelief on her face.

Quinn locked his eyes on Orlando's. 'He's not dead.'

'Bullshit. You saw him die. You gave me his ashes.'

'I know.' Quinn turned to Nate. 'You're sure this is the man you saw?'

'Yeah,' Nate said. 'Maybe a little older now, but that's definitely him. Who is he?'

'Nate's never seen his picture before,' Quinn said to Orlando. 'Maybe you don't believe me, but Nate's got no reason to lie.'

'It can't be,' she said. Only now her voice conveyed more stunned disbelief than defiant anger.

'Think about it,' Quinn said. 'Why would anyone else take Garrett?'

'But Piper's Dahl,' Orlando said, looking for a flaw. 'He's the one who had Garrett kidnapped. He's the one who has been trying to kill you. You saw Piper, not Durrie. Right? That has to be it. You made a mistake. The explosion messed up your head.'

'Durrie?' Nate said, confused.

Quinn shook his head. 'Piper's not Dahl. Durrie's Dahl. I don't think Piper has anything to do with this,' he said. 'Leo Tucker was Durrie's connection in Vietnam. Not Piper. He probably made you when he was following Nate and me. But he never told his old boss. Only Durrie, because he knew Durrie would be extremely interested.'

Orlando fell silent.

'Turn here,' Quinn said to Nate.

A moment later they were nearing the hotel again, only this time on the other side of the building from the main entrance.

The hotel took up an entire city block. While the architecture of the building led Quinn to believe it had been built recently, great pains had obviously been taken to have the building's design complement those of the older stone buildings around it.

'Look for a delivery area,' Quinn said.

'We'll still have a problem with security,' Nate said.

'Maybe.'

Nate steered the sedan past another public entrance, less ostentatious than the front, but no less busy. Apparently all the hotel's non-conference guests were being directed to it. An army of bellhops stood outside the door, a different one peeling off each time a taxi pulled up. And while there were several police officers around, they seemed to only be observing the crowds, not stopping anyone.

'He wouldn't enter through there,' Quinn said. 'Not with the boxes.'

His eyes scanned ahead. Suddenly he pointed.

'That's it.'

There was a large opening in the building, big enough for a delivery truck. A sign mounted to the wall indicated it was the entrance for deliveries and employee parking. There were two more police officers standing just inside the entrance. They were dressed warmly in long overcoats and gloves.

'Turn in there,' Quinn said. 'But don't stop until you are all the way inside. Let the cops walk up to you.' He looked up at the rearview mirror, his eyes momentarily meeting Nate's. 'You're going to have to help me take them.'

'Kill them?' Nate said, sounding surprised and horrified.

'I'm hoping we can avoid that.'

Nate got into the center lane and slowed down to a stop. He waited until the oncoming traffic had cleared, then turned into the entrance of the garage. One of the police officers held up his hand for Nate to stop, but he continued on past them for several car lengths before bringing the car to a halt. They were far enough inside that no one on the street would pay them any attention.

'Get out and distract them,' Quinn said.

As the cops started walking toward them, Nate opened his door and got out.

'Sorry about that,' he said in English. 'I didn't see you at first.' He paused. 'You do speak English, don't you?'

Quinn slid across the back seat and reached for the passenger-side door.

'I'll go,' Orlando said, her face taut.

'You don't have to. I can handle this.'

'I'll go.'

Without another word, she opened her door and got out. Quinn watched as she walked around to the back of the car, joining Nate and the cops. Quinn swiveled so he could see out the back window.

Nate had maneuvered the two police officers so that they stood behind the trunk, their backs to the car. Quinn could only hear muffled voices, nothing specific, but he did see the gun suddenly appear in Orlando's hand. The cops froze, both apparently smart enough to know not to reach for their own weapons.

Orlando said something to Nate, and a moment

later he was back at the driver's door. He reached in and released the trunk, then returned to the gathering at the back.

With the trunk open, Quinn's view of the action was diminished. He heard a few more voices, then the car creaked as it took on extra weight.

'There's not enough room,' a voice said. It was coming through the back of the seat, muffled but clear. Quinn assumed it was one of the cops.

'Kill one of them,' Orlando said, her voice more distant.

There was the sound of a slide release being pulled back on a gun. Almost immediately there was more shuffling and grunting coming from inside the trunk.

'That's better,' Orlando said.

When the trunk closed again, there were only two people standing behind the car – Orlando and Nate.

As the two climbed back in, Orlando threw something over the seat at Quinn. It was one of the long, dark overcoats the cops had been wearing. Once Quinn put it on, it would cover most of his pants, making him more presentable.

'I got these, too,' she said, holding up two utility belts complete with radios, guns, and tools of the cops' trade. Not surprisingly, the handcuffs were missing from each belt.

'IDs?' he asked.

Orlando nodded.

Nate put the car in gear and continued down into the garage. Soon they were on a ramp leading downward into the building. Fifty feet in, the road forked. To the right it veered sharply downward, spiraling farther below the surface toward what Quinn guessed was the employee parking area. The left fork kept going straight for another twenty-five feet, ending at a small parking area to the left and a raised loading dock straight ahead.

There was a single truck backed up to the dock. A linen supplier. Two men were rolling a big basket of towels out of the hotel and into the cargo area of the truck.

Quinn quickly shifted his attention to the small parking area off to the left. There were five cars there: two Fords, a Peugeot, and two BMWs. One of the BMWs was a silver two-door coupe. But the other was midnight blue.

'Stop,' Quinn said.

As Nate stopped their car, Quinn took a harder look at the parked BMW. The windows were tinted all the way around, front and back included.

'That's his car.'

Quinn opened his door and started to swing his legs around to get out, but the pain shooting up from his thigh stopped him.

'Wait,' Nate said. 'Let me check.'

As Nate opened his door, Orlando tapped him on the arm, then handed him an ID and one of the guns.

Nate approached the car cautiously, but it was soon apparent no one was inside.

'What now?' Nate called out.

'See if the boxes are still in the back,' Quinn said.

Nate started trying all the doors.

'Nate,' Quinn said. Once his apprentice was looking over at him, Quinn mimed using his gun as a hammer.

Nate glanced over his shoulder toward the loading dock. The two men who had been rolling out the towels were just disappearing back into the hotel.

Instead of just smashing the gun into the window, Nate removed his jacket first, placing it over the glass. He had to hit the window three times before it broke, but the sound was muffled. Quinn smiled. Nate was getting it.

The tinting held the shattered safety glass together, so Nate just had to fold it in on itself and push it into the car.

'You're sure it was him?' Orlando asked Quinn. Her voice was quiet but demanding.

Quinn kept his eyes on Nate. 'Yes.'

Orlando was silent for a moment. 'That son of a bitch was alive the whole time,' she said to herself.

Nate got the trunk open on the other car and checked inside. Quinn could see the answer on his face before he even came back.

'No boxes,' Nate said.

'Then we need to find them,' Quinn said.

'How are we going to get inside?' Nate asked.

'Nate,' Quinn said, 'we are inside.'

Chapter 41

Quinn had Nate park their car directly behind the BMW, bumpers touching. There was just enough room left for traffic to still get by. In front of the car was a cement wall. If Durrie and Tucker came back for their vehicle, they'd have a hell of a time getting it out.

As Quinn suspected, security at the St. Martin Hotel was localized. Attendees were not high-level enough to interrupt the regular flow of the hotel's business. If heads of state had been attending, the place would have been locked down tight. But because the majority of the conference goers were college professors or other civilian professionals, the perceived threat level would be reduced and, therefore, the security would be designed to fit the situation.

But Quinn knew that didn't mean it was going to be easy.

The St. Martin seemed to be a series of service corridors. At least that was the impression Quinn got as they made their way through the bowels of the hotel. These were the passageways that allowed all the work needed to run a successful hotel to happen seamlessly. Signs were posted at each junction, directing traffic toward kitchens, reception areas, conference rooms, and the like. Hotel staff moved up and down the hallways, some faster than others, but none giving Quinn, Orlando, and Nate more than a single glance.

They weren't the only non–hotel employees in the hallways, either. Conference security, Quinn guessed. Police, or perhaps military, dressed in suits and pretending to work for the hotel.

Unlike the hotel employees, they took more interest in the trio. Twice, Quinn, Orlando, and Nate were stopped. But both times, Quinn flashed his new police ID and explained that they were doing a final check of the areas outside the secure zone prior to the start of the luncheon.

Their biggest obstacle was Quinn's injury. He had a definite limp. He tried as best he could to make it seem natural, an old injury. Often, though, he had to reach out and steady himself on Nate's shoulder.

They found a schedule of the day's events posted on a bulletin board down one of the halls. The conference luncheon was being held in the Athey Ballroom. At the next intersection, they looked for the ballroom on the directional signs and found it next to an arrow that pointed them in the right direction.

'Security check,' Quinn said quietly two minutes later.

They had come down a long hallway and had followed the arrows once again, turning right. The security check was just beyond another intersection. There were two men in dark suits standing next to a walk-through metal detector. Beside it was an X-ray machine for screening bags, similar to those in airports.

Quinn had them slow their pace. His intention was to turn down the hallway just before the checkpoint.

'Quinn,' Orlando said. 'Against the wall. On the other side of the metal detector.'

Quinn looked. There were six boxes against the wall, sitting on a handcart. Six identical cardboard boxes.

He could feel Nate tense beside him.

'Maybe it's not them,' Orlando said.

'It's them,' Quinn said.

His eyes had caught movement farther down the hallway, beyond the boxes. Two men were approaching from the other side of the checkpoint. One of the men seemed to be doing all of the talking. The listener looked like he worked for the hotel. He wore the same mauve suit jacket and black pants Quinn had seen other supervisors wearing. He was nodding his head every few seconds, like he was receiving instructions.

The talker was Leo Tucker.

Quinn stopped. They were still a good twenty feet away.

'Turn around and look at me,' he said to the other two. 'We're having a conversation. Completely normal. Okay?'

Orlando turned first, then Nate joined in, their backs now to the checkpoint.

'Did you see those two men approaching?' Quinn asked.

'Yeah,' Orlando said.

Nate started to look over his shoulder.

'No,' Quinn said.

Nate stopped.

'The tall one is Leo Tucker. It looks like he's giving instructions to the other guy.'

Quinn glanced past Orlando toward the boxes. Tucker was getting closer now. He pointed at the stack. The other man nodded and started to move toward them.

'Shit,' Quinn said. 'Just follow me.'

Quinn pushed past Orlando and Nate.

'Stop,' he yelled in German.

He half ran, half hopped toward the checkpoint. The two men at the metal detector looked up, one of them dropping his hand to the radio at his side. The man reaching for the boxes also paused. But not Leo Tucker. He glanced at Quinn in surprise, then took off running down the hallway.

'Don't touch those boxes,' Quinn said. 'Poison.'

The hotel employee drew back suddenly.

'Stop him,' Quinn said, pointing toward Tucker.

The two security officers weren't reacting quickly enough. Quinn pulled out the police ID and held it high in the air.

'Terrorist,' he said. 'Terrorist!'

That got a reaction. One of the men started running after Tucker, but the other remained at his post. As Quinn ran through the metal detector, it beeped loudly.

'Wait,' the remaining officer said.

Without stopping, Quinn looked over at the man and said, 'Don't let anyone touch those boxes.' Then he was off down the hallway.

Behind him, he could hear Nate and Orlando.

'Hold it right there,' the officer said.

Quinn looked over his shoulder. The officer was standing near the opening of the metal detector, determined not to let Nate and Orlando pass. As he reached for his radio, Orlando charged him, knocking the surprised man backward.

Quinn turned, unable to watch the rest without risking further injury. Ahead the hallway dead-ended at a T intersection. Tucker and the officer in pursuit of him had disappeared, but Quinn didn't know which way they'd gone. He forced himself to pick up his speed. As he reached the T, he turned to the left and was almost bowled over as Tucker ran past him. Down the corridor from which the Aussie had come, the officer was sprawled on the ground, unmoving.

Quinn grabbed at Tucker, getting a handful of jacket and holding on tight. The Aussie continued forward down the right side of the T, dragging Quinn with him. As he did, he tried to struggle out of his coat, but it slowed him enough so Quinn could pull out his gun and jam it into the other man's back.

'Stop it,' Quinn said.

'Go fuck yourself.' Tucker continued to struggle.

'Stop!'

Tucker's jacket slipped off his shoulder. It was everything Quinn could do to not pull the trigger. Just as Tucker was about to free himself, Quinn slapped the back of the Aussie's head with the barrel of the gun. Tucker stumbled sideways against the wall, then fell onto his knees. Dazed, but conscious.

Quinn quickly patted him down. Tucker, obviously not wanting to set off the metal detectors, was unarmed. Quinn grabbed Tucker's chin roughly and raised the man's face.

'Where's Garrett?'

It took a moment for Tucker to refocus his eyes. 'Fuck off.'

Steps approached from around the corner, back toward the checkpoint. Quinn took a step away from Tucker and positioned himself so that he could cover both the hallway and the Aussie.

Orlando raced around the corner, sweeping the area in front of her with the gun in her hand. She lowered it slightly when she saw Quinn.

'Are you all right?' she asked.

'I'm fine,' he said. In truth, his leg throbbed mercilessly. 'The boxes?'

'Secured. Nate's with them.'

'What about the other officer?'

'He'll live,' she said. 'We've got to get out of here.'

Quinn looked down at Tucker. 'You're coming with us.'

'The hell I am.'

'Fine,' Quinn said. He raised his gun.

'You wouldn't shoot that in here.'

'Actually, I would.' Quinn moved his finger over the trigger.

'All right, all right,' Tucker said. 'I'll tell you

where the boy is. But only if you get me out of here and let me go.'

They found Nate back at the checkpoint. He was keeping watch over both the boxes and the terrified hotel supervisor who'd gotten caught in the action. The guard who remained there was slumped against the wall, unconscious.

'Time to go,' Quinn said.

He ordered the supervisor to push the cart. The man's reluctance soon disappeared when Quinn showed him his gun. Since Orlando was the most fit, she had Tucker duty. That left Quinn to lead and Nate to bring up the rear.

They wound their way back into the bowels of the hotel, this time the supervisor advising them on the quickest route to the parking garage. Even Tucker behaved, mostly because every time he took even a slight misstep, Orlando was right there to remind him which way to go.

When they reached the garage, Quinn told the supervisor and Tucker to load the boxes into the back seat of Nate's BMW. When they were through, he had Nate get in the car and pop the trunk.

The two cops were still there, both conscious and looking pissed as hell. Tucker and the hotel employee helped them out as Quinn and Orlando kept their guns trained on them.

'Start it up,' Quinn called out to Nate. As the engine roared to life, he turned to Orlando. 'You and Tucker squeeze into the back seat.'

A few seconds later he was alone with the supervisor and the two handcuffed cops. 'This has been a pretty shitty day. But you're going to have to trust me that it could have been a lot worse.' Quinn walked over to the front passenger door of the BMW and opened it. 'I don't want to see you move until we're out of here. After that I don't care what you do.'

Surprisingly, they did exactly as he said.

Quinn directed Nate back into Tiergarten, approaching the Grosser Stern monument this time from the southeast. Before they reached the traffic circle, Quinn told Nate to pull over.

Outside, the park was covered in snow. There were a few people walking down the sidewalks, but most of the activity was limited to the traffic on the streets.

'We separate here,' Quinn said.

'What?' Nate asked, surprised.

Quinn looked his apprentice in the eyes. 'I need you to get rid of the boxes. Take them to the U.S. embassy. Tell them what's inside. Tell them everything. They're not going to believe you. Not at first. You'll probably be locked in a cell. But at least they'll quarantine the boxes. It may take a day or two, but I'll get you out.'

Quinn expected his apprentice to give him one of his smart-ass remarks, but instead Nate said, 'Okay.'

Quinn put out his hand and the two men shook. 'You've done good. Better than I could have ever expected.'

'Does that mean I get a raise?'

Quinn smiled. 'Doubtful.'

Quinn got out of the car first. Then the back door opened and Orlando emerged, pulling Tucker behind her. But before she closed the door, she leaned down and said to Nate, 'I'm glad we found you.'

Quinn, Orlando, and Tucker walked northwest on Hofjägeralle, the Aussie in the middle.

'Where is he?' Quinn asked.

'You'll let me go?' Tucker asked.

'I won't stop you.'

'It's not you I'm worried about.' Tucker glanced over at Orlando. 'What about her?'

Orlando's face was hard. This was the man who had kidnapped her son. Quinn wasn't sure what she'd do.

'That's the deal, isn't it?' she said.

Her words seemed to satisfy Tucker. 'All right.' He said nothing for a moment, then looked at Quinn. 'He's at the Dorint. Same as you were.'

'Is he okay?' Orlando asked.

'Peachy,' Tucker said.

Orlando grabbed Tucker's arm, stopping him. 'Don't mess with me.'

'He's fine,' Tucker said. He looked at Orlando. 'He's with Durrie. I told him I'd already done enough time with the brat when I brought him here.'

'You son of a bitch.' Orlando forced the words through her clenched teeth.

'Orlando, no,' Quinn said. She was ready to kill Tucker, and for that matter, so was Quinn. But they were still too public. And they had made a deal.

Orlando didn't move. Quinn could see her holding herself on the brink for several seconds before finally easing off.

'You two better get going,' Tucker said. 'I'm sure they won't be there long.'

Chapter 42

On the cab ride to the Dorint, the wound on the back of Quinn's thigh began to feel hot again. He wondered if it was becoming infected, but knew there wasn't much he could do about it at the moment.

'Someday I'm going to kill him,' Orlando said softly, so only Quinn could hear.

He nodded, but said nothing. She didn't have to tell him who she was talking about. He'd seen it in her eyes as Tucker had walked away from them, untouched and arrogant as ever.

When they arrived at the hotel, Quinn went in first, carefully scanning the lobby in case Durrie was there. As he walked up to the reception desk, one of the young ladies standing behind it looked at him and smiled in recognition.

'Mr. Bragg,' she said. 'I didn't realize you were returning. Let me check your reservation.'

'No,' Quinn said. 'I'm actually not staying here.'

'Okay,' she said, a question on her face.

'I'm really just looking for one of your guests. An older man. He has a small child with him. He lent me a book that I'd like to return to him before I leave the country.'

'An American,' she said. Not a question, but a confirmation of knowledge she already had.

'I believe so.'

'Mr. Quinn,' she said.

Quinn looked at her. 'I'm sorry?'

'Mr. Quinn,' she said again. 'And his son, Garrett.'

The son of a bitch had hijacked Quinn's name. No doubt it had amused Durrie to do so. But it was also brilliant, really. Of all the names in the world, that would have been one of the last ones Quinn would have expected to find here.

'Yes. That's right. Do you know where I can find him?'

She looked down at the computer terminal on the desk in front of her, then typed something on the keyboard. 'According to this, he's checking out today.'

'Has he left already?' Quinn asked.

'No,' she said. 'But we have a car coming for him in fifteen minutes.'

'Perfect. I'll wait by the elevators for him.'

Quinn thanked her, then found Orlando tucked into an alcove near the elevators. He shared the new information with her, then located a house phone. Speaking in German, he had the operator put him through to housekeeping. From there it was simple. He pretended to be a disorganized waiter from room service and within moments he had Durrie's room number.

'I'm going to go up,' Quinn said. 'You wait here in case he's on his way down and I miss him.'

'You've got to be kidding,' she said.

'Five minutes. If I'm not back by then, then you come up.'

'No,' she said. 'You wait here. I go up.'

'That idea sucks, and you know it,' he said. He could almost feel the anger radiating from her. 'You go up there, you're not going to be able to think straight. Give me a minute to get into position, then call the hotel and ask to be connected to his room.'

After a quick pause, she said, 'Go on. You're wasting time.'

Durrie's suite was one floor above the one Quinn's room had been on. There were fewer doors here. Quinn guessed that the suites here were larger, perhaps two bedrooms. He found Durrie's not far from the elevator, and he listened at the door. The only sound was that of a television.

The doors of the rooms at the Dorint locked automatically, so he didn't even try it. Instead, he removed the gun from the pocket of the overcoat and aimed it at the lock. He took a deep breath, calming himself.

Just as he finished exhaling, a phone rang inside the room. Quinn held the gun steady, waiting for exactly the right moment.

There was a second ring, then a third.

Maybe they've already left, Quinn thought.

A fourth ring, then nothing. No one had answered.

Quinn pulled the gun back, pointing it upward out of the way. The phone started ringing again, but still no one picked it up.

Break in and see if they were still there? Or go back downstairs?

But the decision was made for him.

The door opened suddenly, swift and wide. Quinn reacted quickly, stepping backward and lowering his gun.

Durrie stood in the doorway. He was carrying Garrett, his left arm supporting the boy against his chest. In his right hand was a knife resting gently against Garrett's back. Quinn could also see a pistol tucked into Durrie's waistband.

Quinn lowered his gun a few inches. If Durrie had been holding the pistol instead of the knife, Quinn might have risked a shot. But with the blade where it was, there'd be no way to keep Garrett from being injured.

'You're a real fucker, Johnny,' Durrie said.

'Are you okay, Garrett?' Quinn asked.

The boy looked over his shoulder at Quinn. His eyes were wide with terror, but he clung to Durrie tightly. Without answering, Garrett buried his head in Durrie's shoulder.

'He's fine,' Durrie said. 'Why shouldn't he be?'

'Because most dads don't use their sons as a shield.'

'Ouch,' Durrie said, mockingly. 'That was a good one. Now get out of the way.'

'I can't let you go.'

Durrie laughed. 'The only way you're going to stop me is if you kill the boy. See, if this knife breaks his skin, it's your hand that's guiding it. Do you really want to do that? Do you really think she'll ever forgive you for that?'

'Let him go,' Quinn said. 'You don't want to hurt him.'

'What are you going to do? Take me in?'

'I'll make sure no one harms you.'

'Jesus Christ, don't act like an amateur.'

There was movement from down the hall toward the elevator. It was Orlando.

'Garrett?' she called.

'Mommy?'

Garrett's head snapped up, his eyes immediately locating his mother. Orlando started running toward them.

'Hey, babe,' Durrie said. He turned just enough so that she could see the knife.

Orlando stopped, her face frozen in shock.

Quinn knew she'd been hoping he was wrong, but now the proof was in front of her. Durrie, her long-dead lover. Alive.

She stammered as she took a few tentative steps toward them, then reached out to steady herself on the wall.

'You look good,' Durrie said. 'Maybe it's the kid.'

'Please, D,' she said. 'Let him go.'

'D?' Durrie scoffed. 'Is that supposed to make me feel all nostalgic or something?'

'Mommy?' Garrett asked, not in excitement, but almost as an accusation.

'Remember what I told you,' Durrie said to the boy.

The boy looked unsure, but he leaned back into Durrie.

'What did you tell him?' Orlando asked.

'I think that's between me and the boy,' Durrie said.

'What did you tell him?' she repeated, her voice rising.

'Quiet,' Durrie said. 'You'll disturb the other guests. You don't want this knife to accidentally slip, do you?'

'There's no need for any of this,' Quinn said. 'It's over. We got the boxes at the hotel. The ones you had Tucker deliver. Just let it go.'

Durrie's face hardened. 'You've got to be fucking kidding me. That's a ten-million-dollar paycheck you just took out of my pocket. Goddamn it!'

'It's over,' Quinn said.

Durrie took several loud, angry breaths. 'No,' he said. 'Not even close.'

'Nobody needs to get hurt,' Quinn told him.

'I'm sorry, what?' Durrie spat the question at his former apprentice.

'We all just need to relax. No reason anyone should get hurt.'

'I didn't start this,' Durrie said. 'You did.'

His eyes moved from Quinn to Orlando.

'What are you talking about?' Orlando asked.

Durrie snorted, then shook his head. 'We're leaving now.'

As he took a step in the direction of the elevators, Quinn moved in front of him.

'Pull your head out of your ass and get out of my way,' Durrie said.

'Quinn,' Orlando said.

As Quinn looked over, she nodded. Reluctantly he stepped back.

Durrie smiled. 'Thanks, Johnny.'

The older man began carrying Garrett down the corridor. As Quinn and Orlando followed him to the elevators, they could see Garrett's eyes peeking over Durrie's shoulder. They were moist and laced with fear and uncertainty.

Durrie stopped on the landing in front of the closed elevator doors.

'Can one of you push the Down button for me?' Durrie asked.

Neither Quinn nor Orlando moved.

'Maybe you can help me,' Durrie said to Garrett. He leaned down, close to the control panel. 'Push the lower button for me.'

Garrett reached over and touched the Down button.

It took less than a minute for an empty elevator car to arrive. Durrie stepped inside, then turned.

'We'll take this one,' he said. He moved the knife a few inches up Garrett's back, then looked at Quinn, a mischievous smile on his face. 'Perhaps, Johnny, you'd like to join us? You come with me, maybe I'll let the boy go.'

Both Quinn and Orlando took a step toward the elevator, but Durrie shook his head.

'Just Johnny, babe.' Durrie pointed at the gun in Quinn's hand. 'Why don't you leave that behind?'

Quinn passed the gun to Orlando.

'You carrying anything else?' Durrie asked.

'No.'

'Okay then.' Durrie motioned for Quinn to step inside.

As Quinn got onto the elevator, he glanced back at Orlando. The same fear and terror he'd seen in Garrett's eyes were in hers, too. Only there was more. Hatred and helplessness and fury.

The door closed, and she was gone.

Immediately Durrie set Garrett down. But instead of punching a button on the console, he let the elevator sit where it was for a moment, unmoving. He replaced the knife with the pistol, closing the blade and putting it in his pocket.

'You created a big mess for me,' Durrie said, his voice surprisingly light, almost playful. 'I wasn't sure at first whether to be proud or pissed off. Given the cash I'm out now, I think pissed off is the better choice.'

Quinn looked at him, saying nothing.

'But I'm going to give you a chance here, Johnny boy. The opportunity to clean things up for me, and make up for your betrayal. It's just a little sacrifice for my employers. Your head in a box should be enough. Don't worry, I'll kill you myself. No more fuckups. I'll even make you a promise. When I'm done, I'll let Garrett go back to his mom.'

'But Mommy's too busy,' Garrett said.

'It's okay. Grown-up talk, all right?'

Garrett nodded slowly, then leaned against Durrie's leg.

'What did you tell him?'

'I told him his mom didn't have time to take care of him, so he was going to be with me now.'

'You're a bastard,' Quinn said softly.

'Better that he learn about betrayal early. Hell,

I've already been a better father to him than you've ever been.'

The comment stopped Quinn. He looked questioningly at Durrie, but his mentor only laughed.

'I saw you die,' Quinn said.

'You saw what I wanted you to see,' Durrie said.

'I saw the bullets hit you.'

'You *heard* a gun fired into a stack of boxes. What you *saw* was a couple of jerks from me, and the contents of a bag of blood. That's it. You never even checked my wounds. Ortega didn't give you enough time before he knocked you out.'

Ortega, the third member of their team. Of course he'd been in on it, too. 'But I did check your pulse. There was none.'

'Come on, Johnny. There are dozens of drugs that'll stop your heart. Me, I was more worried about getting it going again. Thankfully, Ortega was standing by with a shot of adrenaline.'

Quinn knew they'd been idle long enough without entering a destination that the elevator had probably reset itself, allowing it to go either up or down. He reached out quickly and pushed the button for the floor above them. The elevator began to lurch upward.

'Cute,' Durrie said. 'But it's not going to change anything.'

Garrett turned toward his father, burying his face against Durrie. Quinn thought he heard the boy sobbing, but it was faint.

'You said I betrayed you. Why would you think that?' Quinn asked, ignoring the comment.

'Don't fuck with me.'

'Don't accuse me of something I haven't done,' Quinn said. Then a thought hit him. 'It's Orlando, isn't it? You think something happened between us. Nothing has *ever* happened between us.'

Durrie snorted. 'I was blind to it at first, you know,' he said. 'For all I know, you two had been carrying on for years. Then Mexico City gave you away.'

'It was just a job,' Quinn said. 'Nothing happened. Orlando told you that. She wasn't lying, dammit.'

Durrie laughed. 'Oh, I pretended to believe her, but I'm not stupid, Johnny. You two alone, sharing a room, and nothing happened? Right. You don't get something like this from sleeping on the floor.'

The elevator car slowed to a stop and the doors opened.

'Wait,' Quinn said. 'You think Garrett's *my* son?'

'Of course he's your son. That's what you get when you fuck my girl.'

Quinn couldn't believe what he was hearing. 'Garrett is your son. I've never touched Orlando, not like you're saying.'

'Don't even try that bullshit. This isn't fucking high school, Johnny. And I'm not a stupid idiot.'

The doors to the elevator started to close again. Quinn reached out to keep them open, then flipped the stop switch on the panel as he stepped quickly into the open doorway. He faced Durrie.

'What's that going to buy you?' Durrie asked.

'A moment to talk.'

Garrett was crying openly now.

'Shut up,' Durrie snapped at the boy. Garrett only began crying louder. Durrie shot a look at Quinn. 'Tell your kid to knock it off.'

'Garrett,' Quinn said gently, 'everything's going to be all right. Okay?'

The boy said nothing, but after a moment his cries diminished to a soft sob.

'*Nothing* ever happened between Orlando and me. Nothing. I haven't even *seen* her for four years.'

'See what I mean about being a bad father?'

Quinn's eyes narrowed. 'If I had a son, I would never do that to him.'

'You didn't have a choice. With me gone, you probably thought Orlando would be all yours. But you were wrong, weren't you? Once I was dead, she couldn't deal with being with you any longer. She probably took off without even telling you where she was going, didn't she?' Durrie laughed. 'You've got to know the way your woman thinks. I guess that's one more thing I'm still better at than you.'

Quinn stared at his mentor. He wanted to scream, 'You're wrong,' but he couldn't get his mouth to open.

'You want to know the truth, Johnny? I don't really give a damn what you did with her,' Durrie said. 'Hell, you did me a favor letting me see who she really is. I'll tell you what really pissed me off. It was you.' Durrie paused. 'I got you all set up. I gave you everything you needed. Training, experience, contacts. But that wasn't enough, was it? Couldn't just carve out your own niche. You wanted my piece of the action, too.'

'You don't know what you're talking about,' Quinn said. 'I never wanted anything more from you than what you were willing to give.'

'You talked about me behind my back. You got me blamed for insignificant things that could have happened to anyone. Eventually I wasn't getting the jobs I used to. The Office stopped calling. And where did all their work go to?'

This can't be happening, Quinn thought. Durrie's delusion was so complicated, so complete, Quinn didn't know how to fight it.

'You,' Durrie went on. 'You got everything, just like you planned. But it wasn't enough for you, was it? If I was still around, there was always the chance I could be a problem.'

'No,' Quinn said.

'So you got the Office to help. Peter would have been only too glad to see me gone.'

'No,' Quinn said. 'None of that's true.'

Durrie smiled. 'I know the gig in San Francisco was a setup. You were going to get rid of me there, weren't you? But I surprised you. I died before you could even spring your idiotic trap.'

'You're twisting everything,' Quinn said. 'There was no plan. No one wanted to kill you. Peter didn't even want you on that job.'

'I never forgot. No way you can forget deceit like that. Sure, I had to lay low for a couple of years. Then I eased my way back in slowly, planning it out, waiting for the perfect opportunity. When it was time, I was ready.'

'Bioterrorism? Is that what you were waiting for?'

'Fuck. It could have been stealing a truckload of toilet paper, for all I cared. I just needed a few things to line up for me.'

'The Office. Me.' Quinn paused. 'Orlando.'

'The bitch was a problem. I spent my first two years after San Francisco alone, no contact with anyone in the business. I mean no one. I had to make sure everyone believed I'd been killed. By the time I resurfaced, she was gone. I almost sent some people to look for her right away, but I stopped myself. I had bigger plans. Couldn't chance accidentally tipping her off. So I had to wait and use less . . . overt methods. You can understand that, can't you?'

Another Durrie maxim: Never risk exposure unless there is no option.

'It took a while, but I did finally trace her as far as Ho Chi Minh City,' Durrie said.

'Tucker?' Quinn asked.

A laugh. 'Piper, actually,' Durrie said, a smug look on his face. 'He didn't know he was working for me. If he did, I'm sure he wouldn't have been so helpful. Sent Leo with him to be my eyes. But even then, they couldn't find her. Not without making a lot of noise. They could have flushed her out, sure. But that would have tipped her off, and she might have fled. I already knew a better way.'

Quinn stared at his mentor, guessing what Durrie would say next, but not wanting to hear it.

'Even though you'd been keeping your distance,' Durrie continued, 'I had no doubt you knew where to find her. I know the way you think, remember? You wouldn't have been able to handle not knowing where she was. I had no doubt that if I just put a little pressure on you, you'd run right to her.' Another pause. 'And you, Johnny, I knew exactly where you were. I've always kept tabs on you.'

Quinn could feel the anger building inside him, but he pushed it back. 'So you hired Gibson and made me a special request.'

Durrie smiled approvingly. 'His job was to motivate you to leave Los Angeles. Once you were in Vietnam, it was Leo's turn. And all he needed to do was follow you. Poor Piper still doesn't know we found her.'

The elevator buzzed at them, unhappy that its door had been open so long. Garrett was sobbing deeply, almost hyperventilating.

'Decision time,' Durrie said. 'Are you going to clean this up? Or does Garrett stay with me?'

Suddenly Quinn felt a presence just off to his left, outside the elevator. Without showing a sign of having detected anything, he placed his hand on the wall just outside the elevator, as if he needed the extra support.

'You let Garrett go now, right here, and I'll go down with you,' Quinn said as something metallic touched his left hand.

Durrie laughed again. 'I think we'll hold on to him just a little longer.'

Quinn raised his fingers and let the metal slip underneath. 'That's the deal.'

Durrie raised his gun, pointing it at Quinn's head. 'Get back in the elevator. That's the deal.'

Quinn paused for a moment, then stepped back into the elevator, shielding the hand that now held a gun from Durrie's sight. Garrett was still pressed against his father, his back to Quinn.

As Durrie leaned over to disengage the stop switch and push the lobby button, Quinn's empty hand shot out and grabbed Garrett's shoulder. The boy screamed as Quinn first pulled him away from Durrie, then shoved him through the open doorway and out of the elevator.

Durrie turned quickly, but Quinn was already launching himself at his old mentor. He knocked Durrie against the wall with a loud thud. Behind them the elevator doors closed, and the car began its downward plunge.

Durrie raised his knee, using it to push Quinn off, then grabbed for his gun. But Quinn already had his gun pointed at Durrie.

'Don't,' Quinn said.

But Durrie raised his pistol. Quinn kicked out, hitting the barrel of the gun just as Durrie pulled the trigger. The bullet flew harmlessly above Quinn's head, piercing the wall of the elevator.

'I don't want to shoot you!' Quinn said.

Durrie got another shot off, but again Quinn was able to alter the trajectory enough to keep it from hitting him.

'Dammit, Durrie. Stop!'

Again, his mentor aimed the gun at him. Quinn was out of position this time. He wouldn't be able to reach Durrie's gun in time.

He had no choice.

He pulled the trigger on his own pistol, screaming out in frustration. Unlike Durrie's, the cop gun Quinn carried had no suppressor. The roar filled the elevator, deafening him momentarily.

There was no need for him to fire a second shot.

Chapter 43

Getting out of the hotel had been a simple matter of keeping his head down and heading straight for the exit the second the elevator doors had opened on the ground floor. A few hotel employees were looking toward the elevators, no doubt wondering what the odd noises had been. But Durrie's dead body was not directly visible beyond the small elevator lobby. Quinn had even heard the doors close behind him as he walked away, further covering his escape.

He waited across the street in the Gendarmenmarkt, keeping watch on the hotel. From where he was standing, he was able to see both the main front entrance and the service door. A few minutes later, Orlando and Garrett exited through the side door.

They stopped in on Dr. Garber unannounced. He didn't look pleased, but he showed them to one of the examining rooms. He dressed Quinn's wounds, then gave him some medicine to fight any potential infection. Once he was done with Quinn, he gave Garrett a thorough checkup, pronouncing him fit and healthy.

At Quinn's request, Dr. Garber left them alone in the room when he was finished. Orlando held Garrett in her lap. He still seemed a little tentative with her, but he was warming up. Durrie hadn't been with him long enough to do any permanent damage.

At least that's what Quinn told himself.

'Thanks for the gun,' Quinn said.

It seemed to take her a moment to realize what he was talking about. 'Sure,' she said. 'I didn't know what else to do.' She looked at him. 'I didn't thank you for saving him, did I?'

'Don't,' Quinn said. 'He wouldn't have needed saving if it wasn't for me.'

She shook her head and put a hand on his arm. 'Thanks.'

He liked the feel of her touch, but too soon she moved her hand away.

'Can I borrow your phone?' he said.

He called the Mole. 'It's done,' Quinn said.

'Good . . . or bad?' the Mole asked.

'Good.'

'And the boy?'

'Safe.'

'Then I don't . . . need to . . . make any calls.'

'No. But I would like you to send the sample and your results to Peter.'

'Of course.'

Quinn's next call was to the Office. Once Peter was on the line, he filled him in on the basics, then said, 'I'm going to send you a video file. Jansen made it. You'll also be receiving a separate sample you can use to cross-check everything. Those things and the remaining tainted mints Nate delivered to the embassy should go a long way to making some people realize they had a bit of an assessment breakdown.'

'I'd say that's a pretty fair guess,' Peter said.

'Jansen says that HFA backed the operation. Someone needs to deal with them.'

'I'll pass it along.'

Quinn paused. 'I need you to get Nate out.'

'I thought you didn't need me for anything anymore.'

'I'm too tired to argue, Peter. Just get him out, okay?'

'I'll see what I can do.'

'And Kenneth Murray?'

'He's being reassigned. A promotion, actually. The embassy in Singapore. There's a lot of traffic that goes through there. He'll have plenty to do.'

'Thank you,' Quinn said.

'Burroughs isn't happy, though.'

'I'm sure you'll throw him a bone.'

There was a report on the television the next morning. A terrorist plot to strike somewhere in Berlin had been thwarted. The nature of the threat was not revealed. The least surprising part of the story to Quinn was who was taking credit.

'NATO is pleased that our efforts have led to the dismantling of this attempted act of terrorism,' Mark Burroughs said. He was standing in front of a podium overflowing with microphones. Quinn couldn't see the spook's feet, but he imagined one was wrapped in a cast. 'I will be flying to Washington later today to personally brief the President.'

Quinn, Orlando, and Garrett had spent the night in a small hotel owned by a friend of Dr. Garber's. It had been a restless night for Quinn. His mind still seemed to be on overdrive, reliving the events of the previous day. Sometimes the results changed, showing him how close he had come to losing everything.

At breakfast, Quinn and Orlando said very little. In fact, they had said very little to each other since they had left Dr. Garber's. As they were finishing, Orlando's phone began to ring. She answered it, then held it out to Quinn.

'It's Peter.'

'What?' Quinn said once he had the phone.

'They're releasing Nate,' he said. 'You'll find him at the Brandenburg Gate in ten minutes.'

The cab ride from the hotel took them fifteen minutes. Nate was there, alone, standing on the sidewalk. His eyes lit up when he saw Garrett.

'Hey, kid,' Nate said.

Garrett hid behind his mother as she reached out and hugged Nate. 'Good to see you.'

'Good to be seen,' he said, smiling.

'How did it go?' Quinn asked.

'Not something I'd want to do every day,' Nate said. 'I think at first they thought I was just crazy. But a couple key words and phrases always get people moving. Terrorist. Biological weapon. Nuclear threat.'

'Nuclear threat?'

'There was this one guy, I swear to God. He just wouldn't believe me. He wanted to open the boxes and check out the mints himself. It was the only thing that would stop him.'

'Did they treat you all right?'

'I've stayed with worse people since I've been here.'

'I'm glad you're okay,' Orlando said. 'I was worried.'

'Why worry?' Nate said. 'I'm a professional hostage now.'

Orlando smiled. She gave Quinn a quick glance, then stepped to the curb and raised her hand. 'Taxi,' she called out.

Within seconds a tan Mercedes cab pulled over.

'Where are you going?' Quinn asked.

'I need to take Garrett home,' she said as she put a hand on her son's shoulder. 'I just wanted to make sure Nate got out okay.'

Quinn was surprised. He'd hoped for a little more time to debrief, more time just to talk.

'Couldn't we . . . I mean I was hoping . . .' He tried, but couldn't finish what he wanted to say.

She seemed to sense his meaning anyway. 'Give me a little time,' she said. 'I just need to be with my son for a while.' She hesitated. 'I'll let you know when I'm ready.'

'Sure,' Quinn said. 'I understand.'

Orlando helped Garrett into the taxi, then hugged Nate again.

'You're going to do fine,' she told him. 'Listen to what Quinn tells you. At least ninety percent of it's good advice.'

When she turned to Quinn, he didn't know exactly what she was going to do. So he put out his hand. She took it, then pulled him forward and embraced him with her other arm. She kissed him on the cheek. Soft, tender. It was all he could do to keep from turning his lips toward hers. When she let go, she looked at him for a moment. He thought she might say something more. Instead, she finally turned, climbed into the cab, and rode away.

Quinn watched the taxi as it drove through the Brandenburg Gate and disappeared into Tiergarten.

After about a minute, something wet hit his face. He looked up. The sky was covered with clouds and it was beginning to snow.

An involuntary shiver ran up Quinn's spine. He looked over at Nate.

'Have you ever been to Hawaii?'